*To my dear frie
On her 80th* _

*Love,
Dorey*

Wall of Silence

Third Edition

a novel

Dorey Whittaker

ISBN: 1518844995
ISBN 13: 9781518844997
Library of Congress Control Number: 2015920371
CreateSpace Independent Publishing Platform
North Charleston, South Carolina

NOTE: All names, companies, cities and events in this novel are fiction. Any similarity
to anyone living or dead is purely coincidental.

This novel is dedicated to my wonderful husband Bruce. Without his love and support, this story would not have been possible. Thank you, Bruce, for loving each of these characters almost as much as I do.

It is also dedicated to every adult who, as a child, was shamed into silence or worse yet, threatened into silence. May you find your voice and feel the freedom to speak out in such a way that others are encouraged and blessed by your story.

CHAPTER 1

SUSAN'S CAREFULLY ORDERED life began to unravel in the summer of 1985. Accepted into one of Atlanta's most respected families some eleven years earlier, Susan had married well by anyone's standards. She had prestige, beauty, three healthy children, and a husband who adored her. Although those closest to her loved her dearly, Susan remained a guarded person. Her skill at avoiding personal questions had developed into a well-honed art—but that summer, everything was about to change.

After spending an hour settling the children into bed, she watched as they drifted off to sleep. She couldn't really blame them for fussing. The idea of crawling into bed in this miserable heat repulsed her, but her exhausted children needed to sleep.

Susan opened the screen door, being careful not to let it squeak, and then slipped quietly onto the front steps and leaned against the porch rail. Rolling a chilled glass of iced tea across her forehead, Susan stared at the weeping willow in the front yard, hoping desperately to see the drooping limbs move even slightly. In a whisper she pleaded, "Please, move them a little. Can't we just have a slight breeze?" This was one of those smothering summer nights that only those who have lived in the Deep South can truly appreciate. The air hung like a sweat-soaked, woolen blanket. Her every move had to be contemplated, necessity measured against labor.

Susan pondered her present circumstances: thirty-two years old, suffering from the heat, fussing with her children, tormented by her memories, and preparing for a murder trial. Her two worlds were finally about to collide, and she knew she would never be the same.

For the past eleven years, Susan had spent her every waking hour building a life as different from that of her parents as she could. The "code of silence" had been beaten into her as a small child. Needing to talk, Susan had developed the habit of talking to trees. Trees represented everything missing in her life for as long as she could remember—strength, dependability, and tranquility. They were safe; they asked no questions and told no tales. Susan found herself returning to this old habit in order to survive the pressures of her current situation. As she studied this grand old weeping willow, Susan smiled. The tree reminded her of a weary old soul beaten down by life yet stubbornly refusing to yield fully to its outward pressures. Its sad countenance was a strange comfort to her, as if it could understand the unhappiness these memories caused.

Susan told the willow stories she had never dared tell anyone. "I have a wonderful life in Atlanta, but here I am in Jefferson. My sister's murder trial starts in a few days, and I feel like I've been reeled back into my family's hate-filled world."

Leaning her head against the porch post, she pleaded with her silent friend. "You know, it isn't fair. I've spent the past few months giving my sister moral support and trying to help her attorney. I've studied dozens of police reports and reviewed all the depositions with him. After all of my effort to put my past behind me, here I am in front of strangers, spreading it out for everyone to see. This trial is forcing our family secrets into the open, and I have to deal with them all over again. It isn't fair. Wasn't once enough? My sister and I were forced to keep silent. I suffered countless beatings whenever a well-intentioned neighbor cornered me and tried to talk to me. Even though I never said anything, I was still beaten. When you grow up like that, you don't easily break the habit of keeping secrets. Besides, it's intolerable having everyone know what a terrible family we were.

"For three months, I've spent every day in the attorney's office reliving our past, and then I go to the jail and spend an hour with Lisa. No wonder I am emotionally drained! Most importantly, I feel so guilty about uprooting the children and moving them here to Jefferson so I could have them nearby. How they miss their daddy! It doesn't seem fair, but I need to have them to come home to every evening. Their presence reminds me of our wonderful life in Atlanta. As soon as this trial is over, we'll have that life back again. Strange, we are only ninety miles from home, yet it feels like millions."

Not liking the direction of this conversation, Susan picked up the glass, held it up to her silent friend, and smiled. "Every evening, Aunt Gladys has a pitcher of iced tea prepared for me. I don't think I could have endured these past three months without her help." Then, as if her tree might misunderstand the relationship, Susan explained, "Of course, Gladys isn't really my aunt. I mean, she wasn't part of my family. Gladys Carter is my husband's widowed aunt, and she has been living in Jefferson, Georgia, for many years. She is one of those wonderful, gracious Southern women who always seem to know when it is impolite to ask questions. Gladys knows the memories I'm being forced to relive must be ugly, but she would never think of making it worse for me by asking intrusive questions. She comes here every morning to get the children up and dressed so I can focus on readying myself for a hard day. Then she makes us all breakfast and watches my children so I can focus on helping my sister. She always has dinner ready and often has the children fed and dressed for bed by the time I get home."

Taking a sip of tea, Susan studied the ice cubes as they melted into oblivion and allowed her mind to wander, as it did almost every night once the children were asleep. Turning to the tree, Susan confessed, "It's been eleven years since I have spoken to my mother and fifteen since I have seen my father. Having spent the past three days in the attorney's office reading my mother's deposition, her angry and bitter words still ring in my ears as if just spoken. No matter how hard I try to silence them, Mother's hateful words swirl in my head, bringing back to life all the memories I have worked so hard to forget. Reading her deposition showed me that little about Marjorie Miller has changed these past eleven years."

Looking at her tree for comfort, she set down the iced tea and sat up tall and straight, as if to prove that the statement she was about to repeat was not true. "My mother always badgered us with, 'You have nothing, and nothing is going to be handed to you. You two girls had the great misfortune of being born into a Southern, white-trash family, and don't you ever forget it. Don't get uppity, or they'll put you in your place.'" Susan imagined she saw the tree's shoulders slump ever so slightly, as if wilting under the force of her mother's words the way she always had. She felt good sharing, and since the memories were not about to go away, at least the tree would keep her company as she journeyed back in time.

Despite the sweltering heat, remembering the sound of her mother's voice as she repeated this much-resented phrase caused a cold shudder to run down her spine. This misfortune about which her mother had warned her had been reinforced throughout her early years. School friends were friends only at school, and rarely did these friendships carry over to after-school activities. Susan was never allowed, nor did she ever want, to bring friends home.

The combination of this heat and the memory of her mother's warning took her back to a hot June day when "getting uppity" nearly resulted in a severe beating. "I was in the second grade and my best friend, Carol Anne, invited me to come over for a swim. I was so excited I could hardly wait for school to let out at noon that day, so we had the whole afternoon free. Carol Anne's pool had only been recently opened for the summer, and I was curious to see her house. Carol Anne always wore such pretty dresses, and I marveled at the number of pairs of shoes she owned. I tried to imagine what kind of bedroom and toys my new best friend would have."

Susan quickly shot a glance toward the tree, as if studying its reaction. "I wasn't jealous of her. Actually, I never spent any time thinking of such lovely things belonging to me. Even at eight, I already knew my station. My mother had made sure of that. I knew that we came from two different worlds. My mother judged others only by wealth—or the lack of it. But I observed another kind of world that day—one of kindness, caring, and love—a world I had never known."

Susan paused just long enough to listen for her children before continuing her story. "By the time we reached Carol Anne's street, I felt uncomfortable. As we passed one large house after another, I had trouble breathing. I rode in the backseat of our family's old car while my mother drove through neighbor-hoods similar to this one, making deliveries for her part-time job. She would point to various houses, telling my sister and me all about the people who lived in these big houses. She hated *these people* and made sure we knew why." Susan stopped her story for a moment and stared at the tree as she thought about how she had just repeated this part of the story. "That's awful. I can't even repeat her words without sounding like her. No matter how hard I try, they come out angry and hateful. She would spew statements like, '*These people* have more money than God! They probably were born into it and never had to work a day in their lives. *These people* would rather burn their money than give a nickel of it to people in need—unless, of course, they received a tax break. *These people* consider us poor white trash. Don't ever get too uppity, or they'll put you in your place.'

"See," Susan said mockingly to the tree. "I heard that phrase so many times I can't even say it any other way but how she said it. All at once I realized Carol Anne was one of *these people*, and I was no longer so sure I wanted to go to her house. Though not quite sure what my mother meant by the statement, 'They'll put you in your place,' I was certain I didn't want to find out. As we came to Carol Anne's driveway, I stopped and stared at her huge white house. It had dark-green shutters, a big porch that ran the length of the house, and the largest, most beautiful red front door I had ever seen. The house set back from the street, the front lawn was as green as a forest, and huge trees shaded the house."

Leaning back against the porch, Susan slowly allowed her memory to carry her back to that day. Like most of her childhood recollections, she found it a little easier to think of it as if it were a home movie, as if the child in that movie was someone else. Anyone sneaking up and listening would have thought she was talking about some other Susan.

Carol Anne made a dash for the side door, held it open, and waited for Susan to catch up. Susan heard women inside talking, and she quickly froze in place. She had not counted on any adults being there, and without warning, she was consumed with panic. Her fear of what these adults might do to her was greater than her curiosity about what the inside of this beautiful house might look like. Susan stepped back and started to make an excuse about needing to go home. Suddenly, Carol Anne's older brother, Scott, a freshman in high school, came bolting out the door with his bat and glove in his hands and an apple between his teeth. He ran right into Susan, knocking her flat and sending his apple flying.

As he scrambled to his feet and retrieved his bat and glove, his mother came to the door and scolded him for his bad manners. "Scott, please be polite. Help the young lady up and apologize. Don't you realize you could have hurt her?"

Never wanting to be the focus of anyone's attention, Susan was on her feet, apologizing for being in his way before he could respond. Scott, realizing he was off the hook, gave Susan a sideways grin and was gone before his mother had a chance to detain him.

Turning her full attention to Susan, Carol Anne's mother asked, "Are you all right?"

Taking a quick glance at her dress and elbow, Susan timidly responded, "Oh, I'm fine."

After giving Susan a gracious smile, she turned to her daughter and asked, "What are your plans for this afternoon? Did you remember the club ladies are here today?"

Susan looked quickly from Carol Anne to her mother, trying to see if this was some subtle code about her. Carol Anne, seemingly unfazed by the question, answered, "Oh, I forgot." Then, without any sense of dread at having done so, she added, "I invited Susan over so we could swim."

Susan wondered if Mrs. Thomas was going to get angry for being bothered like this. Pushing the screen door wide open, Mrs. Thomas whispered, "That's fine girls, just go quietly." Remembering the chatty women in the great room, she quickly added, "You'd better slip up the back stairs so you don't get trapped into visiting away the afternoon with these women."

Susan noticed the sparkle in Mrs. Thomas's eyes as she almost giggled this suggestion, and she thought, *What a pretty lady. No wonder Carol Anne is always happy.*

Carol Anne grabbed Susan's hand and led her inside. As they reached the bottom step, Mrs. Thomas whispered, "Susan, I'm very glad you were able to come over this afternoon. Carol Anne, be sure to wait for me before getting into the pool. The ladies will be leaving soon, and I will come out to watch you girls."

Carol Anne's bedroom was even lovelier than Susan had imagined. The walls were painted a light, creamy yellow with white trim. It had wall-to-wall carpet, and right across from the door was a beautiful canopy bed. The canopy and spread were a print of soft yellow flowers with dark-green ivy weaving through them, both edged with white lace. Part of her collection of dolls was propped on her bed, and the rest were arranged on a shelf that went around the room. Susan could not believe one girl could have so many dolls. How could she possibly play with them all?

As she walked around touching the dolls, Carol Anne pulled three swimsuits from a drawer and asked Susan which one she wanted to wear. Susan tried to hide her amazement that Carol Anne had three bathing suits. She didn't even have one. After all, they didn't have a pool. When she and her sister wanted to cool off, they wore their shorts and took turns spraying each other with the hose. Her mother always chided, "If it's hot enough to run through the hose, it's hot enough for your shorts to dry off. You don't need a suit; it's a waste of money." Having learned to keep her thoughts to herself, Susan simply replied, "It doesn't matter to me. Any one of them will be fine."

Carol Anne tossed her the blue-and-white polka dot suit, opened a door by the dresser, and ushered her friend into a pretty yellow-and-white tiled bathroom. "You can change in there, and I'll change here in the bedroom."

Susan quickly changed, placing her clothes on top of the clothes hamper and waited until Carol Anne called to say she was dressed. While sitting in Carol Anne's beautiful bathroom, Susan was suddenly overwhelmed with a sense of panic. *What have I done? My mother will find out that I came here. What was I thinking? How can I get out of here without upsetting Carol Anne?*

A gentle knock at the bathroom door made Susan almost jump out of her skin. Catching a glimpse of herself in the mirror, she saw herself in the pretty bathing suit and decided that whatever punishment awaited her would be worth it. She was going to enjoy today and not worry about the cost. She had come this far and was not going to let her new friend see her fear. Looking in the mirror, Susan forced a big smile and opened the door to see Carol Anne in a pretty green suit, almost the same shade of green as her eyes, which complemented her bright red hair. Susan said, "You're so pretty."

Never paying much attention to what she looked like, Susan had no idea people thought of her as a stunning beauty with her jet-black hair and peaches-and-cream complexion. Her dark-blue eyes sparkled if and when she would talk, causing some to say she seemed to be talking with her eyes and some even declared you could see her mind working in them. If ever a person showed her soul in her eyes, it was Susan.

Those expressive eyes are what had attracted Carol Anne in the first place. They sat next to each other in class, and when Susan relaxed into conversation, her sparkling eyes made Carol Anne feel happy. She had invited her over several times, but Susan always declined, saying she had other things she needed to do. Carol Anne was too young to understand that her new friend was actually afraid of her. She had no way of knowing that Susan wasn't like her. Oh, she knew Susan's family didn't have much money, but second graders don't think that's important. At least you don't unless you have a mother like Susan's.

The two girls ran down the back stairs and out the side door where Scott had run into Susan. They ran up the driveway and through the back gate, tossed their towels on a lounge chair, and jumped right into the shallow end of the pool. They could almost feel the sizzle as the heat of their bodies was quenched in the cool water. Within a few minutes, Susan relaxed and began to play. Carol Anne noticed that Susan did not know how to swim and said, "Mother was determined that Scott and I would know how to swim if we were going to have a pool, so she made sure I became a good swimmer. I've taken lessons since I was three. Would you like me to teach you how to swim?"

Susan ignored Carol Anne's offer. While her parents were at work, she and her sister would sneak down to the pond, but she never went in deeper than her knees. The muddy bottom always scared her so she stayed at the edge, content to simply splash around. Since this was her first time in a pool, she made sure she stayed in the shallow end. As long as she could touch the bottom, she was fine. Carol Anne offered again, but Susan declined by saying, "No, thank you, Carol Anne, I just want to play in the water today." Time, for Susan, seemed to stand still, and she was determined to enjoy this afternoon regardless of the consequences that faced her at home.

A beach ball floated in the pool, and the girls began tossing it to each other. After a while, Susan stopped worrying about the depth of the pool. They took turns climbing out after the ball and then jumping back in, trying to make the biggest splash. Their giggles and laughter filled the afternoon air. Susan could not ever remember having this much fun. Reaching for the ball, she gave it a solid hit and giggled as she watched her friend scramble after it. Carol Anne dived toward the ball and batted it back to Susan. Determined to hit it back without the ball's touching the water, she swung but missed, causing the ball to sail past her and leave the pool. Susan scrambled after the ball, tossed it back to Carol Anne and jumped in without paying attention to where she was. She was enjoying herself so much she forgot to be careful. As soon as she hit the water, she realized her mistake. She couldn't touch the bottom and couldn't swim. She frantically grasped for anything within her reach, searching for the side of the pool. In her frenzy, Susan finally felt something beside her and with all the strength she had, she grabbed hold and climbed upward.

Carol Anne had quickly come to help, but she was no match for her hysterical friend. Susan grabbed hold and tried to pull herself up, but in reality, she was actually pushing Carol Anne under the water. Carol Anne struggled to get loose, trying desperately to reach the surface in order to catch her breath.

Susan felt a strong arm pushing her away, and she really began to panic. She wanted to scream, but she was still under water. Her lungs were burning, and she didn't think she could hold her breath much longer. Someone grabbed hold of her again. This time she wasn't being pushed away but was lifted out of the water. All Susan saw was blond hair and blue eyes and then darkness. When she regained consciousness, Carol Anne's brother, Scott, and a man she did not know were kneeling over her. Carol Anne was lying on the lounge with her mother sitting beside her. Susan tried to sit up, but the man, who turned out to be Carol Anne's dad, put his hand on her shoulder and told her to lie down. He explained how they had come very close to drowning, and he was furious they had been in the pool without supervision. He was shouting and crying at the same time. He kept saying, "Scott, if you hadn't come home when you did, they would have drowned."

Carol Anne quickly confessed, "I'm sorry, Mom, Dad. I was so excited to go swimming, I forgot to wait for you."

Susan was shocked at Carol Anne's demeanor while making this confession. She didn't appear nervous as she admitted her mistake, nor did her mother seem to react angrily to it. Susan was imagining how her own mother would have reacted to such a confession. Then she heard Mrs. Thomas say, "Carol Anne, it's as much my fault. I let myself get distracted and forgot I promised to come out here and watch you girls. I'm so sorry."

Astonished by her confession, Susan didn't notice Scott slide over by her. Shaking her shoulder in jest, he grinned as he said, "You look like a drowned rat, but a strong one. I was the one who pushed you away from Carol Anne. I had to make you let go of my sister so I could pull her to safety, all the while screaming for help."

Mr. Thomas chimed in, "Scott's screams greeted me as I drove into the driveway this afternoon. That kind of scream is unmistakable. My heart dropped, and I knew something awful was happening. Because the screams came from the backyard, my first thought was, 'The pool!' and took off running. Caroline here flew out the side door right behind me, and we saw Scott struggling with someone in the water. I dove in shoes and all."

Caroline joined in and said, "By then Scott had Carol Anne at the side of the pool, and I pulled her out of the water. Scott then swam over and helped Bill get you out, Susan, and we laid you on the deck. You had swallowed so much water. You were choking and feeling nauseated, but at least you were breathing."

Susan lay there sick with fear. What were *these people* going to do to her for almost drowning their Carol Anne? Mr. Thomas was so upset, Susan was afraid to look directly at him. He was shouting at everyone except Scott. He kept hugging him and kissing him and thanking him for saving the girls. Scott gave his dad a sheepish grin, and even though Mr. Thomas was clearly upset about the girls' being in the pool without supervision, she noticed Carol Anne and her mother didn't seem stressed or anxious.

Susan struggled to sit up, preparing herself for whatever was coming. She slowly drew her eyes up to this hulk of a man crouched next to her in his dripping-wet business suit. Everyone else breathed a huge sigh of relief as the tension of the moment subsided, but Susan kept staring at Mr. Thomas. She understood, at the tender age of eight, that you can never let your guard down when men get really angry. Just when they seem to have calmed down, a fist comes from nowhere. He's teaching you a lesson. Susan had received many such lessons in her short life; she was certain she was about to get another one now. Although he appeared to be calming down, she was waiting for what her mother called "the next round." She would say, "You'd better learn early on if a man gets hopping mad, give him what he wants and get out of his way." Reluctantly, Susan met Mr. Thomas' eyes as he offered his hand to pull her up. Once she was brave enough to look him in the eyes, she never took her eyes off his face. His eyes weren't mean! He was smiling and didn't look upset anymore.

Once the girls had rested, they were sent upstairs to dry off and change. Mrs. Thomas came up a few minutes later and asked, "Susan, would you like to stay for dinner? I'd be happy to call your mother and ask her permission. Then afterward, Mr. Thomas can drive you home."

Susan knew she couldn't stay for dinner and was sure she did not want Mrs. Thomas to call her mother and tell her what had happened. The less her mother knew, the better. Her mother must never know she had been *uppity* enough to go to Carol Anne's house. If she got home before her parents, they'd have no reason to ask where she'd been. But what time was it? How long had they been playing in the pool? She wasn't very good at sensing time, and she wasn't sure how long it would take her to get home. She knew her parents were always home by six o'clock, and she knew she had better be there when they arrived. Susan faked a phone call home and told Carol Anne's parents she needed to go.

She intended to run as fast as she could and try to beat her parents home, but Mr. Thomas would let her walk home alone, especially not after the events of the afternoon. "You girls finish getting dressed, and then I'll drive you home." The finality in his statement was unmistakable. Susan tried to protest, but he would not hear of it and sent the girls back upstairs to finish dressing. Susan struggled to maintain her composure as she dressed. She'd done it now! Her parents were going to kill her for this stunt. *How could I have been so stupid?* How could she have ever imagined she could get away with this? A familiar sense of terror washed over her, and she struggled desperately to keep her fingers from shaking as she buttoned her dress. She did not want her friend to see how scared she really was. She did not want Carol Anne to know that she was in real danger because she would then have to explain what that danger was, and she was not prepared to deal with that issue.

She forced a smile, steadied her voice, and said, "Your brother sure saved our lives, didn't he?"

Carol Anne, having no reason to question her friend's motive for saying this, chimed in with, "Yes, he did. Wasn't God good to us today? He sent my brother home just in time to save us."

Susan was well-trained at hiding her reactions, but this innocent comment from her friend shot into her like a dagger, causing a frenzy of rage to well within her. Though outwardly calm, her thoughts screamed *God had nothing to do with saving us today. He doesn't care if I live or die; if He did,*

He wouldn't have put me in my family. He probably had to save me just so He could save you. So I guess I got lucky today. He had to help me even if He really didn't want to.

Carol Anne's thoughts had already moved on to other topics and as her eyes landed on her bookshelf, she asked, "Have you ever read the story of *Snow White and Rose Red*?"

Thankful for the change in subject, Susan responded, "No, I don't think so."

Carol Anne went to her shelf, took down a book of fairy tales, and handed it to her. "Take this home with you and read it tonight. I think you and I are sort of like Snow White and Rose Red—you with your black hair and blue eyes and me with my red hair and green eyes. I think we should have secret names for each other. I'll call you Snow White, and you can call me Rose Red. We will always and forever be best friends, okay?"

Susan was amazed that Carol Anne wanted to be best friends with her. Did she think she came from a rich family too? They heard Mr. Thomas calling them, so Susan took the book, promising to bring it to school the next day. They ran down the stairs and out the side door, where Scott and Mr. Thomas were waiting by the car. Carol Anne asked to come along, but Mr. Thomas, concerned the pool episode had been rather hard on her, wanted her to go in and rest. Scott jumped in the front seat, and Mr. Thomas held the back car door open for Susan. Leaning back against the seat, Susan knew nothing could dissuade Mr. Thomas. Unable to talk him out of delivering her right to her front door, she sat back and quietly accepted her doom. She knew his intent was to ensure her safety. She also knew she could not tell him, nor could he guess that, his kind deed would ensure the exact opposite result—a severe beating.

Nearing her house Susan began trembling, a nervous habit that usually showed up only when her father was coming after her. As they drove up her street in Mr. Thomas's fancy new car, not a single person could miss the obviously out-of-place automobile stopping at the Miller house.

Susan saw Steve Reiner, her next-door neighbor, come out on his porch to get a closer look. Steve smiled as he noticed Scott in the front seat and walked over to Scott's window and said, "Hi, Scott. What brings you here?"

Ignoring the question, Scott replied, "That was a great game you played today, Steve. I caught the last two innings after my game was over."

Not noticing Susan in the back seat, Steve said, "I think you'd better make tracks." Giving a wary glance toward the Miller house, he said, "That old Mr. Miller has a really bad temper. If he finds you parked in his driveway when he gets home, there's no telling what he'll do. He's a mean one, you know."

Steve's eyes followed Scott's glance toward the back seat, and only then did he notice Susan's sitting there. If ever someone looked like he wanted to crawl into a hole, Steve did. He hung his head and opened the back door for her, saying, "Sorry, Susan."

Susan gave Steve a slight smile and shrugged. There really wasn't anything to say. After all, he was right. Susan's biggest concern was how to get Mr. Thomas to leave quickly. Her dad would be driving up any minute and she wanted them gone, but then Scott offered, "Susan, would it help if we stayed and explained what happened to your dad?"

Before she could respond, Mr. Thomas opened his door and said, "That's a good idea, Susan. I'll be happy to explain everything."

Though she spoke calmly, her eyes blazed with terror. "You don't have to, Mr. Thomas. I can do it. It's all right—honest. Steve is right; you'd better go."

The expression on Mr. Thomas's face showed he thought he should stay but knew she wanted him to leave. Making her father angry apparently would not help Susan's situation.

CHAPTER 2

A TRAIN'S WHISTLE in the distance jarred Susan back to the present, and she checked her watch. It was eight-thirty, and the neighborhood was ee-rily quiet. Usually when it was this hot, the neighbors were out on their porches, but tonight Susan found herself alone except for her tree and her memories.

She realized her tea was gone, but she shrugged and continued her story. "I remember how scared I was running in my front door that night. I can't tell you my relief when I found only my older sister home. Lisa was seventeen, a junior in high school, and I could always trust her not to tattle. In fact, Lisa was the only person in the whole world I did trust."

As these words came out of Susan's mouth, the image of Lisa's sitting in the jail today burned in her mind. Turning to her tree, she pleaded, "I wish people could see that Lisa—the one who loved and protected me. I still re-member the look of understanding on her face when I ran in the front door that day. She smiled at me and said, 'You're safe; they're not home yet.' "

With that statement Susan again slid into her past.

Lisa had dinner started, the table set, and was busy doing her homework. Susan had no appetite for dinner tonight. She only wanted to go to bed and make this day go away, but she knew that desire wouldn't be allowed—not in this house. Not eating dinner was an insult to Father's hard work of putting food on the table. Asking for seconds evidenced an ungratefulness for what had been given. That lesson had been beaten into her several times. Even during those occasions when she had been truly sick, she sat at the table and ate. Tonight, however, she thought it would be wise to stay out of sight as much as possible.

Susan was leaving the living room when the screen door opened, and her parents walked in. She quickly studied her father's face, trying to judge his mood. He tossed his jacket over the chair and headed for the kitchen to get something cold to drink.

Relieved, Susan thought, "Good, if he had been in a bad mood, he would have ordered Mother to get it." As usual, her mother headed straight for the kitchen to make sure Lisa had dinner ready. Her mother knew he could go off on her if dinner wasn't served on time. Both girls knew better than to be sitting when their parents came home. It was always best to be busy, so Lisa quickly headed for the dining room and began fussing over the already-set table while Susan busied herself filling the water glasses. In their house, it was clearly understood that a five-minute grace period was all that was allowed to get dinner on the table.

Hearing her father open the bathroom door meant time was up, so Susan ran into the kitchen to help her mother. As her father took his seat, her mother placed his dinner in front of him, and Susan quickly set his plate of bread beside his water glass. Until he was served, no one else dared to be served. Susan knew she had to sit at the table and eat—an unbearable task in light of the day's events.

As Susan took her usual place, she noticed that her mother had picked up Carol Anne's book of fairy tales and was thumbing through it. Susan had intended to hide it under her mattress and read it when she went to bed but had forgotten. She was about to explain why she had Carol Anne's book when her mother tossed it on the couch and came back to the table. She glared at Susan as she sat down.

Susan frantically tried to think of an excuse for having the book when her mother groused, "All those snooty rich people think they're so special—giving the school their children's leftovers. They probably made sure their kid's name was in it so everyone would see it. They probably have so much money, the dumb kid hasn't even missed this book."

16

Susan was stunned by her mother's comment. She never could have concocted that lie! Susan breathed a sigh of relief, thinking she had gotten away with it—when the doorbell rang.

Chuck Miller hated interruptions during dinner. He opened the door, and Susan saw the man who lived across the street. Ben was the only neighbor her father considered a friend.

"Hey, Chuck," Ben said with a smirk on his face, "who was the mister big-shot in your driveway this afternoon? I didn't realize the banker himself came collecting in this neighborhood."

Chuck stared at him for a moment. "You're crazy. No banker was here today."

Susan's stomach churned. She looked over at Lisa, but there was nothing her older sister could do to help her now. Ben gave every detail and when he said Susan had climbed out of the car, she knew her fate was sealed.

Chuck didn't even say goodbye; he simply slammed the door and headed for Susan. He grabbed hold of her shoulder so hard, she thought he was going to rip off her arm. Shaking her violently, he shouted, "What's this about you riding in some fancy man's car today? Do you think I like coming home and having all the neighbors thinking the bank is coming after me? Well, do you?"

Susan couldn't think. With a fleeting glance toward Lisa, she knew she had to answer him and soon, but her mind simply would not work. There was nothing she could say that wouldn't get her into trouble.

In a flash, her father spun her around and was right in her face. "So who was this man? And what were you doing with him?"

"I only intended to stay a little while," Susan began to explain while steeling herself against the impending explosion. "Carol Anne has a swimming pool, and it was so hot today. All I wanted to do was have a little fun."

As soon as Carol Anne's name came out of her mouth, Susan sensed her mother's body stiffening. Susan knew she had made a big mistake. One quick glance toward her mother confirmed her fears. She now found herself sandwiched between them, and both were zeroing in.

Susan felt her mother's hot breath on her neck as she almost spit out her words. "So! You were going to sit there and make me think it was only a school book."

She knew very well that her mother, as she often did, was making sure the anger and attention remained focused on one of her girls, and Susan could do nothing to protect herself. She could only let this episode play itself out. She knew not to take her eyes off her father and could only hope her mother would quit egging him on. Susan and her mother studied his face in hopes of predicting the direction of his wrath. She heard her mother clear her throat, which usually meant she was nervously preparing to further incite her husband's rage toward one of the girls.

Without moving her eyes from her father's face, Susan tried to think of a plausible reason for having the book when her father turned around and shouted at her mother, "I don't care about some stupid book. I want to know why some strange big-shot came to my door today."

Closing her eyes so she wouldn't have to see the blow coming, Susan pleaded, "I'm sorry. I was having so much fun, I didn't realize it was getting so late. Carol Anne's father insisted he drive me home."

Sick with fright, she prayed her mother would stay quiet and give her father time to cool off. Time stood still. Gradually, though, an uncertain frown formed on his face, and then with a shrug, he apparently decided this was not such a big deal.

Shoving Susan down into her chair, he growled, "So some spoiled brat let her go swimming. I'm hungry, and all this talk is making my dinner cold."

Without saying anything more, he turned, took his seat, and resumed eating.

Susan felt her mother's continued glare but didn't dare look at her. She was quite sure her mother wouldn't say anything more during dinner since her father had closed the subject, but she also knew this matter wasn't over yet. She silently pushed her dinner around the plate, trying to look intent on eating, but she knew she couldn't swallow a single bite. She was afraid to look up for fear of catching her father's eye, so she had no way of knowing he had moved on from the subject and was busy finishing his dinner. Finally, she heard his chair scoot back and watched as he walked into the living room to watch television.

Susan remained very quiet. She knew her mother was not happy about her going to some fancy girl's house, especially without permission. No one did anything in that house without permission. As soon as her father was out of the room, her mother quickly reached over to take hold of her wrist, digging in her nails, and twisting hard. With a low, hateful voice, she snarled, "Did you like being in that fancy, rich house?"

Lisa gave her little sister a cautious glance as if to say, "Be careful how you answer." Susan knew she needed to be careful. She couldn't lie, but she had no idea what to say. Without any warning, her mother wrenched Susan's arm hard. She stood up and walked out of the room, saying, "I hope you enjoyed yourself because that's the last time you'll ever be in that fancy house. Tomorrow you're taking back that stupid book. You don't need their hand-me-downs. You hear me?"

Saying nothing, Susan simply nodded a yes and quickly started clearing the dishes from the table. She couldn't believe she had gotten away with it. She was certain she would get a beating, but tonight was her lucky night. A special show was on television, and her parents were more interested in getting to that than dealing with her. But just to be safe, she stayed in the kitchen for most of the evening because she would have to walk right in front of her parents to get to her room. She wished she could go out the back door and climb up into her tree, but tonight, she dared not leave the house. She did not want to give her mother any more reason to start a fight, so there she sat. Even though she needed to go to the bathroom, she had to wait until she thought it was safe. She did not want to remind them that she existed. Sometimes her house was way too small. She sat in that kitchen for almost two hours before she heard her father get up and head for the bedroom. When he closed the door, she decided this was as good a time as any to make her way to her room.

Sneaking through the living room, she noticed the book on the couch where her mother had tossed it. She wanted to pick it up and take it to her bedroom, but with her mother only a chair away, she decided it would be better not to draw attention to it. Instead, she went straight to her bedroom.

As Susan got into bed, Lisa came in and gently placed the book next to her. Susan wasn't in the mood to read, so she slipped it under her pillow as her big sister slipped under the covers beside her and softly whispered, "I'm sorry, Suz."

Many nights after the girls went to bed, they made up stories about how they would run away and what they would do. Susan dreamed of finding a family with lots of kids on a big farm up north. She imagined the fun of milking cows and having a dog of her own. Lisa always dreamed of going to California. She had heard lots of kids went there and managed to live on the streets by begging. The school had assemblies informing the kids how awful that life was, but Lisa said those teachers didn't know how awful her present life was or how desperately she needed to get away. At age seventeen, tomorrow's events seem unimportant. Life is only about today and what it brings. Nothing could possibly be worse than her present life, and California would be safer than staying here.

Most of the time Susan understood Lisa was only dreaming, but on occasion, her talk felt more like planning. Susan would cry and beg her sister to promise never to leave her behind. Lisa's reassurance would calm Susan, but deep in her heart she must have known the day would come when she would have to leave in order to survive, and Susan knew she was much too young to take along. If Lisa were to survive, Susan knew Lisa needed to leave soon.

The telephone jolted Susan back to the present. She instantly knew this would be the dreaded call from her mother that Lisa's attorney had warned her about, and she didn't want to answer it. If not for her children sleeping down the hall, Susan would have let it ring until her mother tired of calling. Turning to the willow, Susan explained, "I'm sure that is my mother calling. I'm exhausted and wish to be left alone. My mother has never called me, even once, during the entire eleven years I have been married. Eleven years and three grandchildren have never prompted even one call from her. But now, with the threat of a murder trial, she is furious about being subpoenaed and probably intends to vent her emotions on me."

Frustrated at being forced to answer her mother's call, Susan hurried into the house. "It's funny," Susan called back to the willow, "my friends in Atlanta see my life and are somewhat envious of me. Many were shocked when they learned I had to pack up the kids and move here to Jefferson to help my sister. No one could believe a sister of mine could ever be involved in a murder, nor could they ever have imagined I would have such a hateful woman for a mother." As she picked up the phone, with a sarcastic tone in her voice, Susan cautioned the tree, "People should be very careful whom they envy."

"Susan, I want you to tell that attorney of yours I have nothing to say. I don't see why he needs me on that stand. I wasn't even there. Tell him to leave me alone."

Her mother's tone was demanding, not pleading. As her familiar voice pelted her senses with its hate-filled venom, Susan's mind was flooded with dozens of childhood memories. Struggling even to listen to her, Susan interrupted, "Mother, I have no authority over Lisa's attorney. He wouldn't listen to me anyway. It's getting late. I have to go."

Not waiting for a response, Susan hung up and headed to her children's room to see if the phone call had awakened them. After peeking in, she opened their door wider to relieve the stifling heat building up in their room.

She refilled her iced tea and returned to the porch and her silent companion. Lifting her glass to the tree as if offering a toast, Susan pondered. "Funny how certain smells, tastes, and sounds conjure up feelings— like the smell of Aunt Gladys's cinnamon buns making me feel home-sick, but not for *my* home! The smell of lavender, which reminds me of Grandmother Miller, nauseates me every time I smell it. It doesn't matter who's wearing it. And the sound of my mother's voice always reminds me of a hissing snake."

Shaking her head as if trying to free her mind from that voice, Susan felt a strange need to explain her statement to the tree. "For years I only blamed my father for what was going on in our house. I thought it was all his fault. But as I got older, I realized that even though Mother was his victim, Lisa and I had become hers. It's ridiculous to expect a child to understand the reasons behind their parents' behavior. I have no doubt they had lots of reasons, but their basis didn't help my sister or me. Some people seem to think that simply because something bad happened to them, they are entitled to hurt others. I am not saying there aren't reasons my parents turned out the way they did. I am sure if they ever told their stories, we might feel badly for them. Something in my father's past made him the mean, hateful person he became. As for my mother, what makes some women willing to take that kind of treatment? I never knew her parents, and she never talked about them, but she did tell Lisa and me some of what our father did to her before we came along."

Susan stopped in mid-thought and studied her silent friend. She debated whether or not to continue this dialog. "If only I could tell you these things without feeling them. I feel as if I'm right there again, and I hate it." After a long sigh, she decided to continue. "My dad's name is Chuck Miller, and my mother's name is Marjorie. They both worked on the loading docks of a large freight company in Atlanta, and what I am about to share will reveal why Lisa and I had every reason to fear our parents." With an almost theatrical flare, Susan began anew to distance herself from her memories. Mom, Dad, and even Lisa became like characters in some novel she had read.

Chuck operated a forklift, and Marjorie worked in the office. Their fights about work had spoiled more than one meal. Marjorie's job involved checking the freight list against what had been loaded on the trucks and then signing off on each bill of lading. When Chuck made a mistake and loaded the wrong items onto a truck, Marjorie had to point it out. When this happened, he would stew about her correction all day and blow up during dinner. Chuck Miller was not a man to tolerate anything from his woman—or any woman, for that matter. He was not a big man, and his size had been the cause of many a fight throughout his life. He was constantly trying to prove to everyone that he was as tough as or tougher than the next guy. His hair was jet-black like Susan's, but his eyes were dark-brown. With his face terribly scarred by acne, no one would ever say Chuck Miller was anything but mean-looking.

Marjorie, on the other hand, had been an attractive young girl. All of the boys had hoped to date her, and most of the girls wanted to be her friend in order to be available for those boys Marjorie rejected. During her senior year of high school, Marjorie met Chuck Miller. After their second date, he told her she was not to see anyone else and that he was going to marry her. He did not ask her; he simply told her.

At first she thought he was kidding, that is, until the night he caught her at the movies with another boy. He sat a few rows behind the couple and glared at her. When they left and started walking home, he followed. Marjorie tried to ignore him, not warning her date that they were being followed. She thought perhaps if she did not kiss her date good night Chuck would simply go home and forget it. Marjorie thanked the boy for a nice evening and quickly walked into her house and closed the door.

The next morning a friend called and asked if she had heard the latest. "Doug Marshall got the stuffing kicked out of him after he dropped you off last night, and he's in the hospital. Whoever beat him scared him plenty because he refused to tell the police who did it. He told them he's afraid the guy will do it again, only worse, if he dares tell."

Marjorie knew exactly who had beaten Doug and why. She knew Chuck meant business and that she had better follow his rules if she knew what was good for her for he as much as told her so that night. He said if she ever tried going out on him again, the next guy would wish he had only ended up in the hospital. She never dated anyone else the rest of her senior year, and one week after graduation, they were married.

From the very beginning of their marriage, Marjorie was nervous when they went out together. Whenever some guy made a casual comment about her looks, Chuck went ballistic. People began avoiding him because, should he feel double-crossed, he fought hard and dirty. He would not stop until he had half-killed whoever he was fighting—including Marjorie. One day a new employee at the freight company complimented her attractive hair. That night Chuck stood over her as he heartlessly ordered her to cut off her hair. Being six months pregnant with their first child, she couldn't risk having him hit her again. Marjorie obediently took the scissors and cut it straight across at the neckline, thinking that would be enough to satisfy him.

He glared at her and bellowed, "I said cut it all off!"

Quickly, before he decided to do it himself, Marjorie cut off all of her hair. She did not dare cry, which he hated, and her tears only made him angrier. When she was finished, he turned and walked out of the bathroom, muttering, "Now let's see what he has to compliment next."

Only then did Marjorie understand that her good looks had become her enemy. How could she stop other people from making Chuck this angry? She took a scarf and wrapped her now-bare head. She knew she had to do something, but she didn't know what. Chuck wanted her to look nice because she belonged to him, but he didn't want other men coming-on to her, which apparently included almost anything or everything another man would say or do. If the gas station attendant seemed too friendly, Chuck would get angry and accuse her of leading him on. So by the time Susan came along nine years later, her mother was so physically drab and emotionally beaten down that no one would ever imagine she had ever been pretty. Chuck had long since stopped caring how she looked.

Chuck thought nothing of doing similar things to his two girls, and they were terrified of him. Marjorie had become a bitter person with only one goal in life: to protect herself. She had nothing left inside to care about her girls. She would not even attempt to stop their father from beating them, and worse yet, she would deliberately direct his anger toward one of them in order to spare herself. Lisa and Susan learned early that their mother would never help them. They walked around the house on egg-shells, living in constant fear.

They all understood that you never could say the right things around Chuck Miller because there never was a right thing to say. Avoiding a fight was impossible if their father was in the mood for one. He could make a fight out of anything you said, so they all played "the silent game." The three participants in this deadly game knew the rules: be quiet, don't make eye contact, and stay out of Chuck Miller's way. The two younger partici-pants had one other rule: always feel guilt for hoping that if he were in the mood for a fight, he would pick on someone else. You didn't want the other person to get hurt; you simply didn't want it to be you this time.

Susan tried desperately to make excuses for her mother, needing to believe her mother loved her and cared about her in spite of her actions. Whenever Marjorie sacrificed her girls to their father's rage, Susan be-lieved it was simply because her mother was so terribly frightened of him herself that she could not take another punch or slam against the wall. Both girls panicked whenever it was obvious their mother was struggling to think of something—anything—they might have done in order to de-flect his fury onto one of them. Since this would usually happen during dinner, the girls loathed dinnertime.

Lisa, on the other hand, hated both of her parents. Every time Lisa became the target of her father's rage, her hatred for her mother was rein-forced. Both girls knew Marjorie had a particularly strong hatred for Lisa. For a long time, she thought it was simply because Lisa was the oldest and better able to tolerate the beatings. But one night while in bed together, Lisa told her about life before Susan came along, when Lisa was nine. Susan realized she knew almost nothing about her family, other than the couple of stories their mother had told them. Since all her stories were of their father's beatings, Susan never enjoyed hearing them. But Susan loved her sister, and her heart ached as she listened to Lisa's painful memo-ries. Loyalty forced Susan to listen, but as Lisa became more detailed and graphic, Susan's heart felt like it would break. She knew Lisa had endured some terrible things—many of which she had witnessed. But these stories were so painful to hear. Susan decided she would never subject anyone else to her own horrid memories. After all, she could do nothing to help her sister, and her knowing about these terrible stories wouldn't remove them from Lisa's memory. It just hurt!

So at the age of eight, Susan lay in that bed and formulated a core life decision that would impact the rest of her life: *Never tell those who love you what you've been through. They can't fix it, and it only hurts them.*

Life in the Miller house never seemed to change. At eight, Susan knew the rules and had found her own little tricks for keeping out of harm's way. Seventeen-year-old Lisa, however, suddenly began to ignore the rules. She would slip out their bedroom window as soon as they heard their parents' bedroom door close for the night. Susan pleaded for her not to go, but Lisa was determined and seemed unconcerned about what their father would do if he found her gone. Lisa refused to tell Susan where she was going, saying, "The less you know, the better. If he comes in here, pretend you were asleep and didn't know I left."

Susan knew this explanation would not matter to their father. Lisa's actions were putting her in danger. When their father was irate, he did not care who he hit. For months Lisa got away with sneaking out, but her rebellion took its toll on Susan. She would lie in bed, waiting to get caught. Every time she heard her parents' door open, she would shudder.

One night around midnight as Lisa was climbing into the bedroom window, their mother caught her. Hearing a thump against the outside wall, Marjorie came in to check what was going on. As soon as she saw Lisa, she quickly closed the bedroom door so Chuck would not wake up. Furious that Lisa would pull such a stunt, she grabbed her by the hair, dragging her the rest of the way through the window and shoving her down on the bed.

In a menacing whisper, Marjorie threatened, "I'd like to kill you for pulling a stunt like this! Where have you been, and what have you been doing?"

Susan watched in terror as her older sister took a defiant stand. Lisa had finally had enough and didn't seem to care about the cost to them all for her newfound courage. Calmly, yet forcefully, she pushed her mother's face out of hers as she rose to her feet. "Mother, you will never ever touch me again, you sniveling coward. You may be willing to let him keep beating you and us, but I'm not."

"And just how do you think you can stop him, might I ask?" Marjorie sneered.

Almost spitting the words into her mother's face, Lisa retorted, "I can do what you should have done."

Marjorie's eyes blazed with hate. Only her fear of waking Chuck stopped her from landing a crushing blow into her daughter's face. "I think you'd better remember who's sleeping in the next room. I don't know what you've been doing or what you think you can do, but let me tell you something—he'll kill you if you try anything."

"Let him!" Lisa screamed. "At least it would finally be over. You might have some sick need to live this way, but I don't. I'd rather be dead than exist like this!"

In desperation, Susan shouted, "Stop it, Lisa! You don't mean that."

Turning her anger toward Susan, Lisa declared, "Oh, yes, I do. I'd do anything to keep from becoming like her. Susan, she's as bad as he is. What kind of a mother stands by and lets her husband beat her children half to death?"

Desperate to calm down her sister, Susan tried to reason with her. "What do you expect her to do? Do you actually think she can stand up to him? Can't you see she's scared too? She can't do anything to him. He's too mean!"

"Susan, grow up, will you? She has never cared about us. Face it. All she cares about is protecting herself; it's not our fault she married him. She could get rid of him if she really tried. I'm sick of this. The next time he hits me, I'm calling the cops."

Hearing this final threat, Marjorie flew into a rage. "Don't you get it, Lisa? No one will ever stop your father. You'll only make him madder. Don't you think I've tried? I've called the cops, but no one would listen to me. They always thought it was my fault and that I probably had it coming.

They would pull him outside, have a 'good-ol'-boys' conversation, suggest your dad go sleep off the liquor, and then they'd leave. I tried it twice, and both times he came walking back into the house with a sick grin on his face. Those two beatings were the worst I ever got."

"I don't care!" Lisa screamed. "I'm never going to allow either one of you to hit me again."

Suddenly they both realized how loud their voices had gotten. Courage or no courage, no one wanted Chuck getting into the middle of this.

Marjorie quickly walked to the door and listened for any sign of movement from the next room. Satisfied that he had slept through their argument, she turned and hissed one last threat before going back to bed. "Lisa, you'd better think twice before you do anything. You're not as smart as you think you are. Whatever you do, remember, at the end of it, you'll be in this house and so will he. If you're messing around and get into trouble, he'll not only kill you for shaming him, but the boy as well. Both you girls better learn right now that this world will not protect you. You have *no* rights. Those are only words you hear on television. Those people stir up problems and give you false hope. Then when you need their help, they leave you alone for him to do whatever he wants. If you think that all men aren't the same, you're crazy. The sooner you learn that, the better."

Without even changing clothes, Lisa climbed into bed and stared at the ceiling. She was determined to find a way out of this house…and soon. Her only real problem was her little sister.

"Susan, I've always tried to protect you. When Mother tattled on you, I always tried to step in and draw the attention from you. It didn't always work, but I tried. I can't do it anymore. I know you don't understand, but maybe someday you will. Sis, just remember that I love you."

Susan knew that Lisa had taken several beatings as a result of her efforts, and she loved her for it. Susan also knew her sister was planning to run, and she couldn't blame her. A few weeks later, Lisa quietly slipped out the bedroom window as usual…only this time she didn't come back.

CHAPTER 3

❧

Sitting on the front porch, Susan began to cry as she remembered the desperate feeling of loneliness she had felt when Lisa ran away. Turning to her silent friend for comfort, she explained, "That was the first time in my life I felt totally unprotected. Until then, I knew I could count on Lisa. Her running interference didn't always keep me from a beating, but at least, after it was over, Lisa would be there to comfort me."

Ninety miles from her husband and feeling these raw emotions from her past, she was overcome by that same sense of loneliness. Susan quickly stood and moved to the far side of the porch, as if to escape the haunting feelings. "This is absurd. I can't let the tension of this trial do this to me. After all, it was my idea to move here."

Turning to the tree, as if needing to justify her reasons, she argued, "We didn't know how long my sister's murder trial would last or how much I would be needed here. We—no, I—decided to rent this little two-bedroom house so the children and I could be close during the trial. Besides, Lisa's attorney needed me to fill in the family details. But most importantly, Lisa needed me."

Hearing the phone again, Susan hurried to the living room. As she lifted the receiver to her ear, she heard her mother already spewing her viciousness, not even allowing Susan to respond. She wanted to hang up. *Why can't my mother leave me alone?* She was tired of hearing her threats. As she continued her verbal assault, Susan knew her mother's frustration did not stem from a fear of being put on the witness stand and being exposed as an abusive mother. Her mother had stopped caring what other people thought of her long ago. She was enraged that she found herself forced to do what she didn't want to do, and she was determined to tell her daughter about it again. "Susan, don't you dare hang up on me! I want you to…"

As her mother continued her tirade, Susan rested the receiver against her shoulder so her tantrum wasn't being funneled into her ear. While listening to this voice she associated with so much pain, Susan thought about the countless times she had made excuses for her mother's behavior—even to the point of defending her against Lisa's verbal attacks. Susan had always felt that was the real reason her sister had finally run off without her, abandoning her to fend for herself. While her mother's offensive voice pierced her soul, Susan's thoughts returned to those first few months without Lisa.

At first things appeared fairly calm around the house, but that calmness was deceptive. Chuck seethed in anger, and the Atlanta police were frequently coming around, asking questions and searching for clues about Lisa's disappearance. Some of the neighbors had told the police about the constant fighting in the Miller house and that Chuck Miller should be thoroughly checked out. Some went so far as to suggest that perhaps Lisa hadn't run away after all, that perhaps Chuck had gone too far this time, and he had buried her body somewhere. Because of the neighbors' concerns, the police stopped by often and questioned all three of them. Each time the police left, Chuck would storm around the house, making all kinds of threats, but he knew he was being watched. He was forced to contain his temper. The police began passing out flyers with Lisa's picture. After talking to Susan, they decided it would also be wise to send some out to California, just in case.

One evening, after a harsh grilling by the police, Chuck was so livid he began smashing the bathroom wall with his fists. Susan sat trembling on her bed, listening and waiting. Sooner or later he was going to let loose, and either her or her mother would suffer the full fury of his rage. Susan and her mother kept out of sight as much as possible. Susan felt doubly vulnerable. She not only had to watch out for her father, she also had to contend with her mother. Marjorie's hatred of Lisa for putting her in this dangerous position would surely find its way to Susan.

A full two months passed before the dreaded phone call came. As usual, Chuck punched the loudspeaker so he could pace back and forth to vent his anger. "Mr. Miller, this is the Atlanta Police Department. We received a call today from the Los Angeles Police Department. Apparently, a girl matching Lisa's description was picked up there for shoplifting; however, before they could process her, she walked out of the station and disappeared. The LAPD is sure it was your daughter, Mr. Miller. Even the name was a match. They don't have an address, but they promised us they would pass the bulletin around and keep an eye out for her."

Hearing this conversation, Susan and Marjorie headed for the back of the house and took shelter. They both knew this was not going to be good.

Chuck bellowed at the phone, "You guys can't stand being wrong, can you? You were so sure I did it."

The voice on the other end ignored this response and continued, "We're going to leave her missing-person's file open, but we can do nothing more as long as she's in California."

Slamming the disconnect button on the phone, Chuck Miller began ranting, "I should go outside and rub this news into the faces of all you nosy neighbors. For two months your story-telling has made my life pure misery."

While grumbling about the lack of an apology from the police, his angry gaze fell on a ceramic bunny—a prize Lisa had won at a street carnival when she was little. He removed it from its place on the middle shelf of Marjorie's curio cabinet. The gentleness with which he handled the bunny belied his intentions. He knew Lisa had loved this stupid bunny, prattling on for days about winning it. Suddenly, he spun around and let it fly against the wall, smashing it into tiny pieces. "There! That felt good." Seething with hatred, he muttered, "Too bad it wasn't you, Lisa."

He hesitated only briefly to stare at his handiwork before quickly returning to the cabinet. This time he didn't care whose objects of affection he smashed. With the crashing sounds of each new object, his heart beat a little faster. "You three don't deserve any nice things. You're more trouble to me than you're worth."

Susan could hear her father's thundering around the living room, and sheer terror consumed her. She wanted to run from this nightmare, but she dared not open her door. If only she could fly to her safe refuge. If she could only be high in her tree, where its branches would protect her from her father's rage. She sat frozen, staring at the knob on her bedroom door, praying in silent desperation, *Please don't turn. Please don't turn.*

As Chuck let the last item fly, he grabbed hold of the cabinet, the only item Marjorie had left of her mother's, which heightened Chuck Miller's sick satisfaction for what he was about to do. Chuck tilted it until its own weight carried it the rest of the way to the floor, smashing all of the glass panels as it hit. He stopped for a moment to observe his destruction and felt a fleeting sense of satisfaction, but quickly his anger and restlessness returned. His hands itched with a burning sensation, and he felt the blood pounding through his arms. His rage had smoldered for weeks, and he was not a man to hold back his temper. This whole business had been causing him near physical pain. He was certain the police would leave him alone now because they would not want to admit they had been wrong. He knew they'd never apologize to him, so heading toward the back of the house, he started shouting, "Marjorie, get out here and fix me something to eat."

The dreaded moment had finally come. Susan and Marjorie both knew it. Susan's heart began pounding so hard, she placed her hands against her chest as if to keep it from pounding right out of her body. Finally, she heard the bang of her parents' bedroom door against the adjoining wall and knew he had passed her room. As she heard the first blows landing on her mother, Susan flew off her bed and ran for her closet. In one quick move, she pulled the door closed and huddled in the back corner. Her heart pounded in her ears, mixing with the sounds of her father's rage and her mother's screams. Groping in the dark for something to help muffle these excruciating sounds, she grabbed her winter coat and placed it over her head and pressed her hands against her ears. She could still hear the muffled screams coming from her parents' room.

Months of rage were now being vented on her mother. As the beating began, Susan heard her father scream, "It's all your fault, Marjorie! If you had reared Lisa right, the police wouldn't have humiliated me. Since Lisa isn't here to get the beating she deserves, it's only right that you get it."

Hearing her mother scream, Susan knew she could do nothing to stop her father. If she tried, he would turn on her. All she could do was cower there and hope he would quickly spend his rage and stop. She also knew she was far from safe. Even though her mother was getting beaten, not much would take for him to switch his attention and anger to her. It was such a sick feeling to be glad someone else was getting such an awful beating. Huddled in that closet, waves of panic and nausea flooded her entire body. If only the sounds would stop!

Suddenly she heard a loud crash from the front of the house—more violent crashing and men's voices. Not daring to peek out to find where those other voices were coming from, she placed her ear against the closet door. Several men were shouting angrily, and the house shook. She could only guess and hope that someone was trying to control the situation. Susan heard her bedroom door open. Someone was walking around in her room. She crouched deeper into her corner. Footsteps were coming toward her. Then ever so slowly, the door opened. Susan looked up to see a policeman staring down at her.

Looking past him, Susan saw her father continuing to struggle with two police officers as they tried to pull him toward the front room. Not wanting to leave the closet, she wished the policeman would close the door and leave her alone. But that was not going to happen. The officer leaned down, extended his hand to Susan, and said, "Honey, it's safe now. You can come out."

The ambulance was coming for her mother, and Office Bailey wanted Susan out of the house before it arrived. Leading her into the hall, he noted she barely turned her head to look at her mother before continuing on to the front of the house. He thought it strange that this child did not even ask about her mother. She merely went where he directed and quietly sat.

Susan watched as an officer flagged down the ambulance and directed the crew toward her mother. She kept her head down but heard the officer say to the crew, "I've been a cop for years and have never been tempted to mistreat anyone. Tonight, however, looking into that little girl's eyes, I wanted to thrash her father." His voice was shaking with rage, and Susan felt a strange feeling of comfort as he described his encounter to the crew. "I actually had to push back tears as I looked at this precious little girl crouched like a trapped animal in the back corner of her closet. Her beautiful blue eyes were filled with absolute terror. Hell isn't good enough for these kind of men."

The ambulance crew gathered up their kit and headed in to check on Marjorie Miller. A second ambulance arrived moments later, and the officer directed them inside. Entering the bedroom, the second crew leader asked, "You boys need any help?"

The lead attendant didn't even look up. He was feverishly trying to get a pulse but so far to no avail. His partner, who was busy organizing all kinds of medical equipment, responded, "She's critical. We'll be surprised if she even makes it to the hospital alive."

Another attendant asked, "Why don't we at least help you get her onto a safety board before we move on to another call?"

Grateful for the help, the three closest attendants took their positions supporting her head, neck, and back. Only after rolling her over, did they get their first good look at her face. The youngest attendant grimaced, "Can you believe a man could do this much damage to a woman? He must be some kind of animal."

The others simply shook their heads. Unable to determine how many bones were broken, they were being as gentle as possible while preparing Marjorie for transport to the emergency room at the county hospital. Before bringing her to the ambulance, one attendant suggested, "Would someone make sure that the little kid is taken outside? She doesn't need to see this."

Nodding in agreement, one attendant went into the living room, took Susan's hand, and guided her out to the front porch. As soon as they came through the front door, Mrs. Reiner, the next-door neighbor, came up to Susan, gently wrapped a blanket around her shoulders, and asked if she could take Susan to her house while they investigated.

Officer Bailey, stepping out onto the porch, said regretfully, "I'm sorry. We need to get a statement from her. We'll do everything possible to spare her more trauma."

Tilting his head toward the house, he whispered, "It's pretty bad in there. If you could keep the child distracted while they bring out the mother, I would be grateful."

With a motherly smile, Mrs. Reiner went over to Susan and suggested, "Sweetheart, let's move over to the far end of the porch, so we'll be out of the policeman's way."

Susan didn't even look up. Mrs. Reiner placed her arm around the child's shoulder and nudged her in the direction she wanted her to go and thought, *It's strange, but she's like a little rag doll. It's as if there's nothing inside but sawdust.*

The two sat in silence for a few minutes. Mrs. Reiner kept her arm around the child, pondering her lack of emotions, and whispered lovingly, "You sweet little baby. You've seen so much in your short life, haven't you? Better laws are needed to protect you from people like your parents."

Hearing the screen door swing open, Mrs. Reiner watched as they rolled Mrs. Miller out onto the porch. Susan didn't so much as move. She stared at the ground without expression, without emotion. Mrs. Reiner's head throbbed with pent-up emotion, and she wanted to yell, *Cry, child! Scream! Get angry! Something! Anything!*

Steve, Mrs. Reiner's son, came over as the ambulance pulled away. Approaching the porch, he could see Mr. Miller sitting on the living room couch being questioned by the police. No one in the neighborhood liked Chuck Miller, and with the laws being what they were, the neighbors knew he might never have to pay for his behavior. Taking this into account, no one wanted to attract his attention by speaking against him in his presence, so Steve quietly stood beside his mother and watched. When Officer Bailey asked Mrs. Reiner what she knew about this family, Steve quickly stepped over to the officer and, with a look of deep concern, whispered, "Sir, could you please wait until Mr. Miller isn't around? I really don't want him mad at my mom."

Officer Bailey nodded, agreeing to wait with the questioning. Moments later, a handcuffed Chuck Miller was led out the front door. Finally, he was going to jail. Passing his daughter on the porch, he didn't ask or even seem to care what was going to happen to her. He simply looked straight ahead and glared. When the police car was out of sight, several neighbors came out of their houses to find out what had happened. Steve walked around his mom and sat down next to Susan. He tried to make small talk to divert her attention from the neighbors' discussion. As he was talking to Susan, one of the other officers asked loudly, "Which one of you called the police?"

Steve heard his mother say, without any hesitation, "I did. I couldn't stand the sound of him beating them one more time. I still have doubts as to whether or not Lisa is still alive. I believe it's only a matter of time until one of them dies over here. So, yes, I called."

Steve didn't like the neighbors knowing his mother had done this. She had finally taken her stand, and no one was going to keep her silent now. Mr. Miller had bullied their neighborhood long enough! It was time they stood up to him; however, everyone knew that just because Chuck Miller had been taken away in a police car, it did not mean they shouldn't still be careful.

Steve despised Mr. Miller, but he liked Susan and her sister, Lisa. Susan was only a little kid and not very talkative, but she was sweet. Never having been in this type of situation before, he felt unsure about putting his arm around her—like his mother had done—but he wanted to do something to reassure her. While feebly attempting to make conversation, he began to feel an overwhelming compassion for her and thought, *This must be how big brothers feel toward their little sisters. I want to hug her, but not like a girl, and not like my mom. If only I could stop the hurt in her eyes and get her away from all of this ugliness.* He continued jabbering about anything that came to his mind, hoping Susan would respond. Then to his great relief, she smiled at something ridiculous he had said. *Yahoo! She's coming back. Keep coming, Susan! I'll be as silly as I have to be to get a smile out of you.*

Within a few minutes, Susan was responding to Steve's silly stories. Almost forgetting the other people around, she began talking with him. He had lived next door for as long as she could remember. Everyone liked him and his mom. Susan studied his friendly face. She had often sat up in her tree, secretly watching him and his mother working in their yard. She would listen to them banter back and forth, always being kind and friendly to one another. Steve was one of those boys who usually had a sweet smile on his face and a kind word for her and her sister. Many a night she and Lisa had talked about how different their home was from his. They tried to imagine what it must be like to have a mother as nice as Mrs. Reiner. Though they both liked her, they knew better than to get chummy with the neighbors. If their parents ever caught them talking with anyone in the neighborhood, they would be severely punished. What they did or did not say was irrelevant. Simply talking was reason enough to bring down the reign of terror, so they carefully avoided everyone—except Steve. Lisa had always trusted him, and as long as they sat on his lawn and watched for her parents' car coming up the street, Lisa took her chances because she loved to talk to Steve. And tonight Susan felt the same way. Talking with Steve like this made it feel as if Lisa was not so far away.

Officer Bailey stepped over and sat next to Susan. "Do you have any family we can call?"

Keeping her head lowered, Susan simply shook her head.

"You do understand," the officer explained, "we cannot allow you to stay home alone at your age? We'll find a safe place for you to stay until your mother is strong enough to take care of you."

Fatigued beyond measure, Susan grimaced at this innocent statement and momentarily letting her guard down, replied, "When has my mother ever been strong enough to take care of me?" Without looking up or expecting a reply, Susan followed him and climbed into the police car. They could take her anywhere. She didn't care. This had been a long night, and she was tired. She wanted to go to sleep and make this day end. Sleep had always been Susan's only escape from the pain and sorrow of her life. When the tension in the house became overwhelming, she would go into her room and fall asleep. There was no better way of being invisible. She had discovered this technique when she was three or four years old and had perfected the ability to fall asleep at any time. Her sister could be in their room talking to her, and she could still simply place her head on the pillow and "disappear." After all, she reasoned, you couldn't say the wrong thing while sleeping. More than once her father had come into their room, looking for trouble and seeing Susan was sleeping, ordered Lisa to the kitchen to fix him a snack, which usually resulted in a fight. She was always amazed that Lisa didn't seem to catch on to her trick. At least she never mentioned it. Right now, though, Susan really was tired, and sleep was all she wanted.

C H A P T E R   4

—— ❧ ——

Marjorie's raspy voice jolted Susan back to the present. "Susan! Susan, you answer me! You hear me?"

She lifted the phone to her ear and said, "Mother, I have nothing more to say. I'm tired, and tomorrow's going to be a grueling day. The attorney intends to review the final witness list and the two remaining depositions. We need to be fully prepared for the trial by the end of the day."

Hearing her mother take a deep breath, Susan dreaded another argument ensuing, so she quickly added, "I'm hanging up and going to bed. I suggest you do the same." Not giving her mother a chance to protest, she quickly ended the call and placed the receiver on the table to ensure this would be the last call of the night.

Quietly making her way toward her children's room, she thought about the past eleven years of silence from her mother—not a call, not a card, or gifts for any of her three children. Gently pushing open the bedroom door to peek in on them, she thought, *Mother hasn't changed at all. She assumes she can ignore my children and me and then expect to pick up the phone after eleven years and bully me into doing what she wants. She may not have changed after all this time, but I certainly have. Her power over me is gone; she just doesn't know it yet.*

Susan carefully removed the books and toys the children had fallen asleep playing with and then gently kissed each one on the forehead. Susan's gaze rested in turn upon each child. A cherished ritual for her these past six years, starting the first night they had brought their little Lisa Anne home from the hospital was studying their precious, innocent faces in such sweet, peaceful sleep. Listening to their rhythmic breathing was always a bittersweet experience. Tonight, as on many other nights, she tried to imagine how they must feel.

Hearing her mother's bitter voice shatter eleven years of silence caused Susan to struggle to control her emotions. That loathsome voice pierced her soul like a dagger, breaking through the emotional fortress Susan had erected between her childhood and her adulthood, bringing back to life all of her old childhood feelings. She tried to compare her childhood feelings with those of her children. They never worried about their father's blasting into their bedroom with anything but smiles and hugs for them. They would play for hours and never feel the need to cautiously assess their surroundings for trouble. *What must it feel like,* Susan wondered, *to be able to play without anxiety, never fearing or having to prepare for an attack that came without any warning?*

Hers were such busy little girls, always making pretend dinners and then waiting anxiously for their daddy to come home so they could serve him the "delicious" meal they had prepared. He would make such a fuss over their wonderful make-believe dinners. The thought that Daddy might not want to join them in play never crossed their minds because their daddy could not wait to get home every night to see his beloved little girls.

A favorite game involved their piling on top of him, everyone giggling and wrestling. They refused to stop until Mommy agreed to join them for a family hug, and then everyone received kisses.

Susan loved to watch this family ritual which brought intense pleasure, but also intense pain. A deep ache welled up in the very core of her being. These sweet, precious moments with her husband and girls brought an acute awareness of all she had missed as a child. She could not shake the feeling that this intimate, tender moment was not meant for her. Part of her wanted to turn and leave the room because she felt like an intruder.

In spite of these feelings, Susan was a good mother. She knew this to be true, but she was keenly aware she could be somewhat reserved and slightly aloof with her children. She did wonderful things for them, but how she longed to feel free to shower them with affection as her husband did. She lived so carefully, so cautiously, always fearing that a little bit of Marjorie might one day show itself. Of course, when her family demanded she join in their revelry, she always would. Susan realized, though, that she never initiated affection, and that realization troubled her.

Tonight, after received these phone calls from her mother, Susan was extremely emotional. This trial was resurrecting her old feelings—feelings she hated. She found solace in spending extra time watching her children sleep. But she knew they missed their daddy. She wondered if it would have been better for them to have remained with him in Atlanta. The pre-trial phase had lasted three long months, and the idea of not having them with her was intolerable for Susan, and after all, their daddy came to visit every weekend. Megan, now three, kept busy with play all week and was fine with seeing her daddy on the weekend. Of course, Matthew, being the baby, was so smothered with love from Aunt Gladys that he was perfectly happy. Six-year-old Lisa Anne, who had her daddy's grin and her mother's jet-black hair, knew something wasn't quite right. Although she was usually grinning and giggling and finding the fun in any task her mother gave her to do, Susan could see that Lisa Anne sensed her struggling. Though always cooperative, Lisa Anne was the one who worried Susan. Keeping her from being affected by the trial seemed to be an impossible task.

In the beginning, Susan wanted to shield the children from any knowledge of the trial. She asked her husband to promise that whenever he came for a visit, they would play and have fun with the children. Talk of the trial was to be nonexistent during these family times. But Lisa Anne wasn't a baby anymore, and she asked so many questions. She didn't understand why they had left home for the summer to come here. She could sense the tension and sadness in her mother, and she couldn't understand why her daddy couldn't be with them all of the time. When he did come to visit, she dreaded the moment he would kiss her goodbye and leave again. Susan longed for this nightmare to end so she could pack up the children and go home.

Gladys arrived early the next morning so Susan could meet with the attorney by eight. Gladys never pried, but she always took time to listen if

Susan wanted to talk. This morning, as usual, she went to the kitchen to start a pot of coffee before getting the children up and moving. As she was dressing Matthew, she called to Susan, "Would you like something more than your usual dry toast and coffee today?"

Susan was not one for eating breakfast, and lately getting anything down had been especially hard. What she did eat just sat in her stomach. Dry toast was as much as her stomach could tolerate. "Thank you for the thought, Aunt Gladys, but I think toast and coffee is all I want."

Looking through her closet, Susan was having trouble choosing an outfit. As she checked out her navy-blue suit in the mirror, she was surprised at the weight she had lost since coming to Jefferson. She had always been slim, but now she looked gaunt. As she closely studied her face, she saw the beginning of dark circles under her eyes and ever-so-faint lines around her eyes where none had been before. She had always been careful about cleansing and moisturizing her face, but these days, she was lucky if she managed to change clothes before dropping into bed. She vowed that tonight she would give her face special attention. Right now, though, she needed to decide what to wear.

She settled on a sleeveless light-tan dress with a matching jacket trimmed in white, white heels and a string of pearls. The necklace had been Scott's wedding gift to her, and she wanted something of him with her today. She poured herself a cup of coffee, grabbed her toast, and then went to phone Scott. She had promised to call him every morning because he was so worried about her. At first she had asked him not to come to the trial. Though he was aware of some incidents from her childhood, she preferred he not be present when she and others shared the vivid details with strangers. She wasn't sure if that was for his sake or hers. He reluctantly agreed to remain in Atlanta during the pre-trial discovery, reminding her he was only a phone call and a two-hour drive away. They both knew he was needed in Atlanta, but the entire family planned to be at the trial to support Susan and her sister.

Scott picked up the phone on its first ring, and before she could even say hello, she heard, "I love you, Suz. How's my girl this morning?"

With a touch of forced laughter, Susan responded, "I'm fine. I miss you, honey. I'm sorry I didn't call last night, but yesterday was quite rough. Then my mother called me two times last night." Susan paused and added, "Scott, I couldn't imagine getting through this without you. You always seem to know exactly when I need your words of reassurance, and this is one of those times."

"You know I love you, Susan," he said. "This will all be over soon. We'll have our lives back, and you can put this behind you."

With a sigh, Susan responded, "I'm ready. I want to wake up in our bed, fix breakfast in my kitchen, and watch our children play in our yard."

Scott asked, "I notice you aren't volunteering any additional information about your mother's phone calls. Susan, why did your mother call two times?"

"She seems to think I have some control over whether or not the attorney calls her to testify. No matter how many different ways I told her I couldn't help, she persisted in ordering me to do something."

The lightheartedness was now absent in Scott's voice. "I don't like her bothering you. Eleven years of silence hasn't been so bad, has it?"

With a hostility that surprised even Susan, she snapped, "As a matter of fact, no! You know, Scott, she never even asked about the children. It's as if they don't exist. She's really a piece of work, my mother. Eleven years of silence, and then she picks up the phone and starts ordering me around as if nothing has changed. I'm convinced she thinks I'll still jump when she threatens me."

"Did she threaten you? Are you sure you don't want me to be there today?" The concern in his voice made Susan realize she needed to pick her words more carefully.

"No, Scott, she didn't actually threaten me. Her entire manner is threatening. She doesn't know any other way of communicating. I'm all right. You don't need to drop everything and come down here." She knew he wasn't pressuring her and would do what she felt was best. He was simply letting her know he was there for her and wanted to help. Scott had always been good to her, and she was especially thankful he had never pushed her for the ugly details about her childhood. Besides, he had met her mother enough times to have some understanding of how terrible her life at home had actually been.

"Susan, you would tell me if that wasn't so, wouldn't you?"

Forcing a lilt back in her voice, Susan did her best to reassure him she was fine. As she hung up, she sat by the window and thought about his constant care for her. She had decided Scott did not need to know of her frequent strolls down memory lane, nor was she sure that even his presence last night would have stopped them. Convinced she was protecting him, she argued with herself. *What purpose would it serve to tell him? His knowing won't change a thing; it would only cause him pain.*

Enjoying the warmth of the morning sun, Susan pondered all that had transpired in her life to bring her and Scott together. She was still amazed her every time she thought about it. How had she been so fortunate? At times like this, she wondered if she might wake up one day and find her marriage was only a dream, and she was really in the house with her parents. Eleven years of marriage to Scott, being happy, blessed with wonderful children wasn't really meant for her. Susan always wondered when this dream was going to end.

Before long, Susan's mind was again slipping into the past, but this time she visited a sweeter, happier time. Her conversation with Scott made her realize how lucky she was to have him in her life. As Susan watched the sun's rays dance on the windowsill, she refused to think about how her life might have turned out had he not fallen in love with her. That path was much too painful a journey to ponder right now. Instead, Susan reviewed the years that had brought them together, remembering how Scott had come into her life and changed it.

Scott had left for college right out of high school. His father wanted him to attend an Ivy League school to broaden his life experience and give him a taste of "another world," as they called it. Scott settled on the University of Pennsylvania and had come home that first summer to work for his dad, but after that one summer, he always found summer jobs in Philadelphia.

Although Scott fully intended to return to Atlanta and join his father's company, he was first determined to earn his master's degree in business. He wanted to prove that his future success in his father's company would not be due to nepotism. So during his senior year at Penn, he was accepted by the Harvard Business School.

While at Harvard, Scott began dating an attractive girl from upstate New York who was also a business major. They enjoyed comparing the differences between growing up in the South and the North. She was intelligent and intensely driven, possessing an exhaustive list of goals that did not include being "stuck" in Atlanta, Georgia. She constantly pushed him to apply at one of the prestigious firms in downtown Boston. She had their future all figured out. He would be offered a great job when he graduated; they would get married, and she would also earn her master's at Harvard. She had visions of their hitting Manhattan with their Harvard MBAs in two years and taking over.

Only one problem presented itself: that wasn't what Scott wanted. Whenever he tried to tell her how important it was for him to go back and work with his dad, she would become hostile. She thought he would be throwing his future away. As far as she was concerned, there was only New York. If you didn't work there, you were a failure.

Scott was twenty-five the day he boarded the plane for Georgia with his college degrees in one hand and his father's letter offering him his first official position within the company in the other. He felt anything but a failure, and he couldn't wait to get home.

CHAPTER 5

❧

SCOTT AGREED TO stay at his parents' home for one month to allow his mother to spoil him a little with her wonderful cooking. Then he planned to find his own apartment closer to the office. Except for the first summer and a week every Christmas, Scott had now been on his own for seven years. He was used to fixing his own meals, doing his own laundry, and generally making a home for himself. He never really liked the dorm life at Penn. Even though he enjoyed having fun like everyone else, he tended to be more serious and determined than most. He had never seen the value in getting wasted every weekend and was tired of constantly defending his choices, so shortly before the Christmas break of his sophomore year, he found a studio apartment not far from campus. He had always held down a part-time job, and even though his dad paid for college, Scott wanted at least to be responsible for his rent and living expenses.

Scott felt it was important to show his dad he was growing up. He admired his father and in some ways considered him to be his best friend. He had scores of buddies from high school and college to talk with about sports and girls, but he went to his father with any serious problem. He had grown up watching the way his dad had treated his mother and sister and how they loved him. Even as a boy, Scott remembered going to the office with his dad on a summer day and observing how people responded to his father. Their high opinion wasn't due so much to the fact that he was their boss but more that they liked him. As Scott grew older, he came to realize that what he had seen in these people was the great respect and honor they had for his dad. Somewhere in his early youth, Scott determined that one day he, too, would be such a man. He could not think of anything more worthwhile.

During the month he was at home, Scott enjoyed spending lots of time with his kid sister, who had grown up while he was away. Carol Anne had been ten, almost eleven, when he had left for college. Except for letters, phone calls, and a week home during the holidays, he realized he had neglected to stay in close contact with his little sister. She was almost eighteen and would be graduating from high school in a week or so. Carol Anne had always been a very sweet, kind person, and he greatly appreciated the time they were now able to spend together.

On one of their evening strolls through the mall, Scott was reintroduced to Susan Miller. Carol Anne had known her in second grade, but Susan's neighborhood had been rezoned to another school district. Later, though, their schools were consolidated into Northeast High School, and they had met again.

Carol Anne had approached Susan the first day of their freshman year and with a warm smile said, "Well, hello again, Snow White." From that moment on, the two became inseparable. Susan spent almost every weekend during high school at Carol Anne's where they were always making grand plans for their futures. Both wanted to attend college and have a career, but due to financial restraints, Susan was practical and planned to go to the local community college. Carol Anne, on the other hand, was expected to attend a university elsewhere. As with Scott, her parents encouraged her to experience life outside of Georgia before settling down.

Having received her acceptance letter from USC, she was excitedly telling Susan all about it. "Snow White, can you believe it? I will actually be living in Southern California! I cannot wait to spend time on the beach." They started giggling and began singing one of their favorite Beach Boys songs. They linked their arms together and strolled through the mall. Carol Anne was busy listing everything she was planning to do when she arrived in California, and the girls almost forgot Scott was even there. Susan was sincerely happy for her friend, and she let Carol Anne enjoy this wonderful news. They both knew this summer would end too quickly, but they refused to let this awareness put a damper on their fun tonight.

Scott watched the two girls giggle and talk, seemingly without stopping for breath, and he marveled at their natural beauty. He had always known his sister was destined to be a beautiful woman; she looked so much like his mother that she couldn't help being attractive. However, Susan's beauty was breathtaking. Her eyes sparkled as she talked with Carol Anne, and those eyes melted something inside of him. As he watched her, Scott realized she was unaware of her striking beauty. Her makeup was understated, and her clothes were simple. Something about this girl made him want to spend time with her and get to know her better.

Scott, Carol Anne, and Susan enjoyed a wonderful summer together. Scott was busy during the week getting settled in his new job, but the weekends were reserved for the three of them. They spent every Saturday exploring and having fun.

He found a very nice apartment only two blocks from work, and the three would spend their Saturdays hitting all the yard sales and antique malls, looking for unique pieces of furniture to decorate his apartment. The girls were determined that, before the summer was over, his place would be perfect. None dared mention summer's end, as if ignoring it would make it not happen. But all too soon, their last Saturday together arrived. Scott invited both girls to his apartment for lunch. How he had dreaded this weekend! All day he had struggled to act cheerful and enthusiastic. He had always been quite serious. Sure, he had fun throughout college and grad school, but not like this. This summer had been magical.

Scott ordered pizza, and the trio sat down to talk as they waited for the delivery. Susan shared that she had registered for classes at the community college and would start after Labor Day. With an unusual openness, Susan shared, "I need to get another part-time job now that I have college expenses. With my dad back in prison, finances are tight at home."

Scott knew Susan's father had been sent to prison years ago for his assault on her mother. All of the local papers had carried the story, and since Carol Anne and Susan had been friends, their family had followed the story with great interest. The family felt they needed to explain it as best they could to Carol Anne. Scott also knew Susan never talked about her family. He did not dare ask questions for fear of sending her back into her shell, but he was curious to know why and when her father had been sent back to prison. He did not remember reading anything about a trial in the paper, and he certainly would have noticed if anything regarding her family has been printed.

Carol Anne was shocked to hear her friend talking so openly in front of Scott. Susan was usually guarded about her family. Carol watched her brother's expression, hoping his dismay would not silence Susan. For months, Carol Anne's only real concern about going away to college was leaving behind her best friend. She knew how much Susan depended on her when circumstances became unbearable, and she was unsure what Susan would do without that escape. Knowing how guarded Susan was about her family made their conversation even more puzzling. She did not seem to be struggling for words or acting nervous. Susan's matter-of-fact demeanor was so uncharacteristic, Carol Anne was caught off guard.

"Carol Anne, when I mentioned my plans to attend the community college, my mother became irate. She accused me of wanting to lollygag around campus instead of working full-time to help with the bills. College is my only way out. If I don't improve my skills, I'll be trapped in deadend jobs exactly like my mother. The only way I can go to college is if I find a better paying part-time job so I can give her a little more money. Perhaps then she'll lighten up on me."

Carol Anne stared at Susan, amazed at how calm she appeared in front of Scott. She thought back to a night several months earlier when Susan struggled desperately to share the cruel facts about her father's last run-in with the law. Susan had been unusually quiet that night as the two girls were having an evening swim. Carol Anne was aware that something was bothering her friend, but she had learned not to probe. When Susan was ready, she would talk, so Carol Anne waited.

Abruptly, Susan turned to her and asked, "Carol Anne, you knew my dad went to prison for almost killing my mother when I was a child, didn't you?"

Trying not to act shocked at her question, Carol Anne held a steady gaze and answered, "Yes, I knew. Why?"

Susan smiled faintly. "I was quite sure you did. I want to thank you for not asking me questions. It's not that I don't trust you, honest. I just don't like to talk about what happened."

"I understand, Susan," Carol Anne responded, although she really didn't. Her friend had been through things she couldn't even imagine. She wanted to say something profound, but she had no words.

A few minutes later, Susan paddled up next to her and looked like she wanted to say something. She held onto Carol Anne's raft so the two were floating side by side, while looking at the starry sky. Susan's barely audible voice broke their silence. "My dad spent five years in prison for nearly killing my mother, and then she took him back. Why? Why did my mother do that?"

She knew Susan didn't expect an answer. She remained quiet, hoping Susan would feel free to keep sharing.

Suddenly Susan's voice changed to a tone Carol Anne had never heard from Susan. She was not angry; she sounded almost pleading—as if she dared not say what she was about to. "He had to promise the parole board that he would never hit her again or he'd land right back in prison if he did. Within a few months, the battering all started again. I was eight when he was taken away, thirteen when he returned, and for the next four years, he frequently beat my mother. He simply made sure she never went to a doctor afterward. He did stop hitting me after a gym teacher became suspicious about some ugly bruises on my legs and back and wrote a letter home. The truth is, I was too ashamed and afraid of my parents to tell anyone we were still being assaulted."

Carol Anne knew she needed to say something. "Susan, is it still happening?"

"No. It's finally over. This past October, my father's anger got him into trouble again. He had finally packed up and moved out of the house at the start of my senior year. He got a job with another freight company over in Jefferson, ninety miles from here. He was finally through with my mother and didn't want us to go along. What none of us knew at the time was that my sister, Lisa, had finished her parole in California and had moved back to Jefferson, Georgia."

Susan turned, trying to gauge how shocked her friend was at her news. Carol Anne simply reached over to take her friend's hand and continued to look up into the sky. "You knew my sister ran away from home when I was eight. What I never told you was that while living in California, Lisa got into drugs and was caught selling to support her habit. When she was nineteen, she was sentenced to serve two years in jail and three years on probation. As soon as she had served her sentence, she wanted to leave California, but she had no intention of coming home to live in Atlanta, which was too close to our parents. She settled in Jefferson, but we never knew any of this until this year. Lisa was a great sister to me, but now her life's a mess. She's still on drugs, drinking heavily, and selling herself to anyone with a few dollars to support her habit."

Having shared the worst part of her secret, Susan quickly finished her story. "One night last October, Lisa walked into a bar in downtown Jefferson and ran right into our father. His hatred for her had been smoldering for years, and without any warning, he pulled her outside and beat her beyond recognition. Some guys pulled him off her before he could kill her and held him until the police arrived. His trial was held in Jefferson, and since he was a nobody, the news never made our papers. My mother was forced to sell the house last fall to pay the attorney's fees, but we were allowed to rent it. My father was sentenced to ten to fifteen years, and at the sentencing all he had to say was, 'Lisa better make out her will.' "

Horrified, Carol Anne asked, "Is your sister all right?"

"Sort of, if you can call her life all right. I didn't go to the trial, although I did go to see my sister several times while she was recovering. Lisa needs some intervention, but she doesn't think so and has no intention of getting anywhere near our mother. Besides, Mother wants nothing to do with her and could care less what happens to her."

The doorbell rang, bringing Carol Anne back to the present. Scott went to answer the door and get the pizza. Carol Anne studied Susan's face and thought about that night in the pool. She wondered how Susan could have gone through that much stress and kept quiet for so long. Susan had held in that secret for almost six months, appearing normal even to her closest friend.

Scott grabbed his wallet and opened the door, expecting the pizza delivery boy. Instead, his father, who had been gone on a business trip for almost a week, had stopped by his son's apartment. "Scott, your mother and I would like to invite all of you to join us for a family dinner at the house tonight."

Scott turned and asked the girls, obviously including Susan, if that would be all right with them. Without waiting for their response, he said, "Sure, Dad, we'd love to." Right then, the pizza delivery boy walked up.

Mr. Thomas looked at the large pizza and then at his son and laughed. "Let's make it around eight. That way you'll all be hungry again."

Susan always felt good whenever Carol Anne's family included her in their family get-togethers. Sometimes she felt a little uncomfortable, wondering if she was intruding, but the family never seemed to act like it, and Carol Anne always told her she was silly to feel that way.

Throughout high school, she practically lived at their house; she thought Mr. and Mrs. Thomas were the kindest, most gracious people she had ever met.

Susan excused herself around three o'clock, needing to go home to shower and change before dinner. As soon as she was gone, Scott cornered Carol Anne. "What's the deal with her father? Why was he sent back to prison?"

Carol Anne knew Scott wasn't trying to be nosy. True concern was written on his face; he cared about her friend. Carol sat on the couch, took a deep breath, and carefully weighed her words. "Scott, I was amazed that she talked so candidly about her dad in front of you today. That means she feels she can trust you as she trusts me. If she wants you to know anything more about her family, she'll tell you because I can't betray her confidence. I'm glad she'll have you here while I'm gone. She needs a good friend who will stand by her and, based on this summer, I think that person could be you. Just don't push her. Susan doesn't open up easily." With those words of both confidence and caution, Carol Anne left for home.

CHAPTER 6

SCOTT PULLED INTO his parents' driveway around six that evening. His dad had called a couple of hours earlier to say that because the evening was so warm, his mother had suggested the girls could swim while the men grilled. Scott offered to pick up some ice cream. He wanted to arrive early so he could have a word with his father before everyone else was there.

Scott tossed the ice cream into the freezer and then went out to where his dad was getting the fire started on the grill. Scott sat on the bench next to his dad and asked, "Are there any part-time openings for a general office person at work?"

Bill turned, giving his son a puzzled look. "Why? Who needs a job?"

"Susan said her only hope of attending college hinges on finding another job. She needs a position that provides more hours and better pay." After a thoughtful pause, Scott asked, "Did you know her father was sent back to prison this year?"

"Scott, your mother and I know about Susan's father. You are obviously concerned about Susan's welfare also, so, how about you? Could you use a part-time assistant?"

"Dad, this summer has been wonderful. Carol Anne, Susan, and I have had so much fun together, and I have developed some strong feelings for Susan." Before his father could express his concern about Susan's age, Scott brought it up himself. "I have no intention of dating such a young girl, and because of my feelings for her, I don't think having Susan working directly with me twenty or thirty hours a week would be wise. We can help her, though, and I think we owe it to people like Susan. She has a definite need, and we have been blessed with the ability to fill that need. Isn't that what you've always taught me?"

Bill continued fanning the fire in the grill as they discussed the situation, and Bill agreed to talk to Susan about coming to work for the company.

August nights in Atlanta were usually uncomfortable outdoors, but tonight was turning out to be rather pleasant. The heat wave had temporarily broken, the humidity was unusually low for Atlanta, and a cool breeze was blowing. They could not have chosen a lovelier night to grill outdoors, swim, and have a going-away party for Carol Anne. Bill loved the times his whole family gathered together, but he knew it would be the holidays before they would be together again, which made this evening somewhat bittersweet.

The girls decided to take a swim while Scott busily helped his mother. He knew his parents were struggling with letting go of their baby girl—even though they were the ones who had wholeheartedly encouraged her to venture away from home. Slipping in the side door of the kitchen, Scott silently watched his mother observing the girls through the kitchen window. She had a sad, but sweet, smile on her face. Carol Anne was growing up too fast for her, and he knew his mother was going to miss her only daughter.

Scott quietly walked up behind his mother, slipped his arms around her, and gently kissed her on the cheek. "You did a wonderful job rearing her, Mom. You and Dad reared her to be strong. She will be fine in California."

Caroline didn't say a word; she didn't have to. She simply gave her son's arm a gentle squeeze and then quickly picked up the potato salad and headed outside with a smile on her face.

After dinner, the girls offered to clean up while Scott and his parents took their turn in the pool. While Carol Anne began cutting the pie, Susan brought up the dreaded subject. She walked up behind her best friend, placed her chin on her shoulder, and said, "I can't believe our summer is over. What am I going to do without you?"

Carol Anne dared not turn around to look at Susan. She set aside the dishes and stood very still. "Susan, I wish you were coming with me. I hate the idea of leaving you here with your mother."

Susan quickly hugged Carol Anne as she mused to herself, *Any other time I would have done anything to go with you, Carol Anne. But not now. Though I know I have no chance with Scott, I love just being with him. He makes me feel wonderful.*

Carol Anne had no idea what Susan was thinking. She did, however, have an idea of how strong her brother's feelings were for Susan. She decided to take this opportunity to suggest, "Susan, you've said a million times you're never getting married and that you don't want children. But I wish you would rethink that. Someday you will make some man a great wife." Seeing that familiar look of pain come across Susan's face, she quickly added, "You've come so far and made so many positive changes these past few years."

"Carol Anne, lest you forget, I still have a father in prison, a sister who is a drug-using prostitute, and a mother…well, need I say more? Who in the world would ever want me?"

Carol Anne looked straight at her friend and said, "Any man in his right mind, Susan. That's who!"

Susan shook her head in playful disgust. "If I thought I could have a marriage like your parents, I might consider it. Oh, I know your family isn't perfect, but they are to me, and anything short of what they have simply isn't worth the pain."

Carol Anne smiled. "Susan, you know better than anyone that people's ideas can change. Remember how hard it was when you first started visiting here? You worked so hard to create excuses not to go to church with us, and you were totally offended by anyone talking about God. You were careful not to show your anger to anyone else, but, oh, how you would argue with me back then! Everything I was ever taught was challenged in my efforts to combat your arguments. If I couldn't help you answer your questions, the answers I had always believed in didn't carry much weight for me either. I knew you were blaming God for what your parents did to you, and you considered God your enemy because He allowed the abuse to happen."

With a wan smile, Susan replied, "Yes, I remember. I also remember the great lengths you and your mother went to in order to help me—even when I didn't want help. You two had heard of a Dr. Jacobson and then concocted a story about needing my help at that retreat, stopping just short of lying to get me there. I remember sitting in the back seat of your mother's van as she drove to the campground. I had no intention of attending the retreat. I was simply going to help set the tables and disappear for long walks. I still remember the retreat's topic was "Can God Be Trusted? My immediate response was, 'No He can't!' "

With an embarrassed giggle, Susan quoted the argument she had embraced for so long. "How could a loving God let my sister and me suffer as little kids? If He cared so much, why didn't He stop our parents? If He is so all-fired loving and powerful, why didn't He help us?"

With emotion revealed in her eyes, Carol Anne responded, "Oh, Susan, we all hurt so badly for you back then. You were so hard to talk to, and we wanted to help. We had heard so many wonderful things about Dr. Jacobson and hoped and prayed she would be able to help you."

"I know, Carol Anne, and she did. I had such an attitude back then. I despised it when people with comfortable lives presumed to say that God cared about me. As much as I cared for you and your mother, I would not listen to you. I always thought, *Sure, they have no reason not to believe God loves them!* Did I ever tell you what I did when I found out what kind of retreat you and your mother were dragging me to attend? I spent that afternoon in the van, writing out a long list of questions to challenge the speaker to prove to me exactly how she could know God loved me and cared for me. I was determined to hand this woman my questions and walk away. As I put the paper in my purse, I thought that after she read it, she would have to think twice before she talked about something that my life proved was a lie."

Carol Anne looked puzzled. "You hadn't planned on attending that retreat? What changed your mind?"

"While setting up the literature table for your mother, I read Dr. Jacobson's pamphlet, which described her abusive childhood and how she had suffered loneliness and isolation as a child and young adult. She mentioned she had hated God for most of her childhood. She thought He was either punishing her for something she had done, or He was evil and enjoyed watching her suffer. I had never heard anyone else admit to feeling what I had always felt. I decided to sit in on the lecture and listen to this woman with an open mind. I thought that maybe I could also have my angry questions answered. At least, I was willing to listen for a change."

Carol Anne picked up the dessert tray and, as she stepped through the back door, she turned and commented, "Susan, it was a wonderful retreat, wasn't it? I'm so thankful you finally found your answers—even though I wasn't the one to help you with them."

Susan stepped over to the sink for a glass of water before following her friend. She stood at the kitchen window and watched as the Thomas family huddled around the dessert tray, laughing, talking, and enjoying each other. If not for that retreat, she might never have been able to stand here, knowing that this family was one of God's ways of showing her exactly how much He did love her.

Now almost two years later, she could remember every word shared at that retreat, and Susan allowed her mind to drift back to that wonderful weekend when her life truly began to change.

❧ The Retreat ❧

Dr. Stephanie Jacobson introduced herself by sharing some of her personal background. "I was the fourth daughter in a family of five children. I would describe my father as a working drunk, but in today's kinder, gentler terms, he would be called an *alcoholic*. Our mother, on the other hand, would constantly belittle all of us girls, telling us how worthless we were and how none of us would ever amount to a hill of beans. Neither of our parents were capable of showing love, and I grew up in constant fear of my father."

Dr. Jacobson had Susan's full attention. She was talking about feelings that echoed her own. Dr. Jacobson moved from behind the speaker's podium, pulled up a chair, and sat down. What she would share with these women was much too intimate to be shared from behind a podium. With a smile that warmed the group, Dr. Jacobson began. "If you women are anything like I was, just the title of my talk probably set your teeth on edge."

Nervous giggles quickly washed across the group, giving Susan a sense of comfort as she thought, *Well, I guess I'm not the only one.*

Dr. Jacobson clearly understood the need to put the group at ease. After all, she hoped to shake loose some of their deeply rooted beliefs, and she didn't want formality to get in the way. Leaning slightly forward in her seat, as if sharing an important secret, Dr. Jacobson said, "If you were reared in an abusive home, more than likely you are sitting here tonight with deep-seated anger toward God. I know this because I was too."

With a gentle manner that drew everyone in, Dr. Jacobson began to share more of her story. "When I was little, I came to two very incorrect conclusions that resulted in tremendous damage to me for many years. As a trained therapist, and myself a victim, I have counseled hundreds of adults who struggle with the damaging effects of reaching these same incorrect conclusions. Children growing up in hostile, unloving homes who try to make some sense of their life base their conclusions on their ability to evaluate the world around them. When that world is sick and distorted, their perceptions will likewise be distorted. When their mother or father is beating them, how can a young child understand that this abuse is not happening because something is wrong with him but that his parent is sick? Abused children must, in their young minds, find a reasonable explanation for what is happening to them. These so-called reasonable explanations can cause lifelong damage to a child. I embraced my own *reasonable* explanations, and I'm sure some of you have done the same."

The woman sitting next to Susan nudged her in the ribs and whispered, "She has that right. Both my parents were sick, for sure."

Susan smiled sympathetically but wished this woman would leave her alone. She did not want to appear cold and insensitive toward her, but she wanted to keep her wits about her. If this woman was going to make comments on every point, she would make some excuse to move to another seat. Susan returned her gaze to Dr. Jacobson, trying to focus on what she was saying.

"Ladies, the first wrong conclusion I came to was 'I must be bad. My parents are mean to me because I am bad. If I were good, they would love me. All that is happening to me is my fault.' Everything in my world proved that. I started believing this first lie about myself at a very young age, and though I don't recall exactly how old I was, I do remember the day I said the words out loud.

"I was six years old and in the first grade. It was Christmastime, and my class was busy making decorations for the classroom. My teacher wanted each class member to write our Christmas wish list so we could mail them to Santa Claus. I was only six, but I already knew better than to wish for very much—even from Santa."

Susan's heart immediately jumped to her throat at this comment. *That's exactly how I always felt.* Struggling to control her emotions, Susan swallowed hard and learned forward in order to fully concentrate on Dr. Jacobson's story.

"I finally wrote one small item on my paper, folded it, timidly approached the teacher's desk, and slipped it into the Santa mailbox. I remember how very long most of the other kids' lists were. I knew our family didn't have much money, and my mother was always yelling at my siblings and me, demanding our gratefulness for the food on the table. This statement, by itself, was true. We did need to be grateful that we had food on the table and that we were not starving. The truth was, though, we were starving—only not for food.

"We all felt the sting of the anger and the hatred in our mother's voice. She wasn't attempting to teach us; she was threatening us. The cruelty some parents use to deliver truth is unforgivable. I am sure some of you listeners have memories that are equally as painful, perhaps even more so."

Even at the tender age of sixteen, Susan had become quite adept at camouflaging her feelings, but this woman was speaking to her very soul. She felt almost undressed, as if protective layers she had carefully wrapped around her heart were being peeled away, leaving her vulnerable. She sat, unmoving, totally engrossed in the story.

Dr. Jacobson continued. "Christmas day was fast approaching. My sisters and I did not expect much from our parents. Indeed, that cold, harsh truth had been clearly and bitterly spelled out to us for weeks. But when you are six years old, and the whole world is telling you Santa exists, that he is coming with toys and presents for all the good little children, and well, at six, you still believe!

"I vividly remember that Christmas day. The day before, Mother had brought home a scraggly little tree the grocer had thrown out, and we decorated it with popcorn and paper stars. When we finished, Mother told us we would each have one present under the tree on Christmas morning and that we were to wait until she and Dad were up before opening our present.

"Our baby brother still slept with our parents, while my three sisters and I shared two double beds in the small loft at the top of the stairs. We four girls crawled into bed that night, imagining what might be in our package. We thought we would probably get new dolls; as a matter of fact, we were certain we would. I then confessed to my sisters that I had written a letter to Santa and that my teacher had mailed it. I assured them he would bring what I had asked for because I had only asked for one thing— a shiny pair of black shoes with taps on them. My sisters, not wanting to spoil my excitement and belief in Santa, kept quiet. I fell asleep that night, convinced Santa was bringing me new shoes."

As Dr. Jacobson talked about her sisters, Susan couldn't help but think of her own sister. Lisa would have tried to protect her, and a sudden and powerful sense of loneliness for Lisa overwhelmed her. Carefully controlling her emotion, she allowed Dr. Jacobson's voice to draw her back to the story.

"The next morning I anxiously and hopefully descended the stairs only to discover that no shiny black shoes with taps were under the tree for me. Only the one present from our parents awaited each of us. Our mother had bought each of us a dime-store Betsy Wetsy doll. I remember my sisters being all excited and showing each other their dolls, while I sat quietly, fighting back tears. Mother demanded to know why I did not like my doll. Overcome with indescribable pain deep in my chest, I barely choked out I thought I was getting new shoes.

"Of course, my mother had no idea what I was talking about, nor did she care. She angrily grumbled something about us kids never being grateful and then walked away. I stepped out onto the porch in the bitter cold. I was blanketed under a lifeless, gray sky, and I remember thinking, *This is exactly how I feel.*

"I wasn't really old enough to put my feelings into words, but I understood how the cold air and dreary sky reflected how I felt. I was six years old, and the only reasonable conclusion I could reach was that I must be bad because even Santa wouldn't come to see me. I had only asked for some new shoes while the other kids at school had asked for bikes and expensive toys. What terrible thing had I done that even Santa wouldn't come to my house? I felt a deep sense of shame and guilt but didn't know what I had done wrong. My only explanation was totally substantiated, as I reasoned through my parents treating me bad because I was bad. Santa didn't bring me new shoes because I was bad. It was all my fault."

Several side comments arose from the group regarding this conclusion. A few women near Susan began arguing the error of such thinking, so Susan took the opportunity to slip out of her seat and move to the back row. The silly, nippy responses from some of the women were beginning to frustrate Susan. She understood exactly what Dr. Jacobson was saying and knew how very true the thinking process was.

Dr. Jacobson drew the group's attention back and continued. "By the following Christmas, I had learned Santa did not exist. How wonderful it would have been if I had possessed the wisdom to dig deep within me, find that lie I had believed about myself, and plucked it out. Children don't do that! The lies we tell ourselves as children become the truths we live by as adults. Allow me to repeat this very important statement: the lies we tell ourselves as children become the truths we live by as adults.

"If you grew up feeling responsible for all of the evil that happened in your house, as an adult, you might feel responsible for everything going wrong in your life today. While it was probably something other than Santa Claus that confirmed your conclusion to you, something in your life convinced you to believe, *I am bad.* This lie, which once crippled me, is crippling you. This lie, which resides at the very core of your being, constantly whispers, 'It is all your fault.'

"This lie is such a part of how you view yourself that you and I will probably always struggle against believing this untruth. We need to remind ourselves daily that we are not responsible when others close to us behave badly. We are *only* responsible for how we behave. I believe this horrible lie that abused children embrace as truth is the very reason why some women marry abusive men and stay in abusive marriages. They feel like they deserve it because they believe the lie, *I am bad.*"

Susan was surprised by the sudden silence that filled the room. No one was looking around. Everyone seemed to be pondering this powerful concept Dr. Jacobson was presenting. Susan was glad to be sitting in the back row.

Dr. Jacobson had noticed Susan's earlier seat change and waited until she looked up to make eye contact with her. Giving her a reassuring smile, Dr. Jacobson continued. "The second incorrect conclusion I want to address tonight is 'God just doesn't love me.' I know firsthand this subject is difficult for hurting people to hear, but please understand that if you suffered a harsh, abusive childhood, you probably also came to this incorrect conclusion about God. Most of us did. Please realize that going through life choosing to believe there is no God is vastly different than believing God is out to hurt you. If, as a child, you decided God was your enemy, that formidable enemy still resides in your mind. I would like to help you face that enemy tonight and convince you of the truth that God is not out to hurt you.

"As a very young girl, every night I would pray to God and plead with Him to change my parents—to make my father stop drinking and for the horrifying beatings to stop. I prayed that God would make my mother nice—like my friend's mother. I prayed for His help for years, but no relief ever came. Since He obviously didn't care, I stopped praying."

Tears streamed down Susan's face. Years of desperate childhood prayers screamed in her head, and the pain of realizing they would never be answered was as agonizing tonight as the night she had also decided to stop praying. Trying to subtly wipe the tears from her face, Susan fought to focus on Dr. Jacobson's words.

"With childhood reasoning, I concluded that either God did not exist or God simply didn't love me. If He loved me, why didn't He help me? If He loved me, why did He let those people hurt me? Why didn't God love me? As a child, these questions seemed easy to answer: *I am not worth it* matched up with the other lie I had believed about myself—*I am bad, so God doesn't love me.* Once a child is convinced of these lies, he feels totally isolated. He feels no connection to his parents and now he feels disconnected from God.

You have no doubt heard the saying, 'There are no atheists in foxholes.' Everyone in overwhelming circumstances cries out to God for help. Children who grow up in abusive homes live their lives in foxholes!"

Susan's head jerked up in surprise at this logical description. *That's exactly how it feels!* Suddenly the image of herself crouched down and hiding in the closet the night her father almost killed her mother became strikingly vivid. That closet had certainly been one of her foxholes.

Speaking as gently as she could, Dr. Jacobson proposed, "Children who live in houses with so much hatred and abuse always blame themselves. They naturally begin to believe something they are doing provokes this behavior in those around them, so God is punishing them. When that abuse reaches the unthinkable, God becomes the unthinkable. What are children to do when their world is in utter chaos, and they believe they have nowhere to go for help and protection? What are they to do when they are convinced even God hates them? Most simply hate God right back. Others decide that a god like that simply should not exist, so in their mind, He doesn't. As little children, they have no way of comprehending that the god they are hating isn't God, only their warped conception of

Him. They don't understand He does love them and cares deeply about what is happening to them. If we are to dispel the lie that God is our enemy, don't we have to understand the concept of who God says He is? Once we understand this truth, we no longer need to think of Him as our enemy. We can then be free to seek Him and get to know Him. In this freedom, childhood lies cannot survive. Ladies, please don't leave here tonight still thinking you have to go through life fighting against an enemy as big as God."

Susan's initial resistance to this subject began to melt. This woman's logic, compounded by her own painful childhood, made Susan a willing listener. She did not want to continue feeling as though God hated her.

Dr. Jacobson continued. "I would like to share how those questions were answered for me. Almost all religions teach that we have a choice. We can choose to love God, or we can choose to hate God. This choice, which is a gift from God to mankind, is called 'free will.' God does not want us to be robots, following after Him without any alternatives. Our heavenly Father would experience no pleasure from forced obedience. We all enjoy and, I dare say, cherish our free will. I know I do. We would never want God to take that gift from us.

"One night when I was in my late twenties, I was going through a very difficult time. I was at my wit's end and felt completely alone. As I had done many times before, I began praying, but not as others pray. My prayers were angry accusations toward God. If He truly was a God of love, I challenged Him to answer me and show me exactly how much He loved me."

Susan smiled as she clutched her purse, knowing those very words were written on her piece of paper.

"Ladies, without getting melodramatic, all I can tell you is that in the most calm and quiet manner, a thought, or a voice if you will, came into my mind, which said, 'Stephanie, you're tying My hands.'

"Now I personally don't believe God talks to us out loud, but I am certain that voice was God. He was talking to me, and I wanted to talk to Him. I sensed no anger, only a pleading for me to try to understand. So with more respect than my previous questions had been offered, I closed my eyes and asked, 'How am I tying Your hands? How can I tie the hands of God?'

"My friends, you are certainly free to believe or not to believe this, but in that same sweet, calm manner I heard: 'In one hand, I have given you the same free will that I have given to all mankind. I cannot take back a gift I have given. With My other hand, you are demanding I prove My love for you by taking away another person's free will. Stephanie, your parents had choices. They chose to be angry and hate-filled. Every time they made that choice, I mourned for them, but I also mourned for you. I am God, but man chooses the path he walks. I could not stop them from hurting you, Stephanie, but if you will let Me, I can heal that hurt and replace your hate and anger with love. I am here, and I do love you. Stephanie, you also have a free will and a choice.' "

As Dr. Jacobson paused, the silence in the room was almost deafening. No one spoke or looked around. Susan had heard some preachers talk about free will but never like this. Mulling it over, Susan realized she also had free will, which meant she could free will God away if she wanted to. As this thought crossed her mind, she heard Dr. Jacobson say almost the same thing, and she turned to listen.

"That night I realized I had the power to accept God. I could now set aside the concept that God was my enemy. He wasn't responsible for and didn't want my suffering at the hands of abusive parents. I knew then I had uncovered a huge lie I had told myself. God did not hate me, and He had not put me in that family to punish me. That night was a crossroads for me. The lie was now exposed, and I needed to choose which path I was going to walk: a path devoid of God, no longer my enemy but not my friend, or a path that allowed me to get to know this God I had spent my whole life mistrusting. The choice was mine.

"That night I knew I was being offered something wonderful—not some mystic erasing of my past to give me a different childhood but rather a healing of my soul. Somehow I knew that if I continued to shake my fist in God's face, I was going to remain angry, bitter, and lost. I knew that night I needed to choose healing. I couldn't stay in that place of isolation any longer. If there really was a God who loved me, I knew I wanted to get to know Him.

"Like many of you in this group, I grew up in a house filled with hate and anger. No matter what you did to survive that household, if you have not dealt with your past, you are also filled with hate and anger. No one is more sympathetic to your rage than those of us who have also been there, but that rage is a poison that will eventually consume you. You must choose to let go of the anger. Love and hate cannot dwell together. Before you can welcome love into your life, you must let go of the hate.

"Ladies, the very act of child abuse screams that you had no choice! Yes, as a child, you had no choice, and those who hurt you tried to convince you that you would never again have a choice. But today, as an adult, you can choose to end it. You can choose to live your life as a victim, allowing those who hurt you to continue to continue to control your life, or you can choose to do what you were unable to do as a child—let God help you release yourself from their grip and walk away. You are free to walk a path that does not include God, but I'm here to tell you that *God can be trusted, and God does love you.*"

Susan sat through Dr. Jacobson's talk, almost forgetting anyone else was present. In some strange way, she knew God was trying to tell her something. God was seemingly using this woman to answer the challenges she had written down that very afternoon—the challenges she was still clutching in her purse. She knew Dr. Jacobson was right, and from somewhere deep within her, Susan began to quietly plead with God to help her.

Dr. Jacobson then asked the group to close their eyes and silently remember a time in their childhood when they felt the most alone. Susan pictured herself in that closet the night her father almost killed her mother. She hated remembering that night, but as much as she tried to think of something else, her mind kept returning to that closet. She heard the speaker's gentle voice saying to everyone in the room, "Remember that wherever your memory has taken you right now, God was there! Because He gave man free will, He could not stop whatever happened to you there in your memory place. But God was there crying for you; you were not alone!"

With her eyes still closed, Susan thought about her mother and father. They had a choice to do good or evil because God had also given them a free will. For the first time, Susan began imagining that horrible night from God's perspective. She thought about how He must have suffered as He watched this man who had chosen to live his life so filled with hate there never was any room for Him. If God had tried to reach her mother and father at different times in their lives, she wondered when and how? Of course, she had no way of knowing, but she knew they had obviously turned Him away, and her broken life was the result.

All of a sudden, Susan pictured that little girl huddled in the closet, so terrified she couldn't breathe. Closing her eyes even tighter, Susan began to pray, asking God to hold that little girl, to love her, and to make her feel safe. Without concern about anyone watching her, Susan then allowed herself to cry. For the first time in her life, she allowed her damaged emotions to rise to the surface. Susan began crying for that little girl. The tears seemed to come from deep down to where she had stored that memory, flushing out her lies and pain. She also knew that God's tears were somehow blending with hers, and she felt as if He were wrapping His strong arms around her. A wonderful, warm feeling of peace enveloped her. She was choosing to let go of her anger, and she knew God did care what happened to her.

That night, as she climbed into bed, Susan quietly looked up and, for the first time, prayed, "God, I don't fully understand this free-will business very well, but I know You have also given that gift to me, so I am asking You to help me. Please help me."

Susan fell asleep, but that night it wasn't a sleep of escape. She finally knew God did care, she didn't have to fear Him, and she didn't have to feel all alone. That night, Susan experienced her first really sweet and peaceful sleep.

CHAPTER 7

A NOISE BROUGHT Susan back to the present, and she turned to see Scott's standing in the kitchen. "Susan, aren't you coming out for dessert? Your ice cream has already melted."

Embarrassed at being caught daydreaming, she quickly moved past him and headed out to the backyard. As Scott walked next to her, she thought about the remarkable difference in her perspective on life since that retreat weekend. An "enemy" named God no longer tormented her soul. She no longer felt God was "out to get her," and she had spent the past two years finally getting to know Him.

When everyone finished dessert, Carol Anne collected the dishes and headed for the kitchen while Susan and Scott sat at the table chatting. Mr. Thomas climbed out of the pool and casually wandered over to the table to visit with Susan. Realizing his dad was going to discuss the subject of a job for Susan, Scott excused himself and joined his mother in the pool.

Bill Thomas carefully considered the conversation with his son earlier that day. Not just what he had said but also how he had said it. He knew Scott was falling in love with this girl, and he really couldn't blame him. During most of Susan's high school years, she was like family. Scott had not been around during that time, but Bill and Caroline had come to love Susan as a daughter. He knew more about Susan's childhood than he had ever let on. After that day in second grade when he had driven her home, seeing the terror in her eyes, and hearing the boy next door talk about her father, Bill had asked around town about Chuck Miller. The man was known for his violent temper, and the police had been to their house on numerous occasions. Bill tried to get the police to protect the girl back then, but no one could do anything about

Chuck Miller until he went "too far." The problem was, *too far* was usually too late for most women and children.

Bill had felt helpless and wished he could have done something more for her, so when Carol Anne met Susan again in high school and started bringing her home every weekend, he was grateful. He felt that, at least, he was now able to provide a safe place for her to come when life at home became too tough.

Bill took a sip of coffee and asked Susan what her plans were for the fall. When she mentioned she would need to find a better part-time job, he very casually asked, "Why don't you come to the office on Monday and fill out an application? We have a position that might be what you're looking for."

Susan beamed with excitement as she thanked him for this opportunity. Scott, resting against the side of the pool, smiled at how wonderfully his dad had handled that offer.

Susan had an interview scheduled for the following week at Thomas & Associates. Mr. Thomas had asked his office manager, Mrs. Randal, to create an assistant's position so she could have some much-needed help. He mentioned Susan as a possibility but clearly left the final decision to hire her with Mrs. Randal. She interviewed Susan on Wednesday, and Thursday morning Susan started work.

Life was exciting, and Susan threw herself into her new job. She spent as much time as possible at the office the first two weeks. She wanted to learn quickly to ensure Mrs. Randal would have no regrets about her decision. Susan's community college classes began two weeks later. Keeping up with her job responsibilities and study requirements left her little time to miss Carol Anne.

One week after college started, Susan and her mother were given notice to vacate their house. Because of the expense of her father's trial, he had demanded the property be sold. If her mother had failed to comply, he had threatened to "take care" of her when he got out of jail. Unable to afford the house and the attorney's fees on her meager salary, her mother sold the house to an investor and used the entire equity to pay Chuck's attorney. They rented the house for a while, but now the investors wanted them to move so the house could be renovated and sold.

Faced with relocating, Susan plotted a risky scheme and approached her mother. "I'm earning more money now and am able to help out more with the rent. A very nice apartment building downtown is within walking distance to both of our jobs. It would be nice not to have to take the city bus to work. If they have an opening, I'm sure we can afford it."

Marjorie gave her usual glare to anything Susan suggested. While nervously waiting for her mother's response, Susan weighed the words she had used. *I didn't mention Thomas & Associates, so that shouldn't send her off the deep end. She certainly has no way of knowing Scott—"one of the Thomas clan," as she puts it—lives in that building. So if she explodes, it's simply because she hates anything and everything I suggest. I know I won't be able to keep Scott's presence in the building a secret forever, but I don't care. Living there will be worth it.*

A sudden change came over Marjorie's face. "It would be nice not to have to take the city bus to work, but an apartment building? I would hate having people living right on top of me. I need my space, but I suppose we can go take a look."

Within the week, they had signed a lease on a two-bedroom apartment in Scott's building. Susan made sure Scott understood he would never be welcome to stop by their apartment, but she knew the inevitable would happen. Her mother ran into Scott about two weeks later and exploded in Susan's face for "tricking" her. Marjorie's anger was softened only by her love of the apartment, but regardless of the wisdom of this choice, she was still determined to make Susan pay for tricking her like she had.

Scott had accidentally run into Susan and her mother twice, and he did not like Marjorie Miller at all. She was rude, and her vocabulary was raw.

Susan was horribly embarrassed at her mother's inconsiderate behavior. Susan knew that Scott was aware of her discomfort and intentionally kept both meetings as short as possible. Susan's numerous apologies for her mother's behavior, along with the pain Scott could see in her eyes, made him dislike Marjorie even more. She had such a mean streak, and she seemed to delight in her despicable behavior in front of her daughter's friends. Scott cared little about what Marjorie did or said, other than how she hurt Susan, so when she asked him to stay away from their apartment, he had no problem respecting her request.

Scott kept a busy schedule those first two years. He found it hard to spend a lot of time with Susan because his feelings were so strong, and he was afraid he would scare her. She never hid her fear of marriage and having children. Even though she had changed tremendously in the past several years, he knew she still was not quite ready for a serious relationship—but he was. Scott dated different women in town but always found himself comparing them to Susan, and he would soon lose interest. Though he was determined to avoid her, within days he would find himself making excuses to be with her, so he decided they would simply spend time together as friends. He would rather have the struggle of keeping his feelings in check than to miss out on the time they were able to spend together.

Susan's life had never been this exciting. Her days were filled with work that she loved, dinners with Scott, late evenings studying her college courses, and weekends spent with Scott and his parents. Life simply couldn't get any better. She and her mother had finally settled into a relationship that was workable because Susan was never home. For almost two years, life didn't appreciably change, which suited Susan. Soon after receiving her diploma from the community college, Susan decided not to pursue further college courses. She knew her mother would throw a fit if she wasted anymore time in college instead of bringing more money into the household, but Susan's real reason was personal. She hated the hours that studying took away from her time with Scott.

Late in September, Mrs. Randal invited Susan to take a coffee break with her. Quite unexpectedly Mrs. Randal asked, "Susan, do you intend to pursue a four-year degree?"

Unsure of what Mrs. Randal was hoping to hear, Susan hesitated, afraid to say what she really wanted. "I don't have any set plans. Actually, I'm enjoying my job so much that, at times, I find myself resenting college for interfering with time I could spend here at work."

Mrs. Randal smiled. "Now Susan, I don't want to be responsible for your decision not to pursue further college education, but I don't want to lose you either. I'm offering you a full-time position with the company, and I will look forward to knowing what you decide is the next best step for you."

Susan didn't hesitate; she accepted even before Mrs. Randal could finish presenting the details of the offer. Mrs. Randal chuckled at how quickly Susan had accepted. She hadn't even waited to hear that she was also being offered a significant and much-deserved raise. She loved her job, and now free of the demands of college, she would be able to spend more time at work. Susan thanked Mrs. Randal and could hardly wait to find Scott to share her good news with him. She hoped to invite him out for a celebration dinner.

Scott suggested they drive into the country, outside Atlanta, and have dinner at a wonderful old Southern plantation that had been converted into a restaurant. They had discovered this place with Carol Anne during one of their Saturday treasure hunts that first summer. They both loved its graceful, Southern charm. Each room on the first floor had been converted into dining rooms, some designed for private dining and some for shared dining with other guests. Not wanting to share Susan tonight, Scott called ahead to reserve Susan's favorite, the intimate front reading room with floor-to-ceiling bookcases filled with aged, collectible leather-bound books. Scott reserved this room because it was special to Susan, but he had another reason as well. He wanted to be alone with her tonight because he had decided the time had come to tell her he loved her. After he made the dinner reservation, he decided to go all out and rented a bright-red convertible for the evening. He wanted tonight to be special.

At the close of the workday, Scott eagerly walked into Susan's office. What he really wanted to do was to burst into her office and shout, "I love you, Susan! Will you please marry me?" He resisted this urge, however, and instead, calmly stopped at her door as she was putting away the last items on her desk. "Are you ready, Susan?"

Stepping through the doorway, she reminded Scott, "Don't forget, tonight is my treat." Scott wasn't going to argue the point right now. They chatted as they made their way to the company's parking garage.

The rental agent was already there, standing next to a shiny red convertible. "As you requested, it's all ready for you, Mr. Thomas. Here are the keys. Have a wonderful evening."

Scott held the door open for Susan. "I thought I'd make this night special. I've always liked convertibles." As he closed her door, he looked at her smiling face, and his heart skipped a beat as he thought about what he was finally going to do tonight. He had waited two years for this night, and he wanted it to be wonderful.

Scott quickly made it out of the city, deciding to take his favorite route to the plantation. This particular road had stately old trees that lined each side of the road, forming a canopy with just enough sky at the top to allow a beautiful view of the nighttime stars. Scott had fantasized about this road, this girl, and this night for more than a year! Here he was, Susan beside him, and the radio was playing a love song. He tried to relax and enjoy the moment, not wanting to be so focused on what was coming that he missed the joy of every single minute of this night.

"Susan, why don't you tell me about your new job?"

As Susan began talking excitedly, sharing all that Mrs. Randal had told her, Scott was watching her beautiful face and her happy, sparkling eyes. He wanted to spend his whole life keeping her as happy as she was tonight, wanting so desperately to be the one to protect her and have her eyes shine for him.

Susan leaned back against the seat, closed her eyes, and thought about how much she enjoyed doing things with Scott. As with every major event in her life these past two years, she couldn't wait to tell him all about it and hear his opinion. She loved to sit and listen to him talk about what he was doing at work. She especially loved when he used her as his sounding board when preparing a big presentation. What she didn't enjoy hearing was any information about the women he was dating. Though he never got too personal, Susan always felt uncomfortable whenever he would talk about the different places he was planning to take one of his dates. She knew she had no right to be jealous, but she and Scott always had so much fun together; she wanted to be the one to enjoy those activities with him.

Lately, she found herself inventing reasons to talk with Scott after work, hoping the conversation would keep going right through dinner and into the evening. She especially hated those times when he was forced to go on business trips. Regardless of how busy she kept herself, she missed him. Sometimes when he was away for a day or two, she would walk into his office so she could close her eyes, take a deep breath, and savor the lingering smell of his cologne. Realizing she was falling in love with him produced a firestorm of emotions within her. She had never wanted to fall in love, deciding long ago that marriage was not for her. Then Scott walked into her life, and suddenly she was challenging all of her old rules. Could she really entrust her life in the hands of another person? What if she gave in to these emotions, and he didn't feel the same? What if he simply thought of her as a kid sister? After all, he missed Carol Anne, and she was convinced he was spending all this time with her because he missed his sister. But tonight, she wasn't going to think about that. She didn't care what his reason was. As long as she could be close to him, she was happy.

Susan opened her eyes, turned to look at Scott, and found him smiling at her. "What? Why are you smiling at me?" She felt the blood rushing to her face and knew she was blushing, and she hated it. She felt so juvenile when she blushed.

Scott smiled that familiar half-smile she had come to love and said, "No reason in particular. I just like looking over and seeing you there. You know, I really do enjoy being with you."

She felt herself blush again and looked forward, his words ringing in her ears, *Enjoy being with you.* She thought, *See, Susan, he merely enjoys being with you. So don't let your imagination run away with you. Just enjoy what you have and don't hope for anything more.*

While Susan's mind raced, Scott mentally replayed his comment, *I really enjoy being with you.* His mind screamed, *If I don't tell you soon, I'm going to burst! Enjoy being with you...I can't stand being away from you!* Scott took a deep breath, checked his watch, and mused, *Just be patient, Scott. You'll have your answer soon enough.*

Sweet music greeted them as they pulled into the parking lot of the old plantation. During the summer the restaurant hired a string quartet and positioned them at the far left corner of the verandah. The music was peaceful, and the large old-fashioned fans mounted in the ceiling of the porch sent the sounds flowing through all the windows of the house, softly delivering a warm ambience to the guests inside.

Scott and Susan stopped momentarily to enjoy the beauty of the wonderful old house. Every window was alive with light, and the house looked as if a grand old party was being hosted as in days gone by.

Walking up the wide, wooden steps leading to the large verandah that encircled the entire first floor, Susan gazed at the house and wished it could tell her some of its stories. She tried to imagine women in days past, with their wide-hooped skirts, walking up these same steps. She couldn't help but wonder what this old plantation had seen—both good and bad.

The hostess greeted them as they entered the restaurant and walked them into the reading room. In the center of the room was a charming table set for two. The delicate china rimmed with tiny yellow roses, along with the silver settings, represented the ultimate in Southern elegance. The water goblets sparkled, reflecting the light from the crystal chandelier that hung directly above the table. A fireplace on the far wall housed a large basket of wildflowers. In the winter months, a blazing fire would have greeted them, but during the Georgia summer, the fragrance of wildflowers that filled the room was enjoyable. The lace curtains fluttered in the gentle breeze from the fans outside.

Once seated, Susan noticed a card addressed to her tucked in a bouquet of miniature yellow roses. She glanced at Scott with a puzzled look as she began to read. "Susan, may this be a beautiful evening for a beautiful woman. Love, Scott."

Susan laid down the note and tried to keep her voice from shaking as she said, "Thank you for the flowers, Scott. There is no one I would rather share this special evening with than you."

Scott, who had been unsure of how she was taking the note, had begun to question his timing. *What if Susan isn't ready to get serious?* She had been very outspoken about never getting married. *Am I moving too fast?*

But now he was speechless. Their small talk was agonizing, and he wanted to get to the point. He had intended to wait until after dinner, but that was going to be impossible. As he leaned forward, mentally putting his words together, the waiter walked in, asking for their order. Scott took a deep breath and leaned back in his chair. *This is going to be a long night.* Susan was sitting so close to him—her shiny black hair shimmering around her face, the faint hint of her perfume-filling his senses, her knee gently touching his. He almost wished she would stop staring at him. He couldn't think straight with her eyes smiling at him.

After the waiter took their order, Scott excused himself for a moment and followed the waiter out of the room. As soon as they were out of Susan's sight, Scott stopped the waiter and explained that he did not want to be disturbed for the next several minutes and requested a slight delay in serving dinner or drinks. Scott returned to the reading room, and the waiter quietly closed the pocket doors.

Scott took his seat across from Susan. Before she could say anything, Scott slid out of his seat, came around the table, and knelt beside her chair. Scott gently took hold of her hand and kissed it. He held it to his chest as he began talking. He took a deep breath and said, "Susan, I've loved you for two years now, and I can't keep quiet any longer. I can't stand being away from you, and any thought of living my life without you is inconceivable. I want nothing more in the world than to love you and make you happy. Susan, will you please marry me?"

With that said, Scott kissed her hand again and waited for her answer.

Susan could hardly focus on what he had said. She could actually feel his heart pounding against her hand. She sat frozen, not quite believing what she had heard. She had dreamed of this moment for almost two years but never believed it could actually happen. Scott Thomas was telling her he loved her and that he wanted to marry her. Struggling to find her voice, almost afraid to break the magic of the moment, she barely whispered her answer. "Yes."

In one single move, Scott pulled her chair away from the table and took her into his arms. He smiled down into that face he had come to love and gently kissed her for the very first time. Susan's response to his kiss was more than enough answer for him. He could feel her in his arms, almost melting into him. Her kiss was not timid, and he loved it. There certainly was no fear in her response. They stood in each other's arms kissing, talking, laughing, and kissing again. They were almost talking over each other, expressing the feelings that had been bottled up for so long. They had both forgotten there were other people in the world until the waiter knocked gently on the door.

Keeping Susan in his arms, Scott called, "Come in."

As the waiter pulled open the doors and saw the couple embracing, he smiled a knowing smile. Scott smiled back and said, "She said *yes!*"

The waiter congratulated them both and then asked, "Are you two hungry yet?"

Susan started laughing and admitted, "I'm starving."

Within moments, their celebration dinner was served, and they realized how famished they were. Periodically, Scott would lean back in his chair and stare at his beautiful fiancée. She had actually said yes. He wanted to shout to the world, "Susan Miller is going to be my wife!"

It was almost eleven when they left the restaurant. Neither wanted that evening to end. In contented silence, they drove back toward Atlanta, Scott's arm around Susan, and her head on his shoulder. The memory of this evening would forever be crystal clear in their mind. Every once in a while, Scott bent his head to kiss her. Tonight had been everything he had hoped for and more.

CHAPTER 8

As ARRANGED, SCOTT met Susan at the bottom of the stairs of the apartment building the next morning at seven. They planned to drive to his parents' home and share the good news before breakfast. Susan had not yet shared the news with her mother as she didn't want anything to dampen her enjoyment of this special time. She knew her mother would not like this news and was sure to cause problems—but not this morning—if Susan could help it.

Scott called his mother early that morning to inform her he was coming over but gave no explanation. When the happy couple quietly walked through the side door, the aroma of coffee and the smell of fresh-baked biscuits welcomed them. Scott's mother was slicing a melon at the kitchen sink while his dad was busy setting the breakfast table in front of the bay window, overlooking the pool.

His parents turned in unison as Scott cleared his throat to announce their arrival. Seeing their son arm in arm with Susan and broad smiles on both their faces, what had transpired was obvious. Not allowing time for anyone else to speak, Scott blurted, "We're getting married!"

Without warning, Susan felt a tremendous wave of panic overtake her as she heard him make this announcement. A frenzy of doubts stormed her mind. *How will they react to this news? It's one thing for me to be their daughter's friend. They have always been kind, loving, and accepting of me. But that was different. I was simply a friend. Becoming the wife of their beloved son is quite another matter. They aren't going to want me for a daughter-in-law. If they knew all about my family, they would cringe with shame like I do.*

Dreading that look of disappointment she knew was going to be on their faces, Susan suddenly had an urge to run. Her thoughts screamed, *I can't stand this! I love them too much to be such a burden to them. I can't blame them for wanting their only son to marry well. Scott deserves the best. What was I thinking last night? How could I have ever thought this would be possible?*

Scott felt Susan stiffen and was puzzled to see the fright in her eyes at such a special moment for them. He gave her a gentle squeeze, a reassuring smile and then leaned over to whisper, "Susan, what's the matter? Are you all right?"

Before Susan could respond, Caroline dropped the knife in the sink and came straight to Susan and embraced her. Bill quickly followed, putting his arm around Scott. Except for Carol Anne, Caroline knew more about this girl than just about anyone. She knew about some of Susan's childhood and the pain and suffering she must have experienced. She was aware that adults who suffered through such childhoods nearly always brought baggage into a marriage, but she also knew Susan. She knew her strengths, her loving nature, and her sweet, kind heart that had been opening up, ever so slowly. Susan was the very best choice she could have ever chosen for her son, baggage and all. "Susan, I can't tell you how happy I am that my son had the good sense to ask you to be his bride. I've wanted this for a long time."

Susan tried to return a confident, assured smile. Studying her future mother-in-law's beaming countenance, she searched for any signs of forced happiness in this face she had been studying for years. Bill and Caroline had been a puzzle to her ever since high school. She remembered wondering when Carol Anne's "real" parents would show themselves. They just seemed too good to be true. They were kind-hearted and always considerate of other people's feelings. And though they would discuss how something was upsetting them, it never mushroomed into an angry tirade as it always did with her parents. After carefully observing and studying them for several years, she was finally convinced they actually were for real.

Bill took hold of Susan's hand. "When you were eight, how I wished I were your father so I could protect you, but I couldn't. Then when you came back into our lives during high school, I was so glad to share my home and family with you. Now I am blessed to welcome you into the family as a daughter."

Sitting down to breakfast, they began discussing different options regarding the wedding. Because of her family, Scott suspected Susan was struggling over the idea of a large, formal wedding. Her mother would be impossible to deal with, and her father would not be involved in any way since he was in prison. Even if he were paroled, he wouldn't be welcomed by any of them. She only had three relatives in the world—her mother, father, and Lisa. Scott knew Susan loved her sister, but Lisa's life was in such turmoil. She was using drugs and drinking heavily, and she was still picked up occasionally for solicitation. She would never be able to pull herself together enough to attend her sister's wedding. In reality, Susan had no one. She continually apologized for the difficulties presented in the wedding plans should her family be involved.

The Thomases, on the other hand, had numerous friends and family. Their friends from church would want to attend Scott's wedding, as would Scott's college friends and business friends who would be offended if they were not invited. Though Susan would have preferred to have a small, quiet ceremony, she knew that wish would not be fair to Scott and his family. She would have to make it plain to them that whatever type of ceremony was settled upon, her family would not be part of it, nor would they be able to pay for it. In their discussion, it soon became obvious to the three of them that Susan was making her choices based upon expense—not on what she wanted.

Bill graciously offered, "Susan, we don't want you to worry about the expenses. We are more than happy to help out."

Scott quickly interrupted. "Dad, we appreciate the offer, but save that money for Carol Anne's wedding. I've been making good money for the past two years and haven't needed to spend very much. Besides, I've been saving up for quite a while, hoping and planning for this day. Susan and I will be paying for our own wedding."

He then took hold of his bride-to-be's hand and made a wonderful suggestion. "I know you would feel uncomfortable having a formal church wedding, so how would you like to get married at the old plantation? We could reserve the entire place and have the ceremony in the meadow under the old weeping willow tree. If we set the date for early spring, all of the flowers will be in bloom, and we could have the reception right there in the restaurant. What would you think of that plan?"

"That's sounds wonderful, Scott—except for one thing." An impish look came across her face as she asked, "Do we have to wait until spring?"

Her smile thrilled Scott. "Well, my dear, since it's already early September, what date do you have in mind?"

With that same impish grin, and only half-kidding, Susan offered, "Well, next week would be good for me, but a ceremony under the willow tree does sound wonderful. Also, I know many people would like to come to your wedding, and I realize we don't have enough time to arrange such a large celebration before the weather changes. I guess we have to settle on a spring wedding. Besides, Carol Anne has just started her junior year, and we can't have a wedding without the maid of honor. We need to set the date for the second Saturday of her spring break."

Scott went to the kitchen calendar and looked at April. His mother had already noted the week Carol Anne would be home for her break. "How does Saturday, April 12, sound to you?"

When they had all agreed on the date, he circled the date with a red marker. Returning to his seat at the table, he spoke in a serious tone, "I want to clear up one very important matter right away. This will be 'our' wedding, Susan—not 'my' wedding. All of those people you think are coming for me will also be coming for you. Don't you realize the number of people who would want to come for you? If you think they care only about me, you're mistaken. They all love you and will be there for you as much as they will be there for me. So I don't want to hear any more 'your-wedding' talk from you, okay?"

She loved how Scott always seemed to understand how she was feeling; however, his sensitivity could not shake her uneasiness. "Scott, I appreciate what you're saying, but my family is going to cause problems."

Scott leaned over and took her hand. "If you want your mother and sister included, you and I will do everything we can to help them feel as comfortable as possible. If, however, they are determined to ruin your day, you are not obligated to have them there. I know your mother has intimidated you your whole life, but that was because you were alone. You're not alone anymore. We can't change who she is or how she behaves, but from last night forward, she no longer calls the shots in your life; you do. I'm here to love and support you. You tell me what you want, and that's what we'll do. This wedding will be the way you want it because that is what will make me happy."

Studying his smiling, confident eyes, Susan finally leaned very close to him, placed her cheek against his, and almost whispered, "Scott, how did I get so lucky? You really do love me." Then with a little giggle, she added, "You have no idea what you're getting yourself into with my family. They can be so cruel. We'll do what we can to include them, but I have learned that if I'm going to have happiness, I have to find it outside of my family. So if this wedding goes on without them, so be it."

Scott did not miss the strength of character Susan was displaying by this comment. Having always had love and support from his family, he could only imagine the terrible feeling of loneliness she must feel, having no one to depend on at this important time in her life. He knew he was powerless to change her past, but he was determined to change her future. Susan would never again feel lonely if he could help it.

The couple spent most of Saturday making lists of things they needed to check out, enjoying the excitement of planning the big event. About midday they called Carol Anne so they could include her in some of their plans. Susan told her all about the evening before and how Scott had proposed. She told her about some of the plans they had already made. "Carol Anne, Scott has suggested we have the wedding out at the old plantation."

Susan began describing the large, vine-covered arch they would have set up under the old weeping willow tree in the meadow. Her eyes sparkled as she described some of Mrs. Thomas' suggestions for decorating the grounds. "Carol Anne, remember that exquisite wedding we watched out there last year? They had that huge white canopy set up on the lush green lawn for all the guests to sit under. That's exactly what we are having."

"Everything sounds absolutely beautiful, Susan, but please, will you wait until I'm home for Christmas to pick out your dress? I want to share that time with you. Would you mind?"

"I wouldn't want anyone but you to go with me. Actually, you will be the only person to see my dress before the wedding. By the way, Scott has already reserved the entire plantation for both Friday and Saturday, which includes all of the guestrooms in the main house and the four large cabins beyond the willow. We will have the rehearsal on Friday evening, followed by a barbecue for the wedding party in the big gazebo by the lake. We decided that the entire wedding party will stay at the plantation the night before the wedding so we can relax and enjoy the morning of the ceremony. Your biggest responsibility will be to make sure Scott doesn't see me that morning."

Hardly taking a breath, Susan continued to spill out the plans to Carol Anne as Scott and his parents watched her eyes dance with excitement. She had been so quiet during the planning, always cautioning them about expenses. They realized that now they were seeing her true feelings as she shared every detail with Carol Anne.

"Do you remember your favorite cabin? The forest-green one that was farthest from the main house? You and I will be staying there. Scott and your parents will stay in the main house with his four groomsmen and their wives. The second cabin, the one right next to ours, will be for my bridesmaids. I am planning to ask three girls from work to stand up with me. I haven't decided if I am going to invite my sister, let alone ask her to be in the wedding. I doubt Lisa will come. If there is the slightest possibility of my mother showing up, Lisa wouldn't be caught dead in the same town with her. And, in case my mother does come, we thought we'd save the third cabin for her. I don't want anyone having to share a room with her."

Redirecting the focus from her family, Susan quickly added, "The fourth cabin will be for Reverend Allan and his wife. He'll perform the ceremony, and she'll play the piano. Scott has also booked a string quartet. Oh, and I want Mrs. Randal to attend our guestbook."

Carol Anne responded in amazement, "So much planning has already transpired. Boy, Susan, I wish I could be back there to help, but it seems everything is coming together fairly smooth without me. Did you four decide on all these plans this morning?"

Susan started laughing. "Apparently Scott has been thinking about this for quite some time, and most of the ideas are his. We've simply been responding, 'Sounds wonderful; let's do it.'"

Bubbling over with excitement, Carol Anne said, "I'm so happy for you both. I only wish I could be home and join in the fun. Have you told your mother yet?"

"No, but I'm planning to tell her today." Susan lowered her voice and confessed, "I'm not looking forward to it. It helps that we have so much of the wedding already planned. If I tell her what we plan to do in a matter-of-fact way, perhaps she'll resign herself to the fact that the wedding will happen and accept it."

Carol Anne knew better than anyone how difficult Mrs. Miller could be and how deeply she could hurt Susan. "Please don't let your mother spoil your happiness. I wish I were there to help you, but that will be my brother's job from now on."

"I wish you were here too. I want to share all of our happiness with you. To be very honest, I'm not looking forward to living with her for the next few months. You know how she can be about anything she doesn't like, and you know how easily I crumble under her pressure. The best thing I can do is keep really busy and stay away from her as much as possible."

Finally having exhausted every detail of their planning, the girls said their goodbyes and hung up. Returning to the kitchen table, Susan noticed the big grins on their faces. Slightly embarrassed, Susan asked, "What? What's so funny?"

Getting up to refill everyone's coffee cup, Mrs. Thomas replied, "Susan, we were just commenting to each other how quiet you were during all the planning. We thought we were pushing something on you that you really didn't want, so we were deciding how to back off and let you have your special day—that is, until we heard you telling Carol Anne about the plans."

They all laughed as Susan blushed. Scott took Susan's hand and said, "You're a little hard to read sometimes. I don't know when you're really happy with something or only going along to keep the peace, but I'll learn. I don't want you to be afraid to speak your mind. If there's something you want or don't want, please tell me. I can get pretty excited and go off on tangents and not realize I'm being selfish. If I promise to be careful, will you promise to speak up?"

"Carol Anne told me once that when I get nervous, I turn vanilla. I don't mean to, but I've done that all my life. I'm so afraid of offending people, I get neutral so no one can get angry with me."

Having remained quiet for most of the conversation, Bill Thomas finally said, "You don't have to worry about offending us. You are part of this family, and we all love you—not just Scott. You never need to be afraid of saying what's on your mind while you're in this house. Happy or sad, we love you! And may I add, I think this is going to be one beautiful wedding."

The rest of the day, Susan allowed herself to remain in the moment. She refused to worry about her mother or sister and determined to enjoy the experience of planning her wedding. Several times, as Scott or Caroline were bubbling over with enthusiasm about an idea that came to them, Susan found herself comparing their reaction to that of her mother's and a cloud of dread would fill her for a moment. But she would quickly shake it off and jump into the discussion with her own brand of forced enthusiasm, which would quickly turn to real excitement. She would not allow her family to spoil this event for her. She knew she was going to tell her mother about her plans later that day, but she was determined to enjoy this time and not think about how her mother would react.

CHAPTER 9

SUSAN WAS QUIET as Scott drove back to their apartment building. He made several attempts at small talk, but she was off in a world of her own. He knew she dreaded telling her mother. His thoughts wandered back over the past two years, and he marveled at the incredible change in Susan. Initially, he could hardly get a word out of her. She wasn't shy, but her body language seemed to apologize for even being there. Especially that first summer, she would act as if she was somehow intruding, reminding him of a helpless, frightened little animal. Then, ever so slowly, the real Susan began to emerge. The three of them would get so caught up in one of their treasure hunts that she would forget about herself. Then this radiant, happy person would appearThe real Susan was seemingly buried deep within this timid shell.

On several occasions, while having fun, something happened that reminded Susan of her parents; then he would see her withdraw into her timid shell, and that dreadful look of fear would return to her eyes. Scott thought again about the incredible change in her over the past few years. She had developed such self-confidence at work. He couldn't recall the last time he had seen that timid look, but this evening, the thought of preparing to deal with her mother brought back that frightened little girl.

Susan sat in silence, trying to think of the right words to say to avoid an ugly scene. For most of her younger life, she had made excuses for her mother's cruelty by blaming everything on her father. She needed to have an explanation for her mother's hatefulness. Unlike Lisa, who years ago stopped caring *why* their mother was mean, Susan continued to try to please her mother. She hoped against hope that one day, when everything was good in her life, her mother would become kind and loving. After all, that's what every child needs and deserves from his mother.

When her father was sent to prison the first time, she thought it would be good at home with him gone. It wasn't. Her mother was even more hateful, but Susan, at eight years old, convinced herself the hatefulness was due to their having so little money. She was sure that if her mother had enough money, she would be happy and kind. Lack of money was the problem—not her mother.

It had taken almost eighteen years of enduring this insufferable woman before Susan could finally admit that her mother, for whatever reasons, was a vicious person who had no desire to change. Yes, her mother had many reasons to be bitter and angry. She had suffered horribly for years at the hands of her husband.

When Susan had first started counseling with Dr. Jacobson, she would spend most of her time defending her mother's actions. Her descriptions of some of her most violent memories were dotted with explanations like, "but she couldn't help it." One evening, Dr. Jacobson interrupted her and questioned, "Susan, why do you find it necessary to defend your mother's behavior?"

"Because when people hear what she's done, I'm afraid they'll hate her. I need to help them understand there are reasons she acts as she does."

The counselor paused for a moment and then boldly asked, "Do you hate her sometimes?"

Susan couldn't even look up. She had been denying those feelings for eighteen years. She had always acknowledged her fear of and hatred for her father, but letting go of that last thread of hope to someday have a mother like other girls was overwhelmingly painful. She didn't want to simply walk out of her life as Lisa had done. Somehow, she still felt responsible for her mother. She didn't want to write her off, but she did need to stop making excuses for her mother. In order to live with her as an adult—not as a parent/child—meant facing the probability that her mother might never change.

During the past few years, as long as she paid her share of the bills, her mother basically left her alone, never expressing any interest in her daughter's life. On the rare occasions Susan attempted to share something, her mother would generally respond, "If things had been different for me,

I could have been someone." Everything in Marjorie Miller's world was measured against, "If things had been different for me."

Susan no longer lived in fear of her mother. After all, at twenty-one, she had a good job and a wonderful relationship with Scott. She knew her mother couldn't hinder her plans. At special times, though, she was painfully reminded of what she did not have—a mother who would be happy and excited for her. Susan knew she would not be able to share her wedding plans with her mother. During these times, her feelings of loss were intensely painful. She had come to accept her mother's short-comings in everyday life, but as realistic as she was about her mother, her feelings of loss at these special times were harder to accept. She also knew she had no good way of breaking the news of her engagement. This wedding would represent everything the woman hated. She hated well-to-do snobs, churchgoers, her daughter's *uppity* behavior, and her daughter's having what she had never had. Most of all, Susan knew her mother was going to hate her moving out—not because she would miss her, but because Susan's money had made life a little easier for the past few years.

Susan finally broke the silence. "I think I'd better talk to her alone first. I need to see what kind of mood she's in before we come walking in and drop this bomb on her."

Scott had witnessed Marjorie Miller in action a few times. Once when the building superintendent had refused one of her requests, she had struck back with a venomous verbal attack that upset Scott for hours. He couldn't forget the image of that hateful face screaming at the super. The thought of how many times that bitter face must have screamed into Susan's face as a child hurt him deeply.

Scott detested Mrs. Miller, but he knew Susan wanted to love her and was trying, in spite of her mother's behavior, to be a good daughter. Scott knew she was dreading this meeting and was simply trying to spare him her mother's verbal assault.

"Susan, I know this is bothering you, but please let me be with you when you tell her. I don't want you to face her by yourself. I don't care how ugly she might get. I promise I won't lose my temper with her. I can handle her tirade. Please, I want to be there with you."

"All right, but let me go in first. If she's already in a terrible mood, we'll postpone telling her. If she's civil, I'll call you to come up, and we'll tell her together."

Scott gave her a kiss as they reached her floor and then took off to his apartment to wait for her call.

Susan walked into the apartment, trying to look nonchalant. She wished she didn't have to tell her mother her news. She knew her mother well, and sharing this news was not going to be pleasant. Susan's habit, for the past several years, had been to slip in at the very end of the evening and immediately turn in for the night.

In all actuality, her mother had come to enjoy Susan's absence, often stating that if it had not been for the money Susan contributed, she would have tossed her out as soon as she graduated from high school. But she needed the money, and Susan knew she resented her for it.

As Susan entered the kitchen, her mother turned, clearly surprised at how early she had come home. Snarling, her mother asked, "What are you doing home so early?"

Susan smiled, but as usual, her mother didn't respond. This was no indication of a bad mood; she never responded to a smile.

Her mother walked into the living room, not waiting for a response because she really didn't care what the answer was. Nonetheless, Susan followed her into the living room and took a seat next to the television, placing herself in full view of her mother. Without acknowledging her daughter's presence, Marjorie turned on her favorite program and acted as if Susan wasn't even there.

After a few minutes, Susan slipped out of the room and went into her bedroom to call Scott.

He picked up the phone on the first ring. "Well, do I come up?"

"Yes. It's not going to get any easier. I can't believe something as wonderful as this is going to be so painful. Let's get it over with. Don't ring the bell. I'll meet you at the door in two minutes." Scott took the stairs two at a time and was standing outside her door when she opened it. He forced a big silly grin and then bent to kiss her. "Honey, it's you and me from now on. Just keep remembering that." They walked into the living room, feeling almost as if they were walking into the lion's den.

Marjorie was still watching television. Scott was smiling, and Susan immediately knew that familiar look on her mother's face probably meant she was thinking, *I'd like to slap that stupid grin off your face.*

Marjorie knew who he was. She had been introduced to him a few times around the building and knew he was part of *that Thomas clan*, as she put it. She had resented the whole bunch of them, especially Scott's mother. While Susan was still in high school, Marjorie had run into Mrs. Thomas downtown, and for months afterward, Susan was peppered with her mother's hateful recounting of the meeting. Mrs. Thomas had dared to be polite, but Marjorie took her courtesy as being uppity, feeling as if she was being talked down to; but then, according to Marjorie, everyone talked down to her. The fact that Mrs. Thomas was trying to be gracious was just a cover as far as Marjorie was concerned, and she took every opportunity to repeat her opinion. "Her in her fancy clothes and phony chat, talking as if the two of us were the best of friends." Marjorie hated Scott's mother. She had long since stopped caring how she sounded or what she said. Her attitude screamed, "If you don't like it, tough. They all think they're so much better than me. I don't have to kiss up to anyone."

Marjorie glared at Scott as he took a seat across from her. With a voice that reminded Scott of a growling dog, she inquired, "What are you doing here?"

Susan would have liked to offer Scott some iced tea but didn't dare leave the room. Mrs. Miller sat glaring at the two of them, waiting for an answer. She detested uninvited guests, and since she hadn't invited him, she was seething.

Glaring at Scott, Marjorie said to Susan, "So what's he doing here, and when is he leaving?"

Scott reached over and took Susan's hand and looked directly at Mrs. Miller. Without smiling, Scott simply stated the facts. "Mrs. Miller, I'm not asking your permission or your blessing. I have loved your daughter for two years now, and last night I asked her to marry me. We have set our wedding date for the twelfth of April. We plan on getting married at the old plantation on Highway 19, and we would both like you to come."

Marjorie sat stone-faced. Her eyes were cold and unresponsive.

Susan, on the other hand, glowed with admiration. She had not expected Scott to be the one to tell her mother, but now that he had, she was relieved and so proud of him. He had not even paused to allow her mother to comment. He wasn't rude, but he was certainly not asking for her mother's opinion either.

When he finished, Susan nervously smiled and said, "I love him, and we're getting married. Mother, I would love for you to be part of my wedding."

Marjorie barked back, "And exactly who do you think is going to pay for this wedding? Certainly not me!"

Before they could answer, she turned to her daughter, as if Scott no longer existed, and said, "You are a stupid, stupid girl. Do you really think *those* people are going to accept a poor white trash girl with a father in prison and a sister who's a prostitute? As soon as they find out, *those* snobs will throw you out on your ear." Certain her daughter had not told this fancy guy about her family, Marjorie took great pleasure in filling him in on these tidbits. She sat smirking, waiting for the news to sink in and expecting him to run for the door.

Scott gave Susan's hand a reassuring squeeze before addressing Mrs. Miller. "I know all about your family situation. I have for years. I love Susan, and so does my whole family. As for being poor white trash, Susan may have grown up poor, but she has never been white trash, as you put it. She is anything but stupid, and I want Susan for my wife."

Susan marveled that Scott could sound so determined and absolute without showing anger. His manner was resolute without being haughty. A strange sense of safety flooded her. She realized this was the first time she was not having to face her mother's anger alone. Scott was not only there, he was stepping forward and taking the heat meant for her. She listened as Scott declared his love and admiration for her.

Scott leaned forward as if to soften his final statement. "I love Susan, and because she loves you, I want to try to have some kind of amicable relationship with you, if you will allow it. As for the wedding, Susan and I will be paying for it, so you need not worry about any expenses."

Marjorie was furious at Scott for talking to her that way, and Susan recognized that all-too-familiar look on her mother's face. Marjorie had taken so much abuse for all those years with Chuck, but when he left, she was determined no one would ever again have the upper hand with her. She no longer took anything from anyone. She considered any disagreement with her a personal attack and would attack right back. Whenever anyone dared get in her face, as Scott was doing, she could turn very ugly.

"So! You two are getting married next April. I guess I can't stop you from making a stupid mistake like that, and I certainly don't intend on being there." She glared at Scott while she spit out her words. "I don't want to hear about your plans, nor do I want you coming in here ever again. This is *my* apartment, and you're not welcome here. Do you understand me?"

Scott simply nodded and said, "I understand."

Then she turned to her daughter and said, "When they get tired of you, and believe me they will, don't bother trying to come back here. When you leave, you're gone. Do you get that?"

Susan simply nodded. There wasn't anything more to say. Her mother had made up her mind, and that was that.

Mrs. Miller dismissed them as she focused on the television. As far as she was concerned, they were finished.

The couple quietly left the apartment and went up to Scott's place. Neither spoke until they were in his living room. Only then did Susan allow her feelings to surface, and the tears flowed freely. She felt so humiliated by her mother's behavior. But then, sitting there, so proud of Scott and so ashamed of her mother, all kinds of emotions flooded her.

Feeling the need to say something, Susan finally looked at Scott. "You would think I would be used to her by now. Her response was exactly as I thought it would be. Somewhere deep inside, I must still be holding onto a thread of hope that she might change and that this time she might behave differently. She is so bitter, she has no room for love—not for herself or for anyone. Scott, I really do pity her. She is such a lonely, miserable person."

Although having handled the confrontation well, Scott was now struggling with some strong emotions of his own. He hated how this woman could hurt Susan so deeply and not even care. He saw how Mrs. Miller actually seemed to enjoy inflicting pain on Susan in her eyes. He found it hard to imagine that this woman could actually be Susan's mother. They were so very different. *What could this woman have been like had she made different choices in her life?* He thought about Susan and the millions of others who have also lived really hard lives. Why does her mother think her hard life gives her the right to behave that way? How does a mother become so hardened that she has no feelings—even for her own children?

Susan regained control of her emotions in a few minutes and began talking about the wedding plans. She decided her mother could only ruin her wedding if she allowed her, and she was not going to let her. She sat at Scott's dining room table and started writing out a list of things they needed to start doing. After a few minutes, they realized it had been hours since they had eaten, and they were starving.

Laying the pencil down, Susan started giggling. "You know, I don't have any idea about how to plan a wedding. I've never even been in one. What we need is one of those wedding organizers they sell in the bookstores downtown."

Scott beamed with pride at her strength. She was not going to allow her mother to spoil their excitement. Kissing her tenderly, he suggested, "Great idea! We can go down to the bookstore, and then, how about some pizza? It's right next door."

Susan jumped to her feet and headed for the door. "You know, you've proposed to a woman who really likes to eat. You might want to consider what an expensive venture this may be for you."

As Scott opened the door for her, he said with a huge grin, "I think I can handle it. Besides, this expensive venture is going to be the greatest adventure of our lives, and you and I are going to enjoy every minute of it starting right now."

CHAPTER 10

—⚜—

IT WAS A busy week for Scott and Susan. They asked his parents and sister to promise to keep their secret until they could officially announce their engagement the next weekend. Besides, Scott had another reason. He wanted his ring on Susan's finger when they made their announcement. She had seminars scheduled every night, and he was booked for business lunches every day except Wednesday. The couple agreed to go shopping during their lunch hour on Wednesday. He thought about choosing a ring himself and surprising her but knew it would be better if he let her choose the one she wanted. On Wednesday, they slipped away and went downtown to pick out their rings.

One of Scott's high school friends had become a jeweler in town. Whenever Scott needed to purchase a gift for his mother or his sister, Tim Butler had helped him. Scott quickly phoned him. "Tim, old buddy, I need a favor. I'm bringing my future bride into our store today to pick out a ring."

Without letting his old buddy finish, Tim bellowed into the phone, "Congratulations, Scott! She must be pretty special to snag the likes of you, old buddy."

Scott smiled into the phone. "Tim, it really is the other way around. I'm the lucky one. Susan is so beautiful and charming, I want to get her the perfect ring. Can you help me?"

"Sure. We have a great selection. When are you coming in? I want to be sure I'll be here to wait on you."

Quickly realizing Susan might have a problem with the expense, Scott asked, "Could you do me a favor? When I bring Susan in today, would you have a tray of rings without price tags? Unlike most women, my wife-to-be would make her choice based on the least expensive, and I want her to have the one she really loves."

"No problem. Boy, she sounds like a keeper. I can't wait to meet this girl."

"Another thing," Scott quickly added. "When we come in, please don't let on that we talked. I don't want her to know I arranged this."

"You've got it, buddy. I'll pick out some beauties for you." Then, needing a little more information, Tim asked, "What price range are you thinking about?"

"I guess I'll have to trust you there. All I know is I want something special. I've never done this before, remember?"

Tim's famous belly laugh thundered through the phone. "Okay, leave it to me."

As Scott replaced the receiver, he considered his plan for today. His friend Tim would be the first person outside of the family Scott was going to tell about Susan. He suddenly couldn't wait for the lunch hour. Several times that morning he found himself practicing the exact words he would use to introduce Susan to Tim, and every time his planned introduction made him smile.

Tim was standing behind the ring counter as the couple entered. As agreed, Tim acted as if their visit was a complete surprise. Stepping up to the counter, Scott placed his arm around Susan's waist and announced, "Hi, Tim. I'd like to introduce my bride-to-be, Miss Susan Miller. Susan, this is Tim Butler, a lifelong friend of mine. Tim, we're here to buy a ring. Can you help us?"

Tim played along, acting as if this was the first time he had heard the news, and after congratulating them, he pulled out a tray of lovely rings.

Tim had placed twelve different styles on the black velvet display tray, and Susan quickly noticed none of them were priced. Scott studied her face as she lifted them out, one by one, and placed them on her finger and then held it out for both of them to see. They were all striking, but something about them was bothering Scott.

While Susan continued trying different rings, Scott asked Tim if he had any *special* rings available. "These are all lovely, but you probably have a dozen of each of these behind the counter. Unless she really loves one of these, I was wondering if you might have any one-of-a-kind rings?"

Tim knew exactly what Scott was looking for, and he had it. He excused himself and went to another counter and pulled out an attractive blue-velvet ring box on display. As he placed it in front of them, he explained, "Once in a while, jewelers are offered antique jewelry from estate sales. I purchased this ring from one about a week ago. I doubt you'll find another ring like this one anywhere. I estimate its age to be about a hundred years old. The diamond's color and clarity are almost perfect, and the cut is magnificent. The craftsman's mark indicates it was designed by the best in the business at that time—Himple and Himple here in Atlanta."

He started to mention its investment quality but stopped, remembering that Scott didn't want money to be discussed in front of Susan.

Susan stared at the ring. She wasn't sure she wanted to try it on because it looked very expensive. Scott reached over, pulled the ring out of the box, and slipped it on her finger. He never looked down at it; he simply watched her face. When he saw the look in her eyes as she lifted her hand, Scott said, "Sold!"

Embarrassed, Susan quickly removed the ring. "Scott, this is too much ring for me. I don't need something so expensive. Please, let's keep looking."

Scott knew she absolutely loved this ring, and he had no intention of letting her settle for anything less. She replaced it in its box and handed it back to Tim.

Scott didn't argue; he shook Tim's hand as they left and whispered, "Hold onto that one for me, will you?"

Scott and Susan thanked Tim for his time and agreed to look around before making a decision. Scott then suggested they grab some lunch before going back to the office.

They walked two doors down to a deli and were back at the office well before one o'clock. They agreed to announce their engagement to everyone at the office on Friday afternoon. For the happy occasion, they ordered a large sheet cake to be delivered around three o'clock to have an engagement party. His parents had also agreed to host an engagement party at their home on Saturday evening for all of their church friends. On Sunday, the official announcement would appear in the Atlanta newspaper.

Susan changed her outfit three times Friday morning before settling on a cream-colored linen suit with a royal-blue silk blouse. She wanted to look as grownup as possible. As she was dressing, she could hear her mother in the bathroom also getting ready for work. She wished she could tell her mother what she and Scott had planned for today. She also wished she could have a mother who would want to be there when they made their announcement, but the fact was, she didn't. When she was finally satisfied she had put together the very best outfit, she walked into the living room.

Her mother was having her usual breakfast coffee while reading the morning paper. She didn't even notice that her daughter was dressed especially nice today. Susan casually said, "Goodbye," picked up her purse and keys, and walked out the door to meet Scott.

Scott loved how she looked in that suit. The blouse was almost the same color as her eyes, and the cream suit looked gorgeous against her jet-black hair. As they walked to work, they chatted about going ring shopping the next morning. Both of them had been so busy all week that Saturday morning would be their first chance to try again. They giggled about how today was the last day she would have to be careful what she said to Mrs. Randal so as not to ruin their secret.

They both had a hard time keeping their secret at the office. Twice Susan had forgotten and started talking about their plans with Mrs. Randal. She barely caught herself both times and had been sure she would not be able to remain quiet until Friday afternoon. They agreed to meet in Scott's office at two-thirty and wait there together until his mother had the cake and everything in place. Mr. Thomas would announce over the public address system that everyone was to stop what they were doing and join him in the company cafeteria for a party. When everyone was present, the two of them were to walk out and make their announcement.

Susan wanted to have someone besides Scott and his parents to talk to about their wedding plans. She knew Mrs. Randal would be happy for her, and she could hardly wait to tell her.

Scott was booked with outside meetings for most of the morning, so she forced herself to keep working hard to keep her mind off what was coming. The day seemed to creep by without Scott there to talk to.

Mrs. Thomas came into the office around two o'clock and set up the cafeteria. She kept the doors locked so no one would accidentally walk in and see the decorations and give away the surprise. The bakery delivered the cake at two-thirty as planned, and everything was ready.

Scott returned to the office as the cake was being delivered. He went immediately into his office and waited for Susan to meet him. When she came in a few minutes later, Scott closed his door, took her in his arms, kissed her, and said, "Well, you have one last chance to change your mind!"

She poked him in the center of his chest. "Never! Let's do it."

"Not yet, sweetheart. We need to do one more thing before going out."

He reached into his pocket and pulled out the blue-velvet ring box. He quickly took out the ring and slipped it on her finger. "Susan, you are everything in the world to me. I can't put into words how happy you've made me. I love you and am so glad we will be spending the rest of our lives together. This ring is exactly like you—unique and precious—and the two of you belong together."

Speechless and fighting back tears, she stared at the ring. She knew it must have cost him a small fortune. She wanted to protest, but when she saw the look in his eyes, she knew this gift came from his heart—not from his wallet. She wrapped her arms around his neck and whispered, "Do you know when I first fell in love with you?"

Scott smiled and shook his head no. "I was eight years old. I fell in love with you the day you pulled Carol Anne and me from the pool. You were so sweet and kind, and that grin you have on your face right now was on your face that afternoon. I've loved you for thirteen years, Scott. Let's go tell everyone else."

Walking down the hall, they could hear the excited voices coming from the cafeteria, and the anticipation of what they were about to do was clearly written on both their faces as they swung the large door open wide and entered the room. Dozens and dozens of yellow and white helium balloons covered the ceiling. Mrs. Thomas had tied curly yellow ribbons to each of them, and the ribbons hung like confetti above everyone's head. Hanging from the far wall was an immense banner that read, "Best Wishes, Scott and Susan."

In the center of the cafeteria was the lovely sheet cake they had chosen. Frosted white, miniature yellow roses decorated the cake all around the outside edge. In the center, a graceful and delicate frosting script read, "Best Wishes, Scott & Susan." Little yellow hearts were scattered all over the table.

Before either could say a word, the office personnel started cheering and clapping. Scott took hold of Susan's hand, and they made their way to the table where his parents were standing. He motioned for everyone to quiet down so he could speak. "Well, by the wonderful job my mother has done on these lovely decorations, it seems almost redundant for me to make this announcement. However, because I love the way it sounds when it comes out of my mouth, here goes. Miss Susan Miller has graciously accepted my proposal of marriage. We are planning a spring wedding and would be honored if you all would now join us for cake and coffee in celebration of our engagement."

Mrs. Randal was standing next to Mrs. Thomas, and when Scott finished his speech, she spoke up for everyone to hear. "Well, it's about time. Everyone in the office has known for months that you two loved each other. We were all waiting for the two of you to figure it out! Congratulations and best wishes!"

Finally, when almost everyone had greeted the couple and were busily enjoying the cake, Mrs. Randal came to wish the couple well. "Susan, no one in the world is more deserving of this than you. I couldn't be prouder if you were my very own daughter. Scott is a wonderful young man, and I know he adores you. I'm so very happy for the two of you."

Susan gave her a big hug. "It was so hard keeping our secret from you all week. I wanted to share with you all the wonderful plans we've come up with and get your opinion on some things. I know you have three married daughters, so you've been through the planning of weddings. Would you consider helping Mrs. Thomas and me with my wedding?"

"Well, I can't say I'm an expert or anything, but I would love to help in any way I can. From the looks of this cafeteria though, I think I would leave the decorating duties to your future mother-in-law. She obviously has a flair for decorating. Didn't she do a wonderful job?"

"Yes, she did, and we haven't thanked her yet. If you will excuse us, we need to do that right now!" The happy couple went over to the cake table. "Mrs. Thomas, everything looks so lovely. I can't believe how much you did in only one hour."

"Susan, considering you are marrying my son, I think 'Mrs. Thomas' is a little too formal. I'd feel honored if you would call me 'Mom.' "

Mr. Thomas chimed in. "Hey, wait a minute! If you get to be called 'Mom,' then I get to be 'Dad.' Do you mind, Susan?"

"Do I mind? All my life I've dreamed of having a Mom and a Dad like you."

Scott took hold of her hand and held it up for his parents to see. He had deliberately not told them about the ring because he wanted Susan to be the first to see it. Mr. Thomas could tell his son had chosen an incredible ring. It didn't take a jeweler's eye to see that his choice was something special. He put his arm around his son's shoulder and said, "That is a beautiful ring for a beautiful girl."

Scott was simply beaming with pride. "Dad, life just couldn't get much better than this."

Bill pulled Scott a few steps away from Susan. "We need you to keep Susan away from the house tomorrow," he murmured.

"Why?"

"Carol Anne is flying in late tonight and wants to surprise Susan at the party tomorrow evening. She couldn't wait until Christmas to celebrate with you two."

Scott was thrilled to hear this news. "Susan's going to be so happy. With her taking summer classes this year, she was only home for one week this summer. Susan's really missed Carol Anne. But hasn't she just started her new semester? How long is she staying?"

"She talked to her professors, and she's will only skip her Monday classes, so she must fly out at seven Monday evening."

"Great! I'll make sure Susan doesn't book us for anything on Sunday or Monday. Would you mind if we both took Monday off so we can have more time with Carol Anne?"

"That's fine. Make sure Mrs. Randal knows Susan isn't coming in. Your mother was suggesting the five of us might drive to Jefferson Sunday afternoon and visit with Aunt Gladys. Carol Anne didn't get to see her this summer since Gladys was up north. That way you can introduce Susan and tell Gladys the good news. She doesn't get the Atlanta paper there, but she has so many friends here in town someone is bound to call her since the announcement will be in Sunday's edition. It would be nice if she heard the news from family."

Scott agreed. Besides, he knew he was Aunt Gladys's favorite nephew, and she would want to meet his bride-to-be. He also knew she was going to love Susan.

CHAPTER 11

CARS WERE PARKED all around when Scott and Susan arrived Saturday evening. His mother had told them both that almost a hundred people from their church had called to RSVP for the party. His family had attended that church his whole life, and Susan had been going there since she was a freshman in high school.

Mrs. Thomas had instructed them to use the front door. No one in the family ever used the front door, but since this was a special occasion, Susan didn't think anything about his request. The house was filled with guests. The living room and great room were overflowing with excited people, and the staircase had someone on every other step. There were so many people, Scott and Susan didn't quite know where to go, so they stood in the foyer and greeted people.

Mr. Thomas slipped through the crowd and asked Susan if she would like something to drink. After she had decided on sweetened iced tea, Mr. Thomas suggested, "Why don't you two stay put and keep greeting people? I'll send someone out with your iced tea."

With everyone's pressing in close, Susan gave him an embarrassed little grin and said, "That would be great, Dad."

Everyone wanted to see the ring and give the couple their own best wishes. Susan was chatting with several women as someone stepped up beside her and handed her the iced tea. "I hope it's sweet enough for you, Snow White."

Susan spun around to see Carol Anne standing in front of her, smiling. "Hello, sister. I understand you've stolen my brother's heart."

Squealing with delight, she almost knocked the iced tea out of Carol Anne's hand as she grabbed her and said, "I can't believe you're here! How did you get away from school?"

Knowing her friend needed to circulate, Carol Anne whispered, "Why don't you sleep over tonight so we can have our time to talk?"

"I desperately want to sit down with you and tell you everything that's happened in the past week, but you're right, I do need to attend to our guests. I can't believe you're here! We'll talk tonight."

She hugged and kissed Carol Anne and then moved among the guests with Scott. As they made their way into the dining room, they spotted the cake comprised of five separate tiers joined together by arched stairways. Each tier had been frosted in dozens of yellow roses, except for the one in the middle. On the two arched stairways stood a bride and groom, designed to appear as if the two were coming to meet on the center cake, which had been covered with smooth white frosting with tiny yellow rosebuds all around the edge. The frosting script on the top read, "Scott & Susan, to be joined in matrimony, April 12, 1974."

Carol Anne stepped up behind Susan to also admire the attractive display. "I can't believe all this. Your mother has outdone herself. This is the most beautiful cake I've ever seen. Your parents have been absolutely wonderful to me."

Carol Anne leaned closer and whispered, "I've never seen my parents quite this happy before. Scott is their only son and their first kid to get married. There are loving all of this. Susan, Mother and I talked about you and Scott that first summer he came home. We knew you were perfect for each other; we weren't sure if Scott would be patient enough to wait for you, since you were so young! Mom and I were sure it was a trust issue for you; we just didn't know how long it would take you."

Scott turned to listen to his sister, and placing his arms around them, said, "I would have asked her to marry me back then, but I knew she would have turned me down. Believe me, I tried dating other women, but it was always the one for me. She certainly was worth the wait."

The party continued well past midnight, and when the last guests were finally gone, the girls picked up a few dishes and headed for the kitchen. Scott started making the rounds through each room to look for any stray cups or glasses while Mr. and Mrs. Thomas were urged by all three kids to go relax.

It was almost one in the morning before the house was put back together, and the last of the dishes were dried and put away. Mr. and Mrs. Thomas said their goodnights and had gone to bed a half hour earlier. Scott was preparing to leave.

"Honey, I couldn't tell you before because Carol Anne's coming was a surprise, but Mom and Dad suggested the five of us might take a drive to Jefferson tomorrow after church. You've heard me talk about my Aunt Gladys, Dad's older sister. We all thought it would be good if we formally introduced you to her. She is the essence of old, Southern etiquette and would not appreciate hearing family news from friends or having to read about us in the paper. Besides, she has always been Carol Anne's and my favorite relative. She is the sweetest, kindest woman in the whole world. Would you be up to it tomorrow afternoon?"

"That sounds great," was Susan's only response. She did not relish the idea of going to Jefferson, the place that represented everything she was ashamed of—her sister and her chosen lifestyle as well as the location of her father's trial and imprisonment. The idea of driving there with these sweet people was a little overwhelming. Susan would never say such things out loud, but as Scott continued to talk, she thought, *Why couldn't your aunt have lived anywhere else but Jefferson? When is God ever going to give me a break?*

As Scott finished, she simply nodded, knowing she wouldn't have to see either her sister or her father and said, "That sounds fine to me."

Scott kissed her goodnight and then gave his sister a kiss on the cheek. As he walked out, he called back, "Be sure to lock this door when I leave and don't stay up all night talking."

Of course, he knew better. In no way would these two girls get any sleep tonight. As he suspected, they talked until the wee hours of the morning, finally drifting off somewhere around four. Carol Anne filled Susan in on all of the different projects in which she was involved in California. She told her about several guys she liked and what her college life was like. She especially liked one guy in particular, and it sounded as if Carol Anne was more than a little interested. They talked until they were both so tired they simply fell asleep in the middle of a sentence.

Since Susan hadn't known Carol Anne would be there, she hadn't planned on staying over. She would need a change of clothes for church and the trip to Jefferson. Scott said he would come by around eight and drive her back to her apartment to change, so she set the alarm for seven. She decided to shower there so all she would have to do at home was change and leave. She had been doing that a lot lately. Her mother hadn't acknowledged her or talked to her since Scott made their announcement, which was probably best.

She already knew what she was going to wear. Because it was September, she had only a few more opportunities to wear her favorite summer dress. Quite soon autumn would settle in, and winter clothes would be required; but September in Georgia was beautiful, and the days were still warm and balmy. When she finished dressing, she made one final inspection in the mirror and walked out to the living room. She was sure her mother would still be asleep as she headed toward the kitchen for a quick bite of breakfast. She poured a bowl of cereal and sat down to eat when her mother entered the kitchen. She quickly gave her mother a nervous nod of greeting, but Marjorie ignored her and simply went to the sink and filled a pot for coffee.

She knew better than to attempt any small talk with her mother. Marjorie Miller hated small talk. While growing up, Susan would frequently hear, "If it isn't important, then don't bother me with it," and important to Marjorie Miller was only something that interested her. Since nothing that was happening to Susan interested her, they really had nothing about which to converse.

Susan was almost finished with her breakfast when her mother spotted the ring. She poured herself a cup of coffee and sat across the table from her daughter so she could get a closer look. Susan knew her mother was staring intently at the ring, and her interest made her nervous. Her mother could react in a dozen ways, and none were nice. Susan didn't know what to do with her hands. She did not want her mother to think she was waving the ring in her face, but she didn't want to put her hand in her lap either. Her mother would accuse her of trying to hide it, so she tried to behave normally and finish her cereal.

"So! He's showing off his family's money. Rings like that are a ridiculous waste. But then, people like that have so much money they can afford to waste it."

There was absolutely nothing in the world in which her mother could not find fault. Susan momentarily considered correcting her mother's facts. She wanted to inform her that Scott had purchased the ring with his own money, but realizing the futility of explaining, she remained quiet.

She washed her bowl and put it away and said goodbye as she left the kitchen. She was not going to let her mother's poisoned tongue anger her. *I will not resort to being like my mother.* She picked up her purse and keys and left.

As soon as church was over and they had a bite of lunch, the five of them left for Aunt Gladys's. Jefferson was a two-hour drive on a Sunday afternoon, and Gladys was expecting them around four. Gladys had moved to Jefferson years earlier with her husband, Karl. After Karl's funeral, she had been tempted to sell their house and move back to Atlanta, to be near her beloved brother, but she could not leave all the memories and friends she had made over the years.

Gladys was so happy to have an excuse to make a big pot roast dinner. She seldom made big dinners anymore with only her to eat them. She quickly wrote a shopping list, making sure she had all of the ingredients to make Scott's favorite pie, lemon meringue. She remembered Carol Anne always liked the butterscotch candies she kept in her candy dish, so she made sure they were on the list. As she finished her shopping and headed for home, she felt like it was a holiday. She had almost forgotten how much she liked to fix a big family meal.

As soon as she had the pot roast browned and in the oven, she started on the pie. She enjoyed making pies, but these days almost all of her friends were on restricted diets, so it had been a long time since she had baked her last pie. Gladys was well known for her light-as-air crusts. When her son, Billy, was little, she would make a double recipe so she could roll out a large sheet of crust, poke it all over with a fork, sprinkle it with sugar and cinnamon, and bake it for him. He loved it, and she loved doing it for him.

When dinner and dessert were well in hand, Gladys went into the dining room and opened her hope chest. She still kept all of her cherished linens and crocheted tablecloths in it for safekeeping. She seldom used them anymore, but they represented such good memories she could not think of parting with them. She selected the linen cloth with the exquisite pale-blue embroidery at its four corners. She had done the embroidery herself some forty-five years earlier. She had matching napkins, and as she spread the linen on the table, a wonderfully sweet homesickness came over her. Memories of special dinners floated into her mind. This set had been her husband's favorite because she had embroidered it during their first year of marriage. The first time she set the table with it was the night she told him he was going to be a father. From then on, she would use this cloth for every special occasion.

After setting the table, she went into her backyard to pick some flowers for the centerpiece. Everything was finally ready, so she jumped into the shower and was dressed and ready well before her guests were due to arrive.

Gladys was sitting in her porch swing when they drove up. She walked down to greet them as they climbed out of the car. She first gave her brother a big hug and kiss and then made her way to Caroline. They had been friends for almost thirty years—ever since Bill had married her.

Caroline's family was what is affectionately called "old Atlanta," meaning her family went back several generations and had held prominent positions in the community. Her great-grandfather was a well-respected judge, and at one time, her father held the position of state's attorney. In spite of the prestige with which she had grown up, Caroline was the kindest, sweetest, most unassuming woman Gladys had ever met.

Gladys and Bill, on the other hand, were proud to be hard-working, middle-class people. Their family had also lived in Atlanta for almost three generations but had never moved in the circles with Caroline's family. When Bill first started dating Caroline, Gladys remembered their mother's worrying about the societal differences between them. She remembered her mother's warning Bill to go slowly and to make sure her family was approving of this match. The joke of the family turned out to be that Caroline's father actually pushed Bill to ask him to marry his daughter. He got tired of waiting for Bill to make a move, and since he liked the boy, he brought up the matter first. The family never let Bill live that down, but they were also very proud of him.

Bill would never be classed as "the established wealth of Atlanta," but he was an honest, hard-working businessman who had done very well and was enjoying a comfortable life. He was highly regarded throughout the city, and Caroline never acted like she had married beneath her station. For this courtesy, she had earned Gladys's love and respect.

Carol Anne came around the car and gave her aunt a hug. Gladys didn't think to question why Carol Anne was home from school. She was simply glad to see her.

Scott was out of the car and helping Susan out as Gladys stepped up. "Aunt Gladys, I'd like you to meet Miss Susan Miller, my fiancée. Susan, I'd like you to meet my Aunt Gladys."

"Well, it's very nice to meet you, Susan. I was wondering how long it was going to be before someone captured our Scott's heart. Our Scott is quite a catch, if I do say so myself. But then I've been told I'm more than a little biased! Now since you're joining the family, I expect you to call me Aunt Gladys." Turning to Scott, she added, "So when is the big date? I want to be sure to mark my calendar. I do not want to miss this wedding!"

"We are planning a spring wedding, Aunt Gladys. That way Carol Anne will be home for her spring break. We can't have a wedding without the maid of honor."

Gladys smiled at Susan. "So you and Carol Anne are friends?"

"Yes, Mrs. Carter. Carol Anne introduced me to Scott."

"Oh, sweetie, call me Aunt Gladys."

"Well...Aunt Gladys," Susan responded with some hesitation, "Scott and Carol Anne have told me so much about you. I'm very pleased to finally meet you."

After the greetings, Gladys invited them into the house for some iced tea. Susan offered to help, and Gladys took her up on the offer. Walking through the dining room on their way to the kitchen, they passed the table and noticing the tablecloth, Susan stopped to admire the embroidery. "Aunt Gladys, this is simply lovely. Did you do this?"

Gladys blushed with pride. She had been setting these linens out for her daughter-in-law for years and never got so much as a comment. "Yes, I did that forty years ago, and thank you for noticing."

As they walked into the kitchen, Susan spotted the pie. "Scott bet me you would have a lemon meringue for him. That's all he talked about for the last five miles. Is it a family secret, or would you share the recipe with me?"

With every word, Susan was winning over Gladys. She liked it when young people took the time to notice things and give gracious compliments. She was so disgusted with the way so many young people today didn't seem to have time for manners. When they did bother to give a compliment, they usually sounded either forced or patronizing. Susan's comments were neither, and Gladys liked this girl.

Caroline helped Gladys bring in the food, and the guests took their seats. As compliments began flying around the table about the delicious food, Gladys, with total innocence, asked Susan about her family. Hers was such a common question—especially in communities where families have been established for generations.

Scott was about to change the subject when Susan replied, "I'm sorry to say my family's history is not very noble. We've had some serious problems, and some things are downright shameful. But as is often said, we don't get to choose our family."

Being a gracious, well-mannered woman, Gladys quickly picked up on Susan's discomfort, and not wanting her guest to remain uncomfortable, she smiled and said, "No, that's true. We don't have the opportunity to choose our families, so they shouldn't be held against us. We do, however, get to choose the family we marry into, and you have chosen well. I hope I haven't offended you by speaking out of turn. It certainly was not intentional."

The complete lack of reproach in Gladys's voice put Susan at ease. "You certainly have nothing to apologize for, Aunt Gladys. One day soon you and I will sit down, and I'll tell you all about my family. Just not today."

The rest of the afternoon and evening, the family spent sharing the wedding plans, looking at Gladys's family albums, and enjoying her lemon meringue pie. Around eight o'clock, they said their goodbyes and headed for home. It had been a wonderful weekend, and everyone was exhausted.

Monday was a relaxing, stay-at-home day. They slept in, enjoyed a casual breakfast, and played board games while Caroline stayed busy preparing the last family meal they would share together for several months. Around six o'clock Scott and Susan drove Carol Anne to the airport and saw her off.

As they drove home from the airport, Susan laid her head on Scott's shoulder and groaned, "This engagement business is hard work. I don't know if there will be anything left of us after seven months of this."

"We could always elope," Scott suggested, only half-joking.

"No way. You had your chance last week. Now that you've gotten all of us excited about a wedding at the old plantation, there's no way you're getting out of it. We'll simply have to be patient. Besides, I'm too tired to elope tonight."

CHAPTER 12

———— ⚜ ————

Both Scott and Susan kept busy, and the next several months actually flew by quickly. Between work and wedding planning, the holidays arrived before they knew it. Susan and Mrs. Randal had gone shopping several times to look for bridesmaids' dresses. In late November they finally found the right ones. Susan knew she needed to make a final decision before Carol Anne came home for Christmas break because there wouldn't be any time later for her to get fitted. Besides, she and Carol Anne would need most of their time to look for Susan's bridal gown.

Mrs. Randal had proven to be a wonderful assistant for Mrs. Thomas. Between the two of them, they knew every store in the city, and both were experienced shoppers. By the holidays, the invitations had been ordered, the cake chosen, the menu settled on, and the photographer and music selected. Everything was shaping up nicely, so they all could temporarily set the wedding planning aside and focus on Christmas.

It was mid-December, and Carol Anne would be home in six days. Susan had been going out Christmas shopping almost every lunch hour for the past two weeks. She wanted to shop alone because she was looking for presents for the whole family and wanted these gifts to be only from her.

She found Carol Anne's gift first. While walking by an old doll shop downtown, she saw two dolls on display. Carol Anne had dozens of dolls in her collection but nothing like these, so Susan went in to ask about them. The dolls had china heads and hands, hand painted with delicate features. They were dressed alike except one had dark-black hair and the other was a redhead. The shop owner explained, "This old set is called 'Snow White and Rose Red.' A doll company in South Carolina specialized in fairytale dolls in the early forties. They were very popular with little girls, so not many have survived."

What a perfect gift for Carol Anne!

Buying for Mr. and Mrs. Thomas was proved to be more difficult. She couldn't think of anything. She spent three lunch hours looking for ideas. She knew they weren't expecting something big and expensive from her, but she still wanted her choice to be special. On the third day, she needed to go to the hardware store for some shelf liner. She hadn't been home much these past few months and thought it would be a nice gesture if she changed the kitchen shelf liner for her mother.

As she was leaving the hardware store, she saw a display of brass door-knockers. She immediately thought of their big, beautiful, red front door which did not have a knocker. One she noted in particular had a smooth place reserved for engraving. She asked the counterman to figure out if the words she had in mind could be engraved. When he assured her it would look fine, she ordered the gift. She wrote down: "The Thomas Home, est. July 19, 1943," their wedding day.

She now had gifts for Carol Anne and her future in-laws. She still had Scott, Aunt Gladys, and her own mother and sister remaining. She also wanted to look for something for Mrs. Randal as a thank-you for all of her help.

Her mother and sister would be quick. Every year she had bought a lovely sweater for each of them. Neither had given her a present in years, but she couldn't imagine going through Christmas and not giving them something. She didn't expect kindness or gratitude in return. She knew better. She was determined not to allow their behavior to keep her from doing what she knew was right.

Gladys loved old Southern gospel music, so she purchased her a lovely book that told about famous old hymns, the songwriters, and the story behind the hymn. She was certain Aunt Gladys would enjoy reading the book. As for Mrs. Randal, a pretty pendant was perfect.

She realized that finding the perfect gift for Scott was going to be more difficult. She struggled over what to get him. It was almost Christmas before she found his gift. She was browsing in a downtown bookstore when she saw a large display of books marked "Coffee Table Editions." As she began going through this stack of books, she found the ideal one for Scott—*The History of the New York Subway.* The book contained pictures dating all the way back to the beginning of the construction of the subway system. The pictorial featured black and white pictures of how the city looked at the turn of the century. Stories about the men who had worked on the system as well as the political and financial battles over its construction had been included. The center contained aerial-view maps of the five boroughs, including clear overlays of the subway systems in different colors for each route, giving the reader a perfect picture of all the different subway routes and where they were in the city. She knew Scott would absolutely love this book. Finally, her shopping was done!

On Friday evening, Scott and Susan met Carol Anne at the airport, signaling that Christmas had finally arrived. As promised, the girls spent the next few days shopping. They hit all the bridal shops in the city, and Susan tried on dozens of different dresses. She wanted a traditional style, the fuller the better, but the prices were making her a little nervous. She had never been in a wedding and hadn't thought much about wedding gowns. She didn't realize the dresses were so expensive. They had found one or two that were very nice, but she had no intention of spending so much money on a dress that she was going to wear only once—even if it was on her wedding day.

They discussed the dresses while taking a shopping break and having lunch. Their waitress couldn't help but overhear their conversation and apologized for interrupting, offering a suggestion. "I got married last month, and I found a great little shop out at the edge of town. This woman has three ladies who sew for her, and her prices are very reasonable. They have lots of stunning, very well-made dresses from which to choose. If you'd like, I could jot down the address for you."

Thanking the waitress for the tip, they decided they would go there right after lunch. It turned out to be a small shop in a not-so-great area. They could tell it had been there for years and that the area, at one time, must have been nice. As they walked in, Susan spotted the dress she had been dreaming of displayed on a mannequin.

Tiny pearls and sequins were hand stitched to the lace-covered satin bodice. The lacy sleeves came to a "V" at the top of her hand. The wedding gown featured a dropped waist, and the skirt was made of layers of the most delicate lace. The top layer was randomly dotted with French clear sequins. She knew, even before she tried it on, that this was her dress.

Carol Anne was sitting on a lounge chair by the three-panel mirrors when Susan came out of the dressing room. The look on Carol Anne's face confirmed Susan's opinion of the dress. *This is it!*

She walked in front of the mirrors and slowly turned to see it from the back. The bodice was tapered and fit her perfectly. Tiny satin-covered buttons started at the top of the neckline down the center of the back and then disappeared at the waist beneath the long, detachable train.

"Scott's going to go crazy when he sees you in that dress. You look like you belong on the cover of a bridal magazine. I vote for this one—no matter what the price."

"I love it too, but price is a factor—no matter how much we love it. It bothers me that this dress has no price tag. I am almost afraid to ask how much."

The elderly lady assisting them overheard their conversation and stepped over. "Excuse me, girls. My name is Helen Browden, and I own this shop. I think you might be surprised at its price. I need to tell you that this particular dress was previously owned though it was never worn. The gown had been purchased by a young lady three months ago and taken home. Over the Thanksgiving holiday, the couple broke off their wedding, and she asked us if we would buy it back from her. For that reason, there is no price tag on the dress. We felt the need to explain the circumstances before we discuss the price. If you are not superstitious and don't mind having a previously owned dress, I can make you a very good offer."

Susan was so excited she could hardly stand still. "I'm not superstitious, and yes, let's discuss the price."

"Well, I have one other consideration for you before we talk price. As your friend here mentioned, you do look like you belong on the cover of a bridal magazine. You are a beautiful young lady, and that dress fits like it was made for you. You see, my son, who does all my business advertising and finances, has been pestering me to update my display window and brochures. We have decided it is better to have a life-size photo of a real bride in the window than the lifeless mannequin with a dress that doesn't really fit it. If you would agree to pose for our photographer, I will not only *give* you that dress, I will pay for the photographer to do a bride's sitting for you. Does that offer appeal to you?"

Susan was reeling from the offer when Carol Anne quickly interrupted. "When and where would these photos be displayed? She isn't getting married until April 12, and we wouldn't want anyone to see her in the dress before that date. Would you, Susan?"

With disappointment written all over her face, Susan answered, "I didn't think about that. No, I wouldn't." She stood there thinking she had just lost the dress of a lifetime.

"Oh, you don't have to worry about that. We wouldn't even do the shooting until the end of February, and the print ads wouldn't be ready before the first of April. I wouldn't have any problem holding off changing the window until after your wedding. Do we have a deal?"

"Absolutely! We do have a deal. Thank you so much." Susan took off the dress and watched as it was placed in a clear garment bag and tagged with her name on it. Across the bottom of the tag, Helen wrote, "Sold."

Mrs. Browden then made out a bill of sale with exactly what Susan was expected to do in exchange for the dress. She handed the receipt to Susan and asked her to fill out her name, address, and phone number for her records. Susan decided she should use her company address and phone number; she didn't want Mrs. Browden calling her home and accidentally reaching her mother.

The girls were giggling as they drove home for dinner. They couldn't wait to tell Mrs. Thomas and Mrs. Randal about their great fortune in finding this shop, and now Susan could relax and enjoy the holidays.

Susan was driving down to Jefferson on Christmas Eve afternoon to see her sister, so she arranged to pick up Aunt Gladys and bring her back to Atlanta for the holidays. Her son and his family were traveling to Ohio to spend the holiday with his wife's family, so Mr. and Mrs. Thomas invited Gladys to come to Atlanta and stay at their home for the week.

Susan arrived at her sister's around one-thirty as agreed. Before getting out of the car, Susan slipped off her ring and placed it in a zippered pocket inside her purse. She thought it would be wise not to wear her ring in a neighborhood like this, nor did she want her sister to see it just yet.

Lisa was living in a two-room unit on the second floor of a rundown building in a seedy part of town. An old, half-empty paint store occupied the first floor, and Lisa's room smelled of paint and varnish.

Susan knew her older sister still cared about her, although her attitude would have never revealed her feelings. Lisa obviously felt uncomfortable with her sister, and her discomfort came out as anger. Susan was sure Lisa's feelings came partly out of an old guilt for abandoning her, but mostly because of her current lifestyle. She tried not to show her disapproval, but Lisa knew she did not approve. Lisa always tried to put up a tough, "I-don't-care" front, but she wasn't kidding herself—or Susan. Her life was awful, but she believed she could do nothing about it. Lisa had given up any hope of a better life years ago. Drugs and drinking had been her downfall. She could stay clean and sober for a few weeks, but then the addiction would beckon her back. She hadn't finished high school, so good jobs seemed out of the question. Consequently, Lisa had excuses for every bad decision she had ever made in her life. Everything that had happened was someone else's fault or something else.

"If only my parents had been different, then..."

"If only the drugs would just leave me alone, then..."

"If only I had a better education, then..."

"If only I wasn't an alcoholic, then..."

Susan had tried to help her sister stop her self-destructive cycle. Lisa always grew angry when Susan said, "It's all up to you, Lisa. You have the power to change your life. You can choose to live like this or you can choose to live differently. You know I understand why you're angry. You have every right in the world to be because of what has happened to you. That is not the issue. If you choose to hang onto that hate and anger, you'll become exactly like those who did this to you. You can choose to remain their victim, but I refuse to let our parents keep me their victim. How about you, Lisa? I'm willing to help you, but you have to decide for yourself that you want to change."

Susan knew Lisa hated it when she tried to reason with her. After all, she believed she had no choices, and none of this was really her fault. But what frustrated her sister the most was the fact that she couldn't throw her childhood issues in Susan's face. She couldn't say, "You don't know what it was like in *my* family" because Susan did know. She couldn't say, "I had it worse than you" because she hadn't. None of her arguments worked on Susan, so she usually tried to keep her distance. But the holidays were hard, and she did want to see her sister. She didn't want to be totally alone at Christmastime.

Susan was taking her out for lunch, so Lisa changed her clothes and brushed her hair. Before they left, Susan handed Lisa a present. Many of their planned lunches had ended with Lisa's angrily storming out, so Susan wanted to make sure she gave her the Christmas gift before anything happened.

Lisa tried to act as if this present wasn't important, but it was. No one in Lisa's whole world, except Susan, cared about her. As angry and bitter as she was, Lisa did love her little sister. She opened the box and pulled out the cream-colored sweater with embroidery on the front. The carefully chosen top was very pretty, and Lisa liked it.

Embarrassed, Lisa grinned slightly at her sister and said, "Thank you. I wish I had gotten you something."

Knowing she needed to pick up Gladys by three o'clock, but not wanting Lisa to suspect she was rushing her, Susan smiled and suggested, "Why don't we get going? I'd like to take you to a very nice sandwich shop on the other side of town."

They went to lunch and had a good time together. Susan had decided not to mention the wedding to her sister just yet. She hadn't decided what she was going to do about her and the wedding, but today was about Christmas—not weddings. She asked safe questions and tried to keep the meeting friendly and light.

While dropping Lisa off, she asked, "Why don't you come up to Atlanta for a visit sometime?"

Lisa stiffened and asked, "Is she dead yet?"

Susan simply returned a knowing smile while putting her car in gear and said, "Merry Christmas, Lisa. I love you."

CHAPTER 13

AUNT GLADYS WAS ready and waiting when Susan arrived. Her suitcase was by the door, and all of her Christmas presents were stacked next to it. Susan quickly loaded everything into the trunk, and they were on their way within a few minutes. She had spent several Saturday afternoons with Gladys since their first meeting and loved their time together. Whenever she came down to see Lisa, she stopped by to visit with Gladys.

Scott had told her his aunt would be kind and understanding about her family, and he was right. Although never willing to talk about her own experiences, she did want Gladys to understand and care about Lisa. Susan spent several visits recounting her fond memories of her sister, wanting desperately to have someone understand that Lisa had not always been as she is now. Susan felt better knowing someone like Aunt Gladys also cared about her only sister.

Christmas Eve dinner was ready and waiting when Susan and Gladys walked into the Thomas' home. Scott, Carol Anne, and Susan had decorated the tree three days earlier, and Mrs. Thomas had done the rest of the house. Decorating for Christmas was Caroline's favorite job. She loved pulling out the storage boxes and going through the familiar items that had been used by her family for years. Her mother, before she had died, had given her some special holiday decorations that had been used in their home when she was a child. Every year when she unwrapped her mother's nativity scene and arranged it on the large table in the entryway, she would get a warm, sweet feeling about her mother. She would close her eyes and picture her mother's hands as she lovingly handled these pieces.

This precious time of arranging these pieces made her feel as if her mother were still with her.

Gladys placed her presents under the tree and went into the kitchen. "Everything looks so festive, and dinner smells wonderful. Is there anything I can do to help?"

"Well, as a matter of fact, there is. I have a large gelatin mold on the bottom shelf of the refrigerator that needs to be put on that blue holiday platter of your mother's. I think it's in the cupboard right next to the refrigerator." The two women chatted happily while the last of the dinner tasks were completed.

The Thomas family had a longstanding Christmas Eve tradition. After dinner, everyone went into the great room where Mr. Thomas had set up the movie projector and screen. They watched the family films of Christmases gone by. This tradition had started years earlier when Bill Thomas bought his first 8mm Bell & Howell camera. The next year everyone wanted to see the film that had been shot the previous year.

That first year they had lost Bill and Gladys' grandfather. As the family watched the film and saw Grandpa Thomas waving at the camera, enjoying what turned out to be his last Christmas, they were so happy they had shot that film. They decided that each year they would review all of the past films, remembering family members who had passed away and seeing how the children had grown.

"This year," Mr. Thomas announced, "we'll be adding Susan to the family films."

Susan nestled close to Scott and watched the films. She saw his parents as young people laughing and having fun. She saw his great-grandfather, his grandparents, and even Aunt Gladys and her husband, Karl. She looked over at Gladys as Karl came on the screen, holding their little boy. She noticed the misty tears in her eyes, and Susan watched as Gladys smiled and quietly mouthed, "Hello, sweetheart. I miss you."

The next film was made the year Scott was born. Susan started teasing him about how cute he was, telling him she wanted a little boy just like him. That was the first time he had heard her mention their having a baby, and his heart started pounding. He pictured her holding his baby like his mother was holding him in the film, and he leaned closer and said, "How about four?"

"Four? Well, all right, but I want at least one little girl," Susan teased.

"Absolutely, and I want her to look just like her mommy," Scott ordered.

"Well, I wouldn't mind if she looked like her auntie, Carol Anne," Susan added. "So I guess we need two boys and two girls."

This was the first time Susan had ever seriously thought about having children.

After the Christmas film made when Scott was six, they decided to take a dessert break before finishing watching the rest. Caroline and Gladys went into the kitchen to cut the pies and start the coffee while everyone else took this opportunity to stash their presents under the tree—another family tradition. They always opened their gifts on Christmas morning and then attend church for a one-hour service before coming home to their Christmas dinner.

Dessert was brought in, and the films continued. Carol Anne's debut was a few Christmas films later. She was almost ten months old and was toddling around, her bright-red hair shining. She was smiling and waving at the camera and had on the cutest little dress. Susan watched as Mrs. Thomas scooped up her little girl into her arms, spun her around, and kissed her.

Without any warning, Susan felt herself struggling for control, desperately fighting tears She saw this happy little girl giggling and having fun. She was watching what she never had and desperately wanted. She didn't watch the next few films very closely until she heard Carol Anne say, "Look, Susan, I'm seven here. That's the year you and I met, remember?"

Susan's emotions were flooding her; the films became too painful to watch. Most of the time she could live day-to-day and behave like everyone else. She had all of the same choices and opportunities as any other adult, but no matter how hard she tried to put her past behind her, times like this brought back the pain.

She looked up and saw the Carol Anne she remembered and tried to sound cheerful as she answered, "Yes, I remember that year very well."

In truth, Susan was recalling what that Christmas had been like for her. While watching Carol Anne giggling and opening her presents that Christmas on the screen, she remembered how she had spent her Christmas. That was the year her mother's father died. *That's funny*, she mused. *He never was referred to as Grandpa, just Mother's father.* He had died shortly after Thanksgiving, and her mother had wanted to go home and spend some time with her mother. Susan remembered the horrible fights her parents had had over that request for weeks. Her grandmother kept calling, pleading with her mother to come home. Simply hearing the phone ring set her father off.

Finally, three days before Christmas, her mother slipped out of the house, boarded a bus, and went home without telling anyone, leaving Lisa and Susan to face their father's rage. For two days he screamed and threw things around the house. Then on Christmas Eve, in a horrible explosion of temper, he dragged the Christmas tree and the few presents under it outside and set them on fire. To make matters worse, the neighbors called the police and the fire department, and her father was given a ticket for having an unsafe fire in the backyard.

She and her sister spent that Christmas Day in their bedroom. They didn't come out except to go to the bathroom. Even though they were hungry, they did not want to remind their father they were even there. That was the last tree they ever had, and when her mother finally came home the day after Christmas, he beat her so badly she couldn't go back to work until after New Year's Day.

Susan hated her memories and tried to leave them in the past, but sometimes they would come like a powerful wave, and nothing could stop them. After the memories had spent themselves, she felt drained, and as far back as she could remember, she would sleep to escape them.

Scott noticed Susan had been silent for a while but simply wrote off her quietness to her being tired. He had no way of knowing Susan was preoccupied with her own type of home movies.

When the films were done, everyone pitched in with the dessert dishes and then headed for bed. Gladys was staying in Scott's old bedroom, the girls were in Carol Anne's room, and Scott was relegated to the sofa. He thought about going back to his apartment, but he wanted to be there early on Christmas morning because he had asked Susan to meet him under the tree before anyone else got up.

Bright and early on Christmas morning, Scott was up and had coffee ready when Susan came creeping down the stairs at six o'clock. He had two cups of coffee sitting on a tray next to the tree. He got up and met her at the doorway. "Sweetheart, this is our first Christmas, and I would like to start our own tradition. How about every Christmas morning, no matter how many children we have, you and I meet under the tree before anyone else is up? We can have coffee and give each other our presents. Just the two of us."

Susan loved this thoughtful, sentimental side of Scott. He was so much like his dad. "I love that idea, Scott. It's a date."

Taking her hand and leading her to the tree, Scott excitedly said, "I want you to open this present right away. I don't want anyone coming down during our private time."

As she unwrapped the present, Scott leaned back against the couch and enjoyed watching the girl he loved opening his first of many Christmas presents. He wanted to put this picture in his memory and cherish it.

Scott had bought her an elegant anniversary clock with a brass base and a glass globe. Right below the clock face was a small brass plate engraved, "Only our time together really matters. Love, Scott." Below this line of engraving was the date: December 25, 1973.

Susan loved the gift. She knew it was something she would keep and cherish always. She leaned over to kiss him as she handed him his present. "I hope you like this."

As Scott unwrapped the book, his eyes shined. He absolutely loved it! He started flipping through the pages, seeing the pictures of the city he had come to love, when he noticed she had written something on the inside cover. It said, "Because I know you love this place so much, I would like for you to share it with me on our honeymoon. Love, Susan."

Scott had been racking his brain for a special place to take his new bride. He had not even considered New York, but he realized this would be perfect. "I'd love to show the woman I love the city I love. Thank you for this wonderful present, sweetheart."

They heard people moving around upstairs and knew their special time was quickly coming to an end. Several minutes later, as they were sitting beside the tree, talking quietly, everyone came downstairs. Their first tradition had been established, and they were happy.

As everyone got their coffee and joined the happy couple at the tree, Susan thought about her mother. She had left her present on the kitchen table before driving to Jefferson yesterday. She closed her eyes and wished her mother and sister a Merry Christmas. Whether they had one or not was up to them, but she planned to have a wonderful day.

After all of the presents had been passed out, they formed a circle and watched as each person opened a gift. Everyone loved the presents Susan had bought them. Carol Anne couldn't believe she had found such a special gift. The dolls were marvelous, and she especially liked what they represented. She gave her best friend a big hug as she thanked her.

When Susan's turn came to open a present, she picked the one from Aunt Gladys. As soon as she opened it, she recognized Gladys' linen tablecloth and napkins. She sat in utter amazement for a moment. "Aunt Gladys, I can't take these. They mean too much to you."

"Honey, that's exactly why I want you to have them. I know you appreciate their worth and will take good care of them. Besides, when you and Scott use them on special occasions for years to come, it will be like I'm with you. I *want* you to have them."

"I don't know what to say but thank you. I promise to cherish and care for them just as you have, Aunt Gladys."

Bill and Caroline loved the doorknocker, and Bill said he would install it right after church. Carol Anne had gotten Susan a leather-bound bride's diary with her initials and the wedding date engraved on the front cover.

"It's for your first year of marriage, Susan. The lady at the bookstore said the bride should record everything: the names of your first dinner guests, all the things you do together, and the places you visit during your honeymoon year. Just be careful because someday your children might read it!"

At this comment, everyone started laughing. Mrs. Thomas leaned over to her husband and said, loud enough for everyone to hear, "Right after church I'm burning mine! I'm not taking any chances Carol Anne might get her hands on it."

"Oh, Mother! I'm sure your bride's diary would be very tame."

"Oh, you really think so, do you, daughter? You know, intimacy and romance have been around for a lot longer than you have, my darling."

Gladys laughed. "Young people all think we were born old, don't they? It's hard for them to imagine any of us young and frisky."

Susan loved this family she was joining. They were dignified and respectable without being stuffy or prudish. Even though she was embarrassed, she loved the way they could joke around so openly about love and intimacy without becoming crude or vulgar. As a child, she had been taught that sex was a dirty word, and any discussion of the subject always in a vulgar and dirty manner. She also knew her stiff, uncomfortable attitude about intimacy would eventually cause problems in her marriage if she didn't seek some help. She had thought about talking with Mrs. Thomas. She knew her future in-laws had a great marriage and that they had obviously been open and honest with their kids, but she simply could not bring up the subject with her. Pondering this matter, she thought, *It's probably because I wouldn't just be talking about sex; I would be talking about intimacy with her son. Either way, Mrs. Thomas is out, but Aunt Gladys is a possibility. I love this honest, sweet lady.*

Gladys had been happily married for more than forty years, and she had passionately loved Karl. She loved the way Aunt Gladys talked about him and knew she could talk with her and not be too embarrassed. Who better to talk to than a successful and seasoned woman with a good sense of humor? She decided she would spend a Saturday in January with her and have a heart-to-heart talk.

CHAPTER 14

THE HOLIDAYS PASSED, and Susan stayed busy with work and wedding planning. It was mid-February, and Susan had not yet made a decision about including her sister. She did not want to offend her by not asking her to be in her wedding, but she knew she couldn't trust Lisa. This decision was the most difficult one she would have to make regarding the wedding. She loved her sister, but even having her attend, let alone be a part of it, seemed unthinkable. Did she have to risk spoiling her wedding to be a good sister? Lisa was crude and raw, and exactly like her mother, she enjoyed embarrassing people. The more proper the people were, the cruder she was, and how she loved it.

Mid-afternoon on Friday, a phone call came into the switchboard for Susan. The Jefferson police wanted to talk to the sister of Lisa Miller. Her stomach turned as she picked up the phone.

"Ms. Miller, your sister has been arrested for attempting to sell drugs to undercover officers. Unfortunately, the drugs were apparently tainted, and she had just taken some. The doctors question whether she will pull through, and she's been asking for you."

Susan thanked the officer for calling and asked, "Will you tell my sister that I will be down this afternoon?"

The officer said he would call the hospital and ask one of the nurses to let her sister know she was coming. As soon as she hung up, she called Aunt Gladys. "I just received a call from the Jefferson police. Seems my sister has done it again, but this time she's in serious trouble. The doctors don't even know if she'll live. May I come and stay with you this weekend?"

"Of course you're welcome to come. Would you like me to go with you to the hospital?" Gladys knew all about Lisa and what kind of life she had lived and felt sorry for her.

"I'd love for you to come with me, but I'm not sure they'd let you go in. You see, she's under arrest. Because of her record, the officer said she is looking at some actual jail time for this little stunt. Scott's out of town until Sunday night, so I'm coming alone and could sure use some moral support."

Susan left work early so she could go home, pack, and get on the road before dark. She wasn't looking forward to the ninety-mile drive all alone. It had rained all week but the news on the radio said the roads were clear, so as long as she took it slowly and carefully, she thought she could make Jefferson by six o'clock. Aunt Gladys said she would have dinner ready, and then they could go over to the hospital together.

As she had suspected, only her name was on the visitor list because she was family. The police would not allow Gladys entry to Lisa's room. Susan left her in the waiting room. "Aunt Gladys, I will only stay for only a few minutes tonight."

The nurse at the desk offered, "Your sister is improving but still isn't out of the woods."

When Susan walked into the room, Lisa looked dead. Walking quietly to the bed, Susan tried to smile at her sister, hoping to keep the look of shock from her face. Lisa looked absolutely awful. Her coloring was a greenish-gray, and her eyes were almost sunken into her head, deep black circles extending out to her cheekbones. Her matted hair showed evidence of vomit that someone had tried to wipe away. The stench was sickening.

She gently rubbed her sister's arm, "Hi, Lisa, it's me, Susan. I'm here."

Lisa's eyes slowly opened, and she smiled faintly. She had been intubated, so talking was impossible. She nodded ever so slightly.

Susan gently brushed Lisa's hair away from her face. It hurt so much to see her sister like this. It didn't matter that she had done this to herself; it still hurt. Susan began crying as she gently continued to stroke her sister's forehead. Very few places on her body were free from tubes and needles. "Lisa, the nurse said you're improving, but you need to keep fighting. I know you must be hurting terribly and that you probably don't see any reason to fight, but you have to. Please, Lisa, don't leave me like this. I love you."

Struggling even to open her eyes, she recognized how much her little sister loved her, but like when they were kids, she wasn't sure she could stick around for Susan. *Life is just too hard, and I am so tired.*

"Lisa, the nurses don't want me to stay too long tonight because they want you to rest. I'm staying in town with a friend and will come to see you in the morning. I'm going to ask the nurse if I can wash your hair. That should help you feel a little better. You get some sleep, and I'll see you in the morning. I love you, Lisa."

Lisa nodded and closed her eyes as Susan left the room and went to the nurses' station to ask permission to wash Lisa's hair the next day. The large woman sitting at the desk didn't even look up.

Finally, with a disgusted tone, the woman said, "Why bother? She obviously doesn't care about herself."

Susan was shocked by this seemingly indifferent woman. "I want to bother because she's my sister. I simply need to know if I'm allowed to wash her hair. My sister is a person—not just a druggie."

The nurse looked up as Susan spoke back at her. Taking a good look at her, she quickly determined that this clean, well-dressed lady was obviously nothing like her sister. *That engagement ring is especially quite impressive.*

"Well, as long as you don't have her sit up or lift her head too far, I suppose it would be all right." As if trying to defend her opening statement, the nurse added, "You do realize the staff has cleaned her up several times already? It isn't as if we haven't taken care of her. These patients are their own worst enemies."

Susan refused to allow this woman to make her angry, so she decided not to respond to her phrasing of "these patients." She knew what this woman meant. Her sister was a wreck and was in real trouble, but she was still worth salvaging.

Susan silently turned and headed for the elevator. She remained under control until she and Gladys were in the car. As she started to explain what had happened, her emotions became overwhelming and she simply fell apart and started crying. "I don't know why she does this to herself. It's like she wants to die, and I can't reach her."

Gladys wisely knew Susan didn't really want to talk. She put her arm around her and let her cry. "Why don't we go home? You can jump in a hot shower and get ready for bed while I fix us something to eat. Then we can talk when you're not so upset."

"That sounds wonderful."

Susan started her car and was quiet all the way to the house, but she didn't feel alone. She knew Gladys also cared what happened to Lisa.

When she came out of the bedroom, the hot cocoa was poured, and Gladys had miniature marshmallows floating in it. Even though it was late, Gladys had whipped up a batch of her wonderful biscuits and had spread them with homemade peach jam. Susan tried to thank her for going to so much trouble, but the tears were right below the surface. She knew if she said anything right now, the tears would flow. She wasn't ready to talk yet. She only wanted to sit and enjoy the cocoa and biscuits and let everything slow down a little. The whole time she was in the shower, her mind kept flashing to memories of Lisa and what her life had been like. As much as she tried to force away the images, they would not leave.

After a while, even though she was emotionally drained, she felt a little more in control. They talked about Lisa and her childhood until the wee hours of the morning.

"I know that many people like that nurse only look at Lisa as a drugged-out prostitute who is trying to destroy her own life. They don't see the young girl I remember. They have no way of knowing what brought her to this place. I desperately want to help her, but she always acts as if she doesn't want any help, and now she's going to jail again. That is, if she pulls through."

It was now almost two in the morning. They were exhausted, and Lisa's problems seemed almost insurmountable. Gladys wasn't a naive person; she had experienced her share of pain in her own life. Although she had never personally been around people like Lisa, she knew there were far too many Lisas in this world. As she listened to Susan talk about her sister, something began pricking at her heart. How many Lisas had she treated with disdain, exactly like that nurse tonight, focusing only on the behavior and forgetting this person was probably self-destructing because of feeling lost, unloved, and hopeless? As Gladys listened to Susan talk, this quiet, nagging voice kept whispering to her, "This one is yours. You can't help all of them, but you can love this one. If you are willing, I will help you."

Gladys suddenly remembered a favorite saying of her father's: "This is where the rubber meets the road," and she smiled at the memory. God was giving her an opportunity to show love instead of simply talking about it. Gladys knew God was pushing her to get involved and to trust Him to keep her safe as she followed His direction. Loving the lovable is easy, but loving the unlovable takes courage and strength. After all, some people in her life had loved her through some terrible situations. Gladys knew she could not do anything about the ones she had failed to help, but she knew she was being given another chance to help someone. *I'm going to say yes this time.* Finally, Gladys suggested they get some sleep and visit Lisa in the morning.

After breakfast, Gladys gathered some towels, shampoo, conditioner, and hairbrushes and put them in a bag. She added some lotion and cologne, thinking this might help Lisa feel better. She decided she would try to persuade the police to let her visit Lisa this morning. This girl needed someone here in town who cared what happened to her. She had all the time in the world to go visit with her at the hospital and later at the jail. Maybe she could get through Lisa's tough, protective wall.

They arrived at the hospital around ten o'clock. They quietly walked right past the desk and went into Lisa's room as if they had done it lots of times. Because Lisa was incapable of walking away, the officer obviously felt free to leave his post for a much-needed coffee break, so Gladys was able to slip into the room without a problem.

Lisa was still quite groggy and opened her eyes only when someone talked directly to her. Aunt Gladys took the large plastic wash basin into the bathroom and filled it with warm water while Susan lifted her sister's head very slowly and placed one of the towels under her head and shoulders. Using washcloths, Susan rinsed the vomit out of her sister's hair.

Gladys had to fill the basin with fresh water several times while Susan kept working. When they felt they had her hair rinsed well, they started massaging in the shampoo. Susan carefully lifted Lisa's head while Gladys gently washed the back. Once confident her hair was clean, they began rinsing. They used four basins of water before they were sure they had rinsed out all of the shampoo. Aunt Gladys took a clean towel and gently rubbed Lisa's hair as dry as possible. She then carefully brushed her hair.

Susan got another basin of clean water and sponge bathed her sister. After the bath, she rubbed her sister's neck, shoulders, arms, and legs with lotion. Her skin looked as if it hadn't enjoyed lotion in years. Every once in a while, Lisa would open her eyes but didn't respond. Seemingly, waking required too much effort, and she would drift back to sleep.

When they were finished, Susan went out to the nurse's desk and asked, "May I have a clean gown for my sister?"

The nurse turned and asked, "Why? Did your sister get sick again?"

"No, we gave her a bath and washed her hair. We thought a clean gown would make her feel better." Susan could tell the nurse was surprised at their ministrations, but she wasn't angry.

The nurse went to a linen cupboard, handed Susan a gown, and smiled at her. "I'm sure, even sedated, being clean has made her feel better. That was very kind of you. I know it wasn't a pleasant task."

Susan thanked her for the gown and headed back to the room. As she reached Lisa's door, Susan thought about the difference between this nurse and the one from last night. She thought about what Aunt Gladys had said in the car last night: "It doesn't matter what your job is, we all have times when we can add to someone's burden or we can lighten it. The action we choose shows our true character."

Susan was glad this nurse had been kind and had made this emotional day a little easier for her.

They removed the soiled gown and had finished putting on the clean gown when the nurse came in with an armful of clean bed linens. With a friendly grin, she said, "Since you've gone to all of this effort, why don't we give her some clean sheets too? They're changed daily, but this room isn't scheduled until around three o'clock. I don't see any harm in doing her room a little early. That way she'll be all fresh and clean."

Susan and Gladys stepped away from the bed and let the nurse change the bedding. As she finished and headed toward the door, she said, "She's been a very sick young woman, but I think the worst might be over. She'll feel much better when she wakes up. Being clean and smelling good is sometimes the best medicine there is."

As the nurse walked out of the room, the police officer, who had returned to his post, noticed them in the room. He pushed the door open and said, "Excuse me, but you don't have permission to be in here."

Susan quickly introduced Gladys and herself. "I needed help bathing my sister."

Knowing his charge was incapable of going anywhere, he simply pulled the door closed and allowed them to stay in the room. They sat at Lisa's bedside for about two hours quietly talking, hoping she would come out of the drug-induced sleep so they could talk with her.

Around one o'clock Susan went down to the cafeteria and brought up some lunch for her and Gladys. As they sat eating and visiting, Lisa finally woke up. She was still quite drowsy but was very much aware of them. Susan introduced Gladys and told her sister they had bathed her and washed her hair. Lisa tried to respond but was having difficulty. They sat and talked with her for almost fifteen minutes without her falling asleep. She seemed to understand everything they were saying, although she couldn't talk because of the tube in her throat. Susan explained who Gladys was and how much she had come to love her. She reminded Lisa that she couldn't stay in Jefferson during the week but that Gladys lived there in town and would like to come visit and make sure she had what she needed.

Lisa turned weary eyes toward Gladys. After a long pause, she sort of smiled.

Susan added, "If you would you like Aunt Gladys to visit, she needs to be on your visitor list. Would you approve that?"

Lisa nodded slightly, so Susan went outside and explained to the officer that her sister wanted to allow Aunt Gladys to visit.

He came in and asked Lisa to confirm this request, and she nodded yes. "You'll need to fill out a form, and if you're cleared by the police department, your name will be added by Monday morning. I'm sure you'll have no problem. As a matter of fact, I'll give you a forty-eight-hour pass so you can visit this weekend."

They thanked him for helping and spent most of the day with Lisa. She would drift in and out of consciousness, but each time the conscious periods lasted a little longer, and she seemed more and more alert. Around five-thirty a doctor came in and, after examining her, decided to remove some of the tubes. He said she was definitely out of danger and was a very lucky young woman. Lisa gave her sister a slight smirk at that comment. She didn't feel very lucky, but she was glad she was out of danger.

With a very raspy voice, Lisa tried to thank them for cleaning her up. They helped Lisa with her dinner, and every once in a while, Gladys would pick up the brush and gently go through Lisa's hair. She didn't ask permission; she just did it. Susan could tell her sister was uncomfortable with her attention but also kind of liked it and didn't try to stop Gladys. They stayed until seven, when the staff ordered them out. They promised they would come back around one o'clock the next day and said goodnight.

The next morning started quietly. Both women ate their breakfast in silence and then went to church, and after a quick bite of lunch, they headed over to the hospital. Susan had been amazed that Lisa had not thrown a fit about having Aunt Gladys in the room and that she had actually allowed her to fuss over her a little. She wondered how her sister would behave today, now that she was feeling somewhat better. As they walked into her room Lisa looked up and smiled, obviously glad to see them.

Susan was not sure how much she should tell her sister about Scott's and her wedding plans. She felt uncomfortable, knowing Lisa was in such big trouble and facing jail time, and she felt a little selfish talking about such good happenings in her life. She finally decided she would try to avoid the subject, if possible. However, Lisa was more alert today and was obviously curious about who Gladys was, so Susan ended up explaining everything. Lisa was glad for her sister and hoped everything would turn out the way her little sister dreamed it would. She really did want Susan to be happy and said she deserved some happiness.

Later that afternoon Gladys asked Lisa about the trouble she was in. Her question was kind and non-accusing, so Lisa didn't get angry. "I don't know how much trouble I'm in this time since I never made it to the police station and haven't been interviewed by anyone yet. I suspect the police will probably show up first thing in the morning—or as soon as they find out I am conscious. I am sure to be facing some jail time for this stupid stunt."

Lisa looked at the old woman to see if she were shocked. Gladys was looking directly at her and simply said, "Well, if so, I guess you'll be needing some company. I'd be glad to visit you, and your sister can stay with me on the weekends she is able to come to visit. With the wedding fast approaching, Susan will be very busy, but I have all the time in the world. Would you mind if I came around a few times each week?"

Not accustomed to people's being kind to her, Lisa did not answer at first. She felt uncomfortable, but for some reason, she liked this old lady. Without looking directly at Gladys, she half shrugged to show she really didn't care what she did, but then she mumbled, "That would be okay with me."

They spent the rest of the afternoon telling stories about Scott and Carol Anne, and by the end of the day, Lisa felt like she knew them. Before leaving, Lisa looked at her sister with an impish grin and said, "I'll be unavoidably detained and will not be able to attend your wedding. However, I would like to see some pictures when it's over."

Susan's dilemma regarding her sister and the wedding was now solved, and although she never would have wanted it to happen this way, she was thankful the choice was no longer hers. She promised to bring pictures and save her some wedding cake, and then they said good night and left the hospital.

"Aunt Gladys, Lisa sure warmed up to you. I'm so happy you're willing to keep visiting her. She's never had anyone, except me, care much about her."

"Honey, your sister has a lot of serious problems, and I'm not about to say her problems don't scare me. But she needs to know people care what happens to her and that we'll be there for her. She's the only one who can help herself. If she wants to turn her life around, I'll try to help her. We'll just have to be there for her and show her we think she's worth saving, because she obviously doesn't think so right now."

When they got back to the house, Susan packed her things and said goodbye. She had a two-hour drive back to Atlanta and wanted to see Scott before she went to bed. The weekend had been long, and she needed to feel his arms around her. She kissed Gladys on the cheek and headed for home.

Five days later, Lisa pleaded no contest and was sentenced to six months in jail. The attorney said she might be out in four months if she behaved. Gladys visited Lisa regularly, and they seemed to be getting along.

CHAPTER 15

❧

EVERYTHING ABOUT THE wedding was coming together wonderfully. Mrs. Randal and Mrs. Thomas were doing a superb job keeping everything in order so the bride and groom could relax and enjoy the anticipation of their upcoming wedding. The two planners never pushed their opinions on the couple, and Scott and Susan both knew their day was going to be exactly what they wanted.

On three separate occasions, Susan tried to talk to her mother about the wedding and about Lisa. Marjorie Miller refused to discuss either. Finally, near the end of March, Susan decided she would make one last attempt. She did not want to give up on her mother, but she had come to the point where she needed to settle this once and for all. She decided that no matter what, she was going into April with a clear conscience, knowing she had done her best to include her mother in her wedding. After this attempt, she would not bring up the matter again.

Around six o'clock on Thursday evening, she had dinner ready when her mother got home. She had prepared her favorite meal and had obviously gone to a lot of trouble, but her mother simply dished up her plate, walked into the living room, and turned on the television.

Susan stood in the kitchen for a few minutes, trying to decide what she should do. Part of her simply wanted to scream. Her mother was like a stone wall that seemingly absolutely nothing would be able to penetrate. Susan was so frustrated. There never seemed to be a time when her mother softened—even for a moment.

Determined to break through that wall, Susan walked into the living room, turned off the television, and took a seat across from her mother. If this was going to be the last attempt, she was going to pull out all of the stops and let it fly. She didn't give her mother a chance to react.

Making sure she kept anger out of her voice, Susan confronted her fully for the first time in her life. She took a deep breath and began. "Mother, you and I need to talk."

Susan immediately raised her hand to silence her protests and continued. "I know you don't want to talk to me, but this time you can sit there and listen for a change. I'm getting married in thirteen days and will be out of here forever, but before I go, I have some things I need to say to you."

Marjorie sat back in her chair and simply returned a cold stare.

Without allowing this reaction to dissuade her, Susan pushed on. "All of my life I have tried to get along with you. I have done everything I could to please you, and I have tried my best to help make your life a little easier. Even when I was a little child, you always made Lisa and me feel it was our responsibility to make things easier for you."

Almost spitting the words at her daughter, Marjorie interrupted with a sneer, "When has life ever been easy for me?"

Amazed at her mother's self-centered view of the world, Susan paused. "I know you've had a hard life. I was also there, remember? When I was little, I tried to make excuses for why you did the things you did. I'm not a child any longer, and I'm through making excuses for you."

"I've never asked you to make excuses for me," her mother curtly retorted.

"Mother, you're a lonely, bitter person. Do you want to live the rest of your life, driving everyone away from you with your hateful bullying? What did Lisa and I do that was so terrible that you hate us so much?"

Susan watched her mother slide her tongue across her upper teeth. Susan had detested this habit of Marjorie's since she was a child. Whenever Marjorie wanted to start a fight with her husband, she would slide her tongue across her upper teeth as she pondered which story to embellish.

When it was apparent her mother had decided not to comment, Susan continued. "I wouldn't be sitting here talking to you if I didn't still care. I don't want to walk away from you and leave like this. Can't we find a way to build some kind of relationship? Do you even want to see your grandchildren when they're born? If you do, things must change first. I won't have my children treated the way you have treated Lisa and me. I care about you, Mother, but I have learned how to respect myself. I can no longer sacrifice my self-respect just to get along with you. So for the last time, I am honestly and sincerely asking you to please come to my wedding. Will you please make an effort toward Lisa and me?"

Having finally said all she intended to say, Susan sat quietly as if expecting her mother to respond.

When Marjorie realized her daughter was not going to leave, she set down her plate. Looking at Susan with hateful disdain, she coldly stated, "As far as your wedding goes, I already told you I have no intention of attending. I don't care to spend time with all those stuck-up snobs who think they're better than me. As for you and Lisa...so I screamed and yelled a few times. Life was hard, and I'm sorry if I didn't have time to mollycoddle you two. You had a roof over your head, food in your stomach, and clothes on your back. That's more than many have. If you have kids, what makes you think I would even want to see them? I raised mine; you raise yours. Just leave me alone."

With that diatribe out of her system, she sat waiting, as if daring her daughter to keep this conversation going.

"I'm sorry you feel that way. Someday, when you are old and lonely, if you change your mind, please feel free to call me. In the meantime, I'll respect your wishes, and I'll leave you alone. I'm not angry, and I hope you do call someday." She rose from the chair and left the apartment.

Knowing Scott and his dad were at a business meeting until late, Susan drove over to see if Mrs. Thomas would like some company. As she walked in the side door, she heard Mrs. Thomas in the kitchen. In order not to startle her, she called out, "Mom, it's me, Susan. Would you like some company?"

The two began going over all of the last-minute details and realized that almost everything for the wedding was done, and they were in the home stretch. Mrs. Randal had made a large calendar with everyone's to-do list color-coded and had marked reminders on the calendar for anything someone had to do. She also called to remind them if they had something to do that day. She was amazing. She had even called all of the wedding people and confirmed everything the couple had ordered. The plantation was set, the music, florist, and bakery were confirmed, the photographer reminded, and all of the girls' dresses were finished and tuxedos ordered. Mrs. Thomas had all of the wedding decorations well in hand and was using every bit of her creative energy to make this wedding special. She would be the first to admit she was enjoying every minute of it.

Around ten o'clock, Bill and Scott came home and joined the women. Scott had all the tickets and itinerary for their honeymoon safely locked in his desk at the office and had finished his shopping for some new clothes for the trip. He had not yet decided what to give his bride on their wedding day. He wanted to present her a special gift and was having a hard time deciding. His mother had suggested luggage and his dad had suggested jewelry, but neither sounded special enough to him. He wanted his gift to represent how he felt. He wanted it to be wonderful, and he knew he was running out of time.

Most of that week went fairly well, except for two attacks Susan had to endure from her mother. Marjorie was beginning to turn up the heat, which was very unpleasant for Susan. Having finally stood up to her mother, Susan thought things might change a little around the house, but she was wrong. Marjorie, obviously primed for a fight, was in Susan's face about everything. Susan was beginning to crumble under the constant pressure of her mother's anger. Susan did her best to avoid her and looked forward to her time alone with Scott.

Having had three overnight business trips that week, Scott had not been around much, so Saturday was going to be their day. They did some last-minute shopping and planned to grab some dinner and go to a movie. Although Susan seldom talked about what was going on at home, Scott knew she was struggling and figured Mrs. Miller must be making her life miserable again.

Knowing Susan would never fight back, he suggested, "Honey, I think we need to get you out of your mother's place as soon as possible. We both know she's only going to get worse as the wedding date gets closer, and I don't want her upsetting you. Carol Anne will be flying in next Friday evening, and I know you two have already agreed to stay at my parents' for the whole week before the wedding. I think we should go back to your apartment, pack your things this evening, and move you into my parents' house. We can put anything you don't need for the next two weeks in my apartment, and everything else can go to my parents'. I don't want you to stay one more night in that apartment with her."

Susan understood Scott's concern. She knew he was afraid her mother would start another fight, and the only way to avoid one was to not be there. "I agree with you, but I think we should at least call and ask your parents if they mind. Your mother has been working so hard on the wedding, I feel guilty moving in on her."

"Honey, this was my mother's idea. She knows how hard you work at keeping the peace and how impossible your mother can be. She does not want you to have to think about anything but the wedding. We all want the next two weeks to be pleasant and fun. So let's go get you moved, all right?"

"Okay, but it'll take several hours if we stop to pack, and I don't want my mother home when we do it. It's almost six o'clock. She should be getting ready to leave for her Saturday bowling league and will be gone until around ten o'clock. Let's hurry and take my personal items upstairs. Then we can take our time separating out what I will need at your mother's. We should be able to have everything cleared out well before she gets home. Actually, the truth is, she'll probably be relieved I'm gone. As for the few pieces of furniture that are mine, I'll leave them for her."

They saw Mrs. Miller's pulling out of the garage as they drove in. They hurried and had everything out of the apartment within two hours. After the last load was safely in Scott's apartment, she sat at his desk and wrote her mother a note, explaining that because so many last minute decisions regarding the wedding needed to be handled, she thought it best if she stayed with Scott's parents. She gave her mother their phone number in case she needed to contact her, and she enclosed an additional month's rent. She knew she didn't have to, but she did not want her mother to have any excuses for holding a grudge. When she finished, they went into the apartment and placed the note and her key on top of the television set. After one last look around, Susan kissed Scott and walked out of her mother's apartment.

Susan did not expect to hear from her mother that next week, and she didn't. She was thankful she was so busy she really didn't have much time to dwell on her lack of concern. She and Mrs. Randal were buried at work, trying to get everything completed and ready for her three-week absence. She was taking the entire week off before the wedding and then two weeks for the honeymoon.

Every evening was spent opening wedding gifts that had arrived that day and then writing thank-you notes together. Mrs. Thomas had offered the den as "their space," and gifts were stacked everywhere. By the time Carol Anne arrived home, the house looked like a department store. The girls had the best time going through the gifts and seeing all the lovely items people had sent.

Three days before the wedding, as they were opening the gifts that had come that day, a package addressed only to Susan arrived. All of the earlier gifts were either addressed to Scott and Susan or to the future Mr. and Mrs. Scott Thomas. This one puzzled her until she noticed that the return address was her old street, and the name in the corner was Mrs. William Reiner, her former neighbor. Opening the package, she found a lovely milk-colored glass candy dish. A personal note was tucked inside the gift. Mrs. Reiner had seen the engagement announcement in the paper several months back and knew the wedding was upcoming. Glad to know Susan was doing well, she wanted to wish her lots of happiness. At the end, she wrote, "Susan, you were a sweet little girl, and you deserve some happiness."

Susan was amazed that her former neighbor had remembered her. It was touching that she took the time to send a present. "Scott, I want to invite Mrs. Reiner to the wedding. I know it's awfully short notice, and there isn't time to mail her an invitation. I want to take it to her personally."

Scott could see how excited she was, and this was the first real request she had expressed about the wedding. "Sure! If you want to invite her, let's go right now."

They picked up an invitation and drove to Mrs. Reiner's home. As they drove up the street, Susan felt a strange tightening in her chest. Three years had passed since she had been on this street. As they pulled up in front of the Reiner house, Susan looked over at her former house, and the memories were as fresh as ever. She almost had the feeling her father could come storming out of that front door any minute.

A strange, faraway look clouded her face as she looked over at the fig tree that stood on the property line between her house and Mrs. Reiner's. She remembered climbing that tree many times as a child. She would reach the third big branch, straddle it, lean against the trunk, and pretend no one could see her. She would sit there for hours reading a book or watching the neighborhood kids play baseball in the street. That tree had been special to her. Many times, when her dad was flying around the house in an angry rage, looking for someone to attack, she would escape to her fig tree, climb up, and sit very still, hoping he couldn't see her. She would pretend the tree knew why she had climbed it and made believe it would spread its leaves around her and make her invisible. More than once she sat there, trying to ignore the screaming and yelling coming from her house. She always felt safe in her tree.

As they got out of the car, Susan walked over and studied the tree for a moment. She was surprised at how normal it looked. She remembered it as being so much larger. Scott followed her and placed his arm around her waist.

"I remember this house. This is where you lived the time Dad and I brought you home."

"Yes, I remember that day." Trying to lighten the moment and stay away from that memory, Susan said, "It's funny. All the time I was growing up here, I never saw this tree for the size it really was. It always felt so much bigger."

She hugged Scott tenderly but didn't dare look at him as she thought, *You have no way of knowing the significance of that tree to me. How could you? I don't ever want you to know about all that went on in that house over there. The sooner I forget it, the better.*

With one final glance at the tree, they turned and headed toward Mrs. Reiner's house. They heard the television and knew someone was home, so Scott rang the doorbell. Mrs. Reiner came to the door and immediately recognized Susan. She unlocked the screen door and invited them inside.

As they stepped in, Susan realized she had never before been inside this house—even though she had lived next door for over seventeen years. The furniture was old, but neat and clean. The arms of the sofa and chair were covered with crocheted doilies, and family pictures were displayed around the room.

Susan walked over to get a closer look at a photo of Steve Reiner in his cap and gown standing on the front lawn. "I remember when you took this photo. I was sitting on my front porch, watching you take this. You were so proud of him. Steve used to sit out on your lawn right there"—she pointed to the place he was standing in the photo—"and my sister, Lisa, would sit with him and talk. Steve was always really nice to us, and my sister really liked him."

Remembering that time was always painful. Lisa had been gone for two months when that photo was taken, and life in that house next door was unbearable. Susan remembered how strange it was to sit on her front porch watching this family laugh and take pictures, wondering what it must feel like to be happy. Wanting to get away from these painful memories, Susan walked back and stood by Scott as she looked around the room and then toward Mrs. Reiner. She was always amazed how a house discloses what kind of people lived there. This room was friendly and warm, and so was she.

"Mrs. Reiner, where is Steve these days? I don't see photos of him all grown up."

A pained look crossed Mrs. Reiner's face but was quickly replaced with a gentle acceptance as she said, "The summer after his graduation, Steve was kind of lost. He would never tell me what had happened that so drastically changed his outlook on life, but a mother knows when something is wrong. He had loved baseball his whole life, but suddenly it no longer mattered to him. He had been offered a partial scholarship to the city college but, for some reason, he wanted to get away from here."

Looking over at the last photo she had of Steve, she continued. "Soon after your dad was taken away, my Steve joined the Marines and went off to boot camp. I received several letters from him, and he sounded like things were getting better, but then one weekend he and a friend took a motorcycle ride into town, lost control of the bike, and slid in front of a big semi. They were both killed."

"I'm so very sorry; I didn't know. I liked Steve. He was always kind to Lisa and me." Feeling the need to change the subject, she said, "Mrs. Reiner, I wanted to thank you for sending that lovely candy dish. It was so nice of you to do that. I was wondering—I know it's short notice—but I would love it if you would come to our wedding this Saturday."

"It would be my pleasure." Mrs. Reiner beamed. "I'm so glad that you found such a nice young man. We knew it was very hard for you when you lived over there." She nodded in the direction of the house next door. "I had called the police so many times, they started threatening me with harassment—until that one night. I never understood why they let your father get away with so much before they finally did something. How is your family?"

Feeling quite sure Mrs. Reiner did not know about her dad's returning to prison, she didn't intend to bring up that subject. "Mother is fine. She lives downtown and still has her same job."

Mrs. Reiner sensed that Susan did not want to talk about her family, but she wanted to let this young girl know that she had tried. "You know, I always felt guilty that I couldn't do anything for you girls. The whole neighborhood was afraid of your father, and the police were not doing anything about him. Thankfully, times have changed a little. I think today, if something like that was going on, the police would do something a little more quickly."

"Well, let's hope so anyway." Susan forced a polite smile but made it obvious she didn't want to discuss the past. Her feelings were already a little raw, and sensing her discomfiture, Mrs. Reiner, quickly changed the subject. They visited for a few more minutes, and then, as they were leaving, Susan handed her the invitation. "I do hope you can come. It would be nice to have someone at my wedding who knew me as a child."

Assuring them she would indeed come to the wedding, she watched them drive away, and thought, *I wonder whatever happened to her older sister. I'm curious if Susan even knows where Lisa is these days.*

CHAPTER 16

—— ⚜ ——

Susan and Carol Anne spent Thursday evening packing Susan's suitcase and going over their to-do lists—everything going to the plantation, things for the honeymoon, the items Carol Anne had to bring back home after the wedding, and the list of everyone Susan wanted to thank personally during the reception.

"I'm afraid I'll be so emotional at the wedding that I'll forget someone. So many people have helped make this day special. I want to remember to thank each one of them in person—not just in a note later."

They hung her wedding gown from the canopy, laid out on the bed all of the needed undergarment, and placed her shoes on the floor. Her headpiece was laid across the pillow, and right as they were sure they had everything accounted for, they heard a knock at the door. Fearing someone might see the wedding gown, Carol Anne blocked the door and asked, "Who is it?"

"It's me, Scott. Don't worry, I know I'm not allowed in, but Susan, can you come out for a few minutes? I haven't had five minutes alone with you in days."

His sister and mother had kept them both busy all week with lists of things to do. Even with everyone's help, many last-minute details still needed to be handled. Even when they were together, they were busy doing wedding preparations.

"I'm trying on some new clothes, Scott," Susan called. "Give me five minutes, okay?"

Not wanting him to see any of the darling outfits she had bought for the honeymoon, she slipped on a pair of jeans and the USC sweatshirt Carol Anne had given her and headed downstairs.

Scott kissed her as they met in the kitchen. "I know you have lots to do tonight, and we're both going to be very busy tomorrow. I need five minutes with you without doing wedding stuff. Let's go out back where we won't be interrupted."

The past few days had been hard on Scott, and Susan could see that he was tired. He had three very important projects at work that he was trying to finish before they left.

They walked out to the pool and sat on the swing. She could almost feel his exhaustion, and his weariness worried her. "Are you all right?"

"Sure, what makes you ask?"

"You seem terribly tired," Susan said. "We don't need you getting sick right before the wedding."

She knew he was working on something important, and the pressure was really getting to him. "I honestly don't mind if we have to postpone our honeymoon. We can do it later if there's a problem with work."

Hearing Susan suggest postponing their honeymoon was more painful than he could have imagined. He stood and started pacing back and forth in front of the swing. "Susan, I'm trying my hardest to settle these contracts so that doesn't happen. These people are playing hardball, and if I can't get them to settle by tomorrow, I can't leave town. It would cost my father a lot of money, but even more importantly, it would cost many of our employees their jobs. I simply can't do that to them."

He was obviously very upset about this matter, and she felt awful that she had been so busy all week she hadn't noticed the tension on his face. "Scott, we can go later in the summer. We don't have to go right now. Please, I don't want you to worry about disappointing me. I'm fine with it, honest."

"Honey, I knew you'd understand, and I do appreciate your attitude. I so wanted everything to be perfect. I believe I have a faint chance of closing these dealings tomorrow morning, but I can't push too hard or I'll give us away. I don't dare let them get wind of our wedding and honeymoon plans or they'll really use that against us in a squeeze play. I'm so sorry about this possible delay, but I couldn't wait until we got to the plantation to tell you the honeymoon might be off."

"Sweetheart, we'll still have a honeymoon. It just won't be in Manhattan. As long as we're together, that's all I want."

They sat on the swing for an hour talking about their dreams and enjoying being together. He was so proud of her. He had known she would take the news well, but he planned to do everything in his power to get that contract signed tomorrow.

As he walked her back into the house, he took her in his arms, kissed her, and whispered, "The next time I see you, young lady, will be at our rehearsal. This has been a very long seven months. I can't really believe it's almost here. I need to get some sleep because tomorrow I'll need my wits about me. Goodnight, sweetheart. I love you."

As she quietly headed up the stairs, she decided she would continue packing as if they were going, not mentioning the honeymoon problem to Carol Anne. She knew Scott was upset, and she could see no good reason for anyone else to know.

She and Carol Anne packed and talked until almost one o'clock in the morning. When they climbed into bed, confident that everything that possibly could be forgotten was on a list, and every list had been checked at least twice, they turned off the lights. They continued to talk for another hour or so; after all, they both were much too excited to sleep.

Friday morning was slow in starting for the girls. Since they had plenty of time today, they had decided not to set the alarm. They had everything under control and, besides, they could not check into their cabin at the plantation until two o'clock.

The smell of coffee and fresh rolls greeted them. They tried to stay in bed, going over everything happening that day, but their stomachs were responding to the wonderful smells wafting from the kitchen. They finally got up around nine and headed downstairs.

Mrs. Thomas had been up for hours. She had squeezed fresh orange juice and made cinnamon rolls and coffee. The three of them sat in the kitchen, enjoying the peace and quiet, knowing everything was well in hand. Susan looked over at the clock and realized Scott would be walking into that important meeting right about then. She quietly closed her eyes and asked God to be with him. She wasn't asking God to save their honeymoon. She wanted Scott to remain calm and not to let the outcome of that meeting spoil the wedding for him.

By one o'clock they had loaded everything into the van. Mrs. Thomas stood looking at the van and started to laugh. "With all these clothes hanging everywhere, boy, am I glad I decided to take out all of the decorations to the plantation yesterday. There would not have been any room for us to sit."

Carol Anne did not want to take any chances that her brother would see the wedding gown before the ceremony. "Mom, it's after one. We need to get all this stuff in the cabin before Scott shows up, so we'd better get going."

She was so anxious to see her brother's face the first time he saw his bride in her dress. Not even Caroline had seen it. Helen Browden had carefully wrapped it at the shop and had arranged for one of her workers to come out to the plantation Saturday morning and steam press it. She was so pleased with the results of the ad display, and she wanted to make sure the dress looked absolutely perfect on Susan's wedding day.

The girls spent the afternoon walking around the grounds, greeting the bridesmaids and groomsmen as they arrived, and then they hurried to dress for the rehearsal dinner. Shortly before getting dressed, Susan noticed Scott's car pulling in the drive and wondered how his day had gone. While all the girls giggled and told stories of love and romance, Susan's mind was on Scott. She knew he would not allow his disappointment to ruin this time for her, but she wanted to somehow convince him she didn't care if the honeymoon was postponed. As she pondered her predicament, the phone suddenly rang.

Before she had a chance to answer, she heard Scott's voice. "Ms. Miller, would you care to join me under the weeping willow tree in about fifteen minutes? I have checked with the manager, and the entire wedding party has checked in, so we're all here and ready to go."

She couldn't tell if Scott was really this happy or if he was simply putting on an act for her. Either way she wasn't going to ask any questions. There would be time enough for bad news. Right now they were going to relax and have a great time.

"Scott, I thought the plan was that we would all meet at five."

"That's right. Everyone else will come at five. I want you there fifteen minutes earlier. So tell my sister to stay with the others, and you come alone. Sweetheart, do you realize this is the very last night I will have to kiss you goodbye at the end of the evening?"

The laughter in his voice almost made her want to cry. What a change from last night!

"If I only have fifteen minutes, I'd better hurry. I love you, Scott."

She quickly explained to the girls that she was going on ahead, which made them all start giggling again. This was going to be a fun night, and everyone was excited.

Scott was leaning against the willow when she walked up to him. Because of the barbecue, tonight's dress was casual, and Scott looked great in new dress jeans, a white shirt, and a tan jacket. His hair was blond with a slight curl to it, and his blue eyes were shining brightly as she walked up to him.

She loved to tease him, and he was so cute tonight. "Hello, handsome. You doing anything for the next sixty years or so?"

"As a matter of fact, I'm going to be rather busy. You see, I have this girl. She and I are going to be very busy loving each other." Looking at his bride-to-be, Scott could hardly take a breath. "I can't believe it's here. I'm scared I'll wake up and find out it's another one of my dreams. I've been doing that often these past few months. Why don't you come here and kiss me so I can be sure this is real?"

After a minute or so, Scott cleared his throat. Taking a slender box out of his inside jacket pocket, he looked into those eyes he had come to cherish. "Susan, I wanted to get you something special as a wedding gift. This something represents how I feel."

Opening the box, she discovered an exquisite pearl necklace. She lifted it out, gently rubbing her finger across the pearls. "Oh, Scott, this is gorgeous. Would you mind if I wore these tomorrow on our wedding day?"

"That's why I wanted to give them to you tonight. By the way, I have some news for you. Because I was stressing out and pushing so hard to get those guys to close the deal, they were pushing back. After I told you about maybe delaying the honeymoon, I was able to walk into that meeting more clearheaded. Actually, when I lightened up and didn't push them, they thought I knew something that might stop the deal and they started pushing to sign the contracts! Everything was signed and in Dad's hands by noon. We're going to Manhattan! Thank you for being so understanding. Not every girl would have responded as you did."

A few minutes later, the rest of the wedding party came walking up. Mr. Thomas, seeing the happy couple passionately kissing, oblivious to anyone else, cleared his throat very loudly and said, "Why don't you save some of that for tomorrow, son?"

"Oh, plenty will be left for tomorrow and every tomorrow after that." With all the teasing he had been getting, Scott was getting good at comebacks. "If everyone's here, let's get this rehearsal started."

Mrs. Randal walked everyone through the entry three times, making sure they all understood where they belonged. She then turned the rehearsal over to Reverend Allan, who began reviewing the actual ceremony. When the members of the wedding party were satisfied that they knew exactly what they were to do, the rehearsal was over.

Mr. Thomas then stood and announced, "It is now Mrs. Thomas' and my pleasure to invite everyone to the gazebo for dinner. I don't know about the rest of you, but that barbecue smell has been driving me absolutely crazy for hours. Let's eat!"

All in all, the evening was a total success. The food was great, the weather perfect, and the atmosphere intoxicating. By eleven, the party was winding down, and nearly everyone had returned to the assigned accommodations. Scott and Susan decided to take a quick walk along the lake before saying good night. As they walked beside the water, they talked about how the evening had gone. They laughed at how efficient Mrs. Randal had been and how much fun she was having. They were also thankful for all of her hard work. She had handled details they would have overlooked.

The full moon's shimmering light across the lake was spectacular. the night was so quiet, broken only by the occasional hoot of an owl or a distant sound of a dog and the soothing sound of the water slapping against the trunk of an old fallen tree. They sat on the log and listened to the night sounds.

Scott mused, "In fourteen more hours, you and I will be husband and wife."

They talked until almost midnight, and then Scott walked Susan to her cabin and kissed her good night. "The next time I see you will be when you are walking down the aisle to me. I hope I don't start crying. You'd better keep that big beautiful smile on your face, or I'll fall apart."

She loved how he wasn't afraid to show his emotions. Scott was so sentimental about everything related to love.

With one final good night kiss, a very happy man headed to his room.

CHAPTER 17

SATURDAY MORNING, SUSAN was stirred from her slumber by the sound of workers pounding tent stakes into the ground. She relaxed for a moment or two, realizing this was her wedding day, and that noise was a very sweet sound. Carol Anne was still asleep, so Susan slipped out of bed and sat by the window, watching the men as they lifted the huge white tent canopy into place.

The morning had barely started, but the birds were excited by the men's activity and were singing and chirping. The sky was a clear brilliant blue, and azalea bushes, which lined either side of the grassy meadow, created a colorful and fragrant frame. The huge weeping willow tree standing at the far end was like a master, keeping charge over everything.

She remembered the first Saturday Scott, Carol Anne, and she had driven here looking for treasures. They had stopped to watch a lovely wedding taking place. She remembered watching the bride as she walked from this very cabin and headed for the canopy. Now it was her turn. Today she was the bride, and Scott would be waiting for her.

Carol Anne woke up and noticed Susan's peeking out of the window. "Good morning, Susan. Happy wedding day! Is the canopy up yet?"

Susan turned from the window, jumped on the bed, and gave her best friend a big hug. This was the day for which she had been waiting. Today she would belong to Scott, and he would belong to her. Never again would she feel alone and lost. "You take your time waking up, Carol Anne. I'm going to jump in the shower before breakfast so I'll be ready when the hairdresser comes at ten o'clock. We aren't to go to breakfast until eight o'clock, so when I get out of the shower, there will still be plenty of time to call the girls and make sure they're up and moving."

Carol Anne climbed out of bed and peeked out of the window. "Isn't it great that they put the bride's cabin right at the back edge of the meadow? This way you can see how everything is coming along without anyone seeing you. You'll be able to watch the guests arriving and hear the music. I've been in three weddings, and every time the bride was closed up in some room away from everything. None of them could hear the soloist. This setting is perfectly wonderful, but you'd better get in that shower. We don't want time getting away from us today. Scott would never forgive me if I didn't keep you on schedule."

The morning flew by. At noon the girls were all dressed, had their pictures taken outside and then quickly retreated to the bride's cabin so the guys could have their photos taken. All of the girls, except the bride, kept peeking out of the window, watching the photographer position the men. Susan was dying to peek, but she had promised Scott she would also wait for their moment.

Twenty minutes later, she heard the musicians playing. Carol Anne looked out of the window, saw the first guests being seated, and quickly turned to Susan and squealed with excitement, "It's starting, Susan. It's one-thirty, and guests are lining up at the guestbook. Look, there's Aunt Gladys with my cousin, Billy, and his wife."

The girls stood behind the shirred curtains and watched as guest after guest signed the book and took a seat. Susan was obviously getting nervous, so Carol Anne distracted her by explaining who the different people were and how they were connected to the family.

When the rows were about three-quarters filled, the girls stepped away from the window, checked themselves in the mirror, and waited for Mrs. Randal's signal to start. The music was simply wonderful. A slight breeze stirred. The music quieted the guests' chatter. They sat almost mesmerized, and then the musicians paused. The music changed, as if bringing everyone to attention. This musical variation signaled Scott to escort his mother down the aisle.

A moment later they heard the soloist begin. Susan hushed the girls, wanting to hear the words to the love song she and Scott had selected.

Carol Anne saw Susan starting to get very emotional. "Susan, don't you dare start crying. You'll mess up your makeup, and I don't have time to fix it."

Susan started laughing at Carol Anne's panic. They were still laughing as Bruce Randal knocked and entered. He was wearing a charcoal-gray tuxedo, which looked great against his salt-and-pepper hair. "My wife says you have about two or three minutes. Line up in the order you walk out, and she'll signal when it's time for us."

As they stood waiting to be summoned, Susan remembered the evening almost three months earlier, when Reverend Allan, while discussing this ceremony, asked, "Who will be giving away the bride?" That was the first time she had thought about it. They all knew she had no family—no grandfather, no distant uncles, no longtime family friends, or even her mother to give her away, as some girls were now doing.

Bill Thomas broke the silence that night by offering, "Susan, Mrs. Thomas and I have been talking, and I would be honored to walk you down the aisle."

How Susan remembered struggling with her emotions that day. She was having one of those lonely, lost moments when she was vividly reminded of how alone and detached her childhood had been. The fact there was not a single person she could ask to walk her down the aisle caused her unexpected pain. She remembered how Mr. and Mrs. Thomas smiled at her. She knew they understood what she was going through and sincerely wanted to help.

"Thank you, Dad. I appreciate your offering to walk me down the aisle, but I can't let you do it. Carol Anne has graciously and unselfishly shared her home and family with me for the past seven years. I was part of this family long before Scott and I fell in love, and now I will be part of this family for the rest of my life. This is one thing that belongs only to Carol Anne. I will not ask her to share that. The first and only bride you should walk down the aisle is your own daughter. But thank you for offering."

After some discussion, Mrs. Randal came up with the answer. "Susan, Mr. Randal thinks the world of you. I know he would be honored to walk you down the aisle on behalf of everyone who loves you. Our three daughters are all long-since married, and his escorting you would not be a problem."

Susan loved Mr. and Mrs. Randal. She had worked with Mrs. Randal for almost three years now, spending many a Saturday afternoon at her house planning business meetings. Mr. Randal would fix them sandwiches and make sure their iced tea glasses stayed full. He was always friendly, and she loved to hear his affectionate stories that slightly embarrassed Mrs. Randal. This couple was still very much in love. He was sweet and kind, and she thought he would be perfect. "If you think he wouldn't mind, I'd love for him to escort me."

So here they stood, Mr. Randal and Susan, waiting for Mrs. Randal's signal to start.

The soloist finished and the music changed, indicating that Scott and his groomsmen were now entering.

Mrs. Randal then signaled for the bridesmaids to begin. With a nervous giggle, the first bridesmaid opened the door, turned to Susan with a big smile, and said, "Here we go."

Mrs. Randal had timed this walk about ten times and knew that as soon as Carol Anne reached the runner, Susan needed to begin her walk. It was twenty-five feet from the cabin door to the center back of the canopy. This would give Carol Anne time enough to reach the front and turn.

When Mrs. Randal motioned for Susan to begin, Mr. Randal offered his arm, and they walked toward the canopy.

All of the guests were seated inside the huge white canopy, which comfortably shaded them from the bright sunlight. Scott watched as his sister walked down the aisle. He had not seen her dress and couldn't remember ever seeing her look more lovely. As she reached the front, Scott stepped forward, gave his sister a kiss on the cheek, took her arm, and escorted her to her place in the front.

Because this part had not been planned, Mrs. Thomas was caught off guard, and she started to cry. She was so proud of her children, and seeing the love and affection Scott had for his sister was more than her emotions could handle. Mr. Thomas, well supplied with tissues, reached over and handed her one. "Honey, you'd better pace yourself. or you'll never make it through this wedding."

Scott quickly stepped back into his place, keeping his eyes focused on the end of the runner. He was waiting for his bride to appear. Susan and Mr. Randal stepped to the edge of the canopy. Mrs. Randal quickly straightened her train and then signaled the musicians. While waiting for her cue, Susan could not possibly imagine the effect her standing there had on those who could turn and see her. The sun was shining directly down on Susan as she stood outside the canopy. Her headpiece was a crown of rhinestones with the veil falling like a spray around her head. Her jet-black hair glistened in the afternoon sun, and curls framed her radiantly happy face and cascaded around her shoulders. The dress fit snugly against her bodice and waist, and the skirt seemed to flow out forever. As she stood there with the sun's dancing around her dress and shining off the sequins and pearls, the response from the guests seemed to move across the room like an ocean wave.

Everyone began turning to take their first glimpse of Scott's bride— everyone except Carol Anne. She had her eyes on her brother. She did not want to miss that first look when Scott saw Susan. As she watched his face, she silently whispered a little prayer. *Lord, please send me someone who will love and cherish me as my brother does Susan. Help me have the patience to wait for him. I too want someone to have that look in his eyes for me.*

Carol Anne heard her brother make a slight choking sound as Mendelsshon's "Wedding March" began. He never took his eyes from Susan as she walked toward him. Both were smiling, but their eyes were only for each other. Everyone present hushed as Scott stepped forward and took Susan's arm.

Reverend Allan gave some opening remarks, addressing the importance of marriage, and then asked, "Who gives this woman in marriage to this man?"

"On behalf of all who love and cherish her, I do." Mr. Randal leaned over to kiss Susan on the cheek and then whispered, "God bless you, Susan."

He then took his seat next to Mrs. Randal, who had slipped into her seat, not wanting to miss the ceremony. Reverend Allan spoke about Scott and Susan. He shared a story or two with the guests, showing what special young people they were. He spoke for several more minutes, but Scott wasn't listening. He kept whispering, "You're absolutely beautiful! You are absolutely beautiful…."

When Reverend Allan finished his charge to the couple, he motioned for the bride and the groom to step forward and stand under the arched trellis. They stood face to face until the soloist finished, and then Reverend Allan stepped in front of Scott and Susan and led them in their vows. He prayed a blessing for their lives together, and as he ended his prayer, he announced loud enough for everyone to hear, "In the presence of these witnesses and as an officer of the laws of the state of Georgia, and a preacher of the gospel of Jesus Christ, I now pronounce you husband and wife. What God hath joined together, let no man put asunder. Scott, you may kiss your bride."

Scott lifted Susan's veil and tenderly kissed his bride. Reverend Allan then announced, "For the first time anywhere, I am proud to introduce Mr. and Mrs. Scott Michael Thomas."

The music started, and the happy bride and groom began their walk up the aisle. They had secretly planned ahead of time to stop at the first row to each give Mr. and Mrs. Thomas, Mrs. Randal, and Aunt Gladys a kiss. Then they continued their walk up the aisle.

After the wedding party had cleared the canopy, Reverend Allan announced, "Cold drinks and appetizers are being served on the veranda and patio at the main house. As soon as the photographer has finished taking pictures, Mr. and Mrs. Scott Thomas would be honored to have you join them for dinner in the dining room."

The dinner bell rang at three o'clock as planned. The two hundred-fifty guests were ushered in and directed to their assigned seats. As soon as everyone was seated, Reverend Allan introduced the wedding party as they entered the room. When the bride and groom entered, the room exploded with applause and cheers. Scott's eyes swept the room as they took their seats at the main table. Apparently the guests were enjoying themselves, which pleased him.

At a quarter to five, Mrs. Randal stepped up to the podium, announcing that everyone was requested to begin moving out to the patio for the cutting of the wedding cake. The wedding party went out first, positioning themselves around the cake so the photographer could take pictures. As their guests were enjoying their cake and coffee on the patio, the bride and groom slipped away to change. A few minutes later, they appeared on the veranda in their traveling clothes.

They quickly found Mrs. Randal and gave her a hug and kiss. "You know you missed your calling, Mrs. Randal. Not a single thing was missing today. Thank you so much for all your hard work. We both appreciate so much everything you have done for us."

Mrs. Randal beamed with pride. She knew she had done a great job. She had been overhearing the comments of the guests all afternoon. Everyone was saying what a gorgeous wedding it was, and she was satisfied.

After saying all of their goodbyes, Scott and Susan drove down the tree-lined road that led to the highway. Scott put his arm around his bride, and both were quiet as they thought about their day. Several minutes passed before either of them spoke.

Almost whispering, she said, "Mrs. Scott Michael Thomas. I love how that sounds."

"Well, you just keep saying it because that's your name for the rest of your life. Fifty years from today when we're celebrating our golden anniversary, we'll sit together and remember today."

CHAPTER 18

THE NEWLYWEDS ENJOYED a wonderful time in New York. Scott had always said no place was as awesome as New York in the springtime, and he was right. For their first morning together as man and wife, Scott had scheduled a horse-drawn carriage to pick them up in front of the hotel. They rode through Central Park, sipping coffee and eating a traditional New York bagel. Every tree was absolutely bursting with springtime. The sweet smells of spring simply made any person forget he was right in the heart of a big city. The roller skaters were out early, probably wanting to get in a morning skate before heading off for work somewhere.

As they rode along, Scott watched his new bride's eyes as she had her first glimpse of Central Park. He thought about how special these next two weeks would be, seeing her fall in love with all that he had grown to love here. He could not wait to take her to her first Broadway musical tonight. He remembered how he felt the first time he had attended one. He thought his feet would never hit the floor again. He remembered how he would walk around after the show, drinking in the essence of Broadway and enjoying its magic. Now he was sharing that same wonder with this woman whom he so desperately loved.

Riding along, holding hands, Scott thought about their first night together and smiled. He thought about all of the personal life decisions he had made to get himself to this place. His father had told him how important it was to go against all that society was teaching about safe, free, and open sex. He remembered how his father had talked so openly about the beauty and wonder of sharing this most intimate of acts only with the person with whom you intended to share your whole life. His father had encouraged him to be patient and wait for a wonderful woman, and he had.

Sitting with Susan beside him, Scott remembered how embarrassed he had been by his father's graphic picture of lovemaking. His father had explained, "Boys go for a thrill. Men share love. Son, I can't even begin to tell you what it feels like to hold the woman you have made your bride in your arms for the very first time after making love. Any dog on the street can learn technique. Women want to feel loved, not maneuvered. I promise you, if you will focus your sexual energy on becoming a decent, honorable, and loving man and wait for the right girl, you'll never be disappointed. When you lie beside her beautiful body, exploring for the first time the wonderful gift of sexual intimacy, you won't want the image of some cheap thrill to cloud that moment. Every man has only one such moment to share. You need to save that gift for the woman you truly love."

Scott had always thought his father was a wise man, and now he knew it. Everything his father had promised came true. Although a little clumsy and a little embarrassing, Scott's and Susan's first one-flesh experience was more wonderful than either could ever have imagined because they both knew they had waited for each other.

As the carriage brought them back to the hotel, Scott stepped out and offered his bride a hand. Stepping down onto the sidewalk, she kissed her new husband. She had thoroughly enjoyed their ride together, although she hadn't wanted to get up quite that early.

She too had been anxious about their first night together for most of the past few months. After all, her mother was not the type of person any girl would want to go to for sexual advice. She had wondered about the effects her parents' relationship might have on her and worried if she would be a disappointment to Scott. Concerned about this matter, she scheduled some appointments with Dr. Jacobson, whom she had met at the retreat when she was in her teens.

After Susan shared her concerns of possibly being cold and unresponsive because of her childhood fears, Dr. Jacobson wisely and discreetly addressed the concerns that every mother should share with their daughter. "Susan, there's no great mystery to intimacy. Don't worry about your body. It will know what to do if you simply focus on your husband, knowing how much you love him and that he loves you. Your body will respond. If you get embarrassed or feel a little panic, open your eyes! Look at that face you love, and I can promise, you'll be fine."

As the couple stepped into the elevator to go to their room, she thought about the truth of what Dr. Jacobson had said. Standing there with Scott beside her, she was amazed at how calm and relaxed she had felt. Their lovemaking had felt so natural as they lay together afterward, his arms around her. Knowing Scott wasn't comparing her to a dozen other women made their first time ideal. She thought about how comfortable she felt lying in his arms—much too in love to feel embarrassed.

Entering their room, Susan slipped her hand in Scott's and led him over to the bed. She loved him with all of her heart and wanted to enjoy the feeling of having him next to her again. She lifted her face to his, and with a twinkle in her eyes and an impish grin on her face, she said, "Honey, we have several hours before we need to dress for the show. You aren't really hungry for lunch yet, are you?"

Scott pulled his wife into his arms and kissed her. He knew exactly what she was implying, and her suggestion was fine with him.

The next two weeks flew by. They attended five different plays, toured the Statue of Liberty, visited every art gallery and museum in the city, saw Wall Street, shopped at all of the famous stores, and tasted all kinds of foods. They were much too busy to think about anything but themselves. After all, it was their honeymoon. The only time they thought about anyone else was while they were shopping. They decided to pick out a few small items as thank-you gifts. Otherwise, they were in a world all their own. Soon enough, it would be time to board that plane and head back to reality—but not one minute sooner than was absolutely necessary.

Back in Atlanta, everyone was trying to get back to normal. The family had all of the final tasks to do: returning the tuxedos, gathering up the decorations, stacking all of the wedding gifts in a safe place, and recovering emotionally. The bride and groom never seem to understand the impact a wedding has on all those left behind after the wedding. Even when everyone is excited and happy for the marriage, the months of planning and putting everything else on hold until this magical date has its cost. Suddenly, the event is over. An empty, almost lost feeling replaces the busyness—almost like saying goodbye to a best friend.

Mr. and Mrs. Thomas put Carol Anne on a plane back to California the day after the wedding. Kissing his daughter goodbye, Mr. Thomas had a hard time keeping his emotions under control. He knew it was nonsensical to feel sad. After all, both of his children were well, happy, and doing what they should be doing—getting on with their lives.

As they walked to their car, Bill put his arm around his wife and said, "Why don't you and I go on a honeymoon? We deserve another one after all these years."

Caroline chuckled at her husband, knowing how sentimental and emotional a character he was. "Honey, we've been on a honeymoon every day for that past thirty years. Let's go home."

CHAPTER 19

✤

KNOWING IT WOULD be three weeks before she could visit Lisa, Susan had arranged to take off the first Monday following their honeymoon to drive over and spend the day with her. Her sister had now been in jail for almost two months, and Gladys was visiting her several times a week. Because Lisa was behaving herself, Gladys told the court she would be willing to let Lisa move in with her, and she would help find a job for her. Even with this offer, it still did not look as if Lisa would be released any-time soon. Lisa had a long and colorful record, and the courts were in no hurry to see her back on the streets of Jefferson.

Susan could not really blame them. Lisa was her own worst enemy, and if the truth were known, she also wanted her sister to remain in jail a little longer. Lisa was away from alcohol and drugs, and because she was lonely, she actually looked forward to Gladys's visits. If she had been on the streets, she would never have given herself a chance to get to know Gladys. They all hoped Lisa would be held in jail the entire six months so her body could have time to recover from the drugs and alcohol. They knew she had been in jail several other times and always went right back to her old ways.

Susan arrived at the jail at nine o'clock. Several people turned and stared at her as she entered. In this small town, everyone knew every-thing. She had been coming to visit her sister once a week since Lisa had been jailed, so when she hadn't shown up for three weeks, her absence was noticed. After all, women like her didn't usually come visiting at the city jail. She looked quite out of place, and the officers had grown fond of her visits. Although she was only twenty-one, she carried herself with an air of dignity and class. She was not the type of woman at whom these men would have felt comfortable whistling.

Many an afternoon had been spent comparing these two sisters. The officers knew what Lisa was and what she had done. However, her sister was a puzzle to them. She obviously loved Lisa because she kept coming back to visit, but the two were as different as night and day. The officers affectionately called Lisa "the sailor" because she had such a foul mouth. However, they did notice that when her sister or the old lady came for visits, Lisa cleaned it up a little.

After a visit, one of the officers tried to talk to her about Susan. He wanted to know who she was, where she lived, and how old she was. Lisa blasted him with a mouthful of words that even made him blush. She didn't want any of them trifling with her sister. "She's just a kid, and a really nice one at that. If I find out any of you ever try to get close to her, you'll be sorry."

Lisa loved her sister and was proud of how she had turned out. She hated the fact that Susan had to visit her in this filthy dump and putting up with these creeps in order to see her. In spite of Lisa, the officers had discovered some things about Susan. One had overheard a conversation between Lisa and Gladys. Apparently, the old lady had spent one whole visit describing the wedding. This conversation surprised them since Susan appeared so young and had never worn a ring when she visited. Now they knew she was married and lived in Atlanta.

Finding out about her had become somewhat of a game for them. They all looked forward to her visits, hoping to add more clues. She always behaved like a lady, so they behaved like gentlemen. If one of them engaged her in a polite conversation and found out another piece to their puzzle, he would gloat about his discovery all afternoon before telling the others. So when she came walking in that Monday morning, the officers were especially happy to see her.

Officer Jackson noticed the ring on her left hand as he greeted her. He was certain it had not been there before because none of them would have missed a ring like that. "Good morning, Ms. Miller, how was your drive this morning?"

"Good morning, Officer Jackson, the drive was pleasant. By the way, it's no longer Ms. Miller; I'm now Mrs. Thomas." Susan wasn't used to saying her married name out loud, so it made her smile.

"Well, congratulations, Mrs. Thomas! That news will disappoint several of our single young officers around here." Jackson couldn't help but smile. He had been the first to get the news and couldn't wait to spread it around. "I'm sure your sister is anxious to see you, so I'll take you right in." He did not want the others to have a shot at talking to her. He wanted this information to come from him, so he walked her into a visiting room and said, "I'll be right back with your sister."

Lisa was brought in a few minutes later. She had never met Scott, but as far as she was concerned, all men were alike; they were all dogs. She cynically philosophized that if you are going to marry one, at least marry a wealthy one. If you're going to cry, it's better in a Cadillac than in a Chevy. "So Susan, how's married life treating you?"

"It's wonderful! I can't wait for you to meet Scott. Why don't you put him on your visitor list so he can come in with me next time?"

"Susan, I don't care to meet anyone new while in this jail. If he's still around when I get out, then we can meet. The most important thing is, how is he treating you?"

"Lisa, I've told you, I've known his family for years. They're really great people. Scott is loving and kind. You'll like him."

"I hope so. It's not like I want to be right about him, ya know. I do want you to be happy, but all those wealthy families are the same. They think they're better than everyone else. I hope they don't turn on you after a while."

Susan stared at her sister. "You know, for someone who absolutely hates Mother, you sound exactly like her. That comment is something she would have said. Everyone in the world does not think like our mother. Being wealthy doesn't make someone a snob any more than being poor makes someone honest and hard-working. These are good, kind, and caring people, and I love them."

"I'm glad for you. I really am. You deserve to be happy, but do me a favor…" With this request came a face of steel as she snapped, "…don't ever compare me to Mother again. I'm nothing like her."

Lisa's hatred for their mother was so deep, she simply couldn't see the many similarities between them. Quickly changing the subject, Susan told Lisa about their trip to New York and all the great things they had done there. Her wedding pictures weren't back yet, so all she had were the snapshots the family had taken during the wedding.

Lisa was quiet as she looked through the pictures. As hard a shell as she had developed and as much as she had protested against marriage, she also longed for someone to love her, want her, and marry her, but that would never be. She felt badly that she had made sure of never being married. After all, who would ever want her now? She had really made a wreck of her life.

"Your Scott is a nice-looking man. Everything looks like it was real nice. Did Mother go to your wedding? I don't see her in any of these pictures."

"No, she didn't attend. She's still the same hateful person you always knew. She has no love or time for anything or anyone, especially us. Lisa, our childhood was not our fault, and we didn't deserve the way our parents treated us. We simply had the misfortune of being born into their marriage, but I no longer allow them to control or affect me, and that includes my memories."

With a flash of anger that was meant to end this conversation, Lisa responded, "They haven't controlled me since I was seventeen. That's why I ran away. I will never let them hurt me again."

Susan knew what she wanted to share, but she was not sure if her sister would sit still long enough to listen. "Lisa, why do you believe you're sitting here in this jail right now?"

Not liking the direction of the conversation, Lisa snapped, "That's silly. We both know what I did."

Determined to keep Lisa on this subject, she responded, "No, I don't think we both do know. Why do *you* believe you're sitting in this jail right now?"

Lisa began squirming in her chair. She didn't like talking about herself to anyone, including her sister. "I sold some drugs to support my habit. Do you feel better now? Does that make you happy?"

"No, it doesn't make me happy, but I think you need to ask yourself another question. Why do you feel you need to take drugs and alcohol? We both know you're not taking them for the wonderful feelings they provide. Why do you need them?"

"You've never done drugs, so you can't possibly know how they control you." Lisa always loved throwing the "you-never...so-you-can't-possibly-know" routine at people because it always shut them up. Through the years, many people had tried to deal with her drug and alcohol addictions. Every druggie on the street had a line to throw back at these folks. The truth was she really didn't want to fight it. She wanted everyone to leave her alone.

"You know, I think you use drugs as a shield. First, you take those drugs to numb your pain and hurt. Then when you begin self-destructing, you throw up the drugs as a shield so you can blame them for the mess you're in. That way you never have to look at or talk about the real things that are causing you so much pain. You'd rather kill yourself than face them. I'm through talking drugs to you, Lisa. We need to get to the bottom-line motivators that are driving you to those drugs. Yes, we had a lousy childhood, and no one can ever give us another one. But Lisa, you're allowing our parents to continue cheating you. They cheated you of your childhood, and now you're allowing them to cheat you of your adulthood. As long as you hold on to your bitterness and hatred toward them, you'll continue to destroy your own life."

Lisa's eyes were blazing with emotion. "If you think I'm going to forgive them, you're crazy. They don't deserve to be forgiven. They both can rot in hell for all I care."

"I'm not talking about forgiving them. I'm talking about letting go of your anger. It's killing you. You are killing you, Lisa, and I love you too much to stand by and keep silent any longer. Please, at least think about what I've said." Susan knew she had said enough for today. Lisa was not someone who could be pushed too far or too fast; but between Aunt Gladys and her, they were going to keep at it until they got through that shield someday. Both were determined to keep loving Lisa until she was able to love herself. Standing up to leave, she hugged Lisa goodbye. "I do love you. You're not alone in this place." Susan left for home.

CHAPTER 20

—⚜—

DETERMINED TO GET Susan out of the apartment building and away from her mother as soon as possible, the first order of business was to find a new place to live. Within a month, they found a small charming three-bedroom house and spent their first year of marriage remodeling and making it their own.

By their first anniversary in April, the house was finally finished, and Susan found herself getting anxious for Carol Anne to come home in June. She had applied to all the high schools in Atlanta and had received an offer from her former high school to teach history. Carol Anne was finally coming home for good, and Susan was getting anxious to show off her "new" old house.

A week or so later, Susan suspected she might be pregnant but didn't want to say anything until she was sure. She scheduled a doctor's appointment for the middle of May and carefully guarded her feelings. She did not want to get her hopes up too high in case her hunch turned out to be a false alarm. When the doctor confirmed her suspicions, she went right to the office to tell Scott he was going to be a father. Everyone was so excited; Mr. and Mrs. Thomas were going to be grandparents, and Carol Anne was going to be an aunt. Even Lisa allowed herself to get excited, but one month later, Susan lost the baby.

The loss was devastating to everyone, but Susan was inconsolable. She had so wanted that baby. She found herself weeping all of the time and didn't have the energy to go anywhere. She did what she had always done when the pain had become too overwhelming for her: she crawled into bed and slept. She was resorting to her childhood escape—not a sleep of comfort but one to escape and avoid the pain.

Several times Caroline called to invite her to go shopping or out to lunch, but Susan always turned her down with some excuse. This pattern continued for weeks, and Scott was getting worried. His first experience of seeing Susan's depression and withdrawal scared him. Finally, when more than a month had passed with no improvement, Scott sought his mother. "I don't know what to say to her. How do you help someone get over a loss like this? She's hurting, and I want to grieve with her, but she shuts me out. It's like she doesn't want me near her, and that really hurts. I'm trying to be patient, but I lost my baby too. Why won't she let me hurt with her?" The tears he had been holding back for weeks began to flow. He had been trying so hard to be strong for Susan, he had not allowed his own loss to express itself.

Caroline placed her arm around her grieving son. For a few minutes, they both gave themselves permission to cry together over the loss of this much-wanted baby. She had struggled with her own emotions and understood what her son was feeling.

"Sometimes working through grief simply takes time. All of her life Susan has had to cope with hurt all by herself. She has found her own way of nursing her pain and now has to learn how to let people in. Be patient with her. She's not doing this because she doesn't want you to help her; she doesn't know *how* to let you help her."

"Mom, I love her so much. It kills me to see her hurting. What can I do to help her learn to let me in?"

"All I can tell you is to be there. Let her know you care and don't drive her deeper into her shell by pushing too hard. This is new territory for all of us. No one comes through a childhood like hers without some problems. We both need to keep reminding her that we love her."

Caroline knew what she was telling her son was right. She also knew her son was scared and hurting. "Why don't you try to get her out of the house once in a while? Maybe the four of us could take a weekend trip somewhere."

"I've tried! She doesn't want to leave the house. I guess I simply have to keep trying. Thanks for letting me get out my feelings. I think I just needed to cry with someone. I know she'll come out of this mood one of these days."

As she watched her son drive away, Caroline went over everything she had said to him. It hurt to see her son struggling so, but she also knew that her son and his wife would have to learn to handle these issues if they were going to have a strong, happy marriage. *Life is hard, and everyone has things they have to face.* Caroline also knew this depression was more than just the loss of their baby. Finding a way to help his wife handle hurt would be one of her son's hardest battles, but she knew he was a strong person, and he loved Susan. She knew her son would find a way to help Susan.

A week later, Gladys called and asked if she and Lisa could come for a visit. At first Susan dreaded the idea of having guests in the house. She had gotten used to turning down people and started to do the same to Aunt Gladys when she heard herself say, "That sounds fine. You and Lisa haven't seen the house since we finished it. How is Lisa doing? Has she been behaving herself?"

"Oh, she has her good days and bad days, but overall, I think she's trying very hard to turn her life around. You know, Susan, Lisa didn't want to tell you, but she really took it hard when you and Scott lost that baby. I've never seen her in such pain. She knew how much you were hurting, and she really fell apart. You have always been the strong one, and she has always leaned on you, but when you needed to lean she knew she couldn't help you. Now that some time has passed, I think it would be good for Lisa to come and visit for a day or two."

Listening to Aunt Gladys, Susan realized how much she had been consumed with her own grief. She hadn't thought much about everyone else's loss. Oh, she and Scott had grieved together a little, but then he went back to work and got busy. She had retreated into her own little world of sorrow. That this loss would have affected Lisa had never remotely occurred to her. Then she thought about Mrs. Thomas, and all the phone calls and invitations to lunch Susan had turned down.

She hung up the phone and realized she hadn't thought about how this loss must have hurt Caroline. This child had been her first grandbaby. With the phone still in her hand, she decided it was time to think about someone other than herself for a change.

When she heard the friendly hello on the other end of the line, she responded, "Hi, Mom, do you have plans for lunch today? I thought we could grab a bite and maybe do a little shopping."

"That sounds wonderful, Susan. Why don't I pick you up around ten, and we'll make a day of it?" As Carolina replaced the phone on the receiver, she wondered what had turned Susan around. She didn't know, but she certainly was thankful.

Susan jumped into the shower, and while she washed her hair, she realized this loss had been Scott's and her first big crisis, and she hadn't handled it very well. Instead of trusting him for emotional support, she had retreated into her own little world, trying to drive away her agony and pain. She knew she needed to learn a better way of dealing with hurt. She wasn't quite sure how to go about it, but one thing was certain—she needed to start by apologizing to Scott.

She put on a bright summer dress and had a big smile on her face when Caroline arrived. "Hi, Mom, I thought it was time to stop feeling sorry for myself. I'm sorry for the way I've behaved."

Caroline hugged her daughter-in-law. "The loss of a baby is terrible. Sometimes, time is the only healer."

Susan knew she could always count on Caroline to be gracious. She was never one to rub someone's nose in his or her failure and was always quick to offer a word of encouragement. What a contrast she was to Susan's own mother! She was so thankful to have Caroline Thomas in her life.

The two went shopping that afternoon and enjoyed their time together. When Mrs. Thomas pulled into the driveway later that day, Susan leaned over to kiss her on the cheek. "Mom, I'm sorry about the baby. I know I wasn't the only one to lose something precious."

Big tears quickly rose in Caroline's eyes. Susan saw that her mother-in-law's hurt was raw and real. The two women sat together, momentarily sharing a common loss together, each understanding the other's pain. Caroline reached over to squeeze Susan's hand. "I love you, Susan, and in time, there will be other babies for us to love. I don't know why we had to give this little one back to God, but I know I can trust Him to know what's best."

Susan thought about what her mother-in-law had shared. "Funny, but if you had said that to me even yesterday, I would have been so angry at you. My hurt would not have allowed me to accept that there could be any good in God taking back my baby. I know He did not allow it simply to hurt me, and, yes, there will be other babies."

CHAPTER 21

❧

THE FIRST YEAR after the loss of their much-wanted baby was especially hard on Susan. She began living from month to month, hoping each time this would be it. Her doctor finally told her to stop trying so hard. "You need to relax and set your mind on other matters. It'll happen before you know it. You have to stop driving yourself crazy over this loss. Do anything! Just don't sit home and wait for that baby. You know the old saying, 'A watched pot never boils'? Well, it's the same with babies."

She knew the doctor was right. Except for her monthly drive to Jefferson to see Lisa and Aunt Gladys, she had done nothing but concentrate on having a baby for months. Stopping by the office, Susan invited Mrs. Randal to lunch, hoping to learn if she needed any help around the office. Within a few weeks, Susan had more tasks than she could handle, and life was good again.

Now that Susan was feeling stronger and the house was finished, Lisa and Gladys began coming to Atlanta one weekend a month. Lisa actually enjoyed the visits and was beginning to warm up to Scott, although she would never admit it. Everyone could see the love and respect growing between Lisa and Aunt Gladys. The two had a way of teasing each other that was filled with sweet affection. Somehow, Aunt Gladys was able to praise Lisa in a teasing manner, but if she or anyone tried to praise her seriously, Lisa would stiffen and get upset.

Lisa was working hard to change, and everyone who knew her could see it. She had come to the place where she would never cuss in front of Gladys and seldom did it around anyone else. She and Gladys seldom discussed with the family the weekly drug and alcohol support groups they attended together. Lisa's drug and alcohol addictions were not going to go away by themselves, and they both wanted to understand how to overcome them.

One condition of Lisa's court-appointed parole was her securing and keeping a job. Gladys approached Ruth Bascom, one of the ladies in her church about a job for Lisa. Ruth was a dear friend, and she owned a bakery in downtown Jefferson. After some badgering, Ruth agreed to offer Lisa a job in the back kitchen, away from customers. When Lisa was first released from jail, her mouth and appearance were raw, and Ruth didn't trust her to deal with the public. Mrs. Bascom wanted to help, so she offered to teach her how to bake.

Lisa worked in the back kitchen for almost a year, never missing a single day. She always brought her whole paycheck to Gladys every Friday because she didn't want any money in her pockets during that first year. She didn't trust herself. She knew how easy it would be to mess up and didn't want to be tempted.

Lisa was obviously doing much better and was looking healthier, but she still didn't feel comfortable talking about her struggles. For the first time in Lisa's life she could remember being happy. She finally had something worth fighting for and was determined to conquer her cravings because, this time, she had something to lose.

Lisa loved working with Mrs. Bascom and was amazed at how proud she felt every time a rack of pies she had made was rolled out front for the customers to see. She worked hard at learning all of Mrs. Bascom's special recipes, and by the end of her first year, she was considered the best pie and bread maker at the bakery. Every time she and Gladys planned a trip to Atlanta, Lisa would stay extra late the night before baking something very special for the family. To have others respect and admire something she had done was a new experience, and she liked it.

Gladys loved the fact that she now had someone to cook for every day, and Lisa was looking healthier than Susan had ever seen her. She wasn't skin and bones any longer, her complexion was clear, and she never sported bruises on her arms anymore. The whole family could see that Lisa's living with Aunt Gladys was good for both of them.

One night, almost three months after moving in with Gladys, Lisa asked her why she had taken the risk of bringing a drug-using prostitute into her home.

Gladys smiled and said, "Lisa, God didn't come to save the perfect. He came to love the lost and broken. This time He graciously allowed me to be His hands. When I saw you in that hospital bed, I didn't see what you were, I saw what you could be if you would let God and me help you. In the hospital that first day, while I washed your hair, I saw a young girl who needed to be loved and to be told that God loves her—no matter what she's done."

Almost two years had passed since they'd had that conversation, and Lisa was beginning to thrive. She knew Gladys loved her, and she loved Gladys; she simply wouldn't admit it for fear of losing that love.

In January of the following year, Gladys was hospitalized with pneumonia. For almost a week the doctors were fearful she might not pull through. Lisa was at the hospital every evening, terrified she might lose her. During this period of watching and waiting, Lisa let down her final wall of resistance. One evening, when Gladys was having an especially hard time breathing, Lisa broke down and asked God for help. She had never prayed with Gladys during all of the months they had struggled to get Lisa well, but now that Gladys needed help, Lisa quickly turned to God. She had come to respect both Gladys' and Mrs. Bascom's faith. She had sat quietly listening many times as they talked about God and how He loved them.

Standing by Gladys' hospital room, fearing she might lose this wonderful lady, Lisa lowered her head and prayed, "God, I have no problem understanding that You could love Gladys, but I'm still not so sure why You would want to love me. God, I think You have been loving me for some time now—You have been using Susan, Gladys, and Mrs. Bascom to show me. Gladys told me that before I could understand that You love me, I had to learn what love is—so she has been loving me for You – because she loves You so much. God, I want to love You like Gladys loves You. Please, God, save Gladys right now—and save me."

Around the corner, Mrs. Bascom listened to this sweet, sweet sound of a soul crying out to God for the first time. Her pleas for mercy for someone she loved were heart-wrenching. Mrs. Bascom quietly walked into the room and put her arm around Lisa. "Honey, I can't think of another sound in the universe more pleasing to God than when a lost child turns to Him for help."

Mrs. Bascom knew Lisa had taken a huge step toward healing, and she was certain God would no longer be a stranger to Lisa.

Three more days passed before Gladys's health turned around, and another week slipped away before she was able to come home. Lisa had the house as clean as a whistle, fresh bread cooling on the counter, and a fire roaring in the fireplace when Billy Carter brought his mother home from the hospital.

Lisa had homemade chicken noodle soup warming on the stove and Gladys's winter afghan ready for her lap. Bill started laughing as he made his mother sit on the sofa next to the fireplace. "Mom, Lisa is going to give you a taste of your own medicine. You know, turnabout is fair play. So you behave yourself and let Lisa nurse you for a while."

He kissed his mother and then walked over to Lisa and put his arm around her. "I wasn't really sure my mother was doing the right thing when she first moved you in here, but I was so wrong. My mother loves you, and I can see how much you love her. Thank you."

As Billy walked out the door, Lisa stood watching him leave with big tears in her eyes. Even Bill had accepted her. She went into the kitchen and fixed Gladys a dinner tray, and the two sat by the fire for quite a while talking about life, their futures, and how good it was for Gladys to be home.

The family drove down to visit almost every Saturday until Gladys was back to normal. They had so much fun watching Lisa scurry around the house making sure everything was perfect. They all chuckled to each other as they observed Lisa fussing over Gladys.

She no longer cared how obvious it was that she loved this sweet old lady. Their fondness for each other was no longer a teasing matter because Lisa was no longer ashamed to say she loved her. She had even started enjoying hugging Scott goodbye. As Scott and Susan drove away after a visit, Lisa said, "Aunt Gladys, that Scott is a wonderful man, isn't he? I'm so glad he married Susan."

Gladys simply nodded. An additional compliment about Scott, coming from her, would be redundant. Everyone knew how she felt about him, and now Lisa was beginning to understand.

CHAPTER 22

THE NEXT SUMMER Carol Anne married Harry Stephenson, the assistant principal of the high school where she worked as a history teacher. They had dated for almost two years and were inseparable. All of the students affectionately called Mr. Stephenson "Howdy Doody: because of his red hair and freckles. He had a contagious laugh and steel-blue eyes. He was also the junior varsity football coach, and all of the players respected him.

During football season, Carol Anne sat in the bleachers and corrected papers while Harry directed football practice. All of the boys loved it because they knew she would always have a bag of homemade cookies for them at the end of every practice.

Harry had grown up in Virginia, the youngest of three boys. His oldest brother, Michael, was killed when Harry was a senior in high school. While Michael was working at a convenience store, an attempted robbery had taken place. Michael had been refilling the soda case and apparently did not hear the would-be thief tell him to stand still, so when he turned around, the guy shot him.

Harry's mother was so devastated by the murder, she sent Harry and his middle brother to Indiana to live with their uncle. He had graduated from high school there and then worked on his uncle's farm for an additional two years, earning money for college. Because he had a strong, well-built body, the boys wanted him to lead a wrestling team at the high school. He had wrestled during college and had won several state meets. After lots of begging, Harry agreed to start a wrestling team, along with coaching football and performing his administrative duties.

Carol Anne was madly in love with him, as was the whole family. About once a week, the couple stopped by Scott's and Susan's house, and the four of them always had a great time together. Actually, Scott was the one who walked Harry out to the backyard to ask when he intended to ask his sister to marry him. Apparently, Harry had planned to on several occasions but couldn't go through with it. He had convinced himself she would turn him down.

"You're a nincompoop! Anyone can see my sister is crazy about you. The whole family is. Why don't you march yourself right back in that house and ask her?"

So in front of Scott and Susan, Harry asked Carol Anne to marry him, and four months later they were married. They had a huge church wedding, with Susan as Carol Anne's matron of honor and Scott as one of the ushers. Harry's brother, Randy, served as his best man, and four months after the wedding Carol Anne announced they were expecting. The announcement was given during the Thanksgiving dinner, and even though Susan was happy for Carol Anne, she ached to be pregnant too.

Two weeks later, Scott and Susan announced they were also expecting a baby. Mr. and Mrs. Thomas were overjoyed. They had waited a long time and now were going to be presented with *two* grandbabies sometime in late spring!

Scott was given the honor of telling Lisa and Aunt Gladys. They walked into Gladys' house with a big bouquet of flowers with a big pink bow and a big blue bow. When Lisa answered the door, Scott handed her the bouquet and said, "Congratulations, Lisa, you're going to be an aunt next spring."

Lisa didn't say a word. She grabbed Scott, hugged him, and then took off to her bedroom. They were sitting in the living room when Lisa came out of her bedroom with a package. Without saying a word, she placed it in her sister's lap. Susan opened the box to see a pretty yellow outfit, including a sweater, leggings, a hat, and booties knit in the most delicate pattern she had ever seen.

Holding up the set, she expressed her delight. "Lisa, this is lovely! Where did you get it?"

Beaming with pride, Lisa said, "I made it for the baby. Three years ago, when I needed to keep my hands busy, Gladys worked with me every evening teaching me how to knit and crochet. My nerves were shot, and sitting around was dangerous for me. You know that old saying, 'Idle hands are the devil's workshop.' We have a whole drawer filled with pink, blue, and yellow baby clothes, waiting for this little one."

The girls went into Lisa's bedroom, where she laid everything out on her bed. Dozens of outfits, blankets, and booties had all been done with such love and care.

"Lisa, Scott and I have decided that if this baby is a girl, we're naming her Lisa Anne because you have worked so hard, and we're so proud of you."

"I don't want this baby to ever know what I once was, and I promise I won't ever do anything to bring shame to your baby."

By late spring, Carol Anne and Susan were struggling to get around. They were anxious to see these little faces they already loved so very much. Everyone in the family would tease Carol Anne and Harry, wondering what color of hair their children would have.

"I can't imagine what it will look like," her dad would tease. "Let's see now, both of you have bright-red hair. Do you suppose I'll have another little Carol Anne to love?"

Bill Thomas couldn't think of anything more precious than having another little red-headed girl running around his house calling him "Grandpa." As for Scott and Susan's baby, no one had a clue what their child would look like—him with his curly blond hair and her with jet-black hair.

Everyone was getting impatient, and the weeks seemed to drag. The girls were due within two weeks of each other, with Carol Anne and

Harry's baby due first. Lisa had not taken a single vacation day since finding out about the baby so she and Aunt Gladys would be able to drive to Atlanta when the babies came. Their bags were packed and waiting for the phone call. They were leaving as soon as the babies arrived. Lisa was to care for Susan and her baby while Aunt Gladys cared for Carol Anne and her baby. The waiting was driving everyone mad.

Lisa decided she would keep busy by knitting Carol Anne's baby an outfit. She picked out a soft, yellow yarn, and every evening, while waiting for the phone to ring, she painstakingly worked on the most delicate of stitches she knew. Having finished the sweater, leggings, and booties, she was now doing the final touches on the hat.

Aunt Gladys decided to use the same color, only a shade or two deeper, and knit a matching blanket for Carol Anne's baby. When the gift was completed, they hand stitched a two-inch-wide satin band around the edges, pressed it, and gift-wrapped it for Carol Anne.

The next evening the phone call came; Carol Anne's baby was on its way. Gladys and Lisa drove to Atlanta, laughing and giggling and having a wonderful time. They drove straight to the hospital and met the family in the waiting room. Thrilled to discover they had arrived before the baby, they joined the others playing the final waiting game.

Everyone was excited to know the gender of their babies. Except for Lisa knowing Susan's baby's name if it was a girl, no one knew the names the parents had chosen. Harry came out to give an update. "Carol Anne is doing well but is having some trouble, so the doctors are talking about taking the baby."

Mrs. Thomas began to pace, praying hard for her little girl in the delivery room.

As Harry started back to the labor room, he suddenly stopped, turned and said, "The next time I see you folks, I'll be a daddy."

With a big smile he disappeared, and they were all left to wait. Almost an hour had passed before a nurse came out to tell them that Carol Anne was going into surgery. The baby was experiencing too much stress, so the doctor had decided to perform a C-section.

Not even ten minutes later, Harry walked out beaming. "It's a boy—a beautiful, healthy little boy, and Carol Anne did fine! The doctor said she will be back in her room in about forty-five minutes, and then you may see her. Michael William Stephenson will be available for viewing in about an hour."

Bill Thomas, relieved to hear his daughter was fine, finally relaxed and then realized the significance of the name of his first grandson. "Michael William, I like how that sounds."

Harry allowed everyone to hug and congratulate him. "We decided to name our son in honor of my older brother Michael, with his middle name after you, Dad."

The well-wishers could finally relax a little and, when Carol Anne was ready, they took turns going in to congratulate her on Michael's arrival. Scott and Susan stood at the nursery window, trying to get a good look at little Michael. He had a small patch of dark-black hair, but everyone said that didn't mean anything because his hair color could change. He kept his little fists snuggled up against his scrunched up tight face, as if he were trying to keep the bright lights of the nursery out of his eyes.

Scott put his arm around his extremely pregnant wife and kissed her. "Just think, in a few days, our little baby will be sleeping in one of those bassinets."

"Scott, are you disappointed you weren't the first to make your parents grandparents?"

"To be real honest, a little, but it's all right. I'm just happy we don't have to wait too much longer, and these two little ones will be able to grow up together. Are you sure you aren't feeling any labor pains yet?" Scott grinned at her. He had been good-naturedly teasing her to get the show on the road for almost two weeks. "I think I'll take a bumpy road home tonight. Seeing Michael makes me ache to see our little one's face."

Scott and Susan didn't have to wait very long. Two days later she woke him to say her water had broken. He hollered through the house for Lisa to get up and get dressed. The three of them headed for the hospital, but

Scott managed to stop long enough to quickly phone his parents before leaving.

After checking into the hospital and getting Susan settled in a labor room, Scott came out to the waiting room. "Lisa, Susan and I would like you to scrub and put on a gown and come into the delivery with us. We both want you to be there when our baby arrives."

Humbled by his invitation, Lisa quickly hugged her brother-in-law. She had grown to love him, and his willingness to share this special moment with her was almost more than she could handle. She quickly tried to lighten the moment with a joke. "Okay, Scott, but I want to stand near her head. I don't think I actually want to see the baby arrive."

He laughed and grabbed her hand and led her to the gowns. "I'm not so sure I do either. We'll have to help each other in there."

Within two hours, they were wheeling Susan into the delivery room while Scott and Lisa stood on either side of her, talking to her and wiping her face. The doctor offered to tilt the mirror so they could see the baby's arrival, but all three, almost in unison, said, "No, thank you."

With one final push, little Lisa Anne joined the family. After allowing Mommy a quick peek, the nurse took the baby to the other side of the delivery room to clean her up and take all the birth measurements. Lisa followed the nurse and stood beside her, looking down into the sweet little face of her namesake. Lisa was nine when Susan was born, and Lisa Anne looked exactly like she remembered Susan. Her little hands were so tiny, and her little mouth had the cutest little pucker.

When the nurse was finished, she tightly bundled Lisa Anne and took her back to her Susan. As Susan held her daughter for the first time, Scott put his arm around her and kissed her. Little Lisa Anne was the most beautiful baby Scott had ever seen. Watching this woman he loved more than life, kissing and cooing to his new little daughter, Scott's chest felt like it would burst.

After the three of them enjoyed a few minutes with the baby, the nurse instructed Scott and Lisa to leave so they could get Susan and her baby to their room. Besides, family members were anxiously awaiting news of the baby's arrival in the waiting room.

Bill, Caroline, Aunt Gladys, and Harry were standing around the waiting room as Scott and Lisa walked out. It was too soon after having her own baby for Carol Anne to come, but Harry joined the family to wait and hear all about the new baby cousin. Lisa moved over by Aunt Gladys, allowing Scott to have the floor.

Scott simply grinned at everyone for a second or two. "Susan did great, and we are the proud parents of a healthy, eight-pound baby girl! Her name is Lisa Anne Thomas, and she's beautiful." He barely finished his short speech before starting to cry. He was so overcome with emotion, he had to sit down.

Once she was certain Scott had finished his announcement, Lisa grabbed Gladys' arm and led her to the nursery so they look at the baby. "Isn't she beautiful, Gladys? They named her after me. Can you believe it?"

The two women stayed in Atlanta for three weeks, keeping the two households running smoothly. Almost every evening Lisa baked something scrumptious, and both Scott and Harry dreaded getting on a scale. Auntie Lisa was allowed to help give Lisa Anne her very first bath. The night before Lisa was to leave, Scott decided to take some special photos of the three of them. He posed Susan in the big overstuffed chair in the living room with baby Lisa Anne in her lap. He then had Auntie Lisa sit on the arm of the chair with her arm around her sister. Lisa was wearing a smart box-jacket suit she had knit herself. She radiated with health and happiness. She had gone to the beauty shop that afternoon and gotten her hair cut and styled, and she looked wonderful.

Scott took four or five shots to make sure they had a good picture. When finished, Lisa offered to take some pictures of the three of them, so Scott held Lisa Anne in one arm and put his other around Susan. The photos showed their happiness. Scott promised to send copies to Lisa.

A few days later, without telling anyone what he was doing, Scott slipped several of these photos, plus one or two from their wedding, into an envelope and sent them to Mrs. Miller, along with a note.

Dear Mrs. Miller,

I thought you might like to have these. Both of your daughters are doing well and are very happy. Enclosed you will find a photo of your first granddaughter, Lisa Anne Thomas. You are more than welcome to come by for a visit.

Sincerely,

Scott Thomas

Scott hoped this overture might break the ice with Marjorie. He couldn't imagine any mother not being glad to see her daughters well and happy. He waited for almost a month before telling Susan what he had done. He was angry because there hadn't even been a note or phone call, let alone a visit. He hesitated to tell her at first but knew he should.

"I'm glad you sent them, Scott. I've dropped her notes every once in a while, but I never get a reply. I've told her all about Lisa and her wonderful life in Jefferson, but I have no way of knowing how she is taking it. It's been five years since I have seen or talked to her. I guess she hasn't changed."

They continued to send pictures once or twice a year, regardless of the lack of response. They always sent a picture in their Christmas card and in her birthday card. When Megan was born three years later, they sent her a birth announcement with a picture of Lisa Anne's holding her baby sister. Lisa Anne was now three years old and was a striking beauty. She had her mother's looks and her daddy's smile, and she loved her little sister.

Susan decided to include a photo taken in Mrs. Bascom's bakery. In the picture, Lisa Anne was standing by Auntie Lisa, and they both had flour all over them. Lisa Anne was holding her very first batch of cookies, and she had the biggest grin on her face. Her auntie had patiently helped her mix, cut, and lift the cookies off the pan and onto a platter. Lisa Anne was certain there was nothing her auntie couldn't do. She always loved it when she was able to visit her two aunties. She had even been promised that when she turned six, they would teach her how to knit, which made Lisa Anne very happy.

Tucking the picture of her sister and daughter inside the envelope, Susan calculated how long it must have been since her mother and sister had seen each other. Lisa was seventeen when she ran away, and now she was in her late thirties. Except for a few photos they had sent, more than twenty years had passed since they had seen or spoken to each other. She could hardly believe eight years had gone by since she had spoken with her mother. *You can't force people to love you—not even your mother.*

Megan was such a happy baby with a giggle that was infectious. Her cousin, Michael, had a way of looking at her that sent her giggles exploding through the room, and before they knew it, everyone was giggling. He was three years old, with curly red hair and bright-blue eyes. He would sit on the floor for hours playing with Megan. He had asked his mommy and daddy for a little sister exactly like cousin Megan, and although they couldn't promise a little sister, they told him a new baby would be coming soon.

The next two years were filled with new babies. On Michael's fourth birthday, Carol Anne delivered twins. Michael was with his grandpa for the afternoon because they were busy getting the house ready for his birthday dinner when his mother went into labor. They had known for almost three months that she was having twins but had decided not to tell Michael. Patience is not a strong character quality for a four-year-old. Michael was already driving them crazy with, "When will *my* baby come?"

As Michael and Grandpa pulled into the driveway, Caroline came out the front door and announced, "We need to get to the hospital!" Michael's daddy was waiting for him when they walked into the waiting room. "Hello, birthday boy. How would you like to see your new baby brother *and* sister?"

Michael squealed with happiness. He was getting *two* babies! He couldn't wait to tell his cousin Lisa Anne. Michael took his daddy's hand, and together they walked to the nursery to see his brand new babies. Michael was not happy with the fact that they could not take them home that day. After all, Megan was home with Lisa Anne.

He wanted to name his new sister Megan too, but his daddy shook his head. "We already have a Megan in the family. Michael, our baby girl needs her very own name. Let's go see Mommy, and maybe we can think up a good name."

As they walked toward Carol Anne's room, Harry heard Michael mumble under his breath, "I think Megan is a really good name," but he didn't argue with them.

After a few minutes with his parents, Michael was convinced he had picked out the new names all by himself and wanted to be the one to go out into the waiting room and tell everyone. He walked into the waiting room, puffed out his chest with pride, and announced, "Everybody, I now have two babies, and their names are William and Caroline Stephenson because I love my grandpa and grandma. But I'm going to call them Billy and Carrie."

CHAPTER 23

Busy is the only word to describe everyone's life. Scott was now acting director of the company so Dad could have more time off. He and Mom were starting to take some of the vacations they had always put off. In the spring, they took Aunt Gladys along on a cruise, and the three had a great time.

Harry was promoted to principal after completing a second master's degree, which wasn't easy with three little ones running around the house. Carol Anne had stopped teaching when she found out she was expecting twins, but that didn't mean she stopped working. She had taken on volunteer work and was roping Susan into almost every activity she could dream up. But when Megan was a year-and-a-half old, Susan discovered she was expecting again. Almost thirty, Susan began to panic as she realized that she would be forty-eight, and Scott would in his fifties when this baby graduated from high school. She didn't say anything until she visited the doctor, but once her pregnancy was confirmed, she was surprised at the joy she felt. She loved her two little girls but really did want a little boy.

The house was getting crowded, and they could afford to move to a bigger house, but neither of them could bear to think of leaving their bungalow or their neighborhood. They loved their wonderful neighbors and didn't want to move.

Whether a boy or a girl, they were definitely out of room. Scott dismantled his office, which had been in the third bedroom since they had moved in, and they decided it was better to remodel than lose the house. For the next several months, carpenters, plumbers, painters, and electricians were coming and going all day long. They decided to take the back bedroom, push out the back wall and make it a master bedroom with its own bath. Then the girls could take over their old room, and the baby could have the girls' room.

Susan made sure everyone stayed on schedule, and by her eighth month, everything was ready for the new baby. Caroline wallpapered the girls' new room, and Lisa Anne was allowed to help. She would stand next to her grandma, handing her the smoothing brush whenever Grandma needed it. When the room was finished, Lisa Anne proudly showed everyone what she and her grandma had done. When Michael saw the room, he asked his grandma if she would help him paper his room, but he wanted boats, not flowers. Michael loved his cousin Lisa Anne, but he wanted to make sure that he was always one step ahead of her—after all, he was older.

Scott took off a few days to paint their new bedroom, bath, and nursery. Thinking positively, they picked out boyish wallpaper featuring cars, trucks, and boats. Scott painted the lower wall a deep blue and the chair rail and windowsills a bright red. They finished everything only one week before Matthew Edward Thomas made his grand entrance into the world. He was named after Grandpa Thomas, Dad and Aunt Gladys's father. This time, Aunt Gladys and Lisa came for a whole month, but they stayed with Bill and Caroline to give Scott and Susan some privacy.

Matthew was born with a full head of curly blond hair and looked like his daddy's baby pictures. He absolutely stole everyone's heart. He was such a calm baby, nothing seemed to bother him. The girls could be playing and laughing next to him, and he would sleep right through their chatter.

Life began to settle down a little as Susan became more cautious about how many volunteer projects she could accept. She had three little children at home and didn't want to be out three nights a week. Megan, who was almost three, shadowed six-year-old Lisa Anne everywhere. The girls would play in their room for hours, pretending to bake wonderful dinners for their daddy. Aunt Lisa had given them a play kitchen with all kinds of plastic food, dishes, and pans. The girls would set their play table with all of the dishes, and Lisa Anne would go out in the backyard to pick flowers for the table.

Matthew was now fourteen months old and loved going in and messing up all the girls' hard work setting up their tea parties. He wasn't old enough to understand that this upset his sisters; he simply wanted to be included in their play.

Every evening, Scott would come home eager to have his playtime with his girls. He would smack his mouth as he pretended to eat their delicious meals. Megan giggled as Daddy lifted the tiny teacup to his mouth and pretended to have tea. It didn't matter that they repeated this same game almost every evening, Megan would always giggle. She loved to see her daddy with his big long legs, trying to sit on one of their little chairs. She watched his big hands trying to hold the tiny cup up to his mouth and think how silly he looked, but she loved it.

Matthew would usually come barging in wanting his daddy to pick him up for a hug, and then both girls would tackle Daddy to the floor. Everyone got tickles and kisses. Every night, at bedtime, Mommy and Daddy would each sit on one of the girl's beds while they took turns reading a bedtime story. All four took turns saying their nighttime prayers.

Life was wonderful, and they were happy, except for the few times a year when Susan would fall into one of her black moods and put herself to bed. Susan's moods seemed to start about the time Lisa Anne was three and Megan came along. At first they only lasted an afternoon or overnight. But each year they came more often and lasted a little longer. By the time Lisa Anne turned six, Susan was having sleeping periods almost every month. Scott never could figure out what caused her black moods, but she would become so depressed, begging to be left alone so she could sleep. She never wanted to talk about how she was feeling and couldn't seem to tell him why she needed so much sleep. He worried about her, but when she wasn't having one of her black moods she was perky, happy, and full of energy.

During one of her prolonged moods, Scott felt so desperate he asked his father if he could take some time off to stay home with the children.

Bill and Caroline had noticed this pattern in Susan's life and had been worried for months. They did not know what to do or say. She seemed unapproachable during these black moods, and when they were over, she only wanted to forget them. "Son, what are you doing to help her deal with these moods?"

"Dad, I don't know what to do. If I ask her questions about why she's depressed, she falls apart on me. I'm worried about the kids. Lisa Anne knows her mother is hurting, and she goes around trying to make everything perfect so Susan will be happy again. I don't want her growing up thinking it is all her fault. She already says things like, 'If I had made Megan play quietly, Mommy wouldn't have been sad today.' Dad, I can't let this go on. It's hurting her, it's hurting me, but most of all, it's hurting our kids."

"Son, I think it's about time you encourage her to get professional help. She needs to find out what's causing her moods. Maybe she'll talk to someone outside of the family. It's certainly worth a try."

A few days later, during one of Susan's black moods, Scott tried to think of someone with whom she might talk. He had suggested she talk to someone on several other occasions, but every time she had resisted. Then remembering Dr. Jacobson, who had helped her during her teen years, Scott suggested she go to see her. "You really respected her, remember? It couldn't hurt to talk to her. Honey, I know something is bothering you and making you depressed. Why don't you schedule and appointment with Dr. Jacobson? She might be able to help you understand what's going on."

To his surprise, Susan sat up in bed and gave him a half smile. "That's a good idea. I think I might do that. I know she'd understand, and maybe she can help me deal with this. I'll call her tomorrow morning."

Three weeks passed before Dr. Jacobson could see her. She had been out of town on a speaking trip but had called in for her messages and found out Susan was trying to contact her. Dr. Jacobson gave her an appointment at 10 in the morning. Until then, she suggested that Susan start keeping a journal of her feelings. "I don't need you to analyze your feelings, simply identify them. If you're feeling sad, happy, silly, scared, homesick, it doesn't matter. Whatever you're feeling, write it down. Then write what was going on at the time, where you were, and who was with you. Don't worry about what it sounds like because that isn't important. Also, why don't you drop off your journal at my office on the Thursday before your Friday appointment so I can read it before we meet? Reading what has been happening might help me better understand what you're struggling with."

Susan didn't want this, but she trusted Dr. Jacobson and wanted to get over whatever was causing her depression. For the next three weeks, she kept her journal with her. At first she found herself explaining why she had no reason to feel bad, going on for pages how everything was so perfect in her life. Sometimes though, she was brief and cryptic in her entry, only stating a feeling and nothing else. By the third week, she would almost forget she was writing to Dr. Jacobson and would use the journal to spill out feelings without guarding how they sounded. These particular entries, which most interested the doctor gave her a fairly good idea of how to address some of Susan's struggles.

Dr. Jacobson's office, which was warm and friendly, had been decorated to resemble a living room. After a few minutes, the person seeking counsel could almost forgot she was in a therapist's office. Dr. Jacobsen offered Susan some coffee or tea. Susan was feeling a sense of dread, as if something horrible was about to be exposed.

Dr. Jacobson noticed her wringing her hands and fidgeting, so she took a seat beside her and clasped one of her hand in hers. "Susan, you've gotten yourself pretty upset. Why?"

Susan was about to cry and wished she hadn't come. "I don't know. I feel as if I've been caught stealing something and don't know why."

"Did you read through your journal before you dropped it off?"

"No. I was afraid if I did, I wouldn't give it to you."

"I'm glad you didn't then because I noticed several entries in your journal that were very helpful to me, but before we talk about them, let's catch up on what's been going on in your life for the past several years. The last time we talked, your little Lisa Anne was still a baby. Obviously, there have been some new additions. Why don't you tell me what's been happening to you."

Dr. Jacobson picked up her cup of tea, leaned back against the sofa, and acted as if this time was simply a neighborly little visit between two friends. Early in her practice, Dr. Jacobson had learned that these journeys into personal discovery could not be sandwiched into fifty-minute sessions. Time and patience are required to work with people who are beginning to come face to face with their deepest, darkest fears and pain. After all, most have spent their entire lives denying these feelings and burying them deep in their subconscious. Most of the time, when they came into the office, they had no idea what their real problem was. They simply focused on the symptoms.

During the first five or six visits, Susan spent the time painting a happy, successful picture of her life and family. She talked about Scott's wonderful qualities and what a good father he was. It was obviously important to her that Dr. Jacobson understand there was absolutely no reason for how she was feeling. She knew she had no business being depressed and couldn't understand why she couldn't drive away these feelings.

"Susan, when you feel like this, what do you do to try to feel better?"

"Well, sometimes I try to get involved in a project or something. I'll get out my sewing machine and make one of the girls a dress or make clothes for their dolls. Sometimes I feel like I have to get out of the house, so we go to Grandpa's and Grandma's so the girls can swim. If the weather is bad, we'll walk through the mall and get a treat. Anything that will help me get my mind off how I'm feeling."

"Are those the usual ways you deal with your pain?" Dr. Jacobson knew the answer, but she wanted Susan to say it. It doesn't help a patient to be told what's wrong; the patient has to make this discovery for herself, with a little help.

At first, she quickly nodded yes but then looked over at Dr. Jacobson with an embarrassed half-smile. "Well...no. Lately, I've been sleeping a lot. I can't stand these feelings, and all I can think to do is take a nap. Actually, for the past year you couldn't really call what I do taking a nap.

I've gone to bed several times and stayed there for a day or two. I don't know why I do this. I know it hurts Scott and the girls, but it's like I have this huge weight on me, and I can't breathe."

"Susan, what you're experiencing is not uncommon among adults, who, as children, experienced extremely dysfunctional homes. As you were growing up, you developed certain tools that allowed you to survive an unbelievably harsh home. For you, one of those tools was your escape route. When your life became overwhelming, you would escape the terror of your life by going to sleep—the only place you felt safe. When sleeping, you were somewhere else, with someone else, doing something else. Sleeping was your way of staying out of trouble. After all, a sleeping child cannot say or do something that will bring the reign of terror down on them. Isn't that right?"

Susan was honestly puzzled. "Yes. I understand why I did it when I was a child, but why am I doing it now? Nothing in my life is overwhelming me, and there certainly is no reign of terror in my home."

"Before I address that question, let's talk about another survival tool you used as a child and how that tool is possibly causing you some real problems now. As we have talked together these past few weeks, I have pieced together what you have shared with what you wrote in your journals. I have noticed a pattern each time one of your times of depression occurs."

Dr. Jacobsen needed Susan to recognize these patterns for herself, but she wasn't quite sure Susan was ready to face one of her biggest fears. "Have you noticed any of these patterns?"

Twisting the hankie around her finger, Susan sat on the sofa, trying to come up with an answer. Finally, she turned to Dr. Jacobson and shrugged. "I don't know."

"Susan, do you sometimes feel as if you might be jealous of your girls?"

Susan's strangled answer came out sounding almost like a tortured animal "No! I love my girls. I would never be jealous of them. Why would I?" Feeling a wave of panic sweep over her, Susan began to weep. All of her childhood fears of becoming a bad mother were sitting right at the surface of her emotions. She had always said she would rather never have children than to take the risk of behaving like her mother.

Reaching over to take hold of Susan's hand, Dr. Jacobson gently responded, "I don't think you are either. I don't think you're jealous of your girls. I do suspect you're so terrified of becoming like your mother that your fears are overwhelming you. I do think you're struggling with some very strong emotions that are all tied to your daughters. I believe these emotions are terrifying you, and you are afraid to confront them—fearful of what they might tell you. I also believe you go to sleep so you don't have to address them. Let me ask another question: did you experience any of these black moods before Lisa Anne was born?"

She thought for a moment. "I think the first one came when Lisa Anne was about three."

"That's what I thought. Susan, one of the tools you used as a child to explain or to make sense out of your sick home life was to make excuses for your mother's behavior. You were the obedient, loving daughter who always stood by her side. Your sister, Lisa, ran off, didn't she? She and your mother never got along, and Lisa hated her, whereas you stayed in that house trying to keep her happy until you finally got married. Then she turned her back on you. Isn't that right?"

"Yes, *but* she shut me out. I didn't abandon her."

"I know. I think what has been happening to you is a painful path of discovery. When you were young, you were simply Marjorie Miller's daughter, trying to see your mother's actions from a daughter's perspective. You were an obedient, helpful daughter who wanted to believe her mother really did care about her, but as Lisa Anne began getting a little older, you began seeing the world through the eyes of a mother—a very loving mother. As you began to watch this little girl experience home, family, security and love, your mind couldn't help but compare her life with your own life as a child.

"None of us can remember events much before three years of age, so as your girls got older and closer to ages that are easier for you to remember about your own childhood, your painful memories were triggered. You couldn't help but have some very agonizing memories flood your mind. No, Susan, you haven't been feeling jealous; on the contrary, you have been trying to drive away your painful memories. I think you're finally coming to understand exactly how sick your mother was. You now know what a good, loving mother is. You are one! Could you ever, even for a moment, imagine doing to one of your little girls the things you remember your mother doing to you?"

Susan's response came out of her like a wail from deep in her soul. "No! How could she have done those things to me? I look at my babies, and there's *nothing* I wouldn't do to protect them. I couldn't stand by and watch someone beat my babies into unconsciousness, but that's what she did!"

Dr. Jacobson had watched and listened as many adults had come to similar painful realizations during counseling. No matter how many times she had experienced a hurting person's drawing the right conclusion, it never became any easier.

Susan was staring deep into herself and finally facing the ugly truth she had struggled her entire life to deny. Susan was finally ready to see her mother for what she was. No more excuses. No more hoping. No more denying. Even though Dr. Jacobson knew embracing this truth was exactly what Susan needed to do, it was still hard to watch someone experience such deep sorrow, rage, and loss. Dr. Jacobson waited as Susan's mind raced through the corridors of her memory. She was finally allowing herself to revisit those childhood experiences and see them for what they really were.

With a newfound rage, Susan shared one such memory.

"I remember a time when she turned my father on me. I was in kindergarten. I had left my crayons on the kitchen table, and some of them had rolled onto the floor. She had stepped on one of them. My dad was mowing in the backyard, and one of the neighbors said something to him that angered him. He came storming in and started pushing my mother against the sink."

Dr. Jacobson noticed a hesitation in Susan's voice, as if she weren't so sure she really wanted to go back to that memory after all. These feelings of rage were scaring Susan. She had never allowed herself to feel her outrage at being treated the way she was.

"Susan, what happened in that kitchen?"

Without looking up, Susan said, "I walked in the kitchen to get a drink and saw him slap her across the face for talking back to him. Before I knew it, she was pointing at my crayons, saying I had refused to pick them up. My dad spun around, grabbed me by my hair, and picked me up. I remember my head hurting, but I didn't dare scream. He slammed me against the door, hitting my head hard, punched me in the stomach, and dropped me. As he stepped over me, he screamed, "Now pick up those crayons!" I remember looking at my mother as she stood by the sink with a sick smirk on her face. Even at that age, I knew I had just gotten the beating intended for her. She didn't say a word; she simply turned and went on fixing my dad's lunch. I picked up my crayons and went straight to my bedroom. I don't think I came out that whole day. I could hardly walk because my stomach hurt so much. It was a day or two before I could stand to brush my hair. You know, when I look at my Lisa Anne, someone would have to kill me before I would let anyone hurt her."

Susan was finally seeing her mother for what she really was. Taking Susan into her arms and gently comforting her, Dr. Jacobson encouraged her to let her tears flow. Years of silent rage spilled out of Susan, and she cried out all the questions she had been too afraid to ask because the answers would have been too painful to face. "How could my mother do that to me?"

"I don't know, Susan. Maybe we'll never know all that happened to Marjorie Miller to turn her into the woman she has become. We do know though, she was, or became, a very sick person. But you don't have to wait until you have understood *why* she did what she did before you can be free. My task is to help you—not her. I suspect that once we are able to openly look at your childhood, you will be able to separate your memories from your children. Once you face your memories, they won't have the same power over you. As for your need to sleep, you need to keep reminding yourself that you no longer need to escape your memories."

Susan met with Dr. Jacobsen several more months before they felt they had faced most of her monsters. The black moods were gone, and she hadn't gone to bed during the daytime in months. They both knew she would always have reminders of her loss, but now that she was learning how to recognize her feelings, they would no longer control her. Susan had made excuses for her mother her whole life.

During therapy, Susan went through a period of hating her mother, but then, as her emotions began to settle down, she began to pity her. Her mother was living in a lonely world of her own making, and until she decided to change, there was nothing anyone could do to help her. Susan was finally feeling free of her. She and Lisa were both going to be all right, and that was enough for right now.

What Susan could not possibly know at the time was she would soon need this calm understanding of her childhood. Deadly things were in motion, and Susan would need this calm in order to weather the huge storm that was brewing.

CHAPTER 24

❧

THE COMING STORM hit Susan's house at nearly midnight. The phone rang, and Scott jumped up to answer it. "Who in the world could be calling at this time of night? Oh, I hope it isn't about Dad. Mom said he is recovering well from gallbladder surgery."

Susan stood beside him, anxious to know what was wrong. As he held the phone, the look on his face made her want to take a seat. She was trying not to fall apart, but her mind was racing, trying to figure out what horrible thing could put that look on his face.

Scott replied, "Yes. No. I understand. All right. We'll get dressed and come right away. Don't worry, Aunt Gladys. Everything's going to be all right. We love you!"

When he finally hung up, he turned to Susan, who already knew something horrible must have happened to Lisa. Before he could share the information from the phone call, she began weeping uncontrollably.

"You must pull yourself together. Lisa is all right. She's not hurt, but she's in bad trouble. No one knows exactly what happened, but around eight o'clock tonight, Lisa shot and killed your father."

"My father? What? How can that be? He's in prison!"

"I don't understand either, and Aunt Gladys said the police wouldn't let her see or talk to Lisa. They have her at the police station, trying to piece together what happened tonight. Aunt Gladys cannot get anything out of them because she isn't considered family. I told her we would come right away, so you pack some things for us while I grab some clothes for the kids. I'll call Mother and tell her we're dropping them off on our way out of town."

Susan could hardly think as she pulled out their suitcases and began packing the things they would need. Her mind was fuzzy. All she could think about was Lisa's sitting in that jail again. Every once in a while, she sat on the bed and prayed very hard for her sister. She had no idea what had happened, but she knew Lisa would need her there as soon as possible. She quickly finished packing and helped Scott get the sleeping children into the car.

Mrs. Thomas was standing in the doorway as they pulled into the driveway. She didn't ask any questions, but the look on her face showed inexpressible concern. She had the covers turned down on Carol Anne's bed, and after Scott had tucked in Lisa Anne and Megan, he kissed each of them. As he stood momentarily staring at his little girls, all he could think of was how much Lisa Anne loved her Auntie Lisa. How was she going to handle this news? Susan settled Matthew in the crib Grandma kept in Scott's room, and then the two of them headed downstairs to the kitchen.

They could smell coffee brewing, and Caroline was busy making toast. Bill was still asleep upstairs, so they all tried to keep very quiet. Only that morning he had come home from having gallbladder surgery, and they didn't want him upset. She had already called Carol Anne and told her what was happening—at least what they knew. Caroline needed her daughter to come take the children in the morning so Dad could rest.

Not wanting them driving ninety miles in the middle of the night without being wide awake, she had already filled a thermos, and as she poured them each a cup of coffee, she asked, "So what has happened? Is Lisa all right? He didn't hurt her, did he?"

"We don't know very much right now. They wouldn't tell Aunt Gladys anything, except Susan's dad is dead, and Lisa shot him. As soon as we know anything we'll call, but we need to get going. We don't want Lisa in that jail any longer than necessary. I'm sorry about the timing, with Dad sick, but we'll get the kids as soon as we know what's going on."

They thanked her for the thermos and left immediately for Jefferson. They were quiet for most of the drive, trying to imagine what might have happened. No one had even bothered telling them Chuck Miller was getting out of prison, and Susan was furious. "They knew he had threatened Lisa. Why didn't they warn her he was being released? If they had told Lisa, Aunt Gladys would have known about it. I simply don't understand."

"Let's try to stay calm. We don't know what happened yet, so please try not to worry. At least Lisa's all right."

Even as he assured Susan that Lisa was all right, he knew he was making a big assumption. The police might not have told Gladys if Lisa had been beaten. Unlike the last time, it just might not have been bad enough to send her to the hospital. He didn't want to mention his concern to Susan. She did not need any more trouble right now.

The roads were dry and clear, so Scott drove faster than normal, but it still took almost two hours to get to Jefferson.

As they walked into the jail, Susan recognized Officer Jackson. He had always been kind and helpful whenever she came to visit Lisa eleven years earlier. When he looked up, he immediately recognized her, and a big grin came across his face. "Hello, I'm Officer Jackson, and you must be…"

"Scott, Scott Thomas, and this is my wife, Susan. We're here to see Lisa Miller. I understand she's being held here. Is that right?"

As Scott held out his hand, Officer Jackson thought, *So this is the young man who won the prize. Nice-looking guy; handles himself pretty well. Strange combination, these three. Never could see the connection between these two women.* Officer Jackson suddenly realized Scott's hand was still extended, and he quickly reached out to shake it. "Yes, sir, we have her in back, but you can't see her right now—not until they're finished questioning her, and then she will be booked."

"Booked! For what?" Susan shouted.

"For murder. You're her sister, aren't you?" He was fairly sure he had remembered their connection.

"Yes, I am, but why are they booking her for murder?"

"Well, it seems she shot your father this evening, or last evening is more accurate. Around eight o'clock in a dark alley downtown. Quite a colorful past your sister has."

It was obvious to both of them he had seen Lisa's criminal file and had already found her guilty. This wasn't fair, and she was determined to see Lisa. "That's right! Past! The person you see in that file no longer exists and hasn't for eleven years."

Trying hard to contain her anger, Susan added, "How soon can we see her, and has she asked for an attorney yet?"

"Mrs. Thomas, your sister has been in and out of the system for years. She knows her rights, rest assured of that fact. Why don't you go home, and we'll call you when she wishes to see relatives."

Scott was trying hard to control his temper. This man didn't know what kind of person Lisa had become. He was obviously under the notion she was still a drug-using prostitute and was going to treat her that way. "We're not leaving. I want to talk to someone in authority right now."

Scott didn't take his eyes off the officer and was not going to move until his demand was honored.

Finally, the officer gave in. "I'll see what I can do. Why don't you two have a seat over there, and I'll be right back."

He grabbed his coffee cup and pastry and headed for the back. Susan stared at him as he walked off. "Funny! That pastry wrapper is from Mrs. Bascom's store. That pastry was probably made by Lisa."

Almost thirty minutes had passed before the detective came out to talk with them. "Mr. and Mrs. Thomas, I'm sorry to inform you that last evening, around eight o'clock, your father was shot and killed." He stood waiting for a reaction. He had no way of knowing they were not interested in the victim; they were only interested in the shooter, as he had called her.

Scott was tired and growing impatient with this runaround. "Can we please see Lisa now? Has she called a lawyer yet?"

"Well, actually, no. It's four-thirty in the morning, and we've been talking to her for almost five hours. She'll be arraigned this morning around ten o'clock in front of Judge Kirkley. You might want to see about getting a lawyer to represent her because she has refused to call one herself."

"How do we go about posting bail for her?"

"Well, I doubt if the judge will allow bail, but a lawyer will advise you on that matter. This is a murder case, and she has a pretty extensive record. I would be surprised if he let her out."

This was not what they wanted to hear. They decided they were getting nowhere, so they drove to Gladys' house and waited for morning. Aunt Gladys had not yet been to bed. She had been sitting in the living room praying for Lisa all night. Ruth Bascom had stayed until almost three but finally went home to rest.

Scott, Susan, and Gladys stayed up the rest of the night talking. They wanted to reach an attorney before the arraignment, so around eight o'clock they started calling. They didn't know any local attorneys, so they trusted God to lead them to the right one. The first three didn't answer their phones, so Scott tried the fourth attorney, a Mr. Duncan, listed in the phone book.

Scott was surprised to find a live voice on the other end of the line and doubly surprised to find the attorney himself had answered. Duncan explained that his office didn't open until nine, but he was in early handling correspondence and thought the call was from his wife.

Scott quickly explained their problem and asked if he handled this type of case.

"Yes, I'm a criminal attorney. It sounds like I need to get over to the jail right away. If you can meet me there in twenty minutes, I'll arrange for you to see Lisa."

Aunt Gladys assumed they wouldn't let her go in to see Lisa, so she decided to stay home and pray. She couldn't think of anything more useful, knowing her Lisa was again in that awful place.

Mr. Duncan was waiting on the steps as they walked up. He introduced himself and said, "Mrs. Thomas, I am sorry for your loss. I've already requested a conference room, and you'll be allowed to see Lisa before her arraignment."

Forcing a smile, Susan accepted his extended hand and decided not to comment on the "your loss" remark. They would have plenty of time later to set this man straight. "Thank you, Mr. Duncan. We appreciate your coming on such short notice. The police wouldn't let us see her, nor would they tell us very much."

Opening the door for his new clients, Duncan whispered, "Let's go see your sister and find out from her what happened."

As they walked into the conference room, Susan remembered the last time she waited in that very room for her sister, and floods of old feelings washed over her.

While they waited for Lisa to be brought in, Scott asked Mr. Duncan several questions about his practice, trying to judge what kind of person he was.

"Mr. Thomas, I've been in practice for almost sixteen years. I've defended thirteen murder cases, winning seven of them. You must understand, not all clients are innocent, so even the best attorney cannot always win. I do, however, work very hard for my clients and will defend your sister-in-law with everything I've got."

Susan was exhausted and was having a hard time focusing on everything being said. Mr. Duncan studied her for a moment and thought how attractive she was—even under this stress. He then asked her a few questions. She gave a short background about their father and his prison terms, along with his threat to kill Lisa when he was sentenced. She explained about Lisa's past, making sure he understood that what she was sharing was only in her past. She told him what Lisa had been doing for the past eleven years and what a wonderful person she had become.

Duncan leaned back in his chair and pondered all this information for a moment. Then, turning to Susan, he asked, "Your father was arrested here in Jefferson for that assault on Lisa?"

"Yes, and his trial was here also."

Duncan sort of frowned as he made a note to himself. "I haven't been able to talk to the arresting officer yet, but something doesn't seem right.

They must know of Charles Miller's record by now. I need to find out why they're ignoring his record and pushing so heavily on Lisa's."

With more pleading than anger in her voice, Susan responded, "These men are only looking at her past record. They assume once a prostitute, always a prostitute. After talking to them last night, it sounds like they don't even care what our father was. He's dead, and she did it."

Scott turned as Officer Jackson opened the door and brought Lisa into the conference room. Susan stood up and hugged her sister. Lisa was obviously very upset. Her clothes were torn and dirty, and Susan saw a large bruise on her right arm.

Scott also went to Lisa, hugged her, and introduced Mr. Duncan. "We've hired him to represent you at the arraignment, Lisa."

Mr. Duncan motioned for everyone to be seated and then looked at Officer Jackson, as if to say, "Please leave now." Officer Jackson quickly closed the door and waited in the hall.

Duncan took out a yellow legal pad and prepared to write down everything Lisa was about to say. "All right. Why don't you tell us what happened in that alley last night."

Lisa took a deep breath. "Well, it was around eight o'clock, and I was locking up the bakery as usual. Actually, we close the bakery at six-thirty, but I always have pans and cookie sheets to wash and dry. I had locked up, turned off all the lights, and headed out the back door.

"Because it opens onto the alley, we're always careful to look out to see if anyone's out there before opening that door. When I didn't see anyone, I set the alarm and stepped out. Before I could pull the door closed, someone grabbed me from behind. My first thought was that I was being robbed. It wasn't until he spun me around that I saw who it was.

"His eyes were on fire with rage, and he kept spitting his words in my face. He was so close, I couldn't breathe. He slammed me up against the building and jammed his forearm into my throat. I started choking. Then he pulled a gun from his jacket pocket and shoved it into my cheek.

"Right about then, the alarm started going off. I had set it before walking into the alley, and when the door wasn't closed within sixty seconds, the alarm automatically came on. I guess the noise must have startled him because he took a step back and lowered the gun a little. That's when I grabbed for it. I knew he intended to kill me; he had said he would. He said he'd been waiting for years to kill me and that he was going to enjoy taking his time.

"I didn't intend to shoot him. I was only trying to keep from getting shot myself. I grabbed for the gun and tried to twist it out of his hand, but he kept slamming me against the wall. Then suddenly the gun went off, and he fell. I was standing there with the gun in my hand when the police showed up."

Mr. Duncan asked, "Did either of you know your father was being released from prison?"

Almost in unison, they said no.

Lisa added, "No one from the prison or the DA's office ever contacted me to say he was getting out—even though they had been so ordered by the court because of his threats."

"As far as you knew, Lisa, when you stepped into that alley, you thought your father was still sitting safely behind bars. Is that correct?"

"Yes, sir. I thought he had another four or five years to serve because he had been found guilty of nearly killing a cellmate about six years ago. I don't know why he was out."

For several more minutes, Lisa repeated every detail she could remember.

Several times, Mr. Duncan asked questions, trying to clarify some important point. Lisa was still very upset, but now was the best time to get as many details as possible. Mr. Duncan knew time had a way of clouding a person's memory.

Mr. Duncan was writing quickly, trying to keep every detail in order. "Lisa, have the police had a doctor look at you yet?"

"No, Mr. Duncan, they wouldn't even let me take a shower this morning."

"That's good. I want to get a female officer in here to take some pictures of your back. I suspect your back will be fairly bruised, not unlike your arm. I know the chief of police, and I suspect there's a little 'good-ol'-boys' mentality brewing around here. I don't know how they could possibly believe this is anything but self-defense, but sometimes you find some old-fashioned thinking. It's one thing for a man to beat a woman half to death; it's another thing for her to shoot him. I suspect we're facing a little male preservation here. And by the way, call me Duncan."

Scott, almost afraid to hear the answer, asked, "Duncan, what's your impression of this Judge Kirkley?"

"He's as old as Moses." Duncan chuckled. "He prides himself on running a strict court. Overall, I think he's fair. The law is his passion, and like me, he seems to hate what these young, win-at-any-cost lawyers are doing to our system. You know, there's more than one way to prostitute yourself."

Scott and Susan merely smiled. Duncan's statement didn't really need any response, and Scott already knew he was going to like this man.

Duncan asked for a female officer to come in with a camera, and he and Scott stepped into the hall. Susan helped Lisa take off her uniform, and as it dropped to the floor, she saw what Mr. Duncan had suspected. Two large bruises covered each shoulder blade, where her back had been slammed repeatedly against the building. They were already a deep purple and looked very fresh.

The female officer took several pictures from different angles and then took two more of her arm. She was about to leave when Susan asked if she would also take a picture of Lisa's throat. When she lifted her chin, they could see where someone's forearm had been pressed hard against her throat.

"How long will it take to develop the pictures?" Susan asked. "Do you think we could have them in time for the arraignment?"

"No, she's due to be arraigned in about an hour. I can't have these ready that fast. I'll send copies over to your attorney's office either later today or first thing in the morning."

CHAPTER 25

❧

SCOTT FOUND A pay phone and called Aunt Gladys to let her know they had seen Lisa and that she was all right. "It was definitely self-defense, but the attorney thinks the department is still planning to go after Lisa. They apparently cannot believe anyone with her record could possibly be innocent. Just keep praying. We see the judge in about thirty minutes. Maybe he'll put an end to this nonsense."

Scott and Susan arrived at the courtroom several minutes before the arraignment. The courthouse dated back to Civil War days and, as they walked through the large doors, a musty smell permeated the air. The hardwood floor showed years of wear down the center aisle. Wooden benches capable of seating about eight people were on either side. The floor creaked beneath their feet. At the front stood a large wooden platform with the judge's desk in the very center. Above the platform hung a picture of Anthony Spires Jefferson, the town's founder. On either side of this picture stood a state flag and the American flag. The windows on each side of the courtroom started about three feet from the floor, extending to the ceiling, which was about sixteen feet high. Each window was made of frosted, wire-reinforced glass, and the sunlight coming through gave off a depressing, eerie effect to the room.

The court clerk entered first. He placed several papers on the judge's desk and then went to open the first two windows a few inches. The clerk spun around as he heard the back doors being flung open and watched as a man sauntered into the courtroom. This man was obviously one full of himself and well-practiced at making grand entrances. Susan studied him as he made one or two curt remarks to the clerk and began arranging his papers on the desk provided for the prosecution. By the way the clerk responded, Susan assumed no love was lost between these two.

Bringing a pitcher of water to the prosecutor's table, the clerk mockingly said, "Good morning, Mr. Gordon." Obviously expecting no response, and getting none, the clerk then placed a pitcher of water on the defense table, and then returned to his desk, waiting for the others to arrive.

Susan studied the prosecutor. Mr. Gordon appeared to be in his early forties, thin of frame, and slightly balding, although he had obviously begun parting his hair further and further down to hide this fact. He had one of those faces that held contempt for everyone written all over it. His suit, Susan thought, looked as if he fancied himself a dandy. Her overall impression of this man was of a person who overdresses for every occasion and probably likes the sound of his own voice a little too much.

A minute later, Mr. Duncan walked in. After a nod of acknowledgment to Scott and Susan, he moved to the front and whispered something to the clerk while shaking his hand. Susan couldn't hear what was being said, but she appreciated Duncan's cordial demeanor.

As he turned and headed to his table, Susan compared these two adversaries. Mr. Duncan's suit was clean and relatively new, although it needed to be pressed. His tie looked like it must be his favorite—well-worn and slightly out-of-date. She did notice he had changed his shirt since interviewing Lisa. The other one had sported a noticeable coffee stain. Mr. Duncan had one of those faces that generates trust. Although she approximated him to be only in his mid-fifties, he was a grandfatherly type. Reared in Texas, Duncan told them he had been in Jefferson since graduating law school and had blended into this gracious, slow-moving community.

Hearing Mr. Gordon's thick, New Jersey accent as he again made another demand of the clerk, coupled with his rude, brash demeanor, Susan wondered why he had chosen to settle here of all places; he certainly seemed like a fish out of water.

Susan turned her attention away from Mr. Gordon as Lisa was brought into the courtroom about two minutes later. She couldn't help flinching when she saw Lisa was now in an orange jumpsuit. Her hair was disheveled, and she appeared extremely tired. Struggling to offer Lisa a smile as she was directed to a seat next to Mr. Duncan, Susan slid down on the bench to be directly behind her sister. Every once in a while Susan leaned forward to gently touch her shoulder. She didn't want Lisa to forget she wasn't alone.

Everyone sat quietly for several minutes, waiting for the judge to enter. It was so quiet, the ticking of the large clock above the clerk's desk began to irritate Susan. She was having a hard time sitting still and was about to lean forward to ask Mr. Duncan a question when a buzzer sounded. The clerk ordered everyone to rise, and Judge Kirkley walked in and took his seat at his desk.

Susan was startled by his appearance though she wasn't quite sure what she had expected. She realized she probably had some stereotyped fuddy-duddy, can't-make-it-in-the-big-city kind of person in mind. Judge Kirkley was definitely not what she had imagined. He was a man in his early sixties with a full head of beautiful, neatly-trimmed silver hair. As he entered the courtroom, his steel-blue eyes took in the entire room and, without saying a word, he communicated to everyone that he was in charge. If there is such a thing as emanating dignity, Judge Kirkley was doing it.

While the clerk called out the case number and charges, the judge was busy reading what his clerk had set on his desk. When he finished, Susan saw his eyes narrow as he studied Lisa. He wore a stern appearance and never changed his facial expression. When the clerk finished, the judge asked Lisa, "How do you plead?"

Lisa quietly declared, "Not guilty, Your Honor."

The judge then turned to the prosecutor and asked, "Do you care to address the court?"

"Your Honor, early this morning I received a preliminary report from the coroner's office, which indicates that Mr. Charles Miller, in addition to the gunshot wound, suffered a blow to the lower back of his head. Until the coroner completes an autopsy to determine the nature and origin of this wound, we must assume foul play. Having read through Ms. Miller's criminal file, I feel there is sufficient evidence to warrant holding her. It is the state's contention that Ms. Miller, in an act of revenge, lured Mr. Miller into that alley, waylaid him from behind, and then willfully shot and killed him. We believe this was a calculated and premeditated act on her part, and we have submitted to the court Ms. Miller's extensive criminal history. Because of her prior record, we feel she should be held over for trial without bail."

Judge Kirkley never looked up. He was reading Lisa's court records and apparently found them more interesting than anything Mr. Duncan might say. "Mr. Duncan, would you care to offer a rebuttal to this?"

Duncan, hearing about the head wound for the first time, didn't quite know what to say. "Your Honor, I believe that once we have the completed autopsy report and have done an extensive reenactment of the crime scene, I am sure this head wound can be explained. Last night, everyone assumed we were simply dealing with a shooting death. For all we know, Charles Miller might have hit his head as they struggled or received that injury as he fell to the ground."

Mr. Gordon quickly interjected. "Your Honor, until that time, the state must assume this was a deliberate act, and we request that Ms. Miller be remanded until such time as the head wound matter has been explained."

After a quick glance at Lisa, Mr. Duncan addressed the bench yet again. "Your Honor, Lisa Miller was the one attacked last evening—not Charles Miller. There is sufficient physical evidence on Ms. Miller's body to show she acted in self-defense. It is our contention that Mr. Charles Miller, recently released from prison for having beaten her half to death and having threatened her life, was trying to keep his promise."

"Well, Mr. Duncan, since Mr. Miller is not the one standing before me, and Ms. Lisa Miller is, let us focus on what your client is accused of. I understand her father served time in prison for beating his daughter. Is that correct?"

"Yes, Your Honor. I believe he was to serve a ten-to-fifteen-year sentence for beating my client."

"Mr. Duncan, it is one thing to beat someone. It's quite another to take someone's life. Would you not agree?"

"Yes, Your Honor, but Mr. Miller had every intention of killing my client when he beat her eleven years ago. Actually, he almost succeeded. He was in that alley last night to finish what he had started."

"Well, we can't actually know what Mr. Miller's intentions were, can we, Mr. Duncan? At the time of the beating, it appears as if Charles Miller's daughter was actively engaging in the marketing of her body. Isn't that right, Mr. Duncan?"

"Yes, Your Honor, but my client's lifestyle had nothing to do with the beating her father inflicted on her at that time. He couldn't have cared less what she was doing for a living, any more than he cared that she has been an upstanding member of this community for the past eleven years and has held down the same honorable job for the past ten-and-a-half years. She was doing that same job last night when he ambushed her in the alley behind the bakery where she works."

Judge Kirkley had no way of knowing what kind of man Chuck Miller really was. He quickly reviewed the criminal record of this woman standing in front of him and pondered out loud, "Mr. Charles Miller most likely tried to beat some sense into this daughter of his, and the poor man ended up in prison for it. He was probably trying to get his daughter off the streets, and who could blame him? By these reports, at the time of the beating she had a serious drug problem and had been living a very dangerous lifestyle for years. For all I know, Mr. Miller might have stopped by to check on his daughter—exactly as I would have. Who knows what really happened in that alley?"

With steely eyes directed at Lisa, Judge Kirkley continued. "I feel there is sufficient evidence to warrant holding Ms. Miller over for trial. I suggest the only way we will really learn the truth is in court. I will set July 15 as a trial date and suggest everyone do his homework."

Mr. Duncan was on his feet immediately. "Your Honor, defense re-quests bail be set for Ms. Miller. We can provide ample testimony for her upstanding character for the past eleven years, and Mr. Thomas, the defendant's brother-in-law, is willing to provide any bond the court deems necessary."

Judge Kirkley scanned the police reports in front of him and with a deep, slow breath, turned to the prosecutor, and asked, "Do you have any objections to my setting bail for this defendant, Mr. Gordon?"

With a cynicism deeply rooted by years of dealing with criminals, Gordon assumed everyone was guilty, no matter what. "Your Honor, be-cause of Ms. Miller's criminal history, the preliminary autopsy report that does not agree with her rendition of last night and the serious nature of these charges, I feel the citizens of Jefferson deserve to be protected until we can further investigate this case. It is, therefore, the recommendation of my office that bail be denied at this time. We would not be opposed to re-addressing this issue, say, in a week's time, after all of the investigators have had time to submit their findings. Until then, we request remand."

Nodding, Judge Kirkley turned to Lisa and ordered, "Under the cir-cumstances, I cannot in good conscience allow Ms. Miller to walk the streets of Jefferson. Until this matter is resolved, the citizens of this city expect this court to show caution in setting bail. Therefore, no bail will be offered at this time. Sergeant, please return Ms. Miller to her cell."

CHAPTER 26

Lisa's lawyer had three months to prepare a defense. One week after the arraignment, Mr. Duncan's second appeal to get Lisa out on bail was denied, so Lisa would be sitting in jail until the trial.

One week later, Mr. Duncan had his game plan outlined and called a meeting in one of the conference rooms at the jail to share it with Lisa, Susan, and Scott. "We need to prove two things. One, what Chuck Miller was really like, and two, how much Lisa has changed. The prosecution obviously wants to present Lisa as a drug addict and a prostitute, and as an out-of-control daughter filled with anger and revenge, lying in wait for her father to get out of prison so she could kill him."

He poured himself a second cup of coffee and continued. "Of course, I intend to file a motion to suppress her prior record, but the prosecution will argue that it goes to motive, and I think Judge Kirkley will allow it. Therefore, we need to prepare as if her records will be admitted."

With a puzzled look, Susan inquired, "Mr. Duncan, since that was more than ten years ago, how much could it really hurt Lisa's case?"

"A lot! If we can't prove to this jury that the Lisa in those records no longer exists, they'll convict her—maybe not be for first-degree murder, but it has been my experience that once a jury knows a defendant has been found guilty of any crime, especially for what she has been charged, they will usually find the person guilty of the charges before them. For that reason alone, the courts now tend to prohibit the opening of prior records because of prejudice. Judge Kirkley, being so old school, is hard to read. All we can do is try."

Lisa asked, "So if they allow it, how do we counter it?"

"First, I need to put you two girls and your mother on the stand to show the kind of life in which you had to live and the kind of monster Chuck Miller really was."

Susan shook her head. "I'll be glad to testify for my sister, but my mother will never lift a finger to help Lisa. You don't understand how much she hates her. My dad almost killed my mother because Lisa ran away. She'll probably feel a double sense of justice over this. Her abusive husband is now dead, and her daughter is going to prison for killing him. Her dream has come true."

"Susan, she has no choice. Even if we have to subpoena her and question her as a hostile witness, the jury will read her like an open book. The more hostile she gets, the better. We want this jury to see what you girls experienced. If they can't see Chuck Miller in action, then we'll show them Marjorie Miller instead. You let me take care of your mother."

Susan smiled and responded, "You don't know my mother."

Duncan then turned to Scott and continued. "In order to show the jury how much Lisa has changed, I am going to put you, your aunt Gladys, and Mrs. Bascom on the stand. If I can show them the Lisa you all know, we'll have a chance. This jury has to be convinced they can trust Lisa's testimony. If we can do that, I think we can win."

After a few minutes of lighter conversation, Duncan continued. "One more matter, though. The final autopsy report I received was the reason why the judge denied bail. The head injury was more extensive than first suspected, and since we cannot give a plausible explanation for it, the prosecution is alleging that Chuck Miller may have been waylaid from behind. Judge Kirkley called me into his chambers because of this autopsy report to notify me he was denying our petition for another bail hearing."

Scott quickly sat forward. "That's extraordinary! The man was shot. He was a violent man who was always in fights. Maybe that injury is from another fight."

Mr. Duncan already knew that wasn't possible, but he said, "I haven't had a chance to really study these reports yet. Maybe there is a reasonable explanation. If there is, we'll find it."

Duncan noticed that Lisa did not react in any way to this evidence. She sat stone-faced and silent. He had already told her about the medical findings, and she couldn't explain how the blow could have happened. Duncan wondered, *Maybe she was so traumatized that night, she's afraid to remember. One thing I do know—it wasn't deliberate, like the prosecutor is alleging. This woman is not a killer.*

Turning his attention back to the matter at hand, Duncan began wrapping up the meeting. "Susan, what I need from you is a list of people, outside of the family, who knew what was happening in your house. We have only a few months, so if you could make yourself available to help me put the pieces of this puzzle together, your sister and I would be grateful."

"I'll do whatever it takes, Mr. Duncan. If you feel I could be of help, I'll move down here until this is resolved. I can't let my sister sit in that jail alone. If the authorities only knew what a wonderful person she has turned out to be."

With a tender, grandfatherly smile, Mr. Duncan stood up and placed his hand on Lisa's arm. "Don't you worry. We're going to win this. It's your job to keep your spirits up and trust us to do a good job for you. Can you do that?"

"I'll try. All I can promise is, I'll try."

Mr. Duncan then opened the conference door and signaled the officer that Lisa was ready to be returned to her cell. Susan gave her one more hug and then watched as Lisa was led away.

"I know. But let's give him some time to investigate. Did you notice how Lisa reacted to the news? Or should I say didn't react? She just sat there."

"I don't think it means anything. She's probably so overwhelmed with everything, she doesn't know what to say or feel."

The defensiveness in Susan's voice contradicted her response.

Scott knew she was upset and scared. "All right. Let's leave it alone until we know what we're dealing with."

Wanting to change the subject, he added, "Dad's counting on me to help with the company. The doctors want him to rest for at least a month, so I have to stay in Atlanta and run the company, but Mr. Duncan wants you down here to help him."

Thankful for a different subject, Susan suggested, "Why don't we rent a little house here in town? I'm sure Aunt Gladys would be happy to watch the children while I help Mr. Duncan. By the middle of July, when the trial is to start, Dad should be strong enough to take over the business, and you can come here for the trial."

Scott thought about the logistics of everything for a few minutes and then suggested, "Why don't you and the children stay with Aunt Gladys? She won't understand your wanting to get a place by yourself."

"She will, once I explain. Scott, this is as much for her as it is for me."

Gladys had lunch ready when they arrived. After filling her in on Mr. Duncan's plan, Susan mentioned moving the family down to Jefferson. Just as Scott had suspected, as soon as they mentioned renting a little house, Aunt Gladys offered to have them stay with her.

"That's sweet of you, Aunt Gladys, but with the strain of the trial, I think you'll need a quiet house to come home to. Having my three kids underfoot twenty-four hours a day will be too much. We'll find something close. But could you help watch the children for the month or so before the trial? I wouldn't have to worry about them, and I could concentrate on helping Mr. Duncan."

"You know I will. Helping you will also help me. Caring for the children will give me something to do."

Nodding in agreement, Susan carefully studied this gracious woman she had come to love and silently wondered, *How did you become the sweet, caring person you are? Was it purely an accident of birth? Was it merely luck that you got your family and my mother got hers? Are we all merely the products of our environment with our character, temperament, and future formed before we are even old enough to protest? No. That's an easy excuse offered up by people like my mother because she couldn't, didn't, or wouldn't make different choices. Besides, that kind of thinking discounts all your hard choices, as if you never had to work at being kind, unselfish, and forgiving. People like my mother simply think it's easier for people like you.*

"Susan?. Earth to Susan," Scott teased. He knew her mind was a million miles away.

Roused from her thoughts, Susan gave Scott an apologetic shrug. Years had passed since she had thought much about her mother, but now with having to talk about their childhood, those thoughts were consuming every waking moment. "Sorry. I wasn't listening. What did you say?"

"I said we have lots to do. Can we pencil in some dates? The trial is set for the middle of July, and Mr. Duncan said he wants you here by the first of next month. That schedule only gives us three weeks to prepare."

"Scott, how are we going to find a place and get settled in that time frame?"

Susan was thinking about the timing, but Scott was thinking about their children. "Susan, how can we move you and the kids down here to Jefferson without Lisa Anne's asking lots of questions? She'll never understand why she's staying this close to her Auntie Lisa and not getting to see her. What will we tell the children?"

Susan was already on the verge of tears, but thinking about how this situation was going to affect Lisa Anne was more than she could handle. "I don't want Lisa Anne knowing any of this—at least not until it's over. We'll have to make up some reason."

"I don't mean to be difficult, but I know our daughter. She's going to ask questions, and we need to have some answers ready. How do we explain that she's only blocks from her Auntie Lisa, yet she can't go see her?"

"All right, I promise we'll think of something to tell her, just not right now. I'm too overwhelmed with all of this to think about what to tell Lisa Anne."

"That's fair. I understand you can't handle it right now. Why don't we finish lunch, and the three of us go over to the jail and see Lisa. Then we can stop and talk to a local real estate agent. Maybe we can find something close by."

Picking up the dishes, Gladys said, "I can ask around at church tomorrow. Maybe someone knows of an available house. If you can't find one right away, you can always start out here and keep looking."

CHAPTER 27

ONLY TWO WEEKS had passed since Lisa's arrest, but everyone was already exhausted. Aunt Gladys and Mrs. Bascom visited her every day, and Scott and Susan drove from Atlanta every other night to see her. After their third visit, Officer Jackson arranged to have the rules bent a little for them. He was able to extend the visiting hours to eight o'clock, allowing Scott to work all day in Atlanta and still drive there and have enough time to visit his sister-in-law. By the time Susan and the children moved to Jefferson, Lisa had been in jail for almost a month.

Although he was needed in Atlanta, Scott took a few days off to get his family settled in. Getting ready to leave, he went into the children's room and gave them each a goodbye kiss. They were still sound asleep, but he had promised both girls he would give them a kiss. He jiggled Lisa Anne's shoulder, just enough to make her stir. "Daddy loves you, punkin."

Without fully waking, she lifted her head long enough to say, "I love you too, Daddy," and she slipped back to sleep.

Susan followed him outside to the car and watched as he placed his things on the seat. Turning around, he took her in his arms. "I hate leaving you here alone, Susan. I know these depositions will be painful for you."

"I'll be all right. I have Aunt Gladys, and you'll be back on Friday."

"I want you to call me every night, and I expect you to tell me the truth. If things start getting too hard, I want you to be honest with me. Once the trial begins, Dad should be back to work fulltime, and I'll come down here and stay."

A few days later, Officer Jackson pulled Susan aside. "Mrs. Thomas, I want to apologize for the way I behaved that first night. You see, I had remembered your sister from her other visits with us. She was such a wreck back then. Because of her foul mouth, we all called her 'the sailor.' She could say words that would make the toughest guy in here blush."

"Yes, I remember those days too." Susan halfheartedly chuckled.

With a sheepish smile, he continued. "Well, I've been watching your sister these past few weeks, and I just wanted to tell you there's no way she's putting on an act. I've listened to her conversations with your aunt Gladys and that Mrs. Bascom. I'm telling you, the woman in that cell is not the same person we had in this jail eleven years ago."

"I know, Officer Jackson. It has not been easy for my sister, but she fought her way back from the pit of hell. I'm glad you're here watching after her and that you'll be the one to walk her back and forth to court. I know you'll do everything in your power to make this as easy as possible for her."

For two months, Susan pushed herself physically and emotionally. Every day she visited Lisa at the jail, trying to help keep her sister's mood positive. Daily she met with Mr. Duncan at his office for two-to-three-hours of reading sessions, reviewing the depositions, going over the volumes of police reports, and helping him piece together their family history. With each deposition, she felt herself giving way a little more. How much more could she take? Having to relive these old memories in such detail was draining her of her strength. On top of these legalities was her concern for her children. Each evening, instead of giving in to her waves of overwhelming depression, she forced a lighthearted appearance until the children were put to bed. She was determined that they would remain happy and stress-free, but the energy it took to feign this happy exterior was taking its toll on her.

One week before the trial was to begin, Scott called. "Your mother stopped by the office today looking for you. I told her you were in Jefferson, but I didn't give her our address there. I don't want her showing up at the door without my being there. I don't want her upsetting you or the children."

Susan had been dreading this news for weeks. "Did she say what she wanted? Scott, Mr. Duncan told me how she behaved during her deposition. At first she wouldn't even agree to an interview. Finally, he forced her with a subpoena. He said the deposition went as expected. She was uncooperative and hostile and has no interest in helping us with Lisa's case."

"So what's new? We all knew she would act like that." As soon as this statement of fact came out of his mouth, Scott regretted it. His sarcasm was not only unnecessary, it had been cruel. "I'm sorry, Suz. I didn't mean to say it that way. Her coming here caught me by surprise, and I guess I'm a little more upset than I thought."

"Honey, we all are. This trial is wearing on all of us. I've been going around here feeling so sorry for myself I caught myself getting angry at Aunt Gladys this afternoon. It was over something really stupid. Even though I knew my emotions were so on-edge at the time, I still said something harsh and hurt her feelings."

"What did you say?" It wasn't that he couldn't picture his aunt's doing something that might irritate Susan; after all, she wasn't perfect. The fact that Susan was so stressed she had responded harshly toward this woman she loved so deeply concerned him.

"It's fine. We made up. We're all getting anxious now that the trial is right on top of us." Wanting to get back to the original subject, Susan related Mr. Duncan's story of her mother's deposition. "Even though she was stubborn and hostile, he did make her understand that she has no choice but to come to court. He said she fairly seethed with anger, but that confrontation happened weeks ago. Why do you suppose she's trying to find me now?"

"I don't know, but I'm glad she doesn't know where you're staying, or about Aunt Gladys. If she comes to the office again, do you want me to give her your phone number? It might be best if you knew what she's up to because she obviously won't talk to me."

"I don't much like the idea of getting a call from her, but if she's determined to reach me, the phone is the least threatening way. I guess it would be all right for you to give her this number. I can always hang up on her if she gets abusive. By the way, Mr. Duncan said the prosecution doesn't have her on their witness list, so she shouldn't be in town for the first week of trial. I doubt she would care to come for any part of the trial she didn't absolutely have to."

"I would agree with that." This time Scott made sure his remark wasn't inflammatory. "Susan, we have only one more week before I move down to stay. I've cleared my calendar for tomorrow and will be able to spend a three-day weekend with you and the kids. I'll pack my things and be down around mid-morning tomorrow."

"Oh, Scott, that sounds wonderful. I know it's late, but do you have to wait until tomorrow?" With as much temptation in her voice as she could muster and trying not to laugh, she coaxed, "I'll be more than happy to wait up for you."

"Suz, you know I'd never turn down such an inviting offer. I'll be there in two hours."

Both laughing, Susan ended the phone call with, "The kids will also be happy to have you for three whole days. Having you here when they wake up will be great."

As soon as she hung up, she headed for the bathroom and drew water. She had two hours before he arrived and wanted to soak in a hot bath and drive the weeks of tension out of her body.

Two hours later, Scott quietly slipped into bed and into Susan's waiting arms. She had endured a hard week, and she needed to feel his body next to hers and to have his smell envelop her. Tonight was all they wanted to think about. Tonight there was no trial, no tension, and no fear. Tonight there were only the two of them, speaking in soft, low tones so they would not wake the children. Even though it was late and they were tired, they wanted to take their time, as if by making love slowly and deliberately, they could force the tension of the past two months out of their room.

They were awakened the next morning by Lisa Anne's diving onto their bed. She had gotten up early and, seeing her daddy's car in the drive- way, came running into their room with a good-morning kiss for him. After having her own special time with her parents, she ran into her room to wake up her little sister and help baby Matthew out of his crib. Soon the whole family was snuggled under the covers. None of them were anxious for the day to start. They were all enjoying their private time together. But all too soon, they heard the back door open and knew Aunt Gladys was in the kitchen making coffee and getting the children's breakfast ready.

Scott slipped into the bathroom for a quick shower while Susan grabbed her robe and headed for the kitchen to help Aunt Gladys.

"I noticed Scott's car in the driveway. Did he drive here last night?"

"Yes. He arrived a little after eleven. He decided to take today off so he could have a three-day weekend with us."

Gladys did not miss the lack of tension in Susan's voice. She had been watching the strain building for days and was happy to see a lighter, hap- pier Susan. "Have you changed your plans then? Are the five of you going to spend the day together?"

"No. If it is all right, we still need you to watch the children. Scott will be going with me to see Lisa." After a moment's hesitation, Susan decided to ask, "Aunt Gladys, have you noticed anything different about Lisa this week? Has she seemed distracted to you?"

"Yes, Ruth and I both noticed it. You've been under so much pressure I didn't want to mention it to you. We hoped it was just the strain of being in jail and because the trial is almost here."

Accepting the cup of coffee Gladys offered, Susan said, "That's what Scott said, but I don't know. It's like she's measuring every word she speaks."

Pouring herself a cup of coffee, Aunt Gladys asked, "Have you asked her?"

"Yes. She says she's fine. But you know what that kind of response is really saying, 'Don't ask any more questions.' "

"Well, Susan, maybe it's true. After all, I don't know how someone going through what she's going through is supposed to act."

"Maybe," Susan conceded, although she didn't really think so. She didn't want to upset Aunt Gladys and decided to let it be.

A few minutes later Scott and the children came bouncing into the kitchen with grins and giggles, and the conversation turned to lighter matters. Lisa Anne pleaded with her daddy to take them to the park, but knowing Scott and Susan would be tied up all day, Aunt Gladys offered, "Lisa Anne, they have to see Auntie Lisa today. Why don't you and I make a special cake for your daddy this morning?"

Always eager to help bake a cake, Lisa turned to her daddy and asked, "What kind do you want? Chocolate?"

Giving a wink to Aunt Gladys for saving the situation, he gave his girls a kiss goodbye and said, "You know chocolate is my very favorite kind. I'll think about that cake all day."

While driving to the jail, he filled Susan in on the family's plans. "Mother and Carol Anne have decided they will take turns coming here every day to sit in the courtroom. They both want to be here for Lisa, but they don't want Carol Anne's kids too upset by the disruption. Dad is busy clearing his calendar in hopes of being able to come for at least a few days."

After pulling into a parking space behind the jail, he leaned over to kiss Susan. "Lisa Anne seems to be handling all this pretty well, isn't she?"

After returning his kiss, Susan added, "She still doesn't understand why she can't go to see Auntie Lisa, but she's being good and not fussing about it. Aunt Gladys and I bring her notes from Auntie Lisa almost every day, and that seems to help. I know six-year-olds can't really grasp the situation, but at least she won't grow up knowing we lied to her. It was good that we told her the truth."

Scott took a deep breath. "I hated telling our little girl what's really going on. Things like this make children have to grow up way too fast. I'm glad we kept it simple and matter-of-fact. She understands that everyone who loves Auntie Lisa is going to court and telling what a kind, sweet person she is and that she couldn't have done this bad thing."

Closing the car door after Susan, Scott continued. "It's too bad we adults can't also believe it could be that simple. None of us really trust the court system these days. People who are obviously guilty seem to walk away free, and people, like Lisa, are found guilty. There's no sure thing when the court is blind."

Susan nodded in agreement and repeated something Mr. Duncan had said to her. "It's funny how that term, the court is blind, has been turned around. Once being blind to a person's rank or position in the community so justice was sure to be honest and fair for all was good. Today, *blind* seems to mean that as long as the prosecution, or in some cases an unscrupulous defense attorney, can manipulate the court into allowing only that evidence that supports their position, they can blind the jury from the truth."

Almost as if thinking out loud, Scott added, "It doesn't seem to be a search for truth these days. It has now turned into a contest between opposing attorneys."

Reaching the top step, Scott opened the door and ushered her inside. They had only a few minutes before visiting hours started and didn't want to waste a minute of it.

It was almost noon before they said their goodbyes to Lisa and headed back to the house. It was Friday afternoon, and they had the whole weekend in front of them. As Scott drove through town, a plan began forming in his head. "Susan, we still have most of the three-day weekend. Why don't we pack a few things and take the children to the shore?"

Utterly amazed at the suggestion, Susan could only respond, "That sounds wonderful!"

More determined than ever, Scott started piecing together the plan. "It's only three hundred miles to Savannah. My cousin, Bill, has a place on the shore. I'm sure I could get him to lend it to us. We could be packed and on the road by two o'clock. The children would love the adventure.

We could be there by ten o'clock tonight and have all day tomorrow to play in the water."

With the image of a day at the shore in her head, the excitement in Susan's voice gave her away. "Do you really think we can get ready that fast?"

"Sure. We don't need to pack very much. I'll call Bill and see if his place is available while Aunt Gladys helps you pack. Susan, we need this break. I don't think we'll make it through the next three weeks if we don't get away for a little fun." Scott noticed the excitement leave her face as he said this. "What? Now what are you thinking about?"

Hesitating for a moment while she pondered her thoughts, Susan then gave him a big, reassuring smile. "It's all right, Scott. I only had a pang of guilt for getting to go off for a fun weekend while Lisa sits in jail, but she would be the first one to tell us to do it. The children need this, and so do we."

Within an hour, they were packed and ready to go. Aunt Gladys had packed a lunch for the family as Susan gathered everyone's beachwear. Lisa Anne decided to help Aunt Gladys, wanting to make sure her chocolate cake got packed, while Megan raced around helping her mother. It had been months since she had seen her girls this excited.

Megan gathered up all her dolls and was busily stuffing them into the suitcase when Susan came back into the bedroom with a stack of towels. "Honey, the dolls need to stay here. You'll be so busy playing in the water, you won't have time to play with your dolls."

Seeing the look of disappointment in her little girl's face, Susan reconsidered. "All right, Megan. Pick two dolls to take along. It's going to be a long drive, and you'll have lots of time to play with them in the car."

While Susan and Aunt Gladys got things ready at home, Scott filled the car with gas and picked up the keys from Bill. As they packed everything and left, Aunt Gladys closed up the house and headed for the jail to visit Lisa. No one knew better than she did how much stress this family had been under. Even though Susan worked very hard at keeping up appearances in front of the children, they knew something was wrong. This little outing was exactly what they needed.

The weekend was over much too soon. Driving back to Atlanta Monday morning, Scott thought about what a great weekend it had been. They had played in the waters of the Savannah seashore, built sandcastles with the children, and watched several old movies in cousin Bill's video collection. Anyone observing this young family would never have guessed what was happening in their lives. Susan had been wonderful. She'd laughed and played with the children as if the world were a thousand miles away. He knew she was worried about Lisa, but she was determined that the family would have fun, and they did.

CHAPTER 28

❧

ALTHOUGH THE ACTUAL trial was scheduled to start the following Monday, Susan and Aunt Gladys went to court every day from Wednesday on. Mr. Duncan thought it would take three days to select a jury, and although Susan was dreading this week, she felt strangely relieved when it finally arrived. Scott was glad there would be no more daily meetings at Mr. Duncan's office. He had everything he needed from Susan, so apart from her twice daily visits to jail, she was going to focus on getting the children prepared.

As he reached the Atlanta city limits, he realized this would be the last time he would drive back here alone. It wouldn't be too long before he could pack up his family and bring them home. He wanted to tuck his children into their own beds, sit with his wife on their front porch, and have this feeling of dread finally gone from their lives.

As Scott was reaching Atlanta, Susan was meeting with the new sitter in Jefferson. Since Gladys needed to be in the courtroom every day, Susan had arranged for Mrs. Anderson, a church friend of Gladys's, to watch the children. Susan wanted the children to get comfortable with her before being left in her care for seven or eight hours every day—once the trial started.

Only Susan, Gladys, and Mrs. Bascom were in the courtroom during the jury selection. The rest of the family would be present when the actual trial started. Although the questioning of each prospective juror was at times monotonous and the repetitive nature of the interviews became rather boring, Susan was determined to listen to each and every response. These were the people who would determine Lisa's future. Although tedious, choosing the jurors was the most important battle Mr. Duncan had ahead of him. If he didn't read these people correctly, it wouldn't much matter how good a job he did presenting his case. He had to pick the right jury.

As he had expected, by late Friday afternoon the jury of twelve, with four alternates, was in place. Opening statements would begin Monday morning. The trial was now officially underway.

Scott moved to Jefferson that weekend, and everyone tried to keep busy. The family found it hard to sleep on Sunday night, knowing what they were waking to the next day.

Monday morning greeted them with the sound of rain's hitting the window. Scott woke up first, realized what day it was, and then turned over and put his arm around his wife. She stirred slightly and then snuggled against him. Brushing her hair away from her face, he lay looking at her and remembered something his father once said. "Son, it's seldom the good times that deepen your love. You'll find it's really when things are the hardest that you two will pull together and, in the struggle, you'll find you come out the other side closer and more in love. So don't you be afraid of hard times." Scott smiled as he remembered those wise words and now understood what he had meant. Studying this incredible woman lying in his arms, Scott leaned over to kiss Susan good morning.

Mrs. Anderson arrived almost an hour before they were to leave for court. She wanted to keep the children busy and allow their parents some quiet time before their leaving. She had coffee ready and some toast and melon slices setting on the counter as they came into the kitchen. They sat with the children for several minutes, trying to remain calm. They were as ready as they could be.

After kissing each child goodbye, they picked up Aunt Gladys and headed for the courthouse.

Ruth Bascom and Caroline were standing on the courthouse steps when they arrived, and the four entered the courtroom together.

As they sat waiting for everyone to enter, Scott wondered what the jury would look like. He hoped there would be more women than men because he feared men might have difficulty seeing Chuck Miller's actions with total honesty. A few minutes later, all the attorneys, the court clerk, the court stenographer, and the bailiff were in place. They were now waiting for Lisa, the jury, and then the judge.

Lisa and Officer Jackson came in a side door, and he walked her to her seat next to Mr. Duncan. She looked very nice in the salmon-colored suit that Susan had brought for her. She was almost forty years old with touches of gray at her temples, but she was still very attractive. She had learned to carry herself with an air of dignity that came from within.

Lisa sat up straight as the jury was ushered in and began taking their seats. She looked each one directly in the face, her eyes never wavering as she nodded an acknowledgment to each member. There were sixteen jurors in all, and they sat in two rows of eight. They all seemed to be studying each person in the courtroom as they entered, trying to absorb as much as possible. All they knew so far was that this was a murder trial, and that Lisa Miller was the accused.

Susan quickly looked from face to face. Twelve of these people were actually impaneled, with four alternates. No one knew which were the twelve, since the court wanted all sixteen to pay close attention to the facts of the case. She counted ten women and six men.

Susan studied the men first. Three were fairly young, probably in their early thirties. Two looked like they could be close to fifty, and the sixth one looked to be around his mid-sixties. She could not tell by looking at them what kind of men they were, but she intended to pay close attention to their facial expressions as they listened to the evidence being presented.

The ten women were fairly evenly divided between young and old. Three looked like they were in their early twenties, three in their mid-thirties, and four looked as if they were in their mid fifties. Most nodded back as Lisa nodded toward them, but two jurors, young women, simply stared back with cynical looks. Susan decided she would pay close attention to these two because their expression made her a little nervous.

The buzzer rang, and the clerk ordered everyone to rise. Judge Kirkley entered and took his seat without looking around. The clerk ordered everyone to be seated, and after the clerk read the charges, the judge addressed the jury. "Having heard the charges, it is not your place to speculate as to anyone's intentions in this case. It is your job to listen only to the facts as they are presented to you and to base your verdict on those facts alone. You are not to be swayed by emotional pleas; rather, you will confine yourself to evidence placed before you in this courtroom."

Leaning forward, as if to emphasize the importance of his next few statements, Judge Kirkley perused the jury. "As you know, this is a murder case, with serious consequences. I do not want the court's time wasted because one of you jurors disobeys these instructions. During the jury selection, each of you was questioned about the numerous articles in the local newspaper regarding this case. I expect you to continue avoiding any outside sources while you sit on this jury. You are not to talk about this case among yourselves until the case has been handed to you, and you are not to discuss this case with anyone else until a verdict has been reached. Any misconduct on your part will be severely dealt with by this court. I hope you understand this."

Having sat on the bench in this small Southern town for almost thirty years, Kirkley prided himself as a no-nonsense, total-control judge. He considered it his personal mission to protect the integrity of the legal system he loved dearly, and he was respected and feared by prosecutors and defense attorneys alike. He was not someone to rub the wrong way. He was proud that he came from the old school of law and took pleasure in making life difficult for any ill-prepared attorney who entered his courtroom.

Turning to the prosecutor, Kirkley took note of the new suit Gordon was wearing. The shine on those new wingtips could blind an elephant. Having been forced to socialize with prosecutor Gordon at different political events over the past ten years, seemingly Judge Kirkley had never particularly liked him. Gordon's curt New Jersey attitude had done little to ingratiate himself to anyone in this town. Observing his behavior over the past three months as Gordon turned this case into a small-town circus had only increased Kirkley's contempt for him. That Gordon was parlaying this case into political fodder for his personal career goals had been obvious to many. However, as long as Gordon remained within the legal boundaries, Kirkley would allow him to keep flying high—even though the man's theatrics disgusted him. With a formal smile, Kirkley addressed Gordon. "Are you ready for your opening statement?"

Responding in kind, Gordon nodded and smiled as he rose to his feet and took the floor. Prosecutor Gordon could be described only as a climber. His every move was carefully planned to enhance his career. Having come to Jefferson some ten years earlier, he had had to fight against the "outsider" attitude of this small community from the get-go. For ten years he had been shunned and ignored, making his roots of bitterness and resentment toward this town run very deep. Having lost his bid for district attorney two years earlier, he knew he needed a splashy case to break into this town's protected inner circle, and Lisa's case offered exactly that. For the past three months he had become the toast of Jefferson, being asked to speak at the local men's service club, a club into which he had been denied entry for five years.

For months, with the help of an editor friend, he had been planting stories in the local paper about Lisa's past. The daily editorials read like a dime-store novel, and people were buzzing about the upcoming murder trial. His plan was to make the citizens of Jefferson believe that he, and he alone, stood between this wanton woman and their young sons. Gordon knew that, in a small town like Jefferson, a titillating murder trial does not often come along. He intended to make the best of this opportunity, and he had. This normally half-empty courtroom was now filled with curious spectators.

After a quick sweep of the room, Gordon turned to the bench and responded, "Yes, Your Honor, the state is indeed ready with opening statements."

Walking toward the jury box with an almost theatrical demeanor, Gordon began his opening statement. "Ladies and gentlemen, the state intends to prove that Ms. Miller, a known prostitute and drug abuser, did shoot and kill Mr. Charles Miller, her father. We intend to show how Mr. Miller, trying to reason with his daughter to change her ways, admittedly lost control of himself and beat her, causing some serious injuries to Ms. Miller. Mr. Miller was wrong, but you will learn what Mr. Miller knew. He had an out-of-control daughter who was living a shameful lifestyle, and he was desperate. For this act, he was prosecuted and served time in prison.

"After Mr. Miller paid his debt to society, we contend that he was simply trying to contact his daughter, hoping to find out if she was well and healthy—like any caring father would do. We will show that Ms. Miller, reminded of the severe beating she had received at his hand, took this opportunity to extract the revenge that had been seething within her for more than ten years, and she shot and killed him.

"We will also offer into evidence volumes of court records outlining Ms. Miller's bawdy lifestyle and allow you to see what Mr. Charles Miller saw: a woman in desperate need of correction, yet a woman who had no intention of listening to her father. We will offer into evidence the autopsy reports, which prove that Mr. Miller was struck in the head with an unknown object before being shot. These findings prove that he was not, as Ms. Miller claims, the aggressor in this case, but rather that he was waylaid from behind and then shot.

"We believe, after you study this evidence, you will conclude, as we have, that Ms. Miller's account of that night could not possibly have happened. We will show that she deliberately intended to shoot and kill her father that night."

With his opening statement completed, Mr. Gordon smirked at Lisa as he returned to his seat. Leaning back in his chair, he folded his fingers. With his index fingers pressed against his mouth, he ran his eyes across the jury, trying to evaluate the effects of what he had just said. He was counting on the fact that most people, once they knew Lisa's history, would understand how little her word could be trusted. Besides, the facts simply did not match her account of that night.

Mr. Duncan's opportunity to address the jury now came. Before standing, he reached over to lightly squeeze Lisa's forearm. He thought about how he loved to defend an innocent client, and he had absolutely no question in his mind as to Lisa's innocence. As he rose to address the jury, he pondered the still unanswered questions in this case. *Lisa, Lisa, everything about your story fits together perfectly—except the autopsy report. No matter how many times you replay that night, you cannot explain the blow to the back of his head. What are you hiding? I know you're not guilty, but I'm not so sure you're altogether telling the truth either.*

Giving Lisa a reassuring wink, he turned and walked confidently to the jury box. "Ladies and gentlemen of the jury, the prosecution has painted a very interesting picture of Charles Miller. He would have you believe that Charles Miller was simply a concerned, caring father, trying very hard to win back his wayward daughter. After all, if one of you had a daughter caught up in drugs and prostitution, wouldn't you do absolutely anything in your power to get her back?"

Mr. Duncan had, at this point, positioned himself directly in front of the most elderly looking man on the jury, looking directly at him, as he continued, "The prosecution has made it sound like, in Mr. Miller's over-wrought condition, he simply made the mistake of taking a well-deserved spanking of his daughter a little too far. Ladies and gentlemen, that as-sessment is as far from the truth as one can get. We will prove, beyond a shadow of a doubt, that Charles Miller was never a concerned father.

"We will bring several witnesses, both inside and outside of this fam-ily, who will help you see Charles Miller for the monster he really was. We will produce witnesses and hospital records, for both my client and her mother, showing the extent to which Charles Miller was willing to go when angry. This man was no caring, concerned father. You can be sure we will prove that fact to you before this trial is over.

"Secondly, the prosecution would have you believe that you are sitting here looking at a drug-using prostitute who has simply been cleaned up for this trial. That estimation is as big a lie as the other. We will prove that my client, Lisa Miller, although she once was all those things, has for the past eleven years led an upstanding, honest, hard-working life, with many friends, fellow employees, and family willing to testify on her behalf. We will show that Lisa Miller was not, as the prosecution would have you believe, raging with anger, wanting revenge. Although after finding out what I have about Charles Miller, I would not have blamed her.

"The prosecution will show you who Lisa Miller was. I intend to show you who Lisa Miller has become. And then, ladies and gentlemen, when you understand that fact, you will know what the rest of us know, that Lisa Miller absolutely acted in self-defense, and you must find her not guilty."

Mr. Duncan slowly returned to his seat and again squeezed Lisa's arm. He did not intend to lose this battle.

Judge Kirkley leaned forward in his chair and cleared his throat for effect. He then looked from Lisa to Mr. Duncan to Mr. Gordon and then to the jury. Once again, he was reminding everyone in the room that he, and he alone, was in control of everyone in his courtroom. Slowly his eyes moved back to Mr. Gordon, and after a theatrical pause, he said, "Mr. Gordon, you may call your first witness."

"If it please the court, I would call Detective Joseph Westland to the stand."

The clerk called out the detective's name, and he was sworn in. After he was seated, Mr. Gordon stepped closer to the witness box. He then asked the detective if he was, as the records indicated, the one who had arrested Ms. Miller the night of the shooting.

"Yes, sir. I was the third officer to arrive at the scene but the first to actually approach Ms. Miller after she put down the gun."

The detective had done this before. He was speaking directly to the jury, instead of to Mr. Gordon. Jurors seldom questioned the word of an officer, and he had been instructed to speak with confidence directly to them.

"Detective Westland, where was the defendant standing before she dropped the gun?" Gordon wanted the jury to form a mental picture of Lisa's holding a smoking gun, standing over a dead body.

"She was standing over the victim." Westland's eyes slowly swept the jury box.

"Detective Westland, was the victim still alive when you reached him?"

"No, sir. He was dead at the scene."

Mr. Gordon moved closer to the jury box so the eyes of the jurors would tend to move from the witness to him. He did not want their eyes to focus on Lisa or anyone else in the courtroom as he questioned the detective. "Detective Westland, how many times did you have to yell at Ms. Miller before she was willing to drop her gun?"

"Three times, sir."

Mr. Gordon then walked over to the exhibit table, picked up a handgun, and walked to the witness stand. Handing it to the witness, Gordon asked, "Do you recognize this gun?"

"Yes, sir. This is my mark. This is the gun Ms. Miller was holding as I entered the alley." He purposely held up the gun so the jury could have a good look. They wanted the jury to visualize this gun in Lisa's hand.

"Tell me, Detective, has that gun been tested to determine for certain that it was the same gun that killed Charles Miller?"

"Yes, sir, it was. This is definitely the same gun that was used to kill Charles Miller."

"Were there any fingerprints on that gun?"

Westland had worked with Prosecutor Gordon before and knew better than to jump ahead of his questions. Gordon was a savvy prosecutor, and he loved to build the questions, pulling the jury along, until he was able to stick their noses right where he wanted them.

Westland simply answered, "Yes, sir, there were."

"Tell us, Detective, did you find Charles Miller's fingerprints on that gun?"

"No, sir, we did not."

Gordon slowly returned to the front of the jury box, leaned against the rail, and then looked over at Lisa. His eyes did not leave her face as he asked his next question: "Detective, whose prints did you find on that gun?"

"Lisa Miller's fingerprints were on this gun." He again slightly lifted the gun for effect.

"Detective, is that a registered gun?"

"No, sir. This is commonly referred to as a Saturday night special. The traceable markings have been filed off, giving us no way of tracing its ownership."

"So, Detective, where might Lisa Miller have purchased this gun?"

Duncan was instantly on his feet. "Objection, Your Honor. Calls for speculation on the part of the witness and assumes it was Lisa Miller, and not Charles Miller, who actually made the purchase."

Gordon spun around and gave Duncan a disgusted look. "Your Honor, Detective Westland's responsibility at the Jefferson Police Department is to track down and know where Saturday night specials such as this are bought and sold."

Judge Kirkley's eyes narrowed slightly as he looked over at Mr. Gordon. "Yes, I'm sure he is quite an expert on most Saturday night specials. However, that familiarity does not make him an expert on that particular one, nor does it prove who might have purchased it. Objection sustained. Move on."

Gordon had lost the first tug-of-war. He knew the jury usually kept a mental note of wins and losses, so he didn't want to appear fazed by this. "Detective Westland, is it difficult for an average person to locate and purchase one of these guns, say, here in Jefferson?"

"No, sir. I'm sorry to say it is actually quite easy. Anyone with fifty dollars can have one in two hours."

"Thank you. Now, when you arrested the defendant, was any test ordered to prove or disprove the presence of gunpowder on Lisa Miller's hands?"

"Yes, sir. Within thirty minutes of arriving at the station."

"Can you tell the court the results of that test?"

"Yes, sir. Lisa Miller's right hand had sufficient residue to indicate that she had fired this gun."

Duncan was on his feet again. "Objection, Your Honor. That test can only prove she fired *a* gun. It cannot prove that she fired that particular gun."

Duncan knew this was a moot point, but he could not allow Mr. Gordon's statement to go unchallenged. It was important for the jury to know that Mr. Gordon was attempting to draw a conclusion unsupported by fact. He needed them to remember this fact later, when they might need to question something else Mr. Gordon might have said.

Judge Kirkley leaned forward, looked directly at the detective and then to the court clerk. "Objection sustained. The jury will disregard Detective Westland's response. Continue, Mr. Gordon."

"Detective, did the test indicate that Lisa Miller had fired a weapon?"

"Yes, sir, it certainly did."

"Was a test performed on the hands of the victim as well, and if so, what were the results?"

"Yes, sir, the coroner's report indicated that Mr. Miller had not fired a gun."

Gordon's questioning of Detective Westland was going exactly as he had planned. The questioning lasted for almost two hours, with Mr. Gordon's going over everything from the placement of the body, the direction of the bullet's entry, to the distance of the gun from the body when it had been fired. He produced diagrams, showing the comparative heights of both the victim and the defendant, tracing the bullet angle as it entered Charles Miller.

"Detective Westland, have you had the opportunity to read the autopsy report on Mr. Miller?"

"Yes, sir, I have."

"Are you then aware of his findings that Mr. Miller suffered a fatal blow to the head that night?"

"Yes, sir." Westland didn't take his eyes off Gordon. They had played this out several times in his office, and he knew the questions that were coming.

"Let me ask another question regarding that night, Detective. Were you aware of this blow while still at the scene that night?"

"No, sir. That evening we all thought we were dealing with only a shooting case."

"Why is that, Detective Westland?"

"Because the head injury was not evident. The blow was at the base of the skull. There was no blood, and the skull looked normal. Besides, he had suffered an abdominal gunshot wound that led us to believe that was the cause of death."

"Now, Detective Westland, did you cordon off the crime scene and search the entire area?"

"Yes, sir. Every scrap of paper in that alley was studied."

"To your knowledge, Detective Westland, was anything found in that alley that could possibly have caused that blow to Mr. Miller's head?"

"No, sir."

"Was he possibly slammed backward, say, during a fight, where his head could have struck something in that alley, causing this injury?"

"No, sir. We went over everything and couldn't find anything that matched the injury."

Gordon then questioned Detective Westland regarding the interrogation of Lisa Miller, repeating the dozen or so questions they had asked Lisa that night. "Now Detective, I want you to look through your notes and tell me, did Ms. Miller ever mention striking her father that night?"

Westland dramatically thumbed through his notebook. He knew exactly what Gordon was doing. "No, sir."

"Did she mention possibly pushing him backward, say against something that might have caused this injury?"

"No, sir."

"So let me understand you correctly. Nothing was recovered from the scene that could have produced that injury?"

"Nothing."

Gordon continued his questioning of Detective Westland. He intended to question the witness up until the noon hour so the jury would go to lunch with all this evidence fresh in their minds. He did not want Duncan to have an opportunity to cross-examine this witness before they had time to digest his testimony and lock it in their minds. He knew some things would be clarified under cross-examination, but he had learned that sometimes jurors can be persuaded, and then it is very hard to dissuade them, and the more time between these two, the better.

As he had planned, Judge Kirkley interrupted him as he was about to ask his last question to suggest they break for lunch. Mr. Gordon politely nodded agreement, returned to his seat, and announced that he was finished with this witness. Judge Kirkley again admonished the jury not to discuss the case and ordered everyone to return promptly at one-thirty. The bailiff then ordered everyone to stand as Judge Kirkley left the bench. The bailiff then opened the side door, allowing the jurors to exit as everyone else stood at attention until the jury had been removed.

Duncan had dozens of pages of notes he needed to review during the lunch break in order to have his questions clearly organized so he would be ready to cross-examine Detective Westland. He reviewed his notes while he ate a bite of lunch. There weren't any surprises here, for which he was grateful. But almost three months of investigation and studying the evidence still left some unanswered questions. Westland's testimony bothered him. *Gordon's running a smoke screen. He knows I can handle the gun and fingerprints issue. He probably knows I can explain almost everything about that night except the head injury. No matter how many times I re-enact Lisa's account, I cannot come up with a rational explanation for how that head injury happened.*

Duncan studied the outline of the courthouse across the street. He had been looking out of this window for fourteen years now, and the view still excited him. As if speaking to some invisible audience in his office, Duncan pondered, "The courtroom is still the best thing this country has ever produced. Even with all the lawyer jokes, being able to stand in that courtroom and protect someone's right to a fair trial is the most wonderful job on this earth. But I have found that in doing so, care must be taken. Never ever ask a question without having the answer to that question. I must make that head injury a nonissue. Since I cannot explain it, I must treat it as an unexplained trauma that somehow happened during the life-and-death scuffle. Hopefully, by the time I discredit Westland and Gordon for their underhanded maneuvers, the jury will consider the head injury an unimportant piece of the puzzle—at least I sure hope so."

CHAPTER 29

BACK AT THE courthouse, Officer Jackson moved Lisa to a large conference room adjacent to the courtroom. As they reached the door, he turned to Scott and said, "She'll be having her lunch in here every day. If you would like to grab a sandwich from the lunch cart in the courtyard, you're welcome to eat your lunch with her."

"Thank you, we'd love to." Scott turned to the others and said, "Why don't you go in with Lisa? I'll run out to the lunch cart and get us something."

A few minutes later Scott knocked on the door and was allowed to enter. Before passing out the sandwiches, Scott suggested, "I feel we need to take a few moments and ask God for wisdom and mercy. " As everyone bowed their heads, a quiet, but very firm, "Amen," came from Officer Jackson. Scott lifted his head just long enough to give Officer Jackson a wink and a smile. No one commented on the "amen," and they all sat quietly for several minutes, concentrating more acutely on their lunches than any of the sandwiches merited. Sitting there, trying to keep a light conversation going, none of them could believe how exhausted they felt. The tension of sitting in that courtroom, listening to all of the information being covered, was tiring. Right or wrong, it was tiring. They all agreed they were too exhausted to sit and rehash the morning's testimony, but finding themselves unable to concentrate on anything else made conversation difficult.

As was customary, the bailiff relieved Officer Jackson for a thirty-minute break. When he returned, he picked up his lunch tray and sat at a small table stationed by the door.

Because everyone was emotionally drained, no one knew exactly what to say. Without thinking, Officer Jackson spoke up. "I think Mr. Duncan did a great job with his opening statement, Lisa. It was very powerful, and I think several of the jurors responded positively to him." Suddenly realizing how inappropriate his attempted assurance was, Jackson quickly turned back to his lunch.

An embarrassed Lisa giggled and responded, "I do too, Ben. But Mr. Duncan said his hardest job would be to win over the judge. He said if Judge Kirkley thinks you're a pest, he can make your job really tough; but, on the other hand, if he sees an attorney fighting hard, using the law to fight back, he tends to lighten up. It's way too early to tell, but I feel Mr. Duncan knows what he's doing."

Aunt Gladys shot a quick glance toward Susan. Neither of them missed the fact that Lisa had just called Officer Jackson by his first name, but now was not the time to touch that subject. The two women simply smiled and tucked away this little bit of information for a later conversation.

After lunch, they took turns using the restroom and were sitting around chatting when the bailiff came to get them. Scott, Susan, Caroline, Aunt Gladys, and Mrs. Bascom each kissed Lisa on the cheek and then left to take their seats.

A few minutes later, Officer Jackson brought Lisa back into the courtroom. When everyone was present, the clerk called the courtroom to order, and Judge Kirkley entered and took his seat. After acknowledging everyone, Judge Kirkley ordered the clerk to re-seat Detective Westland and then turned him over to the defense. Mr. Duncan had decided he would remain seated next to his client as he cross-examined the detective. He wanted the jury to see Lisa every time their eyes came back to him as he asked a question.

Duncan also decided he would not address the witness by his title. He wanted the jury to see this person sitting in the witness box as a man—not as a detective.

"Mr. Westland, let's go over your previous testimony, item by item, shall we? You stated you were the third officer to enter that alley. Is that correct?"

The prosecutor had reminded him to keep his responses as brief as possible, and he intended to do exactly that. "Yes, sir."

"Mr. Westland, you stated my client was standing over Charles Miller. Is that correct?" Duncan had no intention of calling him the victim. He wanted the jury to remember the body was Charles Miller—not some *victim*.

"Yes, sir."

"Can you be more specific, Mr. Westland? Was Lisa straddling the body?"

"Well, no."

"Was she standing over his head by any chance?"

"No. No, she wasn't."

"Well, Mr. Westland, if she wasn't straddling the body, and she wasn't standing over his head, where was she? You said she was standing over the body."

Westland quickly glanced toward Gordon and then looked back at Duncan. Because of where Duncan had seated himself, Westland couldn't direct his answers to the jury. "Well, she was leaning against the back door."

"I see. And where exactly was the body in relation to Lisa Miller?"

"Well, his feet were about two feet from hers, I guess."

"You guess? Mr. Westland, didn't the department take photos and markings of the crime scene?"

A flat yes was Westland's only retort, so Duncan stood up, walked over to the same table from which Mr. Gordon had taken the gun and picked up a cardboard sheet with ten to twelve photos on it. He handed it to Westland and then returned to his seat. "Mr. Westland, do you recognize those photos, marked exhibit seven?"

"Yes, sir. They're the police photos of the scene." As he answered, he noticed Mr. Gordon lean forward in his chair. He knew better than to offer any information that was not directly asked for, and he shot a glance at Gordon and then back at Duncan.

"That's right. Using those photos to refresh your memory, how far away from Charles Miller's body was Lisa Miller standing when you entered that alley?"

Westland studied the pictures for several seconds and then laid them on the rail in front of him. He looked over at Duncan. "She was about three feet away from him."

"So let's clear this up for the record. You now say she was not standing over Charles Miller; rather, she was approximately three feet away. Is that right?"

"Yes." Westland had warned Gordon about trying a stunt like this, and he was angry that he was the one sitting up on the witness stand looking foolish.

"Now, Mr. Westland, you also stated that you had to yell at my client three times before she would drop the gun she was holding. Is that also true?"

"Yes. I had to yell at her three times before she would drop the gun."

The smug look on Westland's face as he gave this answer made Duncan's blood boil. He was going to have fun wiping it off. "Now tell me, Mr. Westland, exactly when did one of the officers order the alarm company to shut off the burglar alarm?"

"I don't know. Actually, I think Officer Swanson directed Ms. Miller to turn it off."

"Exactly. And when did Officer Swanson direct Lisa Miller to shut off the alarm?"

"As soon as we had control of the crime scene."

"Now Mr. Westland, would you say you would be in control of the crime scene while a suspect is still in possession of a gun?"

Westland knew where this questioning was going and again looked over at Gordon, who did not look up. "No, sir."

Duncan was enjoying this. "So Lisa Miller must have dropped the gun before she was allowed to shut off the alarm. Isn't that correct, Mr. Westland?"

"I would suppose so. Yes."

"So since Lisa had to drop the gun before she could shut off the alarm, can I assume that the alarm was blasting while you were ordering my client to drop the gun?"

Westland's smirk was totally gone. "Yes."

"Can I also assume that the reason you had to yell at my client three times was not because she refused to obey, but rather that she could not hear you yelling your command?"

By now Detective Westland was keeping his eyes on the prosecutor. He was obviously upset with him, and the jury knew it. "Yah, that's possible."

Duncan then left his seat and went over to the exhibit table. He picked up the gun, walked over, and handed it to the witness. Knowing what his next few questions were going to be, Mr. Duncan took the photos and laid them back on the evidence desk. He intended to be very dramatic in a moment or two.

"Now, Mr. Westland, is that the same gun, exhibit three, that you held this morning?"

"Yes." This time the gun remained in his lap. He did not hold it up.

"You testified, did you not, that the only fingerprints on that gun belonged to my client, Lisa Miller?"

"Yes. That's what the lab report said."

Duncan stood very still for several seconds, staring at the witness. Then, as if disgusted, he returned to the evidence desk, again retrieved the photos, and handed them to the witness.

With all of the disgust he could put in his voice, Mr. Duncan turned to the witness and said, "Mr. Westland, will you please look at exhibit seven again—specifically the photo marked 'D'. Is it not the only photo that shows Charles Miller's hand?"

Westland shot a glance toward Gordon. Both of them had made certain that particular photo had been removed before turning them over to Duncan. *How did he get his hands on it?*

Westland nodded yes, whereupon Judge Kirkley interjected, "Detective Westland, the court recorder cannot record head movements. Please respond using words."

"Yes," was Westland's only response.

Stepping over so he was standing directly in front of the witness box, Duncan asked, "Mr. Westland, look at the photo. Can you please tell the jury what is on that one exposed hand of Charles Miller?"

Westland took a deep breath and let it out very slowly. He did not look up, but rather, with his head down, and looking at the photo, he said very quietly, "A glove."

"Excuse me, Mr. Westland? I don't think the court heard that reply. What did you say?"

Westland lifted his head, looked over at Duncan with a blank face, and calmly repeated a little louder, "A glove."

By now, Duncan had returned to his table and was sitting on the front edge, leaning slightly forward so the jury could be sure to see Lisa sitting behind him. "So the reason why no fingerprints were on the gun belonging to Charles Miller, Mr. Westland, was because Charles Miller had gloves on at the time. Is that a more accurate testimony, Mr. Westland?"

"Yes."

"So can we also assume that the gunpowder test on Charles Miller was negative for the same reason, Mr. Westland?"

"Yes."

"Now, Mr. Westland, did the department do a gunpowder test on those gloves?"

"No, sir."

"Why not? Whatever were you thinking? Did anyone suggest testing those gloves, Mr. Westland? I would be very careful how I answered that question if I were you."

Westland pondered for a moment, trying to decide how he was going to play this. Was Duncan playing poker, or had someone talked to him? He'd gotten his hands on that photo. That wasn't a bluff. Westland's partner, Detective Swanson, had stabbed him in the back before. Swanson always refused to go along.

Deciding he would not perjure himself for Gordon, Westland looked up and said, "Yah, Swanson did, but the lab test was canceled later."

Moving next to Prosecutor Gordon's table, Duncan asked his next question. "Do you know who gave that cancellation order?"

Westland looked from Duncan to Gordon and then back to Duncan. "Gordon did. He said it wasn't necessary and asked us to pull the lab order after the medical report came back about the head injury."

"Is it normal for the prosecutor to control what lab work is done by the police department, Mr. Westland?"

"It is around here when it's one of Gordon's cases," sneered Westland.

Duncan took the photos back and stood staring at them for a moment. Suddenly, he spun around as if realizing something terribly wrong with this picture. "Mr. Westland, if Charles Miller was simply *checking up* on his daughter, why do you suppose he was wearing gloves?"

Gordon was on his feet before Duncan even finished the question. "I object, Your Honor. The question calls for speculation."

Duncan turned and smiled at Gordon, and before Judge Kirkley had a chance to rule, Duncan said, "I'll rephrase it. Mr. Westland, Charles Miller did have latex gloves on that night, did he not?"

"Yes."

"If my client, Lisa Miller, had been found beaten to death in that alley, would Charles Miller, having recently been released from prison, have been a primary suspect by the Jefferson Police Department?"

Gordon was again on his feet. "Your Honor, Mr. Duncan is asking the witness to speculate. We could 'what-if' all day. Lisa Miller was not beaten to death. Charles Miller was murdered."

Duncan stepped in front of the judge's desk to argue. "Your Honor, those gloves go to motive. There is no reasonable explanation for a convicted criminal to be wearing gloves in that alley that night unless he was intending to do something that would land him back in prison. The gloves indicate intent, Your Honor. My client did not have gloves on; Charles Miller did."

Judge Kirkley looked over at Gordon, who was muttering something under his breath. "I'm going to allow this line of questioning. But Mr. Duncan, I'm going to limit your questions to reasonable suppositions. Stay away from the victim's intent, since no one here can speak to that issue."

"Yes, Your Honor." Duncan then returned to the witness box and stood directly in front of Westland, blocking his view of Gordon.

"Mr. Westland, would it be safe to say Charles Miller would have been a primary suspect of the Jefferson Police Department if Lisa Miller had been found dead?"

"Yah, I suppose so."

"Mr. Westland, would the Jefferson Police Department have dusted the area for fingerprints if she had been found murdered?"

"Yes."

Duncan then moved over and stood beside Gordon's seat and asked his final question. "Mr. Westland, you were investigating a murder scene where one of the parties was a recently released convicted criminal wearing latex gloves. A powder residue test on those gloves was ordered and then canceled. Did you ever hear anyone in your department ask why?"

Westland's eyes narrowed slightly, trying to weigh his answer against what Duncan might know. "I didn't ask. I figured it wasn't necessary."

"That's not what I asked you, Mr. Westland. Did you ever hear anyone ask why the test was canceled?" Duncan's eyes never left Westland's face.

"I'm not sure; maybe." Westland knew Duncan was probably fishing, and thought, *If you knew anything, you'd have called Swanson to the stand. But then again, maybe you're trying to trap me into perjuring myself, and then you'll call Swanson up here to contradict my testimony. Swanson's such a twit, always running right by the book. He can't be trusted to cover a buddy's back—like the time I forgot to mirandize that guy. We caught him dead to rights, and the creep got to walk because Swanson wouldn't go along with me and say that I had mirandized the jerk. It would have been our word against his, and he was guilty, so what's the big fuss? Sometimes you gotta bend things a little to accomplish the greater good. Everyone wants us to get the bad guys off the streets; they just don't want to know how we do it.*

Hearing Judge Kirkley addressing him, Westland realized he had not been listening and had obviously missed a question. "Excuse me, Your Honor. What was the question?"

Judge Kirkley leaned in closer, "Detective Westland, Mr. Duncan asked you a question. Did you not hear it?"

With a shrug, Westland turned to Judge Kirkley and said, "I'm sorry. I was thinking about something else." Then looking at Mr. Duncan, he asked, "Can you repeat the question?"

"Certainly." Duncan smiled. "Mr. Westland, you either have or have not heard someone question why the test was canceled. Which is it?"

With a cold stare, Westland sat up in his seat. "Yes, the question was asked."

Duncan knew he had finally split up this duo. Westland had finally decided to break ranks and protect himself. "Mr. Westland, who asked, and to whom did he ask?"

"Detective Swanson asked Gordon why he had cancelled the test. He said he had a problem with the gloves, but Gordon said it didn't matter now that the coroner's report was in. Gordon said this was a slam-dunk case, and the citizens of Jefferson would be grateful to get someone like Lisa Miller off our streets. Everything pointed to her guilt, and we had enough to convict her so we didn't need to bother."

"Again, Mr. Westland, is it customary for the prosecutor to override the working detectives' request for evidence?"

"No, sir, not usually. But Swanson wasn't used to working with Gordon. That's why he questioned it."

Duncan looked at Mr. Gordon, then the jury, and back to Westland. "I have no further questions of this witness, Your Honor."

Duncan then returned to his seat next to Lisa while Judge Kirkley stared at Gordon. "Do you have any redirect for this witness, Mr. Gordon?"

He received a curt, "No."

"Then you may call your next witness, Mr. Gordon."

Duncan sat next to Lisa, smiling. He knew he had stung Gordon pretty well, but he also knew that first strikes don't always win. Much more was coming, and jurors can be pushed back and forth throughout a trial. The side that pushes last is the one the jury remembers. Even though he was feeling fairly good, he had no intention of getting cocky.

Throughout the week, Gordon called every corrections officer who had ever dealt with Lisa. He even subpoenaed her parole officer from California, who painted a graphic picture of a very wild, out-of-control, angry young woman. Gordon also handed the jury page after page of court documents, showing the years of repeat offenses and jail time. He was painting a picture for the jury so they would see what he saw—a woman the good citizens of Jefferson would not want on their streets. He had made sure the citizens of Jefferson knew how hard he was working to protect them from the likes of people like Lisa Miller. He was counting on the common presumption that people don't really change.

On Thursday afternoon, Gordon called the coroner to the stand. After being sworn in, Dr. Kozak carefully answered every question put to him by Prosecutor Gordon.

"Dr. Kozak, did you actually perform the autopsy on Charles Miller?"

"Yes, sir."

Handing Dr. Kozak a stack of reports from the evidence table, Gordon continued. "These reports are marked exhibit six. Are these autopsy findings introduced into evidence on Monday your findings?"

After a quick glance, he said, "Yes, they are."

"Now, Dr. Kozak, the court has heard the findings regarding the bullet entry. We have heard that the weapon was fired from a very close range, in an upward trajectory. Is that in agreement with your findings?"

"Yes. The wound did indicate that the gun was within two or three inches of Mr. Miller when fired."

"Now, Dr. Kozak, can you tell us, was that bullet wound the only life-threatening wound sustained by Mr. Miller that evening?"

Looking at the jury, Dr. Kozak very deliberately said, "No, sir, it was not."

Stepping closer to the witness stand, as if to be filled in on some juicy new tidbit, Gordon, with a look of surprise on his face, asked, "It wasn't? Well, what other life-threatening wound did you find?"

"During the autopsy, it was discovered that Mr. Miller received a substantial blow to the back of his head." Then turning his back to the jury and placing his hand on the back of his own head to indicate the exact spot, he said, "Right here at the base of the skull."

"Dr. Kozak, were you able to determine what type of object might have caused such an injury?"

"Yes. The wound indicates the object was some type of two-inch smooth cylinder; it could have been a pipe of some type. Not having the actual object, one can only suppose."

"Dr. Kozak, is it possible that Mr. Miller, while in a physical altercation, might have been shoved backward? Say, while someone was trying to defend himself or herself from his attack? Could that be possible?"

"No, sir, for two reasons." Dr. Kozak then waited for Gordon to ask what those two reasons were.

Gordon walked over toward the defense table so the jury would look at Lisa as they heard the evidence that would convict her. "Well, Dr. Kozak, would you please tell this court the first reason you feel that would not be possible."

"Yes. If it please the court, may I use a diagram of the alley to illustrate how the body would have had to come in contact with the object, if pushed?" Dr. Kozak knew he would be allowed, and he was prepared. Stepping out of the witness box, he placed a large drawing of the alley behind the bakery on an easel.

Turning toward the jury and speaking directly to them, he said, "We searched this alley. Because of the placement and direction of the wound and the height of the victim, for the wound to be caused by someone's shoving him back against something, two things would have had to happen. First, he would have had to be in a falling movement, not simply a backward movement. A backward movement would have produced a blow to this portion of the skull, at least three inches higher. The indentation at the base of the skull indicates the object would have had to be about three feet from the ground, and that Mr. Miller's head would have had to be slumped forward, his chin almost touching his chest as he fell backward, striking the object."

Gordon leaned forward, still close to Lisa, and asked, "So if that is possible, could the defendant have simply shoved the victim, causing this injury?"

"No, sir."

With mock disbelief, Gordon questioned, "Why? Why isn't that possible?"

Looking directly at the jury, Dr. Kozak gave the same answer Duncan had been coming up with for two months. "Because no exterior pipes are mounted to the walls of that building. There are none."

After allowing this information to sink in a little, Gordon pushed on. "All right, Dr. Kozak. We now know the injury did not occur by the victim's being shoved. What is the second reason?"

Kozak gave a haughty smirk and responded, "The very nature of the wound. This blow rendered Mr. Miller unconscious almost immediately. Death, if no other wounds had been introduced, would still have come. It would have taken between two and three minutes but without the victim's regaining consciousness. The indentation to the skull indicates Mr. Miller's head was forward, as if looking down, and the blow would have come from above."

Gordon then asked the question he had been maneuvering toward for two hours. "Dr. Kozak, is this injury to Charles Miller a wound that is commonly seen in victims who have been waylaid from behind?"

"Yes, sir. It is."

"Dr. Kozak, can you tell which wound came first? The gunshot or the head wound?"

"No, not exactly. We do know the victim only lived two or three minutes after the head wound. We also know his heart was still pumping for one or two minutes after being shot. As to which wound came first, it would be impossible to say with exact certainty."

Stepping back to his seat, Gordon announced, "I have no further questions for this witness, Your Honor."

It was almost five o'clock before Gordon had finished with his witness. The judge, noting the hour, brought the day to a close. As Duncan studied the faces of the jury, he knew his side had received a devastating blow this afternoon. Gordon had painted a perfectly rational explanation of what could have happened that night, making Lisa appear to be the aggressor. The jury's body language was obviously negative. In so many words, they had been told that Lisa was trash, and her story didn't match the facts. Dr. Kozak's testimony was strong and convincing, and they were buying it.

As Duncan packed up his files, he remembered a crude, old-time lawyer who had taught at his law school. This character was a favorite of the students and was famous for his down-home witticisms. One in particular fit right now. He used to say, "Boys, if ever your opponent lays a huge pile of cow manure in front of you, don't never stir it. Stirring won't ever make it go away; it just makes it smell worse." Duncan did not know what Lisa was hiding. All he knew was that he would not cross-examine this witness.

The first thing Friday morning, Dr. Kozak was reseated in the witness stand, and Judge Kirkley turned him over to Duncan to cross-examine. Remaining seated and sporting a more positive attitude than he really felt, Duncan replied, "Your Honor, the defense has no questions for this witness."

Dr. Kozak smiled broadly at Mr. Gordon as he stepped down from the stand.

Judge Kirkley gave Mr. Duncan a long gaze and then addressed the prosecutor. "You may call your next witness, Mr. Gordon."

Mr. Gordon then called his last witness, the doctor who had treated Lisa after Charles Miller beat her. They had blown-up photos taken in the emergency room from that night fourteen years earlier. Several of the jurors had a difficult time looking at these photos and passed them on almost without looking.

The doctor gave a complete account of the injuries, as well as a fairly accurate description of the pain and suffering Lisa had experienced for weeks after the beating. This testimony was hard on Gladys. She was almost sick as the doctor presented a blow-by-blow account for them. To think that this woman she had come to love as a daughter had experienced this physical abuse was too much for her. She had known about the beating. Lisa and Susan had talked about it several times—but never this graphically. Somehow, like so many others who couldn't deal with the painful truth, she must have mentally chosen to think of them as merely bad spankings. As she sat there looking at the back of Lisa's head, she wanted so badly to go up to her and kiss her and ask her forgiveness for not really understanding what she had lived through.

Gordon studied the jury as the doctor finished his testimony. He watched as they all kept looking over at Lisa, as if trying to imagine her in the condition shown in the pictures. Of course, he was not allowed to argue his case, but he believed he had given this jury every reason to think Lisa Miller could hate her father enough to kill him. He simply wasn't allowed to say it yet.

Duncan knew what Gordon was doing in painting such a graphic picture of Chuck Miller's handiwork. Yesterday, he had placed before the jury his suspicion of what Lisa had done. Today, he had placed before them her reason for doing it.

Since this witness could do nothing to help his client, Duncan simply said, "Your Honor, I have no questions for this witness."

After the doctor was dismissed, Judge Kirkley made an announcement. "Ladies and gentlemen, it is now four o'clock, and we have the weekend ahead of us. Since there is not enough time to call another witness, I'll ask the defense to hold off presenting their case until Monday morning. Is that satisfactory to you, Mr. Duncan?"

"Yes, sir. That would be fine."

Turning to the jury, Judge Kirkley said, "I admonish the jury not to discuss this case, and not to draw any conclusions regarding testimony you have heard so far. I wish you a good weekend and will see you back here at nine o'clock Monday morning."

As soon as Judge Kirkley and the jury were out of the courtroom, Aunt Gladys went to talk with Lisa. Scott noticed the look on Officer Jackson's face as the two women sat talking about the day's testimony. The muscles in Officer Jackson's cheeks were twitching, and his eyes were filled with anger.

Scott walked up to him and asked, "Are you all right?"

"No, I'm not. How could anyone do that to such a sweet, kind person as Lisa? I don't care what she was doing back then, no one has the right to do what he did. I can't believe they only gave him ten years. Letting him out to try again was criminal. When is this society ever going to learn?"

As Officer Jackson walked away in disgust, Scott wondered what, if anything, was going on between his sister-in-law and this man, but now was not the time to focus on anything but Lisa's defense.

CHAPTER 30

✤

No ONE RESTED much that weekend. Everyone struggled with a sense of depression, and even though they tried to make sure the children had fun, no one felt much like playing. Bill Thomas came on Saturday and took his granddaughters out to a movie, and Carol Anne and Harry took Matthew back home to Atlanta for the weekend. This gave Scott, Susan, and Aunt Gladys a quiet Saturday to meet with Mr. Duncan. He wanted to go over a few matters before they started their defense on Monday.

Entering his office around nine o'clock on Saturday morning, they smelled freshly brewed coffee and heard Duncan's talking on the phone. A few minutes later he came out and offered them some coffee and directed them into his conference room. Duncan knew these three were counting on him to save their loved one.

With more confidence than the last two days would merit, he began. "I know the last two witnesses did some serious damage, and yesterday was a fairly hard day on all of you. We all knew it would be. As you can imagine, the prosecution has planted some strong motives and suspicions in the minds of the jury."

Scott was looking for anything that would explain how it might have happened. "I don't mean to interrupt you, Mr. Duncan, but how serious is that business about the head wound? Couldn't it have happened during the struggl, e and Lisa simply can't remember? After all, she was terrified."

"Scott, it is possible that Lisa doesn't remember. We've gone over and over every minute of that night. Our problem is, not only does she not re-member, no one can find any evidence that would support an accidental blow."

260

"But the man was trying to kill her. Doesn't she have a right to defend herself?"

"Scott, that's not the issue. The blow, in and of itself, could still be argued to be self-defense, occurring during a struggle. Because Lisa can't, or won't, explain how it occurred, the prosecution is making the assumption that she has something to hide. He has painted a rational picture that fits the evidence. What we have to do is paint a clearer picture of exactly how vicious Chuck Miller really was, how he was always the aggressor, and that he fully intended to kill Lisa that night. I also have to make that jury see your Lisa. If we can paint those two very clear pictures, I am hoping the jury will set aside the head injury as simply something that will never be explained. Because we can't explain it, we need to treat it as a relatively unimportant item in the bigger picture. That's what my approach will be. I think we have a good chance of winning this trial if we keep to the plan and push forward with everything we have."

Then wanting to move away from this line of thought, Duncan smoothly changed the subject. "Susan, I need your testimony. The prosecutor isn't stupid. Gordon wasn't trying to help us yesterday by showing the jury what your father did to Lisa. He intends to use that incident to prove her rage and anger, explaining why she wanted to kill him."

Scott was still having trouble with the images of the day before. "It's funny, someone like Chuck Miller can do what we saw yesterday and someone like Mr. Gordon can look Lisa in the face and say, 'You did not have a right to use deadly force to defend yourself.' "

Duncan understood the anger in Scott's voice. "We need the jury to understand that Chuck Miller did intend to do all that—and more—to Lisa in that alley. If we can keep that matter in front of them, I think we can win.

"Susan, first thing Monday morning, I intend to put your mother on the stand. Then right after her, I want your old neighbor, Mrs. Reiner, on the stand. That contrast should be interesting to the jury. On Tuesday, I will call Officer Kerry Bailey."

Aunt Gladys looked puzzled. She hadn't heard that name before. "Who is that?"

Susan answered before Duncan had a chance to respond. "Aunt Gladys, as Mr. Duncan was going through all the police records, he came across the reports done the night my dad almost killed my mother. Apparently, this Officer Bailey was the one who fought with my dad and rescued my mother. He was the one who handcuffed and arrested my father. Even though it was almost twenty-five years ago, his report was so extensive and detailed Mr. Duncan thought it would be a good example of how bad my dad was."

As Susan explained, Duncan sat there, quietly thinking, *It's strange, but every time I've mentioned this witness to you, Susan, you evade any in-depth conversation. You never want to talk about it or think about it. Getting the truth out of you was a major task. You two girls grew up in a home that demanded secrecy in order to survive. Susan, you have no idea how that night has affected this witness. I wonder how you're going to react when you are forced to finally listen to his testimony.*

Wanting to bring the meeting to a close, Duncan offered, "All right, let's go over this again. On Monday I'll call your mother and Mrs. Reiner, and on Tuesday, Officer Bailey and you, Susan. By then, the jury will have their picture of Chuck Miller. Then on Wednesday, I'll call Scott, Gladys, and Mrs. Bascom."

Duncan paused for moment, weighing his words carefully. "Something has come up, so our schedule will have to be changed for next Thursday and Friday. Judge Kirkley will be closing down the trial until the following Monday, but then I intend to put Lisa on the stand to tell the jury what really happened in that alley."

With everyone's confidence built up and feeling back in control, they left for home. After dropping Gladys off at her house, Scott and Susan returned to their temporary little home for some much-needed rest. The children were already napping, so Susan walked the sitter out to her car while Scott dropped on their bed for a quick nap. Everyone in the house was resting—everyone except Susan. She stayed busy trying to make grocery lists and menus for the next week, anything to keep her mind engaged. Around three o'clock she sat down in the kitchen, waiting for the phone to ring. Knowing she would be under a lot of emotional stress, she had arranged with Dr. Jacobson to call every Saturday afternoon to touch base. Not wanting to disturb anyone, Susan grabbed the phone on the first ring. She quickly explained what had happened that week in court and also that morning with the attorney.

After having been filled in on everything, the doctor asked, "So Susan, how are you doing?"

"All right, I guess. It's hard though—having to sit and listen while others are talking about my life."

"Susan, we've talked about how that dread you feel is coming from deep within your subconscious. Your parents terrorized you with 'don't ever talk.' The level of punishment that came when one of you did let something slip made you always a guarded person. Remember what I told you? Even though your parents cannot terrorize you any longer, your childhood tape is still playing in your head, setting off those feelings of dread whenever anyone gets close to your secrets."

"I know, Dr. Jacobson, but even though I know why I'm scared, that doesn't stop the feelings. I wish I could turn off that tape in my head."

"Every time you reject its message, the tape gets quieter and quieter. You've lived in secret for a long time, Susan. You have to be patient and give yourself time to learn new life skills. In general, how do you think you're doing?"

Susan was somewhat proud of herself. She was doing better than she had expected she would. "Pretty well. We're all tired. Actually, everyone is taking a nap right now. I'm doing pretty well on that subject. I've been tempted to take some naps lately, but I haven't. I know it's my way of escaping, and I don't want to do that anymore."

With a little laughter in her voice, Dr. Jacobson responded, "You know, sometimes when you're sleepy, that's all it is; you're just sleepy. I think you're strong enough to be able to tell the difference between escape sleep and pure exhaustion. You need to lighten up on yourself and give yourself permission to take a nap when you need one. Just because you had a problem with taking naps doesn't mean you can never take a nap again."

The relief in Susan as she heard Dr. Jacobson say such an obvious truth was almost funny. She had been trying too hard. As Dr. Jacobson said goodbye, she ordered Susan to join Scott for a nap, which she willingly did.

CHAPTER 31

⚜

AFTER HEARING WHAT had been happening in the courtroom, Harry and Carol Anne quickly arranged to have his mother come from Virginia. She would care for Michael and the twins so both of them could attend the remainder of the trial. Mr. Thomas had decided that he would clear his calendar, checking in every evening, enabling him to be with his family to show support for Lisa and Susan. Gladys was thankful for the much-needed distraction. Having four houseguests to feed and entertain made coming home from the courthouse a little more tolerable. The five of them, knowing Scott and Susan would need time alone each evening, planned to take out the children every night between five and seven. They felt so useless simply sitting in court every day, but they did know this was one effort would help.

Scott and Susan dressed early Monday morning so they could spend at least an hour with Lisa before the trial started. Both women were dreading today's testimony.

Mr. Duncan came in with his cup of coffee a few minutes later to go over some last-minute details. He knew today would probably be Lisa's most difficult. Lisa hadn't seen her mother in twenty-five years, and both she and Susan worried about how she would feel upon seeing her. Duncan had done a good job filling in both of them about their mother's attitude and demeanor, knowing quite well what her answers would be.

As a final admonition, he said, "Lisa, it's important you don't react to your mother's anger. The jury will be watching you, and if they see hate in your face—even if your mother really deserves it—they will turn on you. No matter what she says or how she says it, you keep a pleasant look on your face."

Duncan was very good at what he did. Every single witness—whether his or Gordon's—Duncan had studied, researched, questioned, and questioned again. He thought of every question Gordon could possibly ask and had an answer for it. His job was to know how Gordon thought, and he had done his job.

A few minutes later, the bailiff knocked on the door. Duncan rose to answer it, and the bailiff whispered something to him. After closing the door, Duncan returned to his seat and announced, "Your mother just checked in with the court. They have her in a witness room ready to be called."

The two sisters glanced at each other. Susan was surprised at the sick feeling she felt to know her mother was there in the same building. Lisa raised her eyebrows and gave her sister a half-smile. "Here we go."

Bill, Caroline, Harry, Carol Anne, Aunt Gladys, and Mrs. Bascom were already seated in the two rows directly behind the defense table. Scott and Susan slipped into their seats and lowered their heads, half-praying while gathering their thoughts. While her head was bowed, Susan heard the familiar sound of the door creaking, which meant Ben was bringing Lisa into the courtroom.

Lisa looked very nice. Aunt Gladys had made her a linen suit especially for today. She had stayed up until well after midnight almost every night the week before to finish it. It was a rich-looking, royal-blue, lined in a cream color, lightweight linen. The blouse had a simple round neckline and was made of the same material as the lining. Aunt Gladys had also placed her favorite brooch on the left breast pocket. Today, she wanted Lisa to wear this prized gift from her husband, Karl. She wanted Lisa to look her very best and feel very special when Marjorie Miller took her place in that witness box. She wanted Marjorie Miller to see what a beautiful woman her daughter had become.

Aunt Gladys had given the suit to Ben Jackson early that morning, and when Lisa walked out of the shower room dressed in that suit, all he could do was smile. He realized he needed to be careful what he said to Lisa when other officers were around. Several had made comments about his obvious favoritism, and he didn't want to give the captain any reason to re-assign him this close to the end of the trial. He whispered, "Lisa, you look very nice."

With a twinkle in her eyes, Lisa simply said, "Thank you, Officer Jackson. So do you."

He then took her elbow and led her to the courthouse. In no way was Ben Jackson going to let any other officer take over this duty. He intended to keep his opinions to himself and guard his expressions because Lisa needed him to be there. Duncan had estimated that the trial would go to the jury by that next Monday, and Ben had no intention of missing it.

When they walked into the courtroom, everyone looked up and smiled at Lisa. As she took her seat, she thought about each one of these people sitting behind her, and she choked a little with emotion. She was so thankful for their being there because they cared about her.

Carol Anne leaned forward, tapped Lisa on the shoulder, and handed her a note. As Lisa unfolded it, she recognized the printing and smiled. The note was from Lisa Anne. She had drawn a picture for Auntie Lisa so she would know how much she loved her. The note contained two stick figures, one large and one small, both with smiles on their faces, holding a cookie sheet with little round cookies on it. At the bottom she had printed, "I love you, Auntie Lisa."

Lisa touched the note to her lips and kissed it, then placed it right in front of her on the table. She intended to focus on that note while her mother was in the witness box.

As soon as the jury had been seated, the court clerk called the court to order. Judge Kirkley came in and took his seat. He nodded a polite good morning to the jury, each attorney, Lisa, and then asked, "Mr. Duncan, are you ready to begin?"

"Yes, sir, Your Honor. The defense calls Marjorie Miller to the stand."

Everyone waited as the bailiff stepped out the back door, walked to the witness room, and returned a minute later with the witness.

Susan heard the door as its hinges squeaked and then the sound of footsteps coming down the aisle. She kept her eyes glued to the back of Lisa's head as the steps passed her by. Lisa's head never moved. They both could hear the sound of their mother stepping onto the wooden platform, and then the sound of the witness chair being slightly scooted as she positioned herself in front of the microphone. Then, and only then, did Lisa's head move. As she lifted her face and directed her eyes toward the witness stand, Susan allowed her eyes to follow.

Susan was shocked at how old and tired their mother looked. In a mere eleven years, her hair had turned very gray and her face gaunt. Susan wondered what Lisa must have been thinking. Their mother was still a young woman when she had last seen her.

Susan watched as Marjorie's eyes looked over toward the defense table, and she took a long look at her firstborn. First came a quick look of surprise, followed by a cold, hard stare. She then noticed her mother's eyes begin to move across the row of people sitting directly behind Lisa. She knew her mother was searching the crowd for her, and her mother's eyes continued to move until they rested on her. Susan did not smile. She simply kept her eyes locked on her mother's until Marjorie finally gave up and turned her gaze to Mr. Duncan. Susan felt the extreme need to show her mother she was no longer intimidated by her. She took a deep breath and returned her attention to Lisa.

After the clerk had sworn in Marjorie Miller, Duncan leaned forward with his forearms resting on the table and smiled at Marjorie. "Good morning, Mrs. Miller."

Without any facial expression, Marjorie Miller simply responded, "Good morning."

Still smiling at Marjorie, Duncan was intent on treating this witness as if she were an ally of the defense. After all, the jury would expect that the mother of the defendant would want to cooperate in her daughter's defense. He intended to pour on the charm and catch the jury off guard when Marjorie, as he knew she would, started showing her true colors. "Your full name is Marjorie Miller. Is that correct?"

"Yes."

Duncan was glad to see Marjorie was still responding as she had during the deposition. Again, with a big smile, he asked, "Please tell the court your relationship to the defendant, Lisa Miller."

Without looking at Lisa, Marjorie simply stated, "She was my daughter."

Duncan shot a glance at the jury. He certainly hoped they had caught that "was" in her last response. "Mrs. Miller, can you tell the court how long it has been since you have seen or talked to your daughter, Lisa Miller?"

Marjorie sat up straight, as if proud of the number, and said, "Twenty-five years."

Duncan looked at the jury as he asked the next question and kept his eyes on them as he waited for her answer. "My, twenty-five years is a long time not to see or talk with your daughter. Have you been living out of the country during those years, Mrs. Miller?"

With as short and flat a response as she could muster, she said, "No."

"Well, Mrs. Miller, if you've not been living out of the country for the past twenty-five years, can you please tell the court where you have been living?"

"Atlanta."

"That is Atlanta, Georgia?"

"Yes. Atlanta, Georgia." Her tone became irritated.

"Well, Mrs. Miller, the court records show that your daughter, Lisa Miller, has lived in Jefferson, Georgia, for the past nineteen years; a mere sixty-one miles from Atlanta. Can you possibly shed some light on what could have been the reason for a twenty-five-year estrangement between you and your daughter?" He watched as several jurors looked from Marjorie to Lisa and back to Marjorie, waiting for her answer.

"She chose to leave. I let her."

Duncan took his legal pad, as if ready to write, trying to do the math. "How old was Lisa when she left home?"

Remembering what Lisa's running away had cost her, Marjorie turned and looked at Lisa as she said, "She ran away when she was seventeen."

Mr. Duncan continued to scribble on the pad, but Lisa could see his pen's tip was retracted and he wasn't really writing. The pad was already filled with detailed notes he had previously recorded.

Suddenly, Duncan picked up the pad, stood up, and walked over in front of the witness stand. He was now only two or three feet from Marjorie Miller, looking directly into her face. "Mrs. Miller, you say your daughter ran away from home when she was seventeen years old, and you have not seen or spoken to her since. Were you aware of the fact that she was living here in Jefferson all of this time?"

"No, I wasn't."

Duncan was surprised that she was trying this same stupid play of words again. She had also done this during the deposition. "No, you were not aware that your daughter Lisa Miller was living sixty-one miles from you? Or no, you were not aware of this for that entire time? Which one is it, Mrs. Miller?"

"I was not aware that she lived here the whole time. She ran away. I didn't know where she went."

Duncan stood looking at Marjorie for a moment. She really did not care what the jury thought of her. She was making no attempt to pretend she was anything but what she was—a cold, hate-filled woman. She was making his job very easy. "Mrs. Miller, what was your relationship to Mr. Charles Miller?"

"He was my husband."

"Were you aware of the beating Charles Miller inflicted on Lisa Miller, your daughter, which resulted in his going to prison?"

Duncan was hoping she would answer this same question just as she had during the deposition, only this time his next few questions were going to be different. "Yes, I knew. I lost my house because of it."

Duncan, pretending to have great concern for her loss, asked. "Oh, what was the cause of your losing your home, Mrs. Miller? Were you helping Lisa Miller with her hospital care after that beating?"

Duncan was looking from juror to juror, thinking, *Come on, jury, remember those pictures of Lisa. Remember the beating Gordon so vividly laid before you on Friday. Think! Remember!*

Duncan's eyes stayed on the jury as Marjorie Miller said, "No, we sold the house to pay for Chuck's lawyer."

Bingo! Duncan thought. "So Mrs. Miller, at the time of the beating, you *were* aware that your daughter was living here in Jefferson. Is that correct?"

"Yes, I knew she was here, but only after that."

Duncan stepped a little closer, as if he was having a hard time hearing her. "*That?* That what, Mrs. Miller? You knew she was here after what?" He wanted her to say it. He needed her to say it. He was going to make Marjorie Miller say it. "After what, Mrs. Miller?"

She glared at him as she answered. "After Chuck beat Lisa."

Duncan walked back to his seat, wanting the jury to again look past him and see Lisa sitting there, a real person, not just a name. "Mrs. Miller, you obviously knew about the trial. You lost your house because of it. Did anyone call and tell you your daughter was in a life-threatening condition after that beating?"

"Yes. The police called me, and so did the hospital."

Duncan leaned forward with his head resting on his right hand. "Yet you never bothered to come sixty-one miles to see your daughter? Can you explain to the court why you did not come?"

Marjorie sat back in the seat, put her hands down on the chair's arms, and looked over at Mr. Duncan. He could feel it coming. Marjorie was beginning to boil, and he intended to keep her thinking about how much she hated Lisa so the jury would see this.

"I didn't *want* to see her. She got what she deserved. Why should I come here and see her?"

"Mrs. Miller, I'm confused. Maybe you were not made aware of how severe that beating was. I'm sorry, you were not in the courtroom when the doctor reviewed the hospital records of all of Lisa's injuries because of that beating. Maybe you were misled and never knew the serious nature of that beating."

Marjorie's response was as cold as ice. "No. My other daughter went down to see her. She told me."

"You have another daughter besides Lisa Miller?"

"Yes."

"And what is her name."

"Susan Miller."

"Excuse me? Is Susan Miller your other daughter's current name?"

"No. Her married name is Thomas. Susan Thomas."

"So your daughter Susan Thomas told you about the severe beating your daughter Lisa had received at the hands of your husband, Charles Miller, and you say she deserved it! Mrs. Miller, will you please tell this court what Lisa Miller could possibly have done to deserve a beating like that?"

It had been fourteen years since Marjorie had heard about Chuck's beating up Lisa. Fourteen years of her having to wait before she was finally able to tell Lisa just how glad she was that Lisa had finally gotten hers, and she was going to enjoy this. She didn't care what any of these people thought of her. Leaning forward, making sure Lisa was looking at her, Marjorie unloaded years of hate. "Lisa, when you ran away, you didn't care what kind of hell you were inflicting on me! The police were coming to our house every night for almost two months, pushing your father around, asking questions, making him mad. After the California police said they had found you out there, the police finally left us alone—just long enough for your dad to beat me so bad I almost died. I almost died getting a beating intended for you, so why should I feel sorry for you when you finally got yours? I'm just sorry I wasn't there to see it."

Susan watched the jury as they studied Marjorie's distorted face. Several of the men had a look of pure disgust while several of the older women glanced at Lisa with a look of sympathy. Susan couldn't see Lisa's face and wondered how she was holding up.

Duncan continued to question Marjorie Miller for almost two hours, asking her to comment on numerous police reports of domestic disturbance calls to their home over the years. He was painting a picture of violence for the jury, showing them what Chuck Miller really was capable of. He was also exposing a picture of a mother who had no love or concern for the suffering her children had experienced. Hers were self-centered, pity-me, see-how-I-suffered comments.

As the noon hour approached Duncan sat back in his seat and announced that he was temporarily through with this witness. "Your Honor, I'll be needing to recall this witness at a later time, so I request the court order her to remain in the courtroom until needed."

Judge Kirkley turned his gaze on Marjorie Miller, and said as coldly as he could, "Mrs. Miller, please remain seated until the jury has been dismissed. After lunch, the prosecution will have an opportunity to cross-examine you. When he is through, you are to remain seated over there until recalled. Do you understand?"

"Yes, sir." Marjorie sat glaring at Lisa as the judge called the proceedings to a close. The bailiff ordered everyone to remain seated until he had removed the jury. As the jury stood up and began filing out, every one of them took a good long look at Marjorie sitting in that witness box.

Duncan watched their faces, carefully trying to measure the impact of his work that morning. As each juror took his turn looking at Marjorie, Duncan screamed in his head, *Good! Now piece that disgust you have for this woman with the feelings you had Friday, seeing those photos of that young girl. Think about how you, or any normal parent, could possibly have stayed away. Ask yourself that question. Could you have stayed away?*

Duncan didn't really believe in mental telepathy, but it had become his habit to concentrate all of his mental energies toward the jury at those times when he most wanted them to think. He couldn't possibly know if this technique actually worked, but he usually got the results he wanted from his juries, so he wasn't going to stop now.

After the jury left, he turned back to Lisa and asked how she was doing. He knew this morning was Lisa's most difficult, and she had handled the proceedings very well. Each time he looked over at Lisa she had a pleasant look on her face. She had followed his orders. He put his arm around the back of her chair and leaned in closely to speak.

As he was finishing his question, he saw Lisa's eyes leave his face and look past his left shoulder. He could hear Marjorie's footsteps behind him as she made her way up the aisle, and he knew Lisa was looking at her.

"Lisa, you handled yourself very well this morning. How are you doing?"

Lisa's eyes didn't return to his face until he heard the sound of the back door opening. And then, as the familiar creak subsided, signaling Marjorie had gone, Lisa's eyes returned to his.

He smiled. He had come to respect this strong, self-controlled woman sitting beside him. Few people have the opportunity to know another person as well as a criminal defense attorney gets to know his client. By the time an attorney has put a case together, he has talked to almost every person, both good and bad, who has ever known the client. The attorney has probably heard every dirty little story there is to tell. During preparation, if he is good, he has pieced together an accurate picture of the client's life. Duncan had done this with Lisa Miller. There were no secrets. He knew it all, and he respected her for becoming the woman she now was.

Lisa quickly assured him she was fine. "Just a little tired. I think I forgot to keep breathing a few times though. When her words became really painful, I focused my mind on the note from my niece and that helped."

"Well, I suspect you have heard the last of your mother for today. I would seriously doubt that Mr. Gordon will want to have Marjorie Miller on the stand anymore than absolutely necessary. He will probably dismiss her almost immediately after lunch. Why don't you go have some lunch and relax during the two-hour break? I need to check with the court clerk and make sure Mrs. Reiner is here, so I probably won't come in and see you during the break. I have some matters to handle, and your whole family is here, so you'll be all right."

Duncan gathered his papers and headed for the court clerk's office.

CHAPTER 32

As Mr. Duncan had suspected, when the trial was resumed and Marjorie Miller was re-seated in the witness box, Mr. Gordon, never looking directly at Marjorie, said, "I have no questions for this witness, Your Honor."

Duncan had read it right. He had intentionally questioned her right up until the noon break so the judge would not have time to offer Gordon an opportunity to begin his cross-examination. The judge, although probably feeling Gordon would want to get rid of her as soon as possible, could not take the chance of Gordon's taking the court over into the lunch break, so Judge Kirkley was forced to make him wait until after the break.

This had been an important move on Duncan's part. He wanted the jury to again see Marjorie Miller's sitting on the witness stand right before Mrs. Reiner was called. He didn't even want to have a two-hour break between these two women in the minds of the jury, and he had accomplished his plan.

As Marjorie took a seat three rows behind the prosecution's table, Judge Kirkley asked Duncan to call his next witness.

"The defense calls Mrs. Bernice Reiner to the stand."

Lisa had read Duncan's transcript of her interview, but she had not seen her former neighbor since she ran away. Lisa turned and watched as Mrs. Reiner came down the aisle, took her seat, and was sworn in.

"Mrs. Reiner, can you please tell the court how long it has been since you have spoken to my client, Lisa Miller?"

"Spoken to her or seen her?" Mrs. Reiner wanted to be careful not to answer any questions incorrectly.

"Either one, Mrs. Reiner. Can you recall for the court how long it has been since you have had any personal contact with my client?"

Mrs. Reiner was a wise woman and knew where Mr. Duncan was going. She was going to make sure the jury heard it loud and clear. "Yes. Well, I lived next door to the Millers the entire time Lisa lived at home. She was born right after the Millers moved in. During the whole seventeen years Lisa lived next door, I cannot recall a single conversation with her. Nothing more than a quick 'hello.' Those girls never talked with any of us neighbors. That is to say, none of the adults in the neighborhood. Lisa did talk with my son, Steve, sometimes—but only when her parents were not at home. So it has been over twenty years since I have seen Lisa Miller."

Duncan knew it was always better to have a witness tell the jury a fact rather than the lawyer. Jurors tended to be distrustful of lawyers, so whenever possible, he wanted the witness to tell them what he wanted them to know.

"Mrs. Reiner, after all that time, can you explain to the court what circumstances transpired that brought you into this courtroom today?"

"I was contacted by you because my name was found on *several* Atlanta police reports over the years." Mrs. Reiner emphasized the word *several* as she directed her answer to the jury. Duncan had also instructed her to address as many of her answers directly to the jury, rather than toward him.

"So Mrs. Reiner, how did your name get to be on several police reports involving the Miller family?"

"I was their next-door neighbor for more than twenty years, and until Chuck Miller was sent off to prison, I had the great misfortune of hearing fights that would turn your hair gray."

"Objection, Your Honor. Please instruct the witness to refrain from adding her colorful colloquialisms."

Judge Kirkley, after giving Mrs. Reiner a polite smile, instructed, "Mrs. Reiner, please simply answer the questions placed before you. I understand it is difficult sometimes to give succinct answers, but please do."

Then turning to the court recorder, the judge instructed, "Please strike her last comment."

"Mr. Duncan, would you care to rephrase your question for the witness?"

Returning a polite nod, Duncan asked, "Mrs. Reiner, over that period the Miller family resided next door, how many times did you call the Atlanta police complaining of fighting?"

"It felt like hundreds…" As Mrs. Reiner saw Gordon start to lean forward, ready to object, she quickly changed her wording. "…but it was probably several dozen times. I didn't keep count."

Duncan stood and walked over to stand close to Mrs. Reiner. Actually, he positioned himself between her and the jury so they could look over his shoulder and still see her face.

"You say these fights went on until Charles Miller, otherwise known as Chuck Miller, went to prison? Now is that the prison term he served for beating his daughter, Lisa Miller, fourteen years ago?"

"No. I know nothing about that time. The prison term I'm talking about was twenty-five years ago when he almost killed his wife. If I hadn't called the police that time, he would have killed her."

Gordon jumped to his feet. "Objection, Your Honor! This witness cannot possibly know what might have happened."

Judge Kirkley, looking at Mrs. Reiner, said, "Will the witness please confine her answers to details that are known to be true, and the court recorder will strike that last comment from the record. Go on, Mr. Duncan."

"Mrs. Reiner, the Atlanta police records show that you called them on five different occasions during the four-year period prior to that incident. You were complaining of violent fighting going on in the Miller residence. Is that correct?"

"Yes, but those were just the five times I couldn't take it any longer. Usually, if the fight didn't last too long I would try to ignore it, but if it kept going, and especially if it was one of the girls being beaten, I would call the police."

"So Chuck Miller did not restrict his fights to only his wife? He also beat his girls?"

"Absolutely." Mrs. Reiner's reaction was pure contempt.

Again Mr. Gordon objected. "Your Honor, Mrs. Reiner was not inside that house and has no way of knowing who, if anyone, was being hit. She simply heard some screaming and therefore made an assumption."

Duncan spun around and looked directly at Gordon while addressing the bench. "Your Honor, if you will allow me to continue my questioning, I will show the court that no assumptions were made on Mrs. Reiner's part."

Judge Kirkley looked at Mrs. Reiner and then said, "I will allow her comment to stand. However, Mr. Duncan, if I am not quickly satisfied that you have met your burden of proof, I will strike her entire comment."

Duncan turned again to Mrs. Reiner, taking a step back so the jury could easily see her face as she told them her story. He wanted them to see the same face he had seen when she told this same story to him two months earlier. "Now Mrs. Reiner, please tell the court what proof you have that Chuck Miller beat his children."

Mrs. Reiner took a deep breath and leaned forward in her chair as if bracing for a difficult task. Her eyes found the most grandmotherly face on the jury, and she spoke directly to her.

"The very first beating I witnessed Chuck Miller give one of his daughters was twenty-seven years ago, and I'll never forget it. My husband and I were in our backyard planting a vegetable garden. It was about lunchtime, and I was getting up so I could go into the house and fix us something to eat when a rock came flying over the fence and narrowly missed my head.

"My husband jumped up and started screaming over the fence at our neighbor, Chuck Miller. Usually, my husband would never think to talk back at that man because the whole neighborhood was afraid of him, my husband included."

"Objection, Your Honor. Mrs. Reiner cannot speak for the entire neighborhood." Gordon almost fluffed his chest as he made his protest. Then he looked over at one or two of the jurors as the judge ordered the comment stricken. He noted his challenging this woman was obviously not sitting well with them.

Duncan then motioned for Mrs. Reiner to proceed.

Turning back to the jury, Mrs. Reiner continued as if never interrupted. "We had ignored three or four other big rocks he had thrown over that morning while mowing his lawn, but when that rock almost hit me in the head, my husband had had enough. The two of them screamed and yelled at each other for several minutes before Chuck Miller turned and stormed off toward his kitchen door.

"My husband and I stood there staring at him as he dared us to do something. When he walked into his kitchen, he didn't bother to close the door, so we could see clearly what took place next. He stepped a little to the right of the door, but we could see everything through the kitchen window. We could see his wife, Marjorie, standing at the sink. We heard him yell something at her, and then we watched as he slammed her against the sink and slapped her across the face.

"As this was happening, their youngest daughter, Susan, who was then just five years old, walked through the door that led from their living room. I watched as she stood against that door looking at her parents. Before my husband and I could do anything to stop him, Chuck Miller walked over to his daughter, grabbed a handful of her hair, picking that child up by her hair a good three feet off the floor and slammed her head against the door three or four times.

"I remember standing there absolutely frozen in disbelief at what I was seeing, and before I could collect my thoughts, with his left hand clenched into a fist, he punched that child in the stomach as hard as he would any man. Then he dropped her, stepped over her, and went through that door into another part of the house.

"You know, that child didn't make a sound. She crawled over by the kitchen table and started picking something up off the floor. Then still bent over in pain, she left the kitchen."

By the end of Mrs. Reiner's accounting of this story, her face was tear-stained, as were the faces of several jurors.

"Mrs. Reiner, what, if anything, happened to Chuck Miller because of that beating?"

"Nothing," was her disgusted response.

"Didn't someone call the police?"

"Yes, sir, we did! That was the first time I called the police on Chuck Miller."

"What did the police do? Did they respond and investigate?"

"Yes, they came. They came to our house first, and we told them exactly what we had seen. Then they walked over and talked to Chuck Miller. We watched them from our living room window, standing there talking to him on his porch. Then they left, and he went back into his house."

"Didn't they talk with the child or check to see if she was all right?"

"No! They never entered the house, and she never came out."

"So what did you do after they left?"

"Well, we sat there for a while talking about how unfair it all was and trying to figure out what we could do. You see, it was dangerous to have Chuck Miller mad at you, and if the police weren't going to do anything, calling them was just asking for trouble. Finally, an hour or so later I called the police station and asked to talk to one of the officers who had come over. He called me back about two hours later with a real attitude in his voice. I asked him what was going to happen to Chuck Miller, and he said, 'Nothing.'"

Before Duncan could ask another question, Mrs. Reiner began repeating that officer's full statement to her in an extremely mocking voice. "He said, 'Mr. Miller just got a little carried away spanking his kid for disobeying. It happens sometimes, Mrs. Reiner. I think that because the three of you had just had an argument, your perspective was a little vengeful. Wouldn't you say that was possible, Mrs. Reiner?' "

Mrs. Reiner sat back in her chair, paused a moment, and then looked at Mr. Duncan. "I have lived with those images in my head for more than twenty years. That was the first, but there were many more. Every time I called the police, they treated me like a malicious busybody until the night he beat Marjorie Miller within an inch of her life."

Knowing Officer Bailey would fill in the jury on that night, Duncan wasn't going to ask Mrs. Reiner to relive her memory for the jury, so he asked, "Mrs. Reiner, I'm not going to ask you to get into any details about that night, other than to ask, why did you call the police that night when they had disregarded your pleas for help so many times before?"

"Well, after years of listening to those beatings, suddenly Lisa disappeared one day. The Millers said she had run away, but none of us really believed it. The police could not find a single person who had seen her. She hadn't taken a bus, a train, or a plane—nothing. They couldn't find one person who had seen her hitchhiking, and she apparently had no money. Even my son, Steve, had no idea where she had gone. After two months of the police coming around all the time, everyone was convinced Chuck Miller had probably gone too far one night and that Lisa was probably dead."

Mrs. Reiner turned her head toward Lisa and smiled at her as she said, "I was very happy to find out we were wrong."

Mrs. Reiner returned her gaze to the jury and continued. "Anyway, when word got around that Lisa had been seen in California, we still weren't convinced. Then around eight o'clock that night, it started. I had heard the noise of many fights coming from that house, but this time sounded different. Almost from the moment of the first scream, we knew this was going to be a really bad one. I remember saying to my son that I couldn't sit there and listen to it. Even if Lisa were safe, one of these times he was going to go too far, and I couldn't have that on my conscience. So I called."

Duncan walked back to his seat next to Lisa and sat down. "I have no further questions of this witness, Your Honor."

Duncan knew Gordon wouldn't have a chance with Mrs. Reiner. He knew Gordon had seen all of the police reports. He had to know he couldn't attack her memory because the reports confirmed everything she had said. He also had to know how powerful her testimony had been and how the jury was simply oozing sympathy for both Mrs. Reiner and the Miller girls. It was quarter to four, and Judge Kirkley was turning Mrs. Reiner over to the prosecution.

Gordon made several attempts to pit Mrs. Reiner's opinions against that of the police officers who had investigated each of these domestic disturbance calls, but he was getting nowhere. He could feel the discomfort of the jury as he tried to imply that maybe the police were a little more trained in the area of domestic problems than, say, a neighbor.

Duncan smiled as Mrs. Reiner responded to this line of questioning. "No, sir, I do not think they know more! An old saying goes 'The proof is in the pudding.' The police were wrong and I was right, I'm sorry to say. That is certainly one time I would have gladly been proven wrong, sir!"

With this response, Mr. Gordon said he had no further questions and sat down. The jury had heard enough for one day.

Everyone was quiet as they made their way out of the courtroom. No one in the family knew what to say after this afternoon's testimony. Susan was obviously upset, and Scott was ready to come undone. Caroline slid her arm around Susan and walked out with her without saying a word, while Aunt Gladys and Mrs. Bascom headed to the conference room to talk with Lisa.

As Scott walked behind his wife and mother, feelings of rage nearly overwhelmed him, but he knew Susan needed him to stay calm. He had promised her that before this trial began, but he had no way of knowing how hard keeping that promise was going to be. He simply had to find the strength to hold himself together—for Susan's sake.

CHAPTER 33

TUESDAY MORNING STARTED with the phone's ringing. Scott reached over to pick it up before it woke the children. Susan sat up, wondering who could be calling at this time of morning. She watched Scott's face, looking for some clue as he answered the person on the other end of the line.

"All right, that's not a problem. I'll be sure to tell her. That's fine, we'll meet you there at eight o'clock. Goodbye." As Scott hung up, he turned to Susan and said. "That was Duncan. I guess he was up half the night working on his strategy and has decided not to put you on the stand today. He said he'll meet us at the courthouse at eight o'clock and explain everything. He wanted to get that message to you as early as possible so you wouldn't be worrying about being on the stand today."

Puzzled by this turn of events, Susan asked, "Why doesn't Mr. Duncan want me to testify? What could have happened that would make him not want to use me?"

Susan rushed around the house, quickly preparing everything so they could be extra early to court. She was concerned something might have happened; after all, she had been feeling as if Duncan had not been totally honest with her. Several times during the past three days, he and Lisa would be huddled together talking, and when she walked up, they would stop. Lisa seemed distracted and worried, but Susan had simply written off that distraction due to all of the testimony she had heard.

Scott and Susan were sitting in the large conference room when Duncan walked in, looking very tired. He set down his papers and poured himself a cup of coffee before sitting down across from Susan.

"All right. I know you must be wondering why I would change the game plan when we're in the home stretch. Well, last night I went over everything that has happened in the courtroom so far. I tried to study it from the jury's position, and I think it would be a mistake to put you in front of them right now."

Seeing Susan about to protest, Duncan lifted his hand to stop her and continued. "Well, that is not altogether true. I intend to keep 'little Susan' in front of that jury. The visual picture Mrs. Reiner painted yesterday was so powerful, I want that jury to be thinking of that five-year-old—not the lovely, poised, grown-up woman sitting across from me right now."

In truth, this reason was not the only one, but this was the only reason he was free to discuss right now. He had been up for days, trying to digest some new information that had only landed in his lap that Saturday afternoon. Before he put anyone else on that stand, he wanted to be sure where this defense was headed. There would be no time to retrace any missteps later on.

"Susan, today Officer Bailey will tell the jury about 'little eight-year-old Susan,' as well as give the jury another profound look at Charles Miller. Therefore, I have decided the best thing you can do for your sister is not to get on the stand."

Understanding she had not had the time to think about the wisdom of this move like Mr. Duncan had and also because she trusted him, she simply nodded in agreement.

They talked about how they thought the trial was going and asked Attorney Duncan for his opinion.

"Even though I feel sure the jury is on our side, you never pull your punches. You hit them with everything you have until the contest is over."

He looked at Susan, who had so wanted a positive, confident response, and added, "Don't mind me. I'm simply one of those over-cautious lawyers who refuses to count the votes ahead of time. Everything is going as planned, so please don't worry. I talked to Officer Bailey early this morning, and he's ready and willing to testify, so let's get out there and do what needs to be done."

He smiled broadly at Susan, hoping her concerns were answered. As Mr. Duncan, Scott, and Susan entered the courtroom, they noticed that everyone was in their seats—everyone except Bill Thomas. Slipping into their seats, Scott leaned over to his mother and asked, "Where's Dad?"

Caroline leaned over and whispered, "Mrs. Randal called very early this morning to let him know about some kind of crisis in Atlanta. He hopes to have it cleared up today so he can be back here tomorrow. He told me to tell you not to worry."

Scott smiled reassuringly at his mother. He knew how much his mother wanted his father there and how much Bill wanted to be there. Only something very important would have made him miss today.

A few minutes later, Marjorie Miller walked into the courtroom and took a seat in the very back row. She sat staring at the back of her daughter Susan, as she sat in the middle of the Thomas clan. Seemingly, she would have felt some kind of relief, knowing her daughter had not only survived her horrible childhood experiences but was obviously loved by these people, but not Marjorie Miller. These people represented everything she had come to hate. After all, they were the "haves," and she was one of the "have-nots"! She knew they had never had to fight for what they had—like she did. To think they had the nerve to look down their noses at her. Those muckety-mucks were all alike, and her daughter had now become one of them. Marjorie Miller was so blinded by her hate that she had long since lost the ability to think rationally about anything—so much so that even while Mrs. Reiner was on the witness stand all Marjorie Miller could focus on was how no one seemed to care that she was the one who had been beaten. Their behavior only proved to her sick mind that she was right. Sitting in that courtroom, she was blind to the fact that she had failed miserably as a mother; however, everyone else there saw her failure.

When the court was called to order, Judge Kirkley asked Mr. Duncan to call his next witness. "The defense calls Mr. Kerry Bailey to the stand."

As Mr. Bailey came in and took his seat in the witness box, Susan kept her eyes on him. He was somewhere in his early sixties, slightly heavy and balding. He had a pleasant manner about him, and after the clerk had sworn him in, his eyes began moving among the rows, as if looking for someone. However, before he could find what or who he was looking for, Mr. Duncan began his questioning.

"Mr. Bailey, can you please tell the court your occupation?"

"Yes, sir. I am retired from the Atlanta Police Department."

"Mr. Bailey, how long did you work for the Atlanta Police Department?"

"Twenty years, sir."

"How long have you been retired from the department, Mr. Bailey?"

"Eleven years this September, sir."

"So if you've been retired for eleven years and you were employed by them for twenty years, then you were employed with the Atlanta Police Department between the years of 1953 through 1973. Would that be correct, Mr. Bailey?"

"No, sir. I was hired in September 1954, right after being discharged from the U.S. Marine Corps. I retired in September 1974. Eleven years ago."

Duncan knew it was important for the jury to have these dates pieced together—before they heard Bailey's story. Duncan didn't want them sitting in their seat trying to do the math in their heads, missing the very reason he was telling the story.

"So Mr. Bailey, how long did you serve in the Marines?"

"I served six years from 1949 through 1954 in the Marine Corp."

"So if you served in the Marines in the early fifties, Mr. Bailey, you must have seen some service time in South Korea. Is that right?"

"Yes, sir. One very hard year, sir."

Gordon had heard about all he wanted to hear of this witness's interesting past. "Your Honor, I cannot possibly see how Mr. Bailey's military record, no matter how honorable, has any bearing on this case."

Spinning around quickly to address his response to Gordon's argument, Duncan fired back, "Your Honor, I feel it's important the jury understand the scope of this witness's experience in order to put his testimony in its proper perspective. I promise I will be brief, Your Honor."

Judge Kirkley understood the dance that was happening in his courtroom. Attorneys love to interrupt each other's train of thought—even if that pause results only in a quick ruling. However, Judge Kirkley also understood something to which Prosecutor Gordon was not yet privy. The judge felt that something gave him cause to allow Mr. Duncan some latitude in questioning this witness. But latitude or not, he needed to keep control of his courtroom. "Mr. Duncan, hurry it along."

"Thank you, Your Honor. Mr. Bailey, the reason you're sitting in that witness box is because your name appears on one of the Atlanta Police reports having to do with the Charles Miller family. Is that correct?"

"Yes, sir. I was the arresting officer in that case."

"Now, since there were five different police reports for five different incidents, will you please tell this court in which of these incidents you were personally involved?"

"Yes, sir. I arrested Mr. Charles Miller for attempted murder in 1961."

"Mr. Bailey, I understand that you have been provided and have reviewed a copy of the police file regarding that incident. Is this true?"

"Yes, sir, I have reviewed the file."

Jumping to his feet, Gordon protested, "Your Honor, Mr. Miller is not on trial here. Wasting the court's time reviewing a twenty-five-year-old case is outrageous."

"Your Honor, this testimony goes to the core of Mr. Miller's character and his violent history. If I might remind the court, the prosecution felt it necessary to spend an entire day going over his fourteen-year-old conviction for assault on my client."

Judge Kirkley thought, *Touché, Mr. Duncan, I wondered why you didn't put up a fierce argument when Gordon took that approach. You must play chess well.*

Gordon was determined to win this round. "But Your Honor, that was allowed because it went to motive."

Duncan smiled and confidently replied, "That is correct, Your Honor! Just as this goes to motive. I intend to show this court the type of man Chuck Miller was. What kind of father, husband, and person he was."

The judge pondered his dilemma for a moment, knowing he had ruled on the prosecution's side to allow the first testimony. "I'm going to allow it. But Mr. Duncan, I suggest you keep to the straight and narrow here."

"Thank you, Your Honor."

Gordon retook his seat, and Duncan picked up the stack of police reports, having them marked exhibit ten. For the next two hours, Duncan produced photos and medical reports. He knew the court would be breaking for lunch in a few minutes, and he didn't want to be in the middle of this witness's testimony when lunch was called. Once all the reports and photos had been discussed and passed among the jury, Judge Kirkley called the morning session to a close. It had been a good morning, but the afternoon was going to get even better. Duncan knew the impact of Bailey's testimony, and he couldn't wait to get into it.

At two o'clock sharp, the court was called to order, and Officer Bailey was reminded he was still under oath. Duncan watched the jury as Bailey took his seat. They obviously liked this retired policeman. As Duncan perused this jury, he happily thought, *Sometimes, for some inexplicable reason, a witness bonds with a jury. Some witnesses can tell the truth the whole day long, and a jury will sit stone-faced, simply disliking him, and almost resenting his very presence in the courtroom. Then there are witnesses, like Kerry Bailey, who have no vested interest in this case except the truth. But it's even more than that. They like him and trust him.*

Duncan again smiled as he walked over and stood in front of the jury box. Giving the prosecutor a long, deliberate stare, he thought, *Gordon, you'd better take a good, hard look at this jury. You try to step on this witness's toes, and they'll turn on you.*

Turning his attention to his witness, Duncan said, "Mr. Bailey, this morning we reviewed a stack of police reports from Atlanta, Georgia, from the 1960s. Many of these happened more than twenty years ago. Having served a total of twenty years on the Atlanta Police Department and then being retired for the past eleven years, wouldn't you find it hard to separate one case of spousal battery from another over the years? What, if anything, can you tell this court that would lead us to believe you are not simply extracting facts recorded in that file and somehow blending those facts with hundreds of other domestic violence calls you had over the years?"

Kerry Bailey sat up very straight in his seat, turned his gaze to the jury, and spoke directly to them. "Every officer, on every force, has one case that stands out in his memory. This was my case. I remember every single detail as if it were yesterday."

"Mr. Bailey, what was so special about this case that it caused you to remember the details so vividly?" Duncan stood back and allowed Bailey to talk, knowing Gordon would be a fool to interrupt.

Turning directly to the jury, Kerry Bailey began. "Well, it started out like any one of a dozen domestic calls we would get every week. Some neighbor calls in, saying the people next door are really going at it. You'd be surprised at how many of these calls we get over the course of a year, so when you've responded to hundreds of these calls—some really nothing, and some pretty bad—you tend to approach them with a wait-and-see attitude. You can't go riding in like a cowboy, acting like you're there to save the town. You have to be skeptical of everyone. Maybe the husband is abusive; maybe the wife is trying to get even for something. Maybe the neighbor has it in for him. All of those are real possibilities, and they have all been true in one case or another.

"That night, my partner and I got the call around eight-twenty and headed over to check it out. As we pulled up to the house, I can't even describe to you the sounds that greeted us. I got to the door first while my partner immediately got on the radio and asked for assistance from the closest available unit. I pounded on the front door twice, trying to get the attention of the people inside. Most of the time, simply having us show up gets their attention, and they stop—not wanting us to see them in action. When they didn't respond to the second blow on the door, my partner and I broke it in and entered. We could hear the fight going on down the back hallway, so we both pulled our guns, yelled that we were the police, and ordered them to stop, but he didn't. We quickly made our way down the hall as the second police car pulled up and joined us.

"It's hard to describe exactly what we saw, the way it really was. Even with all four of us screaming at Charles Miller to stop, he didn't hear us. He had Marjorie Miller on her stomach with her head pulled back until it almost touched her buttocks, and he was slamming his fist as hard as he could into her face and throat. At the same time he was kicking her in the abdomen so hard that her body lifted off the floor.

"Because Mr. Miller did not have a weapon, we immediately put away our guns and tackled him. As we tackled him, he finally turned his eyes toward us, and I can tell you I have never seen a face like his before. His eyes were like pure fire, and even as all four of us were trying to hold him down to get the cuffs on him, he was still trying to kick his wife. As soon as we had the cuffs on him, my partner ran for the phone and requested an ambulance. We didn't think it was going to be necessary though. She looked gone to all of us. You couldn't even make out her face. The two other officers continued trying to control Charles Miller. Because they had moved him out of kicking range, he began spitting at Mrs. Miller and the officers.

"My partner returned to the bedroom and waited with Mrs. Miller until the ambulance arrived while I went around the house, making sure everything was secure. I stepped out the front door to catch a breath of fresh air when a neighbor lady yelled over, 'What happened to the little girl?'

"Suddenly, I had the sickest feeling in the pit of my stomach. All I could think of was, *Oh God, was there a baby in that house?*

"I ran back in and started searching, sort of like the fire department has to do when a house is on fire. Little children hide when in fear. I headed for the second bedroom, which I had peeked in during the quick check. I knew it was a child's room, so I walked over to the closet and carefully opened it."

He was obviously struggling to keep control of his emotions having to tell this story again. At this point, Kerry Bailey sat back in his seat, took a deep breath, closed his eyes, and then continued. "I opened that closet door and looked into the most haunted face I have ever seen.

Huddled in the back corner of that closet was an eight-year-old little girl. She didn't even look up when I first opened the door—probably afraid to see who was standing there. I remember saying, 'It's all right, honey, you can come out,' but she didn't move. Finally, her little face came up, and she looked at me with eyes that have haunted me ever since. Only one other time in my whole life had I ever seen a look like hers, and that was in Korea."

As Bailey kept talking to the jury, Duncan slipped a quick glance at the prosecutor. Gordon was studying the jury's response, and he knew they were mesmerized. He desperately wanted to object to this powerful testimony. The jury was following every word Bailey was saying. Gordon desperately wanted to object but feared the jury's reaction. His was untouchable testimony, and Gordon couldn't do a thing to stop it.

Duncan smiled while Bailey continued.

Looking at the eldest gentleman in the jury, Bailey went on. "Our unit had been out working an area that was heavily entrenched with North Koreans. We had been having to blast mortars and wait them out because they were dug in so well. One by one, we began picking them off, but it still took almost a week of constant shelling. Finally, we felt sure we had secured the area, and my buddy and I were ordered to go lift a barricade cover off one of the pits the North Koreans had dug.

"As my buddy lifted the cover, we both jumped back. A young North Korean boy, who couldn't have been more than sixteen years old, had that same look in his eyes that little girl had. That boy apparently had gotten trapped in there without his gun or any food and had sat in that hole for several days, just waiting for us to come kill him. He had been hearing the sound of the mortars exploding all around him and the sound of other North Koreans screaming in pain.

"I've tried to describe that look to other officers, but to say it was the look of a trapped animal is not sufficient. You see, an animal, unlike humans, can't really reason. Yes, they know they're trapped, but they can't know the sick anticipation of knowing someone is coming after them. A human comprehends full well know what will happen to them when that person gets there. That's the look I saw on that child's face that night. She was hiding in that closet, waiting for her father to come after her."

Officer Bailey turned his emotional eyes toward the prosecutor and asked, "Do you want to know why I remember that night so vividly? It's because I have prayed for that little girl every night for the past twenty-five years."

Bailey sat back, emotionally spent. He intended this to be the last time he would ever repeat this story, and everyone in the courtroom sat in silence.

Very early in his testimony, Lisa had put her head down on the table in front of her. She had never before heard this story. She now realized her childhood fears about abandoning her little sister had come true, and she was devastated. In all those years her sister had continued to reach out to her, caring for her, Susan had never said a word about what she had gone through. Every once in a while Lisa would lift her head and look back at her sister, mouthing the words, "I'm so sorry."

Scott, too, was struggling to keep his composure. Sitting in this courtroom for the past two days and hearing in such graphic detail what had been done to Susan was unbearable. Without warning, a rage stronger than he had ever before felt began building inside him until he couldn't sit still any longer. Without saying a word, he slipped out of his seat and walked out the door. He went out the side entrance of the court lobby and into the courtyard, trying to get control of his emotions. He had prepared himself for Susan's having a hard time listening to all of this, but he had never thought about how it would affect him. He wanted so badly to get his hands on Chuck Miller for a mere five minutes. Hitting his fists against a trash can, Scott let out an anguished cry that sounded like it came from an animal. "How dare he do that to my Susan?!"

The anger quickly turned to tears as he collapsed onto the nearest bench. Every time his mind flashed on images of Susan, either in that closet or in that kitchen, the rage would erupt anew. He allowed his mind to imagine what he would have done to Chuck Miller. But not wanting to stay in that anger, he would force those violent thoughts away and let the tears come. He didn't care who was looking or what they thought. The rage and anger at knowing what this man had done to his wife felt like white heat. Finally, after several minutes of entertaining these thoughts, Scott forced himself to calm down. Once he was certain his rage was under control, he wiped his eyes and walked back into the courtroom. He knew Susan needed him beside her, and he needed to pull himself together for her. As he slipped into his seat, he put his arm around his wife and gave her a reassuring little hug.

Carol Anne, who had been sitting next to Susan throughout the day's testimony, gently held Susan's hand. As soon as Mr. Bailey ended his testimony, Carol Anne fell apart. Susan put her arm around her friend and tried to comfort her, but Carol Anne cried, "I am so sorry you had to live with that monster. All I can think of is that little girl I knew having to live in the same house with him. I really didn't know how bad it was. I'm so sorry."

"Carol Anne, please don't. There was nothing you could have done. You were always there for me. Don't you know you saved my life? You gave me a safe haven. You shared your home and family with me and made me feel wanted. You have nothing to be sorry for."

Seeing the looks of pity and disbelief on everyone's faces, Susan felt embarrassed and naked. She never wanted these people to know what she had been through. As long as they didn't know, she could have gone on pretending it had never happened. Dr. Jacobson had been trying to get her to stop the secrets for months, but she couldn't bring herself to tell the family the truth. She had been denying it for so long, it would be as if she had been lying to them. But everything was all out in the open now, and she was surprised at the sense of relief she felt.

As she looked at Officer Bailey, she felt a strange sense of comfort. She had never looked at her childhood experiences through the eyes of another person until yesterday. Having Mrs. Reiner tell about her very own private memories with such emotion, and now Officer Bailey doing the same made her feel less alone. She realized it helped knowing that people around her—even way back then—had cared. She remembered how alone she felt the night of the beating, sitting on that porch waiting for someone to take her somewhere…anywhere. She had no way of knowing, as she was placed in that foster home for the four months her mother was recovering, that two people praying for her wellbeing every single night.

After Mr. Duncan announced he was finished with this witness, Judge Kirkley offered Gordon a chance to cross-examine Officer Bailey, but he simply dismissed him.

Susan watched Kerry Bailey take his seat and thought how she could never have picked him out of line-up as the officer who had opened the closet door that night. She then realized he probably couldn't pick her out of a crowd either, but her childhood face had been his constant companion all of these years. She kept her eyes on him as he took his seat in the row across from her. She studied that kind, caring face, and then leaned over to Scott and said, "It's time I replace that little girl's face with this one. He too needs to have his monster go away. As soon as court is dismissed, I want to meet Officer Bailey and introduce myself."

CHAPTER 34

———— ✦ ————

SUSAN INVITED KERRY Bailey back to their little rented house to meet her children and have some time to talk. Scott and Susan repeatedly thanked him for faithfully praying for her through the years, but it was when the children were brought into the living room and introduced that Kerry Bailey's real sense of relief came. Lisa Anne looked so much like her mother around that same age, and the resemblance was strong enough to startle him. He sat on the sofa while little Matthew showed him his new toy truck.

Mr. Bailey looked across the living room and stared at this grown-up Susan with Lisa Anne sitting on her lap. Lisa Anne was chatting happily about getting to cut out paper dolls with their babysitter, Mrs. Anderson, and Susan would smile and give her a hug. Mr. Bailey was thankful for this beautiful image and closed his eyes as he tried to imprint it in his memory. Every time the image of little Susan popped into his head from now on, he was going to replace it with the image of these two.

After a short visit, Mr. Bailey said he needed to get back to Atlanta. As he was walking out the door, he turned around and grinned at Scott and Susan. "You know, most of the time we pray and pray and never really know if our prayers were answered. I think God knew it was time to release me from this burden."

He reached out and gently patted Susan's face as a grandfather would and smiled. "Don't worry, Susan, after all this time I'll keep praying for you, but now it won't be painful."

Scott and Susan walked him to his car and waved as he drove off. "Scott, even though these past two days have been hard, I have this tremendous feeling of freedom. Dr. Jacobson said I would, but I didn't believe her. I couldn't think of anything more horrible than for you and your family to find out my secrets. It was hard enough when she forced me to face my memories. I resisted for the longest time, afraid of what it would feel like to really face them."

As Scott put his arm around his wife and kissed her, Susan remembered something. "Dr. Jacobson told me my memories were like a whale in the ocean. She said, 'Imagine trying to hold a giant whale underwater. You might be able to do it for a while, but eventually, that whale is going to decide to come up for air, and all the resolve in the world will not keep him under.' She told me, but I didn't believe her. She said, 'The energy it takes to keep something of that size down is more exhausting than the pain of facing it, once it surfaces.' "

Stopping at the front door, Susan turned to Scott and smiled. "You know, she was right. She and I spent a long time going back over my memories and facing them together, and I felt a real sense of freedom. But somehow, I couldn't take the next step. I was too afraid to tell you about my past. I always entertained this nagging feeling that if you were really ever to find out who I was, you would change your mind about me because, in my mind, who I was—was my family."

Wanting his response to be as gentle as possible, Scott was careful how he worded his question. "Why? Why did you think you had to hide that part of yourself from me? Susan, I'm feeling all kinds of emotions right now. I'm filled with anger at what you had to go through. I'm sorry, but I'm also feeling a little hurt that you didn't trust me with your secret. But most of all, I'm sad that you felt you had to suffer alone. I love you, and I don't want any more secrets between us. Whatever it is, we're in it together from now on." Then with a gentle squeeze, he added, "The whale has surfaced, and we're all breathing clean air. Right?"

"Right."

Hearing the phone ring, they hurried in to answer it. Grabbing the phone, Scott talked quietly for a few minutes and then handed it to Susan. "It's my mom. She wants to talk to you."

Scott and Susan had slipped out of the courtroom so quickly they hadn't had a chance to talk with anyone. After a few minutes of small talk, Caroline brought up the testimony. "Susan, the past few days must have been very difficult for you. I could not let today close without telling you how much I love you. We all knew things were bad at home for you, but we had no idea how bad. It's so painful to think of you as a child, like our little Lisa Anne, being treated like that."

Susan simply shrugged, as if embarrassed. "Mom, I'm sorry you had to hear what you heard. I know the testimony made everyone uncomfortable. That's one of the reasons I didn't tell people. After all, there was nothing any of you could do about it. Besides, I hate when people go around whining about their terrible childhood. So many walk around wearing their wounds like some kind of war medal, repeating every ugly event they ever experienced to any poor soul they can trap into a conversation. I never wanted to be like that."

"I understand what you're saying. That seems to be in fashion these days, but we're your family, and we love you. We should have known. Sure, it's painful to hear something that horrible, but when you love someone, you want to help share that pain so it's less of a burden. I know having it exposed in a courtroom was probably the most difficult way, but don't you feel a little better knowing it isn't a deep, dark secret any longer? Susan, the shame is theirs—not yours. You have nothing to be ashamed of. You survived a horrible childhood. They didn't win! They didn't break you, and I am so very proud of you."

"I love you, Mom. I'm sorry I didn't tell you the truth a long time ago."

Listening to only one side of this conversation, Scott thought, *Why didn't I see this? I was so busy trying to make a new life for her—a happy, safe, wonderful life. I wanted to help her forget her past. I probably told her in a thousand different ways that I didn't want to know what really happened to her. Somehow I helped build that wall she's been living behind but, God help me, I'm also going to help her take it down, brick by brick.*

Before hanging up, Caroline said, "Gladys has something she wants to ask you," and handed the phone to her sister-in-law.

"Susan, would it help if we came over and took the children for the night and gave you and Scott some time alone?"

Susan appreciated the offer but said, "I really don't want quiet tonight, Aunt Gladys. I want my children to laugh, giggle, hug, and kiss all evening long, and the louder the better."

"All right, Susan. I wish there was something I could do for you. How are you holding up?"

Susan felt flooded with the love and support this family always offered her. "You know, Aunt Gladys, sitting in that courtroom, seeing my childhood as an adult instead of through my memories has given me a different perspective. I was able to visualize our Lisa Anne there instead of me. It's strange how age changes your perspective. You know, three women in that courtroom suffered at the hands of Chuck Miller. Two of us survived, but Mother hasn't. As long as she holds onto her hate and anger, he still controls her. I don't hate her, but I don't love her either, and that's all right. Hopefully, someday, someone will reach her—like you have reached Lisa. That too is Mother's choice. But I've also realized that surviving isn't enough. I've carried the burden of that family like a yoke, and I'm through. As long as I kept their dirty secrets, they had control over me. I used to tell Lisa it applied to her self-destruction and anger, but I never realized how the shame was controlling me."

The lightheartedness in her voice thrilled Gladys. Her two girls were going to be all right.

That evening Scott and Susan played with the children and had a picnic dinner in the backyard. Susan filled a basket with hot dogs, watermelon, chips, carrot sticks, and potato salad. She grabbed a large blanket from the linen closet and spread it out under the big tree and tossed some pillows on it.

As she was doing this, Scott took out the new electric ice cream maker they had purchased and allowed Lisa Anne and Megan to help mix the ingredients for fresh strawberry ice cream. Matthew was just happy having everyone outside and was laughing and playing with his toys.

After Susan had everything ready, she relaxed on the blanket, resting her head on one of the pillows and watching her children play. Megan, being only three, had less patience than Lisa Anne and soon left the ice cream maker alone, thinking it was taking much too long to stand and watch.

She walked over to the blanket to question what was in the basket. Without warning, Susan grabbed her and pulled her down. With a giggle in her voice, Susan started tickling and kissing her and telling her what a pretty little girl she was and how much she loved her. Matthew, just a few steps away, never wanting to be left out of a hugging contest, gave a big belly laugh as he plopped down on his mom's legs and tried to tickle her.

Lisa Anne stood frozen, watching this interplay between her mommy and little sister, but every once in a while she glanced over at her daddy. She was six years old and was not used to her mommy starting their tickle contests. As she stood watching, she noticed a big grin on her daddy's face.

Scott noticed Lisa Anne's standing back and wondered if she was sort of waiting to be invited into this much-loved contest. Knowing what a struggle it had always been for Susan, it felt so good to see her initiate this activity with the two little ones. He wanted to somehow get Susan's attention that Lisa Anne needed to also be included but didn't know how to do it without spoiling the spontaneous moment for Susan.

Then as Susan rolled over and pinned Megan to the blanket, holding her down with one hand, Susan reached out and grabbed Lisa Anne around the waist and pulled her down onto the blanket. Matthew had tumbled off as Susan rolled over and was quickly getting up to again jump on his mom's legs. Susan tickled Lisa Anne and kissed her all over her face and neck, which drove Lisa Anne crazy. Her neck was the most ticklish place on her body, and she giggled and laughed until she was crying with pleasure.

Susan lifted her head away from Lisa Anne, giving her a chance to catch her breath before starting all over again. Lisa Anne put her arms around her mom's neck and pulled her down to her ever so gently. With the sweetest smile on her little face, Lisa Anne said, "I love you, Mommy."

Scott, a step away from joining in, stopped in his tracks. He knew this was a wonderful moment for Susan. He had never before seen such a freedom in her response, and he knew Susan had somehow faced another monster and had freed herself.

As Lisa Anne allowed her mother to pull away slightly, he heard Susan say, "I love you, too, Lisa Anne. Mommy loves all three of her precious little angels, and I'm going to tickle you three until you all say 'uncle'!" Their screams of delight filled the summer night. This time, Mommy invited Daddy to join the family in their play, and Lisa Anne did not miss the switch. She was only six, but she knew something good had just happened.

Scott lit a citronella candle to discourage the bugs, and everyone sat on the blanket and enjoyed their hot dog dinner as if it were a banquet. Scott let the girls help serve the ice cream, and when everyone was finished, Susan took out a washcloth and cleaned up the children. She then pulled out their pajamas and changed the two little ones right there in the backyard. Lisa Anne wasn't so sure she wanted to change her clothes where others could see, so Scott held up a large towel while Susan helped her change.

When all three children were ready for bed, Scott and Susan lay down on the blanket and had the children lie down with their heads resting on their parents' tummies. They studied the stars, trying to see if they could make out any faces. Daddy told them some bedtime stories as, one by one, they began to fall asleep.

When all three children were fast asleep, Scott and Susan stayed out back for another hour. They quietly talked about each of their precious little children and thanked God they were theirs to love. Not one word was spoken about the trial that evening. Tonight was theirs, and they were not going to share it.

CHAPTER 35

ON THE OTHER side of town, things were moving in high gear. Duncan had been running himself ragged for three days now. He was desperately trying to keep the trial moving forward during the day and trying to remain focused in front of the jury in case these new facts didn't pan out. An attorney's first obligation is to protect and defend his client. He is obliged to counsel them as to their very best course of action but, if they reject his advice, he must still protect his client.

For three nights, he had been pleading with Lisa to let him defend her properly, but she was not budging. Being bound by client-attorney privilege, he could not enlist her family to help him convince her to listen. It had been a hard week for both of them, but tonight everything was coming together, and soon the truth would be out. Even though Lisa didn't like it, the next day everyone was going to know the truth.

Around eight o'clock that evening, Judge Kirkley called Mr. Gordon into his chambers. As Gordon pushed open the door, he immediately saw Duncan turn from the window. Judge Kirkley was sitting at his desk, and the expression on his face made Gordon's blood run cold. Attempting to feign a confident air, Gordon blustered, "Good evening, Your Honor. What is so important that it couldn't wait until morning?"

Without changing his countenance in the slightest, Judge Kirkley motioned to the empty chair opposite his desk. He didn't say a word; he simply waited for Gordon to follow his instructions.

Gordon shot a quick glance toward Duncan, who simply kept his gaze on the judge. With a nervous tug at his suit coat, Gordon bluffed a "whatever" shrug and took his seat. The seconds seemed eternal as he waited for Judge Kirkley to say whatever was on his mind.

Duncan noticed a nervous twitch, as if Gordon were trying to push up an invisible pair of glasses on his nose. If he hadn't been so angry, Mr. Duncan would have been tempted to feel sorry for him.

Slowly and deliberately, Judge Kirkley began explaining why he had called this meeting. "Mr. Gordon, several days ago Mr. Duncan came to me with some serious allegations—the most serious being obstruction of justice."

Gordon jumped to his feet. He began flailing his arms, threatening and insulting Duncan, desperately trying to play the wounded and offended victim when a loud, thunderous blast came from Judge Kirkley: "Gordon, shut up and sit down."

The tone in the judge's voice brought immediate silence to the room.

Gordon took his seat and stared expressionlessly at the judge.

With almost a whisper, the judge then asked, "May I continue now?"

Gordon merely nodded.

"Gordon, I must advise you that for the past three days, I have been looking into some of these allegations and have found enough to warrant a full investigation."

Gordon tried to protest, but the judge held up his hand and said, "Don't even try, Mr. Gordon. I will not waste any time tonight listening to your explanations. Let me tell you what it looks like from this side of the judicial desk. I have a feeling your thirst for press coverage during this election campaign might have had a great deal to do with your tactics. I suspect you thought you had a career-building, save-the-community kind of case. Then after you blew it up larger than life, expecting to ride it right into the DA's seat, you found your election ticket not only slipping out of your hands, but you were afraid of being exposed as the manipulating conniver you really are. You were willing to send that woman to prison in order to win that election, weren't you? You've known for weeks she didn't do it, but you also knew that she wasn't about to speak up, so you thought you were safe. You didn't count on that girl's coming forward—not after you had threatened her."

Gordon sat quiet and still. He knew he could say nothing that would help right now.

Judge Kirkley began to discuss how they would proceed with this new information. "Duncan, I'm going to keep this trial moving forward, allowing you to call your next two witnesses before we break for four days. That will give you time to review the new information and prepare for putting the girl on the stand next Monday."

Seeing Gordon's reaction, Kirkley exploded, "Mr. Gordon, don't even think about suggesting dropping the charges now. You've done your dead level best to destroy that woman. I suspect, at first anyway, you did think you had a murder case on your hands, but you and I both know that almost a month before this trial was scheduled to start, you learned the truth."

Gordon jerked up his head, and an instant of fear appeared on his face. Quickly regaining his composure, he started to defend himself, but again Judge Kirkley silenced him.

"Don't bother denying it, Gordon. I have your phone logs. That was your defining moment—not now. You made a decision to suppress evidence for *your* greater good. You've sat in that courtroom just like me, hearing what those two women have had to endure in their lives, yet you kept going. I will not allow you to drop the charges and make that woman live in this town with the cloud of doubt you put over her. We both know what this town would do to her. She deserves her day in court. We're going to play this out."

With a look that forced Gordon to turn away, Judge Kirkley laid his glasses on his desk and rubbed his tired eyes. "We have the best legal system anywhere in the world, but people like you could bring it to its knees with your dishonesty. This system will only work if the public believes in it. How many times can they see people like you abusing your position before they totally distrust its ability to serve them?"

Duncan quietly walked over and took the seat next to Gordon. He knew Judge Kirkley's influence in this town. He knew this issue was not going to stop within these four walls.

The judge then turned his gaze to Duncan. "Under these circumstances, I intend to grant Mr. Duncan the greatest of latitude while questioning these last two witnesses"—he checked his witness list to confirm their names—"a Mrs. Gladys Carter and a Mrs. Ruth Bascom."

Looking directly at Mr. Gordon, he chided, "I would seriously advise you to limit your objections during this testimony. You're walking on very thin ice, and I suggest you tread lightly."

At this point, Gordon knew the best thing he could do was keep as quiet as possible. Duncan, on the other hand, needed some additional reassurance from the court. "Your Honor, knowing you will be tied up with other matters on Thursday and Friday, may I ask the court to order the necessary search warrant for the bakery?"

With an understanding nod, Judge Kirkley responded, "Certainly." Then, with an icy stare toward Gordon, he added, "I'll also order forensic tests resulting from any findings at that location be forwarded to both counsel. Inasmuch as this search is necessary before we go beyond these next two witnesses, I intend to call the proceedings to a close at the lunch hour tomorrow. Mr. Duncan, can you be finished with these two witnesses by then?"

"Yes, Your Honor. That'll give me the afternoon to explain all of these new details to Lisa's family."

"That's good." But feeling the need to issue one last warning while gathering his things to leave, Judge Kirkley turned to Duncan. "You do understand this mess is coming from both sides, don't you?"

"Yes, Your Honor, I certainly do." Duncan quickly acknowledged.

"Gordon isn't the only one at fault here. Your client was also wrong, so don't you come walking into my courtroom tomorrow with too smug a face."

Duncan acknowledged this final warning. "No, Your Honor."

"All right, then. It's late, and I'd like to have some time at home this evening. I'll see you two in my courtroom tomorrow morning at nine o'clock."

CHAPTER 36

WEDNESDAY MORNING WAS getting rather heated at Gladys Carter's house. Bill, being filled in on what he had missed the day before, was having trouble keeping his own emotions under control. "I know I had no choice. If I hadn't gone back to Atlanta, thirty-five people would have been out of work next month. These families depend on me to keep the work coming in, but I'm so sorry I wasn't here for Susan. I'm not leaving again. This is too important, and the whole family needs to be here to support all of them—Lisa, Susan, and Scott. I cannot imagine how our son must have felt having to sit and hear about all that abuse. All I can picture is someone's trying to do that to our little Lisa Anne, and I actually feel sick to my stomach."

"Our son knows you were doing what you had to do. I talked to both of them last evening. They're both all right."

"Well, I'm not." Bill hadn't had the time to digest this information the way Gladys and Caroline had. His emotions were raging at the image of Susan's being in that closet. "I should have done something. I knew something was wrong in that house. We had lots of clues. I feel like I let her down."

"Bill, we all feel that way, but you have to remember, this happened in 1960. There were so few laws to protect children back then. This society has come a long way in changing the laws so children can have a voice."

"I know, but the laws are still not enough. Children are not property. We need to find a way to get these children away from the likes of Chuck and Marjorie Miller. Sure, I feel sorry for Marjorie Miller. That woman suffered a lot, but she crossed the line. Somewhere in her sick head, her selfish need to protect herself turned her from being a victim into a victimizer. I don't really care what her sad story is; it's not an excuse. I'm tired of having this sickness passed on to second-generation victims. Their poor damaged past is no excuse for abusing children. Somehow, this society must put a stop to this kind of abuse."

With a calming voice, Gladys interjected, "Bill, I don't think Caroline is suggesting we excuse Marjorie's behavior because it is inexcusable. But if we're ever going to stop this cycle, we must understand that these sick, abusing parents were most likely abused themselves."

Gladys was the last person Bill thought would defend Marjorie Miller. "How can you say that? Why should we have to care why she is the way she is? Isn't that making her not responsible?"

Trying to calm down her brother, Gladys suggested, "No, I don't think so. If our society refuses to acknowledge that the abusive people we are contending with today are the result of sick parenting of the past, they'll never seriously address the causes of bad parenting which continue. It's not to give them an excuse; rather, it's to understand and stop it from continuing."

Reluctantly, Bill admitted, "I guess even Marjorie Miller has a story—not that I care to hear it."

Gladys smiled. "Nor I. We're living too close to her damage, but she was once a child too. Someone should care why she turned out the way she did. Maybe understanding that past could help the next Marjorie from taking her same path."

It was getting late, and they needed to get to court. Starting to laugh, Bill placed his arm around his sister and kissed her as they headed out the door. "Gladys, after these past few days, hearing everything we've heard, only you could make me feel pangs of sympathy for a woman like Marjorie Miller. I'm not quite sure if I'm ready to stop hating her exactly yet, but I am sure you'll keep after me. You're a good person, Gladys. Better than I am."

Everyone was seated in the courtroom promptly at nine o'clock. The family was eager to get on with the trial, sure that the worst was now behind them.

Mr. Duncan met with Lisa before coming into the courtroom. In one sense, things were falling apart for his client, but in another, everything was coming together. He understood the stress she was feeling but advised, "I don't want you to say anything, or act as if anything is going on until after Mrs. Carter and Mrs. Bascom testify. Lisa, these women's testimonies are critical. The jury will be asked to decide what kind of person you are. These women can tell them. We cannot drop this bombshell on Mrs. Carter and Mrs. Bascom just before they get up on that stand and expect them to do a good job. This new information wouldn't change their testimony, but it might make them seem confused. Do you agree?"

Lisa's world was unraveling, and she could do nothing to stop it. "I'll try. I thought the day I had to sit there and listen to my mother testify was hard. Today, having to sit emotionless as if nothing is going on will be harder, but I'll try."

As planned, Mr. Duncan was able to get both Gladys and Ruth on the stand that morning. He carefully worded each question so their answers were always facts they knew to be true, rather than opinions or conclusions. He did not want to give Gordon any more opportunities than absolutely necessary to raise an objection before the jury.

Gladys talked about meeting Lisa in the hospital after her drug overdose and jail time eleven years earlier. She told how Lisa and she had attended alcohol and drug addiction support groups three times a week for the first two years and then how Lisa had become a group leader four years later.

She shared how hard it was for Lisa to get through each day that first year. How she would wake up at night with nightmares, and they would sit up the rest of the night talking so she could make it through. She explained how Lisa had chosen to hand over all of her hard-earned paycheck every Friday for the first two years. "You see, she wanted to help with the household expenses, but even more, she didn't want to take even a single chance of being tempted to stray."

The jury heard how much Lisa loved her sister and her children, especially Lisa Anne, and how hard Lisa had worked to make the children proud of her. Gladys never actually said to the jury that she was proud of Lisa, but she didn't have to. The pride on her face as she talked about what this young woman had accomplished was unmistakable.

Mr. Duncan stood in front of the jury box so Gladys could look directly at them as she answered the last few questions. "Mrs. Carter, were you aware that Charles Miller was released from prison almost a month before that fateful night?"

"No, sir."

"Do you know whether Lisa was made aware of his release?"

"No, sir."

"Mrs. Carter, during that month, did you detect any change in Lisa's behavior? Any anger, change in routine, or suspicious behavior?" He knew Gordon wanted to object to this line of questioning but wouldn't dare.

With great confidence, Gladys scanned the jury, allowing her eyes to move from face to face as she answered, "Absolutely not. She was calm, happy, and looking forward to her first trip to Savannah. She and I were going to spend a whole week at my son's place at the shore. We'd been planning it for almost three months."

Stepping closer to the witness box, Duncan asked his last question. "Mrs. Carter, will you please tell this court who you think Lisa Miller is?"

Gordon could remain silent no longer and was on his feet. "Your Honor, I object. Mrs. Carter is not an expert in human behavior. Her opinion is simply that—an opinion."

Duncan started to respond, but seeing the look on Judge Kirkley's face, decided to remain quiet. The judge leaned over toward Gladys, studying her face for a moment, and then said, "I think I'll allow it. More than ten years of personal experience should qualify her to answer that question. Mrs. Carter, you may answer."

Gladys turned toward the jury and took a deep breath. "I know Lisa Miller to be a strong, wonderful, loving woman. She has fought back from the very brink of self-destruction and self-loathing. As you have heard, this woman suffered horribly at the hands of her father, but I do not think she deliberately intended to kill him. I've watched her grow to appreciate herself, accept love from others, and learn to trust people again. She has become a woman I would proudly call my daughter. There's no way she would have done anything to throw away that relationship."

Stepping back to his seat, Duncan announced, "I have no other questions," and Gordon wasn't about to ask any. Aunt Gladys gave Lisa a reassuring smile as she took her seat next to Susan.

Duncan then called Ruth to the stand. As she came forward and was sworn in, the jury studied her confident air. She was a black woman, appearing to be in her mid-seventies, was well-dressed and sure of herself. Lisa noticed several puzzled glances from the jury as if wondering where this black woman fit into all of this. Lisa chuckled as she thought, *She fits just fine, just you wait. She'll show you.*

Duncan decided to remain seated beside Lisa as he questioned Mrs. Bascom. He wanted to connect her and his client, as her testimony would no doubt do. "Mrs. Bascom, will you please tell this court what you do for a living?"

With great pride in her voice, Ruth looked directly at the most senior juror. "I own and operate the bakery where Lisa has been employed for the past ten years."

"Can you tell the court what brought you to hire someone with Lisa's record?"

With a quick smile toward Gladys, Ruth gladly told her story. "Gladys Carter and I go way back. We've been friends for more than fifty years. Our husbands worked together at Hastings Furniture Factory in Atlanta. Gladys's husband, Karl, was the one who loaned me the money to start my bakery in Jefferson the year after my husband passed. Everyone who knew me knew I could bake, but when I couldn't find a single bank willing to take a chance on me, Karl put a mortgage on his house and got me started."

Lisa spun around in her seat and stared at Gladys. She was amazed that she never had heard that story. Gladys sat smiling. She was obviously proud of Karl.

Ruth continued. "Anyway, I struggled at first. It's one thing to know how to turn out a beautiful pie, but it's another thing running a business, especially for a black woman in the white business district. I worked hard, took some business classes, and made it work. I repaid Karl every single penny. Gladys and I have been part of the same church for years. We were both widows and enjoyed each other's company. That's how I heard about Lisa. Gladys told me she was thinking about inviting this girl into her home, but I didn't like it. I was afraid for her. The girl was dreadful. She couldn't say one sentence without using foul language. Besides, she was on drugs, and I was scared she would hurt Gladys.

"Well, Gladys didn't listen to me or her son. She wanted to help this girl and wanted me to help her too. At first I said no, but Gladys kept after me and wore me down. I agreed to hire her, but only for her to work in the back kitchen at first. You see, when she first came to work, everyone had to walk gingerly around her because she had a flash temper and a sailor's tongue."

Officer Jackson looked over at Susan when Mrs. Bascom made this comment and gave her an embarrassed little shrug. Susan chuckled quietly but quickly returned to a more serious demeanor.

Duncan interjected, "Mrs. Bascom, did you have trouble with Lisa?"

Turning her gaze toward Lisa with an obvious look of pride, she answered, "Yes, for quite a while. You need to understand. Lisa didn't trust anyone. She was angry, hostile, and her nerves were shot. She had a hard time cleaning up her body from years of drugs and alcohol abuse, but she was determined to beat it. I never saw a girl want to get clean as much as she did."

Duncan stood up and walked over to the witness stand. "Mrs. Bascom, how long did it take Lisa to win you over?"

Ruth Bascom, being a very savvy witness, knew what Duncan was asking. "Mr. Duncan, it took her two years—but not because she messed up, but because I couldn't afford to make a mistake in judgment. I worked that girl hard. For the first whole year she stayed in the kitchen cleaning every pot, pan, cookie sheet, and oven I owned. I slowly started teaching her how to bake, and you should have seen the look on that girl's face the first time a customer complimented one of her cakes. You would have thought she'd won a beauty contest."

Several of the jurors chuckled at this comment, and Duncan knew she was winning them over. He stepped over and stood beside her and asked, "So when did you feel comfortable giving Lisa more responsibility?"

Ruth knew the jury was responding to her, so she was going to take full advantage of her age and experience. "Well, Mr. Duncan, for three whole years I watched that girl like an old hound watches a raccoon he's treed." Several of the jurors smiled at this familiar colloquial Southern saying.

Ruth smiled back and then continued. "I couldn't afford to make an error in judgment; my livelihood was at stake. After watching that girl grow and change, I realized the girl I'd hired three years earlier no longer existed. In her place was a lovely, trustworthy, hard-working woman whom I love dearly."

Duncan smiled at her comment. She was doing a great job. "Mrs. Bascom, after that three years, you started giving Lisa more and more responsibility. Can you tell us some of those responsibilities?"

"By her third anniversary, she was already my lead baker. Although she enjoyed the front counter, baking was her passion. By the end of her fourth year, she had become the chief baker, with five other women taking their directions from her. She was responsible for everyone's schedule, as well as large-party orders such as weddings and banquets. She even got us the standing orders for the fire department and city hall cafeterias. Everyone at my bakery, including all of my customers, absolutely adore Lisa. For the past five years, Lisa has been responsible for all the bank deposits and bakery security."

It was almost noon when Mr. Duncan finished with Mrs. Bascom. He knew Mr. Gordon was furious at the freedom the judge was allowing him. As he took his seat, he wondered if Gordon would dare cross-examine Mrs. Bascom. Sure enough, as he sat next to Lisa, Gordon stood up, straightened his jacket, and swaggered up to the witness box with arrogance that surprised even the judge. Duncan glanced at Judge Kirkley and gave him a look like, "What is he doing?" He received in return a shrug of the judge's shoulders, a puzzled look on his face.

Stepping up to the witness box, Gordon asked, "Now, Mrs. Bascom. Are we to believe you were willing to hire a drug-using, drug-selling prostitute and hand over the keys of your business to her, allowing her to handle your deposits, and there was never any money missing?"

Mrs. Bascom had listened to about as much from this man as she could stand. Deciding to simply ignore Mr. Gordon, Mrs. Bascom turned confidently to the jury, smiled, and responded, "Do you really think I would entrust my life's work into the hands of a person like he just described? I have watched this woman grow into a respectable, caring, loving person over these past eleven years, and she could not have done what they say she did."

Mrs. Bascom then smiled at Gordon, like a mother smiles at a disobedient child she is about to scold. "Mr. Gordon, like I said, I didn't automatically turn anything over to Lisa Miller. I worked her like a dog in the back kitchen for almost three years before she was even allowed to see one of my customers, let alone be responsible for having a set of keys or touch my money. I'm not a stupid person, Mr. Gordon, but sometimes in order to stay human, you have to take a chance on people. Lisa Miller had never been given a chance in her whole life. Gladys and I thought it was time somebody did. I know this world does not believe people can change and, without some real help, maybe they can't. But one thing I do know. If a person is willing to let God help them, and people like Gladys Carter are willing to trust God to help and protect them while they love these people in Jesus' name, anyone can change. I have come to love that woman sitting over there like my own daughter, as has Gladys Carter. Personally, I think it would take the two of us treating her as a daughter for the rest of her life to make up for having had that woman"—she pointed toward Marjorie Miller—"for a mother her first seventeen years of her life."

With this final lengthy explanation, Mr. Gordon dismissed Mrs. Bascom.

Duncan couldn't help but chuckle as Gordon returned to his seat. *Boy, did he pick on the wrong woman!* If he wasn't so angry at the man for deliberately trying to hurt his client, he could almost feel sorry for him—almost.

Banging the gavel on his desk, Judge Kirkley called the courtroom to order. "Ladies and gentlemen of the jury, some court business has come up that requires a two-day delay of this trial, which will carry us into the weekend. Because of this matter, I have decided this is a good time to stop today's session since I do not want to be in the middle of testimony with a four-day break coming."

After reminding them to refrain from drawing any conclusions or talking about the case with anyone, Judge Kirkley instructed, "Bailiff, please escort the jury out of the courtroom while everyone else remains seated."

As soon as they were removed, Judge Kirkley gave Lisa a fatherly smile, knowing what was now ahead of her, and then removed himself to his chamber.

Duncan quickly signaled Officer Jackson to remove Lisa before the family came to talk with her. "I'll give them a one-hour break and then assemble them in the conference room. You go to the restroom, have some lunch, and get yourself ready. I'll call for you when we're all in there. Lisa, it's going to be all right. They'll understand once you explain. Don't worry; it's almost over."

As prearranged, Officer Ben Jackson escorted Lisa out of the courtroom while Mr. Duncan played interference. Stepping into the aisle in front of them, he raised his hand in a halting fashion. "Lisa won't be having lunch with you today, but she'll see you in a little while." Trying to distract their attention from Lisa, he said, "You ladies were amazing. Did you see those jurors looking at Lisa, obviously filled with respect and compassion? They were told, and they believed, that Lisa has changed. You did a wonderful job."

After giving everyone else a chance to chime in and add their own bravos, Mr. Duncan suggested they all take a few minutes to use the restrooms, get a quick bite to eat at the lunch cart, and then meet him in the conference room at one o'clock. "Since we've been given this afternoon off, I feel we need to cover some matters before we dismiss for four days. It's important, so I'd like all of you to attend."

Obviously this was all he was going to say for the time being, so the family members picked up their things and headed out. He had said it in such a matter-of-fact manner, no one suspected anything was afoot. Duncan studied them as they enjoyed the exuberance of this morning's testimony, thinking, *You're quite a family. If ever anyone needed to find and be accepted into a family like yours, these two girls did. You have quite a shock ahead of you, but you'll be fine. You'll handle it just fine.*

CHAPTER 37

AT ONE O'CLOCK Scott, Susan, Bill, Caroline, Aunt Gladys, Mrs. Bascom, Carol Anne and Harry were all seated and talking quietly in the large conference room at the end of the hall when Duncan entered the room. The seriousness of his expression immediately unnerved them.

As he took his seat, Susan asked, "Mr. Duncan, what is going on? I know something is. In fact, I've suspected something for days."

"Yes, Susan, you're right. Something has been going on. But before I have Lisa brought in, I wanted to talk with you all. Over the past several days, some startling new information has come to my attention. I haven't been able to talk about it until now because Judge Kirkley needed to help me clear up some possible problems that might occur as a result. I needed some assurances that certain people would be protected, and I needed some help getting the timing of this information properly coordinated. What you're going to hear will shock you, but I wanted you to hear it in here—not out there in the courtroom. I also wanted you to hear it from Lisa."

A thousand questions were flying around in Susan's head. She tried not to jump to conclusions, but this vagueness was scaring her, and knowing how Lisa had been behaving wasn't helping.

Mr. Duncan stood and asked the officer to bring in Lisa.

A few moments later she walked in and took a seat. She was visibly nervous, and as soon as the officer left the room and closed the door, Susan blurted out, "Lisa, what's going on?"

Lisa didn't look up or comment.

Scott looked from Duncan to Lisa and then back to Duncan. "So can you tell us what's going on here?"

Duncan took his seat next to Lisa, and placing his hand on her arm to reassure her, he started the ball rolling. "Well, I've suspected something for several months. I wasn't sure if Lisa was so traumatized that night that she couldn't remember everything—or worse, that she could be keeping the truth from us. As you have heard in the courtroom, something was not right about her story, but she stuck by her account of that night, even though the evidence contradicted her. I'm obliged to defend my client the way she mandates—that is, as long as she doesn't ask me to lie or expect me to put her on the stand and allow her to knowingly lie." Duncan then turned to Lisa and asked, "Would it be easier for you if I tell them?"

With an almost inaudible voice, she sighed. "No. I will. I caused all of this mess."

Looking over at her sister for the first time, Lisa took a deep breath and began to tell what had really happened the night of the murder.

"I let the girls leave a little early that night because they had dinner plans, and I knew they wanted to get home and freshen up. Besides, business is always slow the last two hours on Saturdays. I knew I'd have my two regular customers picking up their Sunday morning baked goods but didn't really expect more than one or two other stray customers stopping in. I didn't mind cleaning up the kitchen alone, so they finished up around five-thirty and left. My regulars came in around a quarter to six, and then I went into the kitchen and started cleaning the cookie sheets.

"Around six-fifteen I heard the entry bell signal that someone had entered the shop. I headed out front to service the person and didn't really look at the customer at first. I noticed she was a fairly young woman and headed behind the counter to where she was standing."

Glancing over at Gladys, Lisa hesitated for a moment and then continued. "That's when I got my first really good look at her. I instantly knew who she was and why she was there. I could have picked her out of a thousand people. I had feared this day of reckoning for twenty-two years."

As Duncan placed his arm around her for moral support, Lisa looked directly into her sister's eyes and said, "I was looking into the face of my one and only daughter."

Seeing the look of pure astonishment on her sister's face, Lisa struggled on. "Her name is Hope. Can you believe it? They named my little girl Hope. I love it, Susan."

Looking over at Aunt Gladys and seeing that same supportive smile she had always known helped Lisa continue. "Aunt Gladys, she's a lovely young woman—not a stunning beauty like our Lisa Anne, but very pretty. She reminds me of myself when I was young. That is, before my life took its toll on me. She finished college last spring and is engaged to marry a young man she has known most of her life."

Seeing hurt and disbelief mixing on Susan's face, she turned directly to her sister and pleaded, "You don't know how many times I wanted to tell you about her. I just couldn't. At first, I didn't want to. I was such a wreck back then, and you were such a goody-goody. Susan, I couldn't keep her. As much as I hated Mother, I knew I was too much like her to trust myself with a baby. Besides, I was living on the street. How could I care for a baby? As it was, I had to steal to keep myself fed while carrying her. I couldn't go to anyone for help for fear of being sent back home because I was still a minor. You see, I knew I was pregnant when I ran away. I didn't get pregnant on the street, Susan. I know who the father is. He was the only person, besides you, whoever loved me. When I discovered I was expecting, I knew I had to run. We were both still in high school, and you know what Dad would have done to him for bringing shame to his house. I couldn't risk being beaten again—not for me—but for the sake of my baby."

Susan nodded in agreement. She knew exactly what their father would have done to both of them for bringing such shame upon him. As she listened to her sister talk, she tried to figure out how she was feeling. Hurt, definitely. Maybe a little angry for not being trusted with the truth, but mostly bewildered. This was so out of the blue, so unexpected.

"Susan, I didn't start the drugs and prostitution until after I gave her up. At least I did that one thing right. I didn't hurt my baby. I gave her a chance at a better life than we had. After I gave her up, I didn't really care what happened to me. I found if I kept myself doped up, I could sort of forget about her and didn't have to think about what I had to do to keep myself supplied. Then days turned to months, and months turned to years. I know it was stupid, but in a sick way, it helped. As you know, I spent some time in jail and then on probation. When I was finally free, I wanted to get away from California. I didn't want to watch every little girl passing by and wonder if she was my little girl. I wanted to get far away. That's why I came back to Georgia."

"Lisa, why didn't you tell me then? I would have understood." There wasn't anger in Susan's voice, only confusion and disbelief.

"By the time I moved here, she was five years old; I didn't want to think about her. My life was over. I was twenty-two but felt like one hundred. It's strange, but from day to day I didn't think about how I felt about myself. It wasn't an issue. It was only when you came around to see me that I struggled with what I was doing. I would only feel when you were around. That's why I didn't like having you around.

"Anyway, the longer I went without telling you, the harder it got. You and Aunt Gladys were so good to me. Then you and Scott lost your baby. How could I tell you I had given mine away? I watched you struggle with your grief and couldn't tell you I knew how you were feeling. I couldn't share the pain your loss was causing me. You had forgiven me for so much, but I didn't quite trust this wouldn't get past. Why should you? I never have."

"But Lisa, I've always forgiven you. When have I ever turned my back on you?"

Wanting desperately for her sister to understand, Lisa pleaded, "Remember the night Lisa Anne was born? I was so happy for you. You were finally getting your little girl, and then, Scott, you invited me into the delivery room. Watching you in labor flooded my mind with the memory of my own labor, knowing I had to give away my baby when it was over. Then standing there looking into Lisa Anne's little face, I ached for my own little girl. I wanted to scream, 'I have one too,' but it was too late. I had waited too long to tell the truth, and I found myself a prisoner behind a wall of silence I had built. I was a prisoner of my own making."

Duncan gently suggested, "This is a lot to absorb. There are lots of issues, and we aren't going to be able to settle twenty-two years' of secrets here today. Why don't we get back to that night?"

Lisa cleared her throat and slowly began the story of what had really happened that night. "Well, at first she pretended to be interested in buying some baked goods. She ordered a dozen cookies and then some pastries. I knew she was testing the water, telling me she was in town to visit some long-lost relatives. She said something about thinking it would be nice to bring along some baked goods to warm up the meeting. I knew she was studying me, and I had no idea how to respond. I found myself groping for casual words, while in my head I was pleading, *Don't pursue this. I don't want you to know what I was. Why didn't you just leave it alone?*

"All of a sudden I heard sort of a choking sound come from her throat. I knew she was trying to get up the nerve to say something. I wanted to help break the tension but didn't know how. As casually as I could, I simply smiled at her and asked, 'How have you been?' "

Relief flooded her face, and she took a deep breath and said, "I've been fine. You know who I am, don't you?"

"I told her I was pretty sure. I told her I had wondered if this day would ever happen—how in lots of ways I had longed for it, but in other ways I had dreaded it. I suggested she follow me into the kitchen so I could make a pot of coffee and continue cleaning as we talked. At first we talked about her. Was she happy? Were they good to her? Where did she grow up? Was she married? Were there grandchildren?

"Anyway, she told me all about her life. How she loves her parents and that they were good to her. She was reared in a good home with two other adopted children. She said that since they were all adopted, it was always an open topic of conversation. The oldest, a boy, didn't have any interest in finding his birth parents, but she and her younger sister did.

Their parents told them when they reached eighteen, if they still wanted to find their birth family they would help them. Because of my fear of our parents' finding out about her, I had lied about my age and had demanded a closed adoption. I wanted the records sealed. I couldn't take the chance of our parents getting their hands on her. As a result, they had a hard time tracking me down. It took them several years of letter writing and petitioning the courts for access to her birth records. When they finally got the information, they had to find me, which took a while. Once they were sure I was the Lisa Miller they were looking for, Hope wanted to come alone. She didn't want to write a letter or make a phone call because she was afraid I would turn her down. She wanted to meet me face to face."

With a face filled with pain at remembering that night, Lisa said, "Then it was my turn. My chance to answer her questions—questions like, 'Why did you give me up?' and 'What is my real family like?' And then she asked the hardest one of all: 'What kind of person are you?' How? How do you look into the eyes of an innocent young woman and tell her what I had to tell her?"

After a long pause, she said, "As it turned out, I didn't have the chance. We'd been in the kitchen talking for more than an hour. I hadn't yet gone out front to lock up. Neither of us heard the entry bell jingle. He must have silenced it as he came in. I spun around as he bumped the tray of clean cookie sheets, sending them crashing to the floor. Instantly, a night I couldn't imagine getting any worse suddenly did for our father was standing there with a gun in his hand, hate in his eyes, and my daughter not three feet from him."

Aunt Gladys was almost beside herself with emotion. Hearing Lisa's voice filled with the same fear she must have felt that night was heartrending. She wanted to move closer to her and to reassure her that she was there for her, but this was not the time. She knew Lisa was using every bit of strength she had just to get through this story. All she could do was sit there and listen as Lisa struggled on.

Everyone watched as Lisa closed her eyes, trying to drive from her mind that horrible image of her father and her daughter in the same room.

Finally, Lisa continued. "At first, I think Hope thought it was just a robbery. He was obviously surprised I wasn't alone. He said something about my always being alone at the bakery this time of night. At that point, I realized he must have been watching me for some time. I was trying to think of a way to get between him and my daughter, but my brain wouldn't work. I was so scared, I couldn't think.

"Hope begged him not to hurt us. While offering him her purse, she said, 'Please, take whatever you want and leave.' She had no idea she was pleading with her own biological grandfather.

"He slapped the purse out of her hand, shouting, 'I didn't come here for money. I came for justice. I've waited a long time for this, and I'm going to enjoy every minute of it.'

"I stood frozen while Hope continued pleading for us. 'Please, don't shoot us. Why would you want to hurt us?'

"Hope's face was filled with fear and bewilderment and then error as she heard his response, 'I don't intend to shoot her. That would be much too quick. I intend to take my time. I'm going to make sure she feels every single blow.'

"The way he emphasized the word 'her' suddenly set me in motion. I knew he wouldn't let my daughter out of there alive. He intended to beat me to death, but he was also going to kill her. He had to. So I grabbed the copper pot we melt chocolate in and let it fly, hitting him on the upper arm. The blow startled him, and he jumped back, hitting his elbow on the doorjamb. That jarred his hand, and the gun fell to the floor. All three of us dove for it, but while I struggled with him to get the gun, I was also screaming at Hope to run. I kept screaming, 'Get out of here! Run!'

"She jumped up and ran, but right when she reached the back door leading to the alley, he slammed me backward and went after her. She had unlocked the door, but as she pushed it open, he was grabbing her with one hand, and he had the gun in the other. All I could think of was saving her. I jumped up, grabbed my marble rolling pin, and ran out into the alley where Hope was struggling to get free of him."

Wiping the perspiration from her lips, Lisa tried to maintain her composure. This was the third time in three days she'd had to repeat this story, and she wasn't sure she'd be able to finish. Taking a deep breath, she leaned forward for a moment. Duncan offered her a glass of water while everyone else sat stunned.

After gathering her composure, Lisa continued. "I needed to get him off her. He was wild with rage, screaming all kinds of horrible things. I thought if I could knock him out cold, I could get her out of there, but I was afraid I might hit Hope. So I forced my body between them, shoving the gun away from Hope's face. I again screamed at her to run, but this time she wouldn't. That's when he grabbed me by the throat with his free hand and slammed me up against the door. I couldn't breathe, and I couldn't fight back. I dropped the rolling pin. Hope started pulling his hair, trying to get him to let go of me. I was trying to wrestle the gun from him when she picked up the rolling pin and hit him. Just as she hit him, the gun went off. At first, I didn't know who, if anyone, had been shot. I stared at Hope's face, praying not to see pain. Then he slumped down, and I knew he'd been the one to get shot."

Duncan quickly interjected, "That's why the autopsy reports didn't jell. The prosecution knew he had been hit from behind, but Lisa wouldn't explain how."

Jumping to his feet, Scott shouted excitedly, "So it was self-defense! She can prove it! Hope can tell them."

Duncan leaned forward and offered, "That was our next problem. Lisa didn't want Hope involved."

At that Susan shrieked, "What? You're kidding! Lisa, she was there. She knows what happened, and you're not going to let her testify? Why?"

"Because I didn't want her life destroyed because of me. I begged her to leave. I wanted her to get back on a plane for California and forget about this. She didn't want to, but I convinced her it was the only way. After I persuaded her to leave, I locked the front door, tossed the rolling pin behind some boxes in the storage room, wiped the gun clean of her prints, tripped the alarm, and waited for the police to come. I didn't want her involved. I decided I would tell the truth, leaving her out of it. If she hadn't been there that night, it still would have happened. I would have rather spent the rest of my life in prison than involve her."

Finally the truth was sinking in. Scott looked into Lisa's face and saw the look of a lioness desperately trying to protect her cub. It wasn't fear of their finding out about Hope that had kept her quiet all these months. She was trying to protect her daughter from being hurt. As gently as he could, Scott suggested, "Lisa, she's already involved. You can't change that fact."

During this meeting Aunt Gladys had remained quiet, but now she knew she needed to speak up. "Lisa, the shame and secrets your parents forced you and Susan to endure almost destroyed the two of you. If you force this girl to keep this secret, you're placing her behind that same wall of silence you just told us you've been living behind. It'll destroy her much more than the truth will. Give this girl a chance to know you and forgive you. But most of all, give her a chance to help you. You owe her that."

Not waiting for Lisa's response, Gladys turned to Mr. Duncan and asked, "How much trouble could Hope be in for running? And if Lisa agrees, how do we get her back here to testify?"

Mr. Duncan gave Gladys a big smile and then filled them in on his secret. "That's what we've been working on for the past week. You see, the only reason I found out about this is because Hope's attorney contacted me last weekend. Apparently, she did keep quiet for almost two months. Her parents wrote off her strange behavior to her having a bad meeting with her birth mother. When she didn't want to talk about it, they decided to leave her alone. After some time had passed, she couldn't stand it and told them. They weren't really sure what they were dealing with. At that point they weren't even certain the assailant been seriously injured. Hope's father made a few phone calls and discovered that not only had he died, but the victim was Hope's natural grandfather, and her mother was on trial for his murder."

Everyone sat still. Bill Thomas leaned forward and asked, "So where is she? Why didn't they tell the police the truth when they found out?"

Almost shouting his answer, Duncan said, "They did!" Then a little calmer, he continued. "When they found out what was going on here, Hope's father called and talked to Gordon himself. They offered to bring her back here and tell what she had witnessed, but they were told to 'sit tight.' They waited another week then called again. This time they received a not-so-veiled threat of serious repercussions if it was discovered that their daughter had indeed been involved. At this point, Hope's father hired his own attorney, fearing Hope was in serious trouble."

"Is she? Can they go after her for running?" Bill's question quickly brought everyone to attention. Suddenly, they had another serious issue to address.

Mr. Duncan sat back in his chair and grinned like a Cheshire cat. "Well, she could have been in real trouble. Leaving the scene of any crime is serious; leaving the scene of murder is even more serious. When her attorney called me to find out what was going on, I immediately went to Judge Kirkley with my suspicions. He ordered a quiet investigation and discovered that Gordon's phone records showed he knew about Hope a full month before the trial. Judge Kirkley has ordered a full investigation, and I wouldn't want to be in Mr. Gordon's shoes right now. In any event, he wouldn't consider going after Hope now, so she's safe."

"I never did like that man," Ruth Bascom thundered. "But why did he go after Lisa like that?"

Duncan then offered up his and Judge Kirkley's full suspicions. "Yesterday morning I had breakfast with someone in city hall. He wants to stay off the record, but apparently Gordon has had his eye on running for district attorney. He tried unsuccessfully a few years back. Around the first of March, word got around that Sam Crane, the current DA, had been diagnosed with cancer and would be stepping down soon. This person I talked to said Gordon was anxious to put together a case that would give him some press time. He needed to gain what they call in politics 'curb appeal.'

"Not one month after finding out the post was coming up for grabs, Lisa's case was dropped into his lap. Apparently, he was going around to his friends in city hall bragging how this case had all the titillation of a dime-store novel, how he could keep the papers filled for weeks with new tidbits of information. He thought he had the perfect vehicle to keep his name in front of the public for most of the summer. Then with this conviction, he thought he could ride right into the November election as the great defender of the streets of Jefferson."

Scott's response reflected most everyone's reaction to this news. "That creep! So he was behind all those ugly articles in the paper?"

Duncan nodded an affirmative and then continued. "I think Gordon did believe Lisa had done it, at least at first. Remember, Lisa was lying, and the evidence didn't jell. He really thought he had a strong case. But after two months of shooting off his mouth, living the life of guest speaker around town, and a few weeks before his career-changing trial, this new information dropped out of nowhere. It threatened to turn him into a laughingstock. I think he felt he could scare these people into staying quiet and staying out of town. After all, Lisa wasn't stepping forward with this information. He saw that she had her own reasons for keeping quiet, so I think he felt he could get away with it. Imagine his surprise when he found out they showed up on Saturday."

Almost in unison, everyone responded, "They're here?"

Then Susan stammered, "You mean they're here in Jefferson? Can we meet her?"

"Well, yes and no. Yes, they're here in Jefferson, but no, I don't want you meeting with or talking to any of them until after she testifies on Monday." Duncan then added, "I want to be able to ask her if, before coming to court, she has talked with any friends or members of Lisa's family. I want a resounding 'no' out of her. Therefore, I want you all to keep a clear path of this family until after she testifies."

It was getting late, and Duncan had a lot to do. Bringing the meeting to a close, he turned to Ruth Bascom and said, "This morning, while you were here in court, a search warrant was issued and executed at your bakery. They recovered the rolling pin and are doing all the necessary tests to verify that Lisa and Hope's story is true. I'm sorry I wasn't able to warn you, but I didn't want either of you upset and second-guessing yourselves while on the witness stand."

"I understand. They can take anything they need if it'll help." Ruth then turned to Lisa. "Honey, you were going to let that horrid Mr. Gordon put you in prison in order to protect your child? You do beat all."

As everyone was preparing to leave, Bill Thomas asked, "Mr. Duncan, why can't Gordon simply drop the charges against Lisa?"

Putting his things back down on the table, Duncan felt it important to explain this point. "Yes, Gordon could drop the charges. That would be the safest path for Gordon, and it would ensure Lisa's freedom, but it wouldn't really free her. This town would always think of her as a murderer who got off. We need to put Hope on that stand Monday morning and allow the jury to hear what happened. Hope needs the closure, Lisa needs the vindication, and Gordon needs to be stopped. We're talking about one more day in court. We can do this. We will do this, and we will win."

As much as he wanted to give this family some more time to talk with Lisa, Duncan had mounds of work waiting for him back at his office. "I'd love to let you stay here and talk, but Lisa's time is up; Officer Jackson needs to get her back next door. If you would quickly say your goodbyes, I'll buzz the officer."

Susan was the first to move. Everyone gave the sisters a moment alone. Neither said a word at first, they just fell into each other's arms and hugged. Both were drained of emotion after this unusual day.

Lisa kept her arm around her sister as she turned to everyone and apologized.

"I'm so sorry I lied to you. I was stupid to think I could protect Hope by lying. I do hope you can forgive me, but I do want to say something before you leave. These past few months sitting in that jail, knowing I was lying but also knowing I was innocent, gave me lots of time to think about my life. It's been hard eating my meals with girls who are living the kind of life I used to live, hearing those same old sick excuses for why they're doing it. I've been reliving some terribly painful memories in here, but I am daily reminded exactly how fortunate I am that you people reached out to me, even though I didn't deserve it. I don't even want to think about what might have happened to me if you had left me in my misery. You all loved me until I could begin to love myself. I'm sorry I didn't trust you with the truth. I want you to know how much I love you and how very thankful I am that you never gave up on me."

When Lisa finished, Susan stepped back slightly, and taking Lisa's face in her hands, kissed her on the cheek. "We're quite a pair, aren't we? Until this trial forced it all out into the open, I never realized how much our parents were still controlling us. They so terrorized us about keeping secrets, we've both been afraid to look at the truth. Secrets were our way of protecting ourselves. A little while ago you said something about ending up your own prisoner. When you said that, it all clicked with me. I remembered something I heard Dr. Jacobson say once during a lecture. She said, 'The lies we tell ourselves as children become the truth we live by as adults.' For her, the lie was that God didn't love her because she didn't think He cared what she was suffering through. For you and me, it was the lie that secrets will protect us. Until you said that, I never understood that if you let your secrets build up in you, they become a wall that holds you prisoner. For us, it has sort of been a wall of silence. At first it protected us, but then we became its prisoner."

Coming up behind them, Scott put his arms around them both. "Yes, but now that wall is down, and there are no more secrets."

With a steady voice, Lisa made one last confession. "Scott, not all my secrets are out. I have one last one to confess, but this secret belongs to Hope first. Once I tell her who her father was, I'll be ready to tell the rest of you."

Susan looked at her sister, studying her face as she made this last declaration. She knew it would only be a matter of time before she knew who Hope's father was, but wanting to take the pressure off Lisa, she said, "Right now we need to be content that you are finally safe. That's enough for now."

Beaming with happiness that her two girls were finally going to be all right, Aunt Gladys slapped her hand on the conference table and said, "I'll say a hearty amen to that," bringing a round of tension-releasing laughter from everyone, including Mr. Duncan.

After giving everyone a minute or two more, Duncan buzzed for the officer, and Lisa was escorted back to jail.

Four long days lay ahead for everyone, days of knowing Hope was somewhere in town but miles away from all of them.

On Friday afternoon, Duncan called the house to let them know that the forensic report had come back. "Susan, Hope's fingerprints were found all over the rolling pin. I'm so thankful Lisa didn't think to wipe it clean as she had the gun. She couldn't remember whether or not she had."

"Mr. Duncan, how is Hope holding up? This must have been an unimaginable few months for her."

Susan's concerns for this girl were justified. All this had hit the girl hard, coming as it did out of nowhere.

"Yes, she's quite upset. I haven't told her the whole story yet. I want her to get on the stand and tell what happened from her perspective of that night. The less she knows, the better she'll be able to focus on the events of that night. There will be plenty of time afterward to tell Hope the whole story."

Almost afraid to hear his answer, Susan then inquired about Hope's parents. "What kind of people are they? I mean, do you think they'll understand, once they know?"

Duncan decided it couldn't hurt to tell her now, so he filled her in on a little secret of his own. "After promising me they wouldn't discuss anything with Hope until after the trial, I agreed to let Mr. and Mrs. Winslow sit in the courtroom all last week. While Hope stayed hidden in the hotel room, they were sitting right behind your mother all week. They have a very good picture of what went on."

"Winslow. That's their name? Hope Winslow." Straining her brain, Susan tried to picture the courtroom and who was sitting where, but she couldn't place them. So many townspeople were always sitting there, enjoying the daily soap-opera atmosphere that she had simply tried to tune them all out. Now she was sorry she had.

"Susan, don't worry. They're good people. Dan and Jean have been good parents, and they'll help their daughter get through this. I have to go, but I'll see you Monday morning."

He excused himself and all Susan could do was to wait for Monday to come.

CHAPTER 38

THE ANTICIPATION IN the courtroom as the family took their seats seemed felt almost palpable. They studied every face as the spectators filed in, jockeying for the best seats in the house. They were concerned only with couples, trying to see if they could pick out Mr. and Mrs. Winslow. They had no idea what they looked like, so they studied the faces, looking for a clue to their identity.

As Susan looked from couple to couple, the door opened, and she watched her mother come in and take the same seat she had occupied throughout the trial. Quickly, before her mother looked over, Susan spun around and looked forward. She did not want to make eye contact with her. As she sat thinking about what was going to be said today, she wondered what her mother's reaction would be. All through the trial she had sat stone-faced, never responding to anything. Susan pondered her mother's insensitive demeanor. *You're so filled with hate, you can't feel anything else. I guess as long as you keep yourself filled up with hate, you have no room to feel guilt, but if you never allow the guilt feelings to come, you'll never be able to put the past behind you. I feel so sorry for you, Mother.*

The familiar sound of the side door's opening drew Susan's attention and she watched as Lisa was escorted in, obviously quite nervous but glad the trial was almost over. Lisa was barely in her seat when the jury filed in, and the courtroom was called to order.

Judge Kirkley entered a moment later, and after a quick formal greeting to the jury, he asked Mr. Duncan to call his next witness.

"Your Honor, the defense would like to call Ms. Hope Winslow to the stand." Duncan remained seated with his arm around Lisa. He knew this development was killing her.

The bailiff pushed open the back door and signaled the officer standing outside the witness room to send in the next witness. The whole family turned and stared at the door, waiting to get their first look at Hope. They could hear her footsteps as she made her way across the lobby of the courthouse, and as she stepped through the door, Scott heard a gasp escape from Susan.

Susan's eyes were riveted on the girl, and she was having difficulty breathing as she watched Hope walk up the aisle toward the witness stand. Leaning close to Scott, she whispered, "She looks like Lisa," and then she began to cry.

Scott slipped his arm around her and held her tightly. The image of this young Lisa was unmistakable.

After Hope was sworn in, Duncan stood up and approached her. With a reassuring smile he asked, "Will you please tell the court your full name?"

"Hope Spencer Winslow." Her voice sounded anxious, and she didn't take her eyes off Mr. Duncan. She was afraid to look at Lisa.

Trying to loosen her up a little, Mr. Duncan stepped a little closer and said, "It's all right, Miss Winslow, take your time. Now please tell the court how old you are and where you live."

Hope knew she needed to relax a little, so she forced a smile and said, "I'm twenty-two, and I live in Culver City, California."

"Have you always lived in California?"

"Yes. Except during college. I lived in Colorado during college."

Leaning against the jury box, Mr. Duncan knew the jury was probably busy trying to figure out what a girl from California had to do with this case. "Miss Winslow, have you ever been to Georgia before coming here to testify?"

Hope finally let her eyes move to the jurors. Duncan had deliberately placed himself in front of them so she could let her eyes wander in their direction as she answered, "Yes. Once."

"Can you tell this court when that was and for how long?"

Hope's gaze drifted over to Lisa, "It was last April. I was here for one day."

Stepping forward, Duncan handed her a copy of her airline tickets. "Hope, are these the airline tickets you used for that visit?"

Taking them from Mr. Duncan, Hope flipped through the tickets and handing them back, she answered, "Yes. These are mine."

Turning to Judge Kirkley, Mr. Duncan asked, "I'd like to place these airline tickets into evidence as defense exhibit twelve, Your Honor."

Judge Kirkley simply nodded.

Setting the tickets on the desk, Duncan turned to face the witness. "These tickets were originally booked for a three-day layover in Atlanta. You were to fly out of Los Angeles, arriving in Atlanta on Saturday morning. Your return booking was for the following Tuesday. Is that correct?"

Hope nodded. "Yes. That was the plan. I was to return to Los Angeles on Tuesday morning."

"But that's not what the airline records show, Ms. Winslow, do they? When did you return to Los Angeles?"

Putting her hand on her knee to keep it from shaking, Hope answered, "No. Instead of waiting until Tuesday, I caught a standby flight."

Leaning forward ever so slightly, Duncan asked, "When?"

Realizing she hadn't been clear, she quickly said, "Oh, I'm sorry. It was that Sunday morning."

"Ms. Winslow, you flew all the way from Los Angeles to Atlanta, arriving Saturday morning around nine o'clock and flew back that very next morning? Is that correct?"

"Yes, sir."

Duncan walked over to sit on the edge of his desk so the jury could watch both Hope and Lisa. "Now Hope, will you explain to this court why you wanted to come to Jefferson last April?"

After a quick glance at Lisa, Hope again looked at Mr. Duncan. "I came to Jefferson to meet my birth mother. My parents had adopted me when I was three days old. I've always known I was adopted, and I only wanted some questions answered. I wanted to see what she looked like and ask her why she gave me away."

Duncan didn't have to look at the jury. They were already ahead of him. It was obvious who her birth mother was. "Ms. Winslow, can you point to the person you believe is your birth mother?"

Lifting her hand, Hope pointed to Lisa. "I know she is."

Duncan nodded. "Hope, was Lisa aware that you were coming?"

"No, sir. I was afraid she wouldn't see me. I had no way of knowing what her story was and didn't want her to tell me to stay away. I wasn't going to move in with her. I just wanted to talk to her."

"So did you two meet?"

"Yes, at the bakery. She acted like she was glad to meet me." With this statement, Hope broke down in tears. Months of stress were showing, and she couldn't maintain control any longer.

Putting his hand up to stop the next question, Judge Kirkley bent down and asked, "Ms. Winslow, do you need a break?"

Without looking up, Hope shook her head no; she wanted this questioning to be over.

Duncan picked up a photo from the evidence table, walked over, and handed it to her.

"Hope, do you recognize this man?"

Barely looking, as if never wanting to see that face again, she answered, "Yes, sir. That's the man who came into the bakery kitchen that night."

Taking the photo from her and passing it among the jury, Duncan then asked, "Hope, that night, did you know who he was?"

"No, sir. I thought he was a robber."

"Ms. Winslow, do you now know who the man in that photo was?"

"Yes. He was her father," she said, pointing at Lisa.

Susan noticed Hope didn't refer to him as her grandfather. She also noticed she referred to Lisa as "her."

Leaning against the jury box, Duncan clarified, "Ms. Winslow, either before or after that night, have you talked with Lisa Miller about that night?"

"No, sir."

"Have you talked with any friends or family members of Lisa Miller regarding that night?"

"No, sir."

Stepping closer to Prosecutor Gordon's desk, Mr. Duncan folded his arms in front of him and asked, "Ms. Winslow, in your own words, would you please tell the court what happened that night after Charles Miller entered that kitchen?"

The family sat listening mesmerized as Hope told the jury the same story Lisa had told them four days earlier. Several times her emotions started to get away from her as she relived the terror of that night. Once or twice she had to stop and take a drink of water before continuing. Her voice shook with emotion as she gave detailed information about where each of them was standing, what was said, and how she felt. Her description of Charles Miller was gut-wrenching, and the jury was again witnessing one of his victims.

The jurors kept their eyes fixed on Hope. They were struggling right along with her. Yet again, a witness was drawing them right into one of Charles Miller's tirades, and they were having absolutely no trouble believing every single word. As she reached the point in her testimony where she was sharing her sense of panic that he wouldn't let go of Lisa's throat, she stopped.

Duncan waited, expecting her to continue when she had gathered her composure, but she didn't. She sat staring at him. He walked over and gently probed, "What happened then, Hope?"

Hope ignored his question. She turned her gaze toward the back of the courtroom. Susan knew she must have been looking at her parents for some kind of moral support. Then slowly, her eyes returned to Mr. Duncan. With almost a whisper, came, "I hit him. I picked up the rolling pin, and I hit him. He was killing her. She couldn't breathe and was turning blue. I had to stop him, but when I hit him, the gun went off and he fell. I killed him."

At this declaration, Lisa began to cry. All her sacrifices of trying to protect her baby from Chuck Miller had failed. Her baby had now been poisoned by him as well.

Stepping over to the evidence table, Mr. Duncan picked up the rolling pin that had been retrieved from the storage room at the bakery and walked over near the jury. On other occasions with other witnesses, he would have placed that rolling pin right in the witness's hands, but not this time. Hope was traumatized enough simply having to tell this story. To make her hold the object she knew she had used to take a person's life would be an unnecessary cruelty. "Hope, do you recognize this marble rolling pin?"

With a flash of a peek, she nodded and said, "Yes."

"Hope, is this the rolling pin you picked up in that alley and used to protect your birth mother? The object you used to stop Charles Miller from committing murder?"

"Yes, sir."

Duncan then walked over to the evidence table, placed the rolling pin down and returned to his desk. He picked up a stack of reports and offered them to the court. "Your Honor, these reports show that a search warrant was issued and executed at Bascom's Bakery. They found this rolling pin, and the forensic findings matched Chuck Miller's head wound. This report also indicates that the fingerprints belonging to Hope Winslow were found on this object."

Returning to the witness, Mr. Duncan then asked, "Hope, why didn't you stay here and tell the police what happened?"

As the tears came unabated, Hope pleaded, "I wanted to, but I was just so scared. I have never seen anyone like that in my whole life. I knew he was going to kill both of us. Then when the gun when off, I panicked, and she was telling me to run because she didn't want my life ruined because of what had happened. I know I shouldn't have, but I was so scared. All I could think of was getting home where I'd be safe. I ran back to my rented car and left for Atlanta. I got there around two in the morning on Sunday. I caught the first flight back to Los Angeles that morning. I wasn't even sure he was seriously hurt until two months later. I'm sorry. I'm so sorry."

The jury now had all of the pieces they needed. Duncan noticed several of them looking at Lisa with comforting smiles. They now understood what had happened that night. They didn't care that Lisa had lied. It no longer mattered. That was for someone else to deal with; they knew what they had to do.

Duncan wasn't going to bring up what Gordon did right now. He didn't want the jury to have to deal with any more facts. Gordon's guilt was a matter for another day. "Your Honor, I have no other questions for this witness."

Judge Kirkley looked at Gordon, who quickly waived away his opportunity to cross-examine this witness. As Hope stepped down from the witness box and passed Lisa's seat, she paused to say, "I'm sorry I waited so long," and then took her seat next to her parents.

Susan turned and watched as Hope fell into her mother's arms. *So you're her parents*, she thought. *I hope you give us a chance, although I wouldn't blame you if you didn't.* Susan watched as Jean Winslow gently comforted her daughter. As Susan's gaze remained locked on these two women, Jean lifted her eyes from her daughter's face and turned to face Susan. Susan felt embarrassed, as if being caught scrutinizing an intimate moment. A sweet smile of understanding appeared on Jean Winslow's face, and Susan returned it with a nod of acknowledgment. Much had been said in that smile, and content to let that be enough for now, Susan turned back in her seat and faced forward to hear the closing arguments.

The judge quickly swept the courtroom. As his eyes stopped on Duncan, he thought, *Good job, Duncan. I wondered how you were going to introduce this girl to the jury. You gave them just the information they would need to protect your client. If you had given in to the temptation of drowning the jury with the minutiae of details because of your personal animosity for Gordon, you would have made their job harder. Yes, the details would certainly have embarrassed Gordon, but that's not your job.*

Turning to Prosecutor Gordon, he thought, *That, I'm happy to say, will be my job.*

Warning them both to be ready with their closing arguments, Judge Kirkley turned to Duncan and said, "Mr. Duncan, if you please."

Duncan quickly gathered his closing notes and walked over to the jury, as if to have a personal conversation with them. He knew he did not need to beat them over the head with the evidence.

"Ladies and gentlemen, at the beginning of this trial I told you the prosecution would show you who Lisa Miller was, and that promise has been fulfilled. I also told you I would show you who Lisa Miller has become, and I have. You have also been told who Mr. Charles Miller was and what he was capable of doing. You have seen the nightmare his wife and children were forced to live through. It is now time that you, the jury, put an end to Charles Miller's reign of terror. You, and you alone, can stop the nightmare for Lisa Miller.

"Yes, my client lied. Yes, our witness ran. Was that wrong? Yes, but did my client commit murder? No! Was the action taken by my client and her daughter in self-defense? Absolutely! I could repeat many issues during closing arguments, but you have already heard them. Hope Winslow had nothing to gain by stepping forward. The forensics reports verify her account of that night.

"I would like to put before you only one matter as you deliberate. Ask yourselves, why was Charles Miller wearing latex gloves that night? Could it be that he knew what he was intending to do and knew he would be the logical suspect? Did he not want the police to find his fingerprints anywhere near that bakery when Lisa's body was found beaten to death? Ask yourself, what other reason could he have had to wear those gloves?

"Ladies and gentlemen, life is complicated for all of us. But for people who have had to grow up being terrorized, the complexities of life sometimes simply boil down to survival. My client was forced to live with secrets in order to survive that home. Is it any wonder she would revert back to her childhood method of survival when placed in a terrifying situation? She did not intend to shoot and kill her father in that alley. She was simply trying to save the life of her daughter and herself. If, in the aftermath of that action, she was guilty of poor judgment, that is not for you to decide. Yours is only to decide if Lisa Miller did intentionally, and with forethought, take the life of Charles Miller. Understanding all of these facts, it is your duty to find my client, Lisa Miller, not guilty."

Duncan confidently returned to his seat next to Lisa and gave Gordon a polite, but mocking, smile. He knew Gordon was in a tight spot. Judge Kirkley had all but taken the wind out of his sails, and Gordon needed to pick his words carefully. Duncan sat back, preparing to listen with interest to Gordon's faulting attempt to wrap up his closing statement.

Judge Kirkley nodded for Gordon to begin, but there was no movement at the prosecution's table. Duncan studied Gordon's body language as his fingers slid up and down the edge of his prepared statement. Gordon's nervous twitch, which he'd observed in the judge's chambers, was back, and it made Duncan want to walk over and remove those invisible eyeglasses Gordon was nervously trying to twitch into place.

Finally, tired of waiting, Judge Kirkley ordered Gordon to begin.

Gordon gathered his notes, and, knowing he needed to weigh them carefully, he remembered how, in the beginning, he had been so convinced of Lisa's guilt. He had prosecuted many of these wretched women and honestly felt society was better served by getting them permanently off their streets, even if that required closing your eyes to suspicious evidence. After all, it was for the common good of the community. He had been so arrogant and pompous; he wouldn't listen when Officer Swanson tried to tell him he was wrong about this woman. Once he had read through her criminal file, he closed his ears to everything else because he had a case that would put him on the front page.

As he stepped in front of the jury to give his closing arguments, his haughty demeanor was gone. He knew his political agenda had trapped him, and now they were gone. He knew Judge Kirkley was a bulldog and wouldn't let go of this.

Certain that Kirkley would call for an investigation, and with almost a sigh, Gordon began his closing arguments. "Ladies and gentlemen of the jury, we have a witness who admits to leaving the scene of a crime. She remained silent for sometime while we were forced to draw conclusions of what happened, based on the available evidence. Please keep in mind that the defendant herself did not tell the truth, and the evidence was telling us this fact. The defendant's criminal record strongly suggested we were dealing with a person who was out of control and a danger to society. Only you, the jury, can decide if that is still true. It is up to you to decide whether or not the testimony of this witness is credible."

Taking his seat, all Gordon was thinking about was protecting himself and silently mused, *I wasn't the only one responsible for this mess.* Quickly reviewing his closing statement, he thought, *Words are what a lawyer uses. I didn't say anything that wasn't true. Kirkley, if you bring me up on charges, you'll have to prove I knew the truth; you'll have to prove malice. Yes, this woman got a raw deal, and I feel bad for her. But if they hadn't tried to hide the truth, none of this would have happened.*

Everyone listened intently as Judge Kirkley instructed the jury. Because it was almost noon, he ordered them not to discuss the case during their lunch break but to wait until they were seated in the deliberation room.

As soon as the court was dismissed, Susan quickly made her way to Hope. Of course, Hope had no way of knowing who she was. All Hope knew was what had been said in the closing arguments. Cautiously approaching her, Susan extended her hand and said, "Hello, Hope. I'm your Aunt Susan. I'm very glad to finally meet you."

With a look of amazement, Hope clasped her aunt's hand. "You're Lisa's sister? You don't look much older than me."

"I was eight when she had you. I sincerely want to thank you for stepping forward. I know you've been through a horrible ordeal, and Mr. Duncan has purposely kept you in the dark about certain matters, but I am certain your mother will fill you in."

Pulling back her hand, and in an emotional voice, Hope's responded, "I'm not so sure I want to be filled in. If I hadn't been so obsessed with getting some answers, I never would've been there that night. I have great parents. I had a great life. I should have left it alone."

Appreciating her feelings, Susan stepped back as if giving this girl some space. "But, Hope, if you ever want to know what giving you up so you could have these great parents and great life cost your birth mother, I'll always be available. We'll understand if you never want to, but I do want you to know we would love to have the chance to know you."

When Hope didn't respond, her mother stood up and took Susan's hand. "She's not ready to deal with anymore right now. This entire ordeal has pretty much shattered her Wonder-Bread image of life. We always worked hard to give our kids a love-filled world to live in, and this has been a crash course in reality for her."

Susan appreciated Mrs. Winslow's attempt to soften Hope's reaction. "Well, at least some people's reality. I'm glad Hope has a solid foundation to fall back on." With one last attempt to reach out to Hope, Susan added, "I'm glad a wonderful family adopted you. The lucky ones get born into them. Some, like you, get adopted into them, or like me, marry into them, and some, like your birth mother, get accepted into them. There are lots of wonderful people in this world. I sincerely hope you always live up to your name. Please don't let that horrible night make you stop hoping. A family lives here who wants to get to know you. I hope someday you'll give us a chance."

"Maybe someday," Hope responded. "I don't want to hurt her."

Dan Winslow stepped into the aisle and cleared a path for his daughter to leave. "I think we should take her back to the hotel where she can rest. This morning has been very hard on her."

As her family left the courtroom, Jean Winslow stayed behind. Obviously she wasn't finished talking. As the door swung closed behind her husband and daughter, she turned back to Susan. She was about to say something when she caught the image of Marjorie Miller making her way up the aisle.

Susan turned to see at whom Jean Winslow was looking. The two women watched as Marjorie, still stone-faced, made her way out of the courtroom. Marjorie was now free to go and had no intention of talking with anyone.

Both women remained quiet until Marjorie was gone, and then Jean turned to Susan before leaving. Placing her hand on Susan's arm, she said, "Dan and I understand. Let us talk to her. She'll come around. She simply can't get past the fact that she killed a man—no matter how justified."

CHAPTER 39

No one was interested in eating lunch. The family gathered in the conference room and tried to keep the conversation on a light note. The absence of any talk about Hope was understandable. No one could think of anything to say about her without feeling they would have to comment on the obvious stress that having to testify was causing her. For most of the recess, Lisa sat quietly pondering the damage all of this was causing her daughter. She appreciated the fact that everyone was there to give her moral support. She was also thankful they respected her need to remain quiet. These next few hours would be difficult, and all the talking in the world wasn't going to make it any easier.

Susan carefully watched her sister's expressions. She knew Lisa's thoughts were probably focused on when she might have an opportunity to talk with her daughter again than reflecting on what the jury was doing. But knowing how Hope was struggling, she worried some pain was still ahead for Lisa. After seeing Hope's reaction, she knew she was not likely to rush into Lisa's waiting arms—even if the jury came back with a not-guilty verdict. As much as she would wish it to be so, there was not likely to be a fairy-tale ending to this. Then it dawned on her. *Lisa knows this! That's what she's doing. She's not worried about the verdict; she's preparing herself for Hope's rejection.*

Lowering her head and pleading from a heart aching for her sister, Susan prayed, "Oh, God, give Lisa the strength to get through this."

At one-thirty the bailiff stuck his head into the conference room and signaled to Mr. Duncan that the jury had just buzzed, which meant they had reached a verdict. While the family quickly filed out of the conference room, Susan stood up and hugged her sister. She then followed the rest out to their seats. As the courtroom was called to order and the jury was being seated, Susan looked around the room. The seat her mother had occupied for the past week and a half was now empty, which did not surprise her. She scanned the crowd, trying to see where Hope was sitting.

As the clerk called the room to order, Susan heard the familiar squeak of the back door and turned to see Dan and Jean Winslow quickly enter and take a seat. Hope was not with them. Susan kept her gaze on them until Jean looked at her and mouthed the words, "She didn't want to be here." Susan simply smiled an understanding response and returned her attention to the front.

Lisa was standing straight and tall next to Duncan. She faced the jury with a calm that belied her real feelings—not fear of their verdict but of what was ahead.

Everyone watched as the foreman passed the verdict to the bailiff, who, in turn, passed it to the judge. After reading it, the clerk repeated the charges, and then Judge Kirkley asked, "Mr. Foreman, having heard the charges before you, what is your verdict?"

With a sympathetic smile toward Lisa, he loudly and clearly said, "We find the defendant, Lisa Miller, not guilty."

Even though they had been sure of the outcome, the relief at hearing the not-guilty verdict sent the whole family into celebration. They clapped and hugged each other and thanked the jury.

Judge Kirkley gave everyone a minute or two before banging his gavel so he could talk. "Ladies and gentlemen of the jury, the court would like to thank you for your service in sitting on this trial, and I would personally like to thank you for your wisdom. Thank you. You are dismissed."

Each juror who stepped out of the jury box walked over to Lisa, shook her hand, and wished her well. Gordon, knowing people were watching, extended his hand and offered an official, nevertheless insincere, expression of regret. "I'm glad it turned out this way. I'm sorry we made you go through this."

Lisa simply smiled. She knew he had made her go through this, but she also knew most of it had been her own fault.

The whole family crowded around Lisa, all of them trying to have their turn to give her a hug. Mrs. Thomas and Carol Anne were laughing and crying at the same time. Bill Thomas stood with his arm around his sister, Gladys. Harry and Scott kept talking about what a sense of relief it was to finally have this over.

Mrs. Bascom walked up to Mr. Duncan, and with the sweetest look on her face, she thanked him for all of his hard work. Everyone chimed in and agreed that he had indeed done a wonderful job.

Susan noticed Lisa was straining to see beyond the crowd of people. Knowing who she was looking for and wanting to protect her, she leaned close and whispered, "Lisa, Hope isn't here."

A knowing look washed over Lisa's face, and Susan watched as that determined strength began to appear. She wasn't going to fall apart. She had dealt with pain and heartache before, although this time her pain was not for herself, but for her daughter. "It's all right, Susan. I can't blame her."

When everyone had finished celebrating, Scott and Susan came to Lisa and suggested they take her home. "After all, Lisa, three little children are sitting at Aunt Gladys's house, waiting to see you. They have missed their Auntie Lisa for three whole months, so let's go see them."

As they prepared to leave, the Winslows stepped forward. "We're sorry she's not here for you."

Seeing the tears beginning to fill Lisa's eyes, Jean quickly added, "Please be patient. Dan and I intend to tell Hope everything. Once she knows what you two girls lived through, she'll see her birth mother differently. Lisa, because you loved your baby, you gave us a wonderful daughter. We'll do everything in our power to give her back to you." With a momentary half-smile, she added, "Well, at least we'll *share* her. Please give her some time to process all that has happened."

Lisa choked back her emotions as she took hold of their hands. "Thank you for giving her what I wanted for her. She told me how much she loves you and how good you've been to her. All I ever really wanted was for her to be happy. Thank you."

Dan quickly let go of Lisa's hand to wipe away the tears that were running down his face. With great confidence, he said, "You'll get more than that, Lisa. You have a great kid. She'll be so proud of you when she learns what you have done with your life. I'm terribly sorry it won't be tonight. She's not ready."

With tremendous composure, Lisa smiled as she reached over and squeezed Dan's arm. "I understand. I've waited this long; I can be patient. At least now my family knows about her, and I can finally talk about her. That alone will help."

Scott put his arms around Susan and Lisa, guiding them through the crowd. As they reached the side door, Officer Jackson, with a huge grin on his face, stepped into their path. "Lisa, I couldn't let you leave without telling you how happy I am about how things turned out. You have become a strong, kind person, and I'm proud to have met you."

Lisa stepped forward and stood right in front of him. "Ben, you treated me with dignity and respect—even when you weren't sure whether or not I was guilty. You and I have had some great talks in that jail. I'll miss that."

"You don't have to miss them, Lisa," Ben responded shyly. "Our talks don't have to end. Would you mind if I called on you sometime? After hearing about your baking skills, I'd sure like to taste one of your specialties."

Without the slightest embarrassment, Lisa said, "Ben, I'd love for you to call on me. I'll be looking forward to it."

Susan was shocked, but pleased, when she heard Lisa suggest this. She shot Gladys a quick wink but made sure Lisa didn't see it. No one dared tease Lisa about Ben, at least not tonight.

Every time Gladys thought about it, though, she couldn't help but smile. Maybe God had finally sent a man strong enough to see beyond her past, understand why Lisa had done what she did, and love her because of it—not in spite of it.

The family decided to have an impromptu party at Aunt Gladys' house. Ruth Bascom nearly emptied her store of baked goods in celebration, and ladies from the church brought platters of food. All afternoon and well into the evening, people stopped by as word got around that the trial was finally over.

When the party finally came to an end, Aunt Gladys walked with Scott and Susan out to their car. Feeling a confession was in order, Gladys said, "You know, when this difficulty started, I have to admit I questioned God. I couldn't understand why He would allow this to happen to Lisa after everything she had gone through. It took me days before I could stop shaking my fist in His face, demanding He show Himself to be the God of love and power I knew Him to be. I wanted Him to stop this horrible trial and return her to me so I could protect her. I must say, I'm so very thankful He didn't listen to me. He knew exactly what He was doing. He didn't want me to protect her. He wanted to heal her. He used this trial to force out the darkness, bring the evil to light, and free you two girls from your secrets."

With their final goodbyes spoken Scott and Susan headed back to their small rented house Susan had called home for the past three months. Mrs. Anderson had graciously offered to take the children home earlier, allowing Scott and Susan to remain at the party. Lisa Anne had resisted leaving Auntie Lisa, but upon the promise that the two of them would have a special breakfast together the next morning, Lisa Anne finally agreed to go home with Mrs. Anderson.

Scott slipped into the children's rooms to kiss them goodnight while Susan walked the sitter out to her car for the final time. As Mrs. Anderson drove up the street, Susan walked up the driveway and stopped for a moment to admire her much-loved weeping willow tree. Even though she was looking forward to packing up her family and finally going home, she knew she would miss this faithful confidante.

Susan slipped under the drooping limbs and leaned against the tree's strong trunk. She looked up through its beautiful canopy to the stars above, allowing the quiet of the summer evening to envelop her. She closed her eyes and felt the stillness, not only of her surroundings but also of her spirit. Without opening her eyes, she leaned her head against the tree and asked it, "Can you feel the difference in me? Three weeks ago I couldn't have imagined this trial doing anything but harm, remember? I was so full of secrets, but as we all found out, I wasn't the only one. I wonder, will Hope give Lisa a chance to get to know her? I wonder, might Lisa finally find love with Ben Jackson? I wonder, will our mother ever learn that hate is never the answer? Allowing yourself to face your guilt so God can begin to heal you is not bad. Most of all, I'm thankful Lisa and I are free. Our healing has never been dependent on Mother's choices. She may never find her truth, but Lisa and I have, and we're going to be fine."

Patting the tree's strong trunk one more time, Susan mused, "I've always had a tree to confide in. I imagine I'll always do this, but from now on, I won't be sharing shame-filled secrets." With one final pat, Susan said goodnight and headed into the house.

That night, as she and Scott slipped into bed, Susan thought about all of the different people God had put in Lisa's and her life to bring them to this point. She wondered what her mother must have thought, being forced to listen to all of these wonderful people talking about Lisa. She wondered if her mother had ever had a Gladys Carter or a Ruth Bascom in her life. She felt sure that some of the neighbors had wanted to help her. The big difference was that she and Lisa had chosen to accept help from people who had been willing to let God use their hands to bring love and healing to two very hurt and troubled girls.

Snuggling up close to Scott, Susan thought about all the different lessons she had needed to learn before she was willing to step out from behind that wall of silence she had erected around herself and to finally lay her past to rest. She thought about all of the pain Lisa had suffered throughout her life and how hard Aunt Gladys had worked, sharing God's love and forgiveness with Lisa while she nursed her back to health. Susan wondered, *Would we have ever found out about Hope if it hadn't been for this trial?*

Finally, thinking about Lisa's last secret—the one still not shared— she understood why Lisa had decided to keep that last secret to herself for now. Lisa had told the whole family that Hope would be the first person to whom she would reveal that secret. Still, Susan wondered who it was. She remembered all those nights when Lisa had climbed out that bedroom window and how angry she was at her for putting her in such danger. Who was she climbing out the window to see?

Scott was already half asleep. Susan studied his face and marveled at his strength of character and smiled, knowing how much he loved her. "No more secrets" she had promised him. She also knew how hard it would be to let go of lifelong habits. After all, she knew that little girl still lived inside her, still whispering those dreaded warnings: "Be careful, don't trust anyone; guard yourself."

Lying next to Scott, feeling so relaxed, she prayed, "God, how long will it take before that little girl inside me finally feels safe enough to stop the whispering? Probably never; maybe that little girl will always be here, but with Your help, I don't have to listen to her whispers anymore. Maybe now that the truth is out and there are no more secrets for her to hide, that little girl can start living too. God, thank You for freeing me from my secrets, for sending so many people into my life to show me Your truth, and thank You, most of all, for not giving up on me, for loving me even when I didn't trust Your love."

Susan kissed Scott, said one final prayer for both Lisa and Hope, and then snuggled close to her husband and allowed the sweet, sweet sleep of a soul finally at peace to come.

About the Author

Dorey Whittaker

Dorey lives in central Virginia with her husband. She and Bruce have been married for forty-seven years, reared two daughters, enjoy their four grandchildren, and have partnered together in lay ministries for over forty years.

Accidently poisoned by arsenic at age three, Dorey was left practically deaf until age twelve and illiterate until age sixteen. She knows how it feels to face tremendous obstacles. She was told, "Just get over it and move on." Dorey knew how broken she was. She also knew that God was her only hope. What once was her greatest shame, has now become one of her greatest victories.

We all must decide our life path. Either accept the label of victim, with all its excuses readily at hand, or choose to follow God on His path to real self-worth. Dorey shines a light on God's path to living a victorious life.

Hope Returns: Book #2

- *How will Lisa survive in a small town that knows all of her secrets?*
- If love finds its way to Lisa's door, will she dare to open it?
- Will Officer Ben Jackson pursue Lisa now that the trial is over?
- Will revealing the name of Hope's birth father spell trouble for Lisa and Ben?
- How will Hope react once she learns about Lisa's past?
- How will Hope's well-connected fiancé react to this troubling news?
- Will Hope return to Georgia to give her birth mother another chance?

Treasure in a Tin Box: Book #3

- This novel is a stand-alone prequel to Wall of Silence
- Learn about the man who won Ruth Bascom's heart
- Find out how Tobias influenced Gladys Thomas Carter
- Discover the truth behind the old plantation
- Follow the Bascom family through four generations
  - Slavery
  - Emancipation
  - Reconstruction
  - Self-determination
  - Family and faith

Made in the USA
Columbia, SC
03 June 2017